"YOUR LORDSHIP!" MARISA IMPLORED, SEEING THE PASSION STIRRING IN HIS EYES.

She rose from the sofa, trying to back away as he advanced even closer, but soon found herself with nowhere to go.

All at once, his mouth rushed passionately against hers in a long and savage kiss. She fell limp under the overwhelming power of his arms, and then his lips found their way to her cheek, her ear lobe, her neck and the hollow of her throat.

"No. . . no," she whispered urgently. "No, no, . . . Please, stop. The servants. . ."

Straeford recoiled at her pleading. "Of course. Tonight it is the servants—and what excuse will you use the next time?" Without another word, he lifted her into his arms, muffling her cries. It was impossible for her to think clearly as he swiftly took the stairs, her entire being firmly in his grip. Entering her room with a kick of the door, he dropped her on the bed and followed her down. . .

Also by Alicia Meadowes

Sweet Bravado

Published by
WARNER BOOKS

Tender Torment

Alicia Meadowes

WARNER BOOKS

A Warner Communications Company

Tender Torment

Prologue

Driving wind and snow forced Marisa Loftus to pause momentarily and snatch at the fur collar of her pelisse in a vain attempt to protect herself against the biting thrust of the frigid winter weather. She linked her arm through her maid's and together the pair pushed against the determined wind and picked their way cautiously over the slippery walks of the Inns of Court.

The pelting snow impeded visibility, and rounding the corner of an ancient stone building that had stood since the days of Elizabeth, Marisa was rudely jostled by a tall, dark man in a heavy black cape. His head was hunched into his shoulders against the piercing cold, and he jerked it up impatiently to stare with penetrating green eyes into the startled face of the young woman obstructing his pathway. Marisa, who was struggling to regain her precarious footing on the icy walk, was shocked by the darkling glance—a bitter blend of anger and misery—which her haughty jostler cast upon her before muttering something indistinguishable and hastening on his way.

Ignoring the icy blast of wind that almost tore the bonnet from her head, Marisa stood with her hands on her hips to stare after the stranger until he disappeared into the swirling snow.

"Well, I never!" claimed the lady indignantly.

"Bully," added the shivering Lucy, who urged her mistress into the somber gray building and up the creaking stairs to the solicitor's chambers on the second floor.

Henry Saunders greeted the girl warmly, kissing her cheek and clasping both her hands in his. "Why my dear, whatever has disturbed you?" he queried, noting the annoyance marring her usually serene countenance.

"I just met the rudest man outside this building," she claimed as Mr. Saunders seated himself at his desk.

"Ah, the earl," he sighed heavily.

"He practically knocked me off my feet and never offered an apology."

"He probably wasn't aware of what he was doing, my dear. That one is a very troubled young man."

Marisa's expression grew perplexed as she tried to call forth the features of the stranger in the snow, but his visage was lost to her.

"Never mind him now," Saunders suggested. "Tell me why I have the pleasure of your company on such a blustery day."

The young woman's sparkling blue eyes brightened gaily. "Uncle Henry, I had to come to thank you for the marvelous birthday present. I adore the Worthington. But I have no idea where I shall hang such an impressive painting. I love those sweeping landscapes of the English moors, but its proper setting should be in a great hall somewhere."

"I am sure you will preside over a grand establishment of your own one day soon, Marisa, my child. No doubt the proper setting will turn up." A mischievous grin wreathed his homely face.

"I wish you may be right in your predictions, Uncle, but I do not foresee that day in the near future." Marisa's face lost its happy animation as her thoughts turned inward to the obligations her present life forced upon her.

"It will come. It will come," Saunders insisted heartily. "If ever there were a young woman meant to reign over a happy home, surrounded by an adoring husband

and a covey of young, it is you, my dear. It is time you stopped playing nursemaid to your sister and brother, and I shall tell your father so."

"Father would not take it kindly if you did, sir. And besides, it would serve no purpose. At four and twenty I am already on the shelf."

"Nonsense."

"Dear Uncle Henry." Marisa wagged her finger at the man playfully and changed the subject to the dinner party she was hostessing for her father's associates next week.

Saunders pledged his attendance and shortly afterward escorted his charming visitor to the outer chamber, where she took her leave with her maid, Lucy. From a narrow window overlooking the street below, he watched Marisa as she scurried out of sight, wishing he might be instrumental in bringing that lovely young woman to the attention of the proper matrimonial match.

1

The carriage rumbled through the iron gates and swung up the circular drive of gravel to the front door of the earl's country estate. Halting the team, the driver jumped down, opened the door and peered into the darkened coach.

" 'Ere ye be, m'lor'," he said and withdrew to collect the luggage.

Without a word the earl climbed out and looked about him.

"Looks like no 'uns ta 'ome," the coachman commented.

The Earl of Straeford ignored the coachman's remark and simply dismissed the man by placing the required coins in his hand.

Time and neglect had eroded much of the charm of his boyhood home. Even the climbing ivy and dimming light could not hide the desperate need for repairs. As Straeford scanned the crumbling stone structure dark clouds gathered overhead to warn of an approaching storm. Straeford recalled the storms of his boyhood.

"It's going to rain any minute now. Where are those boys?" Lady Straeford asked in annoyance.

"Here we are, mama." Justin ran into the room followed by his brother Robert.

"Justin, what have you been up to this time?" Lady Straeford frowned at her younger son. "Look at your clothes!"

"Mama, he rescued Emily!" Robert explained excitedly.

The Earl of Straeford chuckled as he regarded his two sons. "Where was that stupid cat this time?"

"On the roof," Justin said proudly, stroking the cat. "I climbed out the dormer window . . ."

"I don't wish to hear about your escapade," Lady Straeford interrupted. "Go change your clothes at once, young man. You look like a chimneysweep. I cannot bear the sight of you!"

"Come here, son," the earl beckoned to Justin who was now attempting to scrub his face with a handkerchief. "Don't get yourself into a dither, Marian," he said as he finished wiping the dirt from the small boy's face.

"He's irresponsible risking his neck that way, and you encourage him to do it!"

"Justin can take care of himself," the earl retorted with thinly disguised impatience.

"What if we'd had guests and the boy had walked in here looking like that?"

"Is that your only concern?" he asked disdainfully.

The countess ignored his question and placed her arm about Robert's shoulder. "You're fortunate that Robert knows how to behave, and that he is your heir."

"I'm proud of both my sons, and I know if the responsibility for Straeford were Justin's, he'd be an excellent earl."

"Why?" she sneered, "Because he patterns himself after you?"

"And that's not to your liking, is it, Marian?"

Straeford reached the door of the old house just as the rain began to fall. He grasped the heavy brass knocker and heard it resound through the empty house.

"Who be it?" a rusty old voice asked as the door creaked open.

"It's me, Manners, open up."

"Who?" The old man raised the candle in his wizened hand and squinted at the caller.

"St. Clare." Straeford rarely referred to himself as the earl. In his mind the title belonged to his father and brother before him.

"My lord, we weren't expecting you. It's been such a long time."

"Yes, it has," Straeford replied as he stepped into the entrance hall. Immediately he was arrested by its somber appearance. The darkened oak paneling and unlighted tarnished chandelier threw the room into shadow and the aged portraits on the walls peered at him out of the gloom. As he crossed the slate floor, his booted feet echoed solemnly. In the center of the foyer stood a cracked marble table, and to his right was a grandfather clock that no longer chimed. Upon entering the east drawing room his attention was riveted to the portrait above the fireplace. The late Lady Straeford, his green-eyed, black-haired mother, stared boldly, defiantly out at him.

"I'll have the covers off the furniture at once, my lord." Manners shuffled his ancient body about the room as he removed the dust cloths.

Crossing to the corner window, Straeford opened the tattered blue velvet draperies, letting in the dwindling twilight. Then turning his back on the threadbare furnishings, he stared out of the window at the meadow and sloping landscape where he had played as a boy.

"William?" a woman's voice called from the hallway.

Manners went to the door. "It's all right, Bess. It's his lordship."

"Lordship?" An elderly plump woman came into the room and stopped abruptly as she recognized the earl. "Well glory be, if it ain't Master Justin."

"His lordship the Earl of Straeford!" Manners corrected indignantly, and she bobbed a curtsy.

"Bess, you haven't changed in all these years."

Straeford remembered this good-natured cook with kindness and gave her a half smile.

"Ah, I only wish it was true, m'lord, but if you don't mind me sayin' so you look the same as the day you left the Park. You be the image of your mother with those green eyes and black hair . . ."

"Yes! Yes!" he cut in shortly and changed the subject. "Could you provide me with a cold supper?"

"I'll see to it at once, m'lord." Bess withdrew hastily, knowing she had overstepped herself.

"Is there anything left in the wine cellar, Manners?"

"Yes, your lordship, there be several fine clarets and burgundies."

"Good, bring me one . . . a . . . make it two."

Manners nodded sagely into the stormy green eyes. "Right away, your lordship." And he shuffled out of the room.

"Goddamn," Straeford swore under his breath as he caught a glimpse of his face in the Chippendale mirror and saw his mother's eyes reflected there. Suddenly a deep scornful laugh erupted from him, and he swung about to face the portrait of the countess. Bowing mockingly, he spoke aloud, "I will always be haunted by you, Madam. Does that satisfy you, I wonder?"

The sardonic picture remained silent.

Later, the better part of two bottles of claret downed, he managed to climb the creaking stairs to his bedchamber. An inviting fire was burning in the grate and the tartan coverlet had been turned back. Starting across the room towards the washstand, his boot caught in the carpet, almost tripping him. Catching himself, he glared at the frayed rug. "Damn!" he swore. "Is the whole place going to come down about my ears?" He threw himself on the bed fully clothed and fell into a fitful sleep. Only a few moments passed when he sensed a presence in the room. "What is it?" He rose on one elbow and blinked at Manners, who hovered at the foot of the bed.

"Would your lordship wish to have his boots removed?"

"You'd be surprised how often I've slept with them on."

"Your batman?"

14

"Doesn't disturb me unless I call for him." He studied the old man's solemn face and shrugged his shoulders. "Go ahead if it will please you." Immediately Manners began to struggle with the earl's right boot. "You did a bit of valeting in your younger days, didn't you, Manners?"

"That I did. For your grandfather before I became his major domo." He managed to pull the boot free, and then started on the other one.

"There's not much you don't know about the Straefords, is there, Manners?"

The ancient servant observed his master's eyes before offering his guarded reply. "I've seen much in my time, my lord, and I've forgotten what is best laid to rest."

"A very convenient mind, and a wise one too, I might add." The earl allowed Manners to take his jacket and hand him a robe.

"Would your lordship be requiring anything else?" he asked as he hung the uniform in the wardrobe.

"Go to bed, old man, you need your rest more than I do."

"That's what I do most of these days, rest."

"There's not much to take care of at Straeford Park now, is there?"

"Oh, there's much to be done, and Bess and I are glad you have come home, so that we can get to it."

"Don't count too heavily on my straightening this mess out!"

"You'll find a way, my lord. I was telling Bess when I heard you were in London, 'He'll come Bess. Straeford Park is the earl's home. He'll set it to right.' "

"Did you now?" The earl raised his eyebrows and frowned at the old man. "Well, we'll see," he mumbled, "we'll see."

"Yes, my lord. Goodnight." Manners permitted himself a smile before closing the door behind him.

The old reprobate! the earl thought as he closed his eyes and stretched on the bed. He was trying to manipulate him. Well, why not? Manners's loyalty to the Straefords and the Park was well known.

A crack of thunder followed by a streak of lightning

caught his attention, thrusting him backward in time to another stormy night when, as a boy of seventeen, he had made the shattering discovery that set his life on its lonely course.

Dear mama! She had done her hatchet-work well. He could not remain at Straeford once she had spewed forth the full poison of her hate. The knowledge was too bitter a burden. He tried to explain his reasons for enlisting in a letter to his father; but it was a futile effort. Lord Straeford had written an angry summons demanding a further accounting for Justin's rash action. But Justin remained in India, the full horror of that confrontation with his mother forever sealed within his heart.

The morning light streaming into the dining room did little to enhance its shabby appearance. The chipped wainscoting and dull rosewood table showed up pitifully in the merciless light. Straeford sighed ruefully. The only things that remained the same were Bess's good cooking and the quiet peace of country life.

Manners removed his plate and informed him that he had a visitor in the drawing room.

"Grandmother." Straeford walked into the room and bowed formally to the thin, white-haired lady seated on the sofa. His father's mother. Dressed all in black except for a white lace ruffle about her high-necked dress and holding an ebony cane in her gnarled right hand, she looked every bit the formidable dowager she was. Having survived two husbands and reached the grand old age of eighty, Lady Maxwell commanded respect and sometimes obedience even from this obstinate young man.

She eyed him sternly, her ebony eyes flashing. "So you've finally decided to come home."

"For the moment, Madam." He remained standing.

"Don't try to put me off, Justin St. Clare. I'm not frightened by that glacial stare."

The earl's face was a study in stern dignity. The luminous green eyes gazed out from inner realms that the observer sensed were inviolable. Few dared trespass the private sanctum of that inner world where the proud spirit reigned in isolated disdain. Many a foolish female had sought to probe those depths only to suffer so thorough a rebuke as never to broach the edges of that gentleman's personal being again.

Despite his austerity, he was a handsome man. His well-shaped head carried a rich crown of crisp black curls that owed nothing to art other than a hasty brush carelessly applied each morning. The mouth was well-formed but severe. The chin and nose firm, strong and manly. It was a beautiful face for all the hardening years of exposure spent in the deserts and jungles of India.

To Lady Maxwell's surprise, a smile creased his mouth as he replied, "You were always perceptive, ma'am."

"And you were always obdurate!" She decided to press her advantage. "Sit down, boy, I don't like having to look up at you. You are taller than I remember."

He sat opposite her and stretched out his long legs in front of him. "To my knowledge I'm still six feet, ma'am." He smiled lazily. "Shall I ring for refreshments?"

"I informed Manners we would call for the tea tray later." She studied him closely before adding, "Although you might want something stronger."

"Perhaps, but it is much too early."

"Never acquired the vice, eh?"

"Not that one, at any rate."

"Gammon! You don't think I believe for a minute those scurrilous attacks in the papers."

"Past or present ones, ma'am?"

"Both! And don't try my patience with a lot of balderdash about your reputation. When that tiresome hearing is settled, we must think to your future."

"My future?" His eyebrows rose a fraction. "I thank you for your concern, but it is misplaced. I have always done very well for myself, and I shall continue to do so."

"So you're telling me to mind my own business."

Her candor disarmed him momentarily, and he found himself able to respond to her directness with a short laugh. "Again I bow to your perception."

"But I won't be hushed that easily, Justin," she said in that confident manner which irked him. "It's time someone took you in hand."

The earl's annoyance surfaced and his politeness quickly vanished. "I warn you, Madam!" he said in rising tones, and punctuated his words with a thrust of a pointed finger.

"Don't threaten me, young man!" Lady Maxwell stomped her cane on the floor. "It's time some plain speaking was done! Your mother has been dead . . ."

"Madam!" He came to his feet, but Lady Maxwell ignored him.

"If you had remained to defend yourself against your mother's insinuations at the time . . ."

"I would still be branded a scoundrel!" he said through clenched teeth. "Now have done with it!"

"I don't wish to cause you pain, my boy."

"Pain!" he laughed harshly. "Don't you know I have no such human feelings? Try my patience no further, Grandmother, I desire nothing more than to be left alone."

"That's just my point! You can no longer be left alone. Your obligation as the Earl of Straeford supersedes all else."

He turned his back on her and walked toward the window without replying, but Lady Maxwell was not deterred. She plunged on. "You must marry!"

"Marry!" he said with deep sarcasm.

"The line must be secured and the Park saved!"

"I shall save Straeford in my own way."

"I already have the solution." Lady Maxwell rose and walked slowly toward the tall slender chair behind which he had positioned himself.

He eyed her suspiciously under half-closed lids. "Very well, Grandmother, I see I shall have no rest until you have your say. So tell me your scheme."

A triumphant sparkle lit her eyes and lips. "There is a wealthy merchant who is mad for the *ton*. He has two daughters . . ."

"My God!" He threw up his hands. "Not only do you condemn me to matrimony but to a climbing heiress!"

"If my calculations are correct, you will be thirty-five come August. Do you intend the line to end with you?"

"I'll cross that bridge when I come to it." Turning, he pulled the bell cord hoping to close the discussion.

"Are you afraid of women?"

Straeford whirled to face her and hissed, "This is beyond endurance, Grandmother."

"For heaven's sake, Justin, all women are not like your mother!"

"Enough!" he roared, slamming his fist into the wall. She had pushed him too far! But with superhuman effort he dropped his arm. Then wheeling on his heel, he stalked out of the room as Manners entered with the tea tray. Lady Maxwell sighed heavily. She had been hard on him, but it had to be said. If only he would drop that protective armor he had built about himself and permit himself to feel again. The tragedies of the past had forced her grandson down a bitter, lonely path for too many years. And she was determined to change all that somehow!

Since Justin left home at the age of seventeen, he had returned only twice. The first time was for his father's funeral. There was no assuaging the grief Justin suffered for never having explained himself to the man he idolized. There was no way possible to explain without disclosing the shame that had sent him fleeing in the first place. Sometime later he had sold out and returned from India at the hasty summons of his grandmother. His brother Robert was dying. But Robert was dead by the time he reached England. The deep personal loss, along with his mother's disastrous remarriage, had placed the seal of destruction on the family.

Straeford stood in the long gallery before the portraits of his distinguished ancestors. Holding a glass of port in one hand and the bottle in the other, he walked down the gallery to the picture he had come to view. Lord Straeford, seated beside his wife, with Robert standing next to him and Justin on his mother's knee, presented a false picture of family tranquility. Justin thought about that coldly beautiful woman, his mother, and how he had tried to warn her.

"Justin, you don't know what you are saying!"
"And I told you I have written proof!"

19

"You were always a headstrong boy," she laughed weakly.

"I am no longer a child, Mother, you can't put me off!"

"So much like your father . . ." she went on.

"And that ploy won't work either! I'm here to talk to you about Huxley . . ."

"No! Don't you dare speak those filthy lies again! You hate Ellis because I love him!"

"No, I hate him because . . ."

"Isn't it enough for you that you are now the Earl of Straeford?"

"Do you think I give one blasted damn for the title? For God's sake, don't you see anything?"

"I will not be talked to in such a manner! You were a bad, unfeeling child, Justin St. Clare, and you have grown into a cruel, heartless man. That's why I could never love you."

The glass of port cracked in his hand, pouring wine onto the floor and carpet, mingling with his own blood. Becoming aware of his aching hand, Straeford pulled a handkerchief from his vest pocket and wrapped it about his palm before quietly withdrawing from the gallery and the memories it engendered.

Straeford was going through the strongbox in the library when Major Edward Harding, a tall, well-built man in his early thirties, walked into the room. He was an attractive man with tanned features, sandy hair and hazel eyes.

Easy-going and good-natured, Edward Harding had been Straeford's friend since boyhood. If there was one person the earl trusted and respected, it was this confidante of his youth and companion of his military years in India. Straeford was in need of cheerful company and Harding was precisely the one to provide it.

As they vigorously clasped each other's hands, Harding admonished his friend for not having called on him and his new wife in London. Major Harding had married Ann Cromwell, his colonel's daughter, shortly after returning to England. He had requested a transfer to the western front when Ann's father retired and the family came home. Harding had followed them soon afterward, and Straeford had not seen him since that time.

"I went to your lodgings to see you but found Billings instead. Your batman was concerned about you."

"Billings is turning into an old lady," the earl stated in exasperation. "So that's what sent you hotfooting it down here."

"Thought you might need some company. After all, the press has been pretty hard on you."

"Believe me, I'm not going into a decline over some scoundrels who write libel," Straeford jeered. "I simply came down here for some solitude, but between Manners and Lady Maxwell bending my ear about saving Straeford, I might just as well have stayed in London."

"What are your plans for the Park?" Harding asked as he surveyed his surroundings.

Straeford threw back his head and laughed, causing the major to smile sheepishly. Then in a more sober vein the earl explained that he had just finished an inventory of the family jewels to discover that besides the legendary Straeford emeralds, which were entailed to the estate, there were a few good pieces he could pawn along with the last of the Van Dycks. After that he would try his luck at the gaming tables.

Harding was not enthusiastic about this plan, but he had to agree with Straeford that there was little else he could do under the circumstances. They speculated about his chances of winning a fortune, and Harding volunteered to investigate the clubs most likely to accommodate his friend in this matter.

"When do you return to London?"

"The inquiry begins next week." Straeford scowled.

"Just, I've been thinking. You ought to defend yourself against these attacks in the press. Cromwell and I are only too willing to give character references for you."

"But you and Cromwell were not there when the Nangore incident took place."

"Yet we know what Seton is like!"

"Hearsay. The facts will have to speak for themselves."

"And if they don't?"

"I've survived slander before."

21

"Damn! I'd like to tell them a thing or two."

"But you won't. I can count on you."

"You know you can."

Straeford smiled and brought the discussion to a close by inviting Harding to join him for dinner.

2

"And did you not on the morning of February 18, 1807, two days after the total rout of the rebel forces under the leadership of Dashrami al Singhe, deliberately order the public execution by hanging of twenty-three of those rebels? And was not that order in direct disobedience to the express orders of General Seton, your commanding officer in charge of the expeditionary forces to the Madras territory of continental India?" Major Ross Covington of the Judge Advocate's Office droned on in the near-empty chambers of the military court at the Horse Guards.

"The statement as read by Major Covington is in partial error—the execution was ordered by me, but *not* in direct disobedience to General Seton's orders." Lord Straeford directed his reply to the seven-man board before him.

"My lord, I hold here a direct communiqué from General Seton, charging that you were given explicit orders to take no reprisals in reestablishing British control over the village of Nangore." The major regarded the earl with a quiet disdain.

"I take it you have those exact charges in writing, sir?" Straeford's reply in the form of a question was not what Major Covington had expected.

"I have here General Seton's letter . . ."

"But does the general make formal charges of misconduct, Major Covington?"

"They are not charges by writ of military code, but this represents the word of your commanding officer. Do you choose to question the word of General Seton, sir?"

"I choose to defend myself, Major. Do you deny me that right?" The cold authority in Straeford's voice struck the assembled board with surprise. Whatever Lord Straeford had done in that distant Indian village, it was obvious that shame bore no part in it.

"I should think your right to defend yourself is apparent since it is an inquiry and not a court-marital we are conducting here, sir," Major Covington sneered.

"In that case, I assume I have the right to explain my actions during that operation and why I ordered the execution of twenty-three Indian rebels." Again a statement delivered with absolute authority.

"Very well, my lord, suppose you tell us your . . ." the major paused significantly, ". . . version."

"I will tell the board the facts, Major. I do not deal in versions."

"Pray then, proceed."

"It is necessary that I start with the attack on midnight of February 15, preceding the battle at dawn on the sixteenth. It was shortly after the midnight attack that twenty-three members of His Majesty's 74th Foot were captured by Dashrami . . ."

Straeford disregarded the startled looks of the board as he thought back over the events of that dark night. The jungle blackness had been so intense that it was impossible for him to see his hand in front of his face. Straeford had struggled to prevent General Seton's midnight attack, knowing in advance that it was a disastrous tactic, but it was impossible to penetrate the fog of inebriation that clouded the general's brain.

The order to attack was given by Seton to Bradwick, and by the time Straeford received word of it, it was too late. The earl knew he should never have left Seton's side that night, but there was no way of covering every hole in that ill-conceived operation. Calamity was inevitable despite Straeford's vigilance.

It had been only a matter of time before the general committed an irreversible blunder. Seton's drunkenness had been a scandal of growing magnitude, and no effort of Straeford's could conceal it. But the earl's obsession with duty was a habit of too many years to alter. And Seton had once been a first-class soldier—that Colonel Lord Straeford could not disavow regardless of the enmity between them. The earl would try to pull them both out with honor if it were humanly possible; nevertheless, this inquiry was an humiliating blow. How could the fool have dared create such a fracas? Seton was probably beyond salvation, but Straeford would not be the one to expose him.

". . . and it was because of our attempt to rescue those captured troops that the battle was enjoined at dawn on the sixteenth . . ." he continued calmly.

The looks of increasing dismay from the board finally caused the earl to halt in his recitation.

"Lord Straeford, is it your contention that there was a predawn attack on the fifteenth in which British soldiers were captured by the enemy?" This was from General Belvoir, who was also a veteran of the Indian campaigns.

"But of course, sir. The success of the attack on the morning of the sixteenth was due in large part to surprise. Dashrami did not think we would regroup and counterattack so speedily. Unfortunately the scoundrel escaped capture, or it would have been *his* neck we stretched later."

"But my lord Straeford," this time it was Lord Carstairs of Castlereagh's office who interrupted, "there is nothing in the record concerning a predawn encounter with Dashrami's forces. This is a most shocking report you bring forth at this time."

The earl received Lord Carstairs's statement impassively, in no way betraying the dismay and anger this piece of information caused him.

The seven-man board appointed by the Secretary of

State for War, Major Covington and the court recorder all stared in consternation at the implacable countenance of the earl, who regarded each man silently.

After some passage of time, Straeford spoke quietly. "If I may be allowed the opportunity of reading through the record—it seems there is need of clarification."

"Indeed, sir, there is," Lord Carstairs replied. "However, I feel it necessary to put some questions to you before we adjourn and reconvene to consider this revelation."

"As you wish, my lord."

"There are any number of matters to cover here, sir. Let me briefly state them as I see them. First, there was a predawn attack in which twenty-three British soldiers were captured?" Carstairs had taken over, relegating Covington to the sidelines.

"That is correct, my lord."

"And the attack at dawn was partially a rescue effort?"

"It was."

"And did you indeed rescue those men?"

"No sir."

"No!" Carstairs was aghast.

"No, we found their mutilated bodies following the defeat of the enemy on the afternoon of the seventeenth."

"Before God, Lord Straeford, these are most serious charges!"

"You have me at a disadvantage, my lord. I do not regard these as charges, but merely as the facts."

"Well, well, sir, we shall leave that till later. I don't wish to get into the matter of facts versus charges just yet."

Straeford nodded.

"Now then, was your order to execute the twenty-three Indian rebels a matter of punishment for the atrocities?"

"Only in part, my lord. It was primarily to issue a public warning to all other rebels—as you know, Dashrami's band is only one of many. The rebels must be made to understand that British justice is swift and harsh and that acts of murder will not be condoned as part of military combat."

Lord Carstairs and his colleagues regarded Lord Straeford angrily. "My lord, why did General Seton not agree to these measures if what you say is true?"

"I am afraid you will have to question General Seton on that matter, my lord."

"You may be sure that I will. But *he* is in India, and *you* are here and I am questioning you *now*. Why did General Seton not agree to your course of action?"

Lord Straeford paused, gathering his thoughts before replying. "There was great confusion in Nangore at the time. Many inhabitants of the village were fleeing into the countryside."

"Where was General Seton when you ordered the executions?"

"On his way to Bengal."

"He left you in charge of occupational forces?"

"Yes, sir."

"But he ordered no reprisals?"

"I . . . General Seton gave no exact orders to me on that matter, Lord Carstairs."

"But we have here his own deposition."

Straeford cursed inwardly. "General Seton preferred that no reprisals be taken."

"Can you tell me why?"

The earl groaned silently. "He believed it might stir up greater hostility among the native population . . . and the general was aware of public opinion in England regarding the treatment of Indian nationals."

"But this was a situation involving warring natives and the restoration of public order."

"So I believed, my lord."

"How real was the danger of stirring up further native hostility, Lord Straeford?"

"Very real, sir. It *still* is a great danger, and likely will continue to be."

"Then there was some wisdom in General Seton's position, I take it?"

Again Straeford paused. "Not . . . not as I viewed the situation, my lord." His reply startled his auditors once more. "The control of India requires inflexible strength, Lord Carstairs. Especially in dealing with the countless brigands who roam the countryside attacking not only His Majesty's representatives, but the peaceful citizens of the Indian continent as well. However, those are problems of state, my lord, which I do not pretend to answer. My training is that of a soldier, and as a soldier I knew the necessity of setting a harsh example before the people. The safety of the British soldier in India is risky, at best, and it was my concern to take whatever measures were necessary to ensure our men of at least minimal safety—prisoners of war should not have to risk mutilation!"

This final statement was pronounced with such deadly finality that even Carstairs dared not refute it.

"Of course, of course, my lord. However, I feel there is much that is still cloudy in this matter. The predawn attack which you state resulted in the capture of British soldiers—how did that come to pass?"

For the first time the earl displayed visible indecision.

"Lord Straeford, there is nothing in the record about such an attack. There is nothing in the record about the atrocities you describe. Our loss of some eighty men in the encounter at Nangore was attributed to casualties of battle. This is a serious alteration to the facts as written up by General Seton, and the record must be set straight. I'm sure you will agree."

Straeford nodded curtly.

"Now, if this attack did occur as you claim, I cannot, for the life of me, understand General Seton's intentions in bringing charges against you."

The explanation was one the earl chose not to go into. Seton's hatred of Straeford went back over many years, ever since Straeford's growing success in battle began to overshadow the general's record. As Seton's blunders increased, Straeford was forced to assume more authority, which only served to further embitter the man whose career was eroding steadily.

The earl took up the recitation of the night's events without preamble. "We had been on the march five days prior to our arrival at Nangore. General Seton, believing that an attack under cover of darkness would have the advantage of surprise, ordered a charge at midnight on the fifteenth. Unfortunately al Singhe was prepared and

28

waiting for us. Our men were badly shot up and twenty-three taken prisoner before General Seton called off the attack and retreated."

"Was there no reconnaissance of the area to determine the readiness of the enemy?" Lord Carstairs questioned.

"We arrived at sundown and attacked at midnight. There was no opportunity to reconnoitre the situation."

"Excuse me, my lord," General Belvoir, who was restraining himself with great difficulty, interrupted, "but I must ask Lord Straeford to repeat what he has just said. Did you in fact say that General Seton ordered an attack during the dark of night without first having sent advance patrols into the area to determine enemy strength?"

"It was as you say, General Belvoir," Straeford replied without explaining that that had been exactly what he himself was preparing to do when the noise of the attack reached his ears.

"Infamous! That was an infamous piece of work," General Belvoir sputtered. "By the lord of hosts, General Seton barely redeemed himself with victory the next day." Then, as if further infamy dawned on him, "He did lead the counter-attack, did he not, Lord Straeford?"

A sudden silence fell on the near-empty chamber where the Earl of Straeford had been summoned to give an accounting of himself. The sound of wind fretted bare branches against the windows, and voices drifted faintly from the streets below. Finally, his reluctance apparent, Lord Straeford answered General Belvoir's question.

"The entire expedition to put down the rebellion at Nangore was under the command of General Seton." He hesitated. "If I may interject my thoughts here, gentlemen, the purpose of this inquiry is to investigate the execution of those twenty-three Indian rebels. I readily admit that the execution was carried out by my command when left in charge by General Seton. I also admit that our viewpoints differed sharply on the necessity of such action. However, I am ... ah ... surprised that General Seton's deposition states that my actions contravened his orders. If I could have some time to read over that deposition, perhaps I could clear up the misunderstanding to the board's satisfaction."

"It is more than a mere misunderstanding, Lord Straeford. Your testimony has brought forth disturbing information which cannot be lightly cast aside. Perhaps it would be best to adjourn this inquiry until further study of the matter can be made. I suggest, gentlemen, that we call a recess of indefinite duration and reconvene when the facts are better known on all sides."

Lord Carstairs's suggestion was readily accepted and the hearing adjourned—the principal participants hastening to their clubs to speculate on the startling revelations brought forth by the afternoon's testimony.

The earl pushed his way through a throng of journalists crowding outside the hearing room and ignored their determined questioning with grim silence. It was left to Lord Carstairs to quiet their clamor with a brief noncommittal statement.

The reporters scurried to their home offices to ready their accounts which, as usual, relied heavily on conjecture and libel to appease the appetite of a public eager for scandal rather than facts. Over the years, the fortunes of Lord Straeford and his family had been the source of much scurrilous entertainment of a people avid to enjoy the comedown of so mighty a house. "The Infamy of Nangore" was seized upon by working men and gentry alike as topic for heated debate.

The Earl of Straeford had been the target of journalistic assault before, but none had been so vicious and unremitting as the current affair over the rebels of India. They were represented in the popular press as ignorant natives suffering oppression and brutality at the hands of an unfeeling monster. Several years ago there had been a tremendous furor raised over Straeford's treatment of the Bedloes boy, but fortunately evidence had proved that the then Major St. Clare had acted correctly in having the blackguard drummed out of the corps. And now it was vastly more satisfying to shred the reputation of that same St. Clare whose elevated station as the Earl of Straeford enhanced the sport. The earl suffered little at the hands of his detractors, however. He had long ago steeled himself against the barbs of public obloquy, and there was little the scandal mongers could say to wound him.

Once in his room at the Stephens, Straeford ordered a light supper to be sent him, preferring solitude before a small fire to further contact with a world he scorned.

Ever since the estrangement from his mother and the consequent notoriety, Justin St. Clare had steadily removed himself from a society so eager to brand him an unprincipled villain. He had become a loner who cherished his isolation.

The solitary man sat regarding the bright flames in the grate, musing at the red lights glinting from the ruby signet ring on his left hand. It should be Robert, not himself, wearing the ring of the Earl of Straeford. But Robert was dead too many years to allow that bitter memory to pain him further.

And yet the pain did not abate with the passage of time. Robert had been too close and loving a brother, and the bond between them had not been severed by death. Deep within, Straeford maintained a vigil of mourning he would never admit to anyone. In truth, he wished that his brother had married Adele and supplied the necessary heir to the earldom which now laid so heavy a burden upon him. He much preferred to steep himself in his life as a colonel of the Horse Grenadier Guards to a life circumscribed by the conventional duties that went with a title.

Reluctantly, the earl applied himself to the lengthy records containing General Seton's charges. It would take a miracle to extricate himself this time from the tangle created by Seton's folly. No doubt the old dog had sent off the deposition in a condition of alcoholic excess and was probably regretting it at this very moment. But what to do to salvage the situation honorably was Straeford's burden, not the general's. Just how long the board would delay until the next hearing was not possible to ascertain.

Whatever the board's timing, Straeford decided he had had enough of the rebels of Nangore by the next evening and was ready to join Ed Harding in an excursion to the Golden Hazard, a discreet gaming hell. Entrée to the Bloomsbury establishment depended mainly on the size of the client's purse, and many a well-heeled cit rubbed elbows with gentlemen from the upper strata of society under circumstances not prevailing elsewhere in such a class conscious world.

No-limit betting drew the inveterate gamblers of London to the Hazard's tables, and extravagant sums were won and lost there. It suited the earl's purposes perfectly, since he hoped to gain a fortune to restore Straeford Park through his efforts at cards. His cold control had served him rather well in past games of chance, and he saw no reason why he should not succeed in applying that same style now.

"My dear Lord Straeford! How uncommon surprising to find you patronizing such plebeian environs." It was Harold Foxworth, an improvident fop whose supercilious manner placed him high on the earl's list of fools to be avoided.

"I cannot say that it surprises me to find you here, Foxworth."

The gentleman tapped Straeford lightly with his silver-headed cane and jeered, "You were ever quick on the uptake, Straeford. I should not have forgotten. But let me introduce you to Angus Loftus, the luckiest chemin de fer gamester in London."

Straeford's attention was instantly alerted. The middle-aged man before him was exactly the opportunity he was seeking. "Indeed sir, I trust your friend Foxworth speaks with authority on your gaming."

"Aye, he does. I've won more than my fair share, and I'm not ashamed to admit it. I hear you don't do too badly neither, my lord. Care to match your game to mine?"

The earl's eyes narrowed shrewdly as he realized the affluent cit with penetrating blue eyes was sizing him up too.

"Chemin de fer is not exactly my game," Straeford drawled, dissembling his interest.

"If Dame Fortune smiles on you, it don't matter what the game, I always say."

Was this a frontal attack or merely a skirmish, Straeford wondered.

"Very astute, sir. I shall be delighted to join you in a

game," the earl agreed and followed Loftus to the table.

As he walked, his friend Harding whispered, "Lord, Justin, that's not your game. Stick to Hazard. You've always been lucky with dice."

"The big money tonight is at the chemin table."

"But Angus Loftus wins more than he loses," Harding warned.

"Did you not hear the gentleman's notions about luck? If the lady grants me her favor, I may be able to reclaim the Van Dycks and jewels I pawned as collateral to the moneylenders and refurbish Straeford Park. I think the risk is worth it."

Several hours later Straeford and Loftus were the only two players left at the chemin de fer table. Although they had attracted an interested crowd of bystanders, the room was very quiet. Cautiously and accurately they had gauged each other's plays, but it was the earl who controlled the bank now with £15,000 at stake. Straeford had refused the opportunity of passing to his opponent after the last hand. He was gambling that Loftus would declare "banco" and match his £15,000. If the earl should win, Straeford Park was secure.

Betraying none of his inner feelings, he sipped calmly at his wine and smiled genially at the older man who was studying this imperturbable stranger.

"Banco," Angus claimed, shattering the stillness and placing his money beside the earl's. The winner would take all.

The operator handed the box with the cards in it to Straeford, who slid one card out and dealt it to Loftus face down. Then one to himself. A second card to his opponent, and finally another card to himself. Each man examined his hand with no change of expression.

Did Loftus have an 8 or 9, Straeford wondered. If so, it was all over for him because he held a total count of four.

"Pass," Angus Loftus called. The earl sighed silently as he too passed, returning the play to Loftus.

"I'll stay," the sturdy cit claimed.

Straeford raised his cigar to his mouth and puffed on it before taking his cards. His opponent probably had a count of seven. If so, he must draw a 3 to tie or a 4 or 5 to beat him. Anything over a total count of nine and he would lose! He drew a 2 of clubs.

Harding shifted uneasily behind him although Straeford remained unflinching with defeat yawning before him. There was still one chance! Loftus had taken the option to stand pat at five points.

"Gentlemen?" the operator questioned.

Loftus studied his cards for one more moment, hoping to stir the younger man to some display of emotion, but the earl remained impassive. Exasperated, Loftus flipped his cards over one at a time—a 3 of hearts—a 4 of spades!

The earl did not hesitate in revealing his own hand. Although his face paled slightly, his hands remained steady as he tossed the cards onto the table—an ace of hearts, a 3 of spades and a 2 of clubs for a count of six.

"Mr. Loftus is the winner," the operator announced.

There was a moment of confusion as the onlookers broke into a noisy babble, and the operator scooped up the money for the winner.

"Congratulations, sir." Straeford extended a steady hand to his opponent as he rose.

"You play well, my lord. Perhaps a rematch at another time?" Loftus squinted up at him.

"I doubt that, sir. My blunt is spent."

"You will oblige me by having a drink with me?"

"Of course," the earl nodded and dropped into a chair beside him. "Harding," he looked up at his friend who was frowning unhappily, "sit down and join us. I'm sure Mr. Loftus won't mind."

"Not at all, not at all. I think your friend needs a brandy more than you do, my lord. You too, Foxworth," he motioned to the dandy and turned his attention to the earl. "You take your loss admirably."

"Do I? And how else should a gentleman behave?" Straeford claimed arrogantly as he quirked an eyebrow at the older man.

"I have been witness to many gambling displays in my day, and your coolness surpasses them all."

"I assure you I have no intention of cutting my throat—or yours, for that matter."

34

The old man chuckled. "No, I'm sure you don't."

"That's not the good *Colonel's* way, is it, Straeford?" Foxworth cut in grinning slyly. "Don't you know, Angus, this man never displays any emotion. Some claim he don't have any. Do you, *Colonel?* Cool as a cucumber while your whole career hangs in the balance," the silly man taunted.

"If I did have any emotions, you might be enjoying the back of my hand right now, Foxworth," Straeford warned.

"Be quiet, Harold," Angus spoke sharply, "or go away. No one is amused by your attempts at humor."

Harold pouted angrily as he drew a lace handkerchief from his sleeve and touched it to his lips. "It does grow late, and I do have a morning engagement." He looked meaningfully at Loftus. "So I shall wish you a pleasant goodnight, gentlemen. Of course, one wonders how pleasant the *Colonel's* night will be . . ." he let the thought dangle. Then, pausing behind the earl's chair, "Does tonight's loss mean you will be forced to sell Straeford Park, *Colonel?* Such a pity, I'm sure. But you've spent so little time there it's not much use to you, is it? Unless you plan to marry soon . . ." Again he let the thought hang in mid-air.

"Goodnight, Foxworth," Loftus claimed sternly while Straeford ignored his antagonist.

Foxworth laughed affectedly and sauntered off.

"Pay him no heed, my lord," Loftus suggested.

"The man's a popinjay," Harding added. "His points are so high he risks stabbing himself every time he tries to turn his head."

This produced a spurt of laughter from the three of them. When it died away, Straeford and Harding rose and took their leave of Loftus, but as they turned to go the man called to Straeford.

"A word in private, my lord?"

Harding shrugged and left them while the earl eyed Loftus suspiciously.

"Don't look so fierce, my lord. I have a slight proposition to put to you."

The earl's guarded look intensified but he did not speak.

"The sum you lost tonight—an inconvenient amount, I take it." Loftus waited for the earl to acknowledge his statement, but Straeford did not reply. Shrugging his heavy shoulders, the merchant continued, "Perhaps a loan. . . ." He waited again, letting his eyes rest on the taller man's impassive face.

Finally Straeford spoke. "And for this loan . . . you would require some service." It was not a question but a statement.

"You come straight to the point, my lord. Yes, you might call it a service," he temporized, "but it is late and we are both tired. Would you find it convenient to call upon me at my offices about three this afternoon?"

Straeford accepted the proposal. "So be it. Until three."

After dropping Harding at his home, the earl continued to his hotel, all the while mulling over his dilemma. He was not a sentimental man, he told himself, and as Foxworth had pointed out, Straeford Park had not been his home for years; nevertheless he could not contemplate losing it. The pride of the St. Clares was too ingrained in him. The estates must be saved, and the line secured, whatever sacrifice was demanded of him. He would have to marry, as his grandmother suggested, but he'd be damned if it would be some climbing cit. His will to sacrifice stopped short of that particular comedown—no matter how great the fortune of his grandmother's particular candidate. He'd find an heiress from the *ton*.

If only Robert had married Adele and provided an heir. Ah well, that was a dead end, and Adele's qualifications for Countess of Straeford left much to be desired. She had proved little better than a slut, coming to him the very night of Robert's funeral and offering herself to him. At least he did not have to contend with that bitch!

Women! They were all alike. The meaning of loyalty beyond their perfidious natures. Best restrict one's amorous pursuits to those ladies of the night who made no pretense of their intentions.

Yet marry he must. And the lady would understand from the start that his only motive would be to secure an heir. There would be no romantic illusions clouding the

36

picture. God grant he find some sensible female willing to accept the bargain he was girding himself to make.

Of course, there was the slim possibility that Angus Loftus would offer him a worthwhile proposition . . . But what did he know about the man except that he was a wealthy textile merchant who had used chemin de fer as a pretext for meeting him? Well, he would learn more on that score before too many hours elapsed. Dawn was already creasing the eastern sky.

That same afternoon Straeford was escorted into the merchant's plush office, which was richly decorated in red velvet and brown leather. The center of the room was dominated by a huge desk behind which sat Angus Loftus. The gentleman welcomed him and offered the earl a cigar from a heavy bronze box inlaid with a darker metal in a scrollwork pattern.

"Now, let us get down to business," Loftus proposed confidently.

"By all means."

"I don't mind telling you, Lord Straeford, I have had my eye on you for some time, ever since your return from India."

"Indeed." Straeford regarded his host blandly.

"Hope you don't mind my saying that I don't hold with the raking-over you're getting in the press these days. A lot of puffed-up nonsense pandering to the noisy rabble. Experience has taught me not to judge on the appearance of things. There are always deeper currents than meet the eye." He paused. "There now, I've said my say and you'll hear no more from me on that score."

The earl nodded noncommittally, not allowing himself to react.

Loftus observed his guest and leaned forward confidingly. "I'll come quickly to the point, my lord."

"Please do."

"You and I, Lord Straeford, can be of service to each other in meeting needs . . . needs each of us is capable of satisfying for the other. To be blunt about it, you need money, my lord, and I . . ." he paused again.

"Yes?" Straeford queried, but the merchant was not quite ready to reveal his full proposal.

"I'll see that Straeford Park and your town house are restored. Also the paintings, jewelry and land which have been sold over the years are bought back—under the following conditions . . ."

Straeford displayed no enthusiasm or agitation at Loftus's words, but commented levelly, "I'm listening."

"A commission in the army for my son John and . . . marriage to one of my daughters. Make one your countess and see that she is presented to the *ton*."

The moment of silence following Loftus's terms was abruptly shattered by Straeford scraping his chair across the floor as he rose to his feet, swearing softly to himself.

Angus rose too and spoke before Straeford could put into words his opinion of this scheme. "My dead wife was the daughter of Sir Harry Bradshaw, an impoverished lord from the North Country. It is my wish to see that my children take their rightful place in society."

"And I am to provide that entrée!" Straeford laughed scornfully.

"Why not? It's more than a fair proposition to you."

"You're willing to sell one of your daughters to me for a place in the *ton?*" Straeford jeered.

"Don't set me down, Lord Straeford, for something that is a common practice among the gentry; marriages of convenience are arranged all the time." Loftus betrayed a touch of anger as he spoke.

"But not for me," Straeford's voice was laced with steel, "they aren't."

"My girls are dutiful and know what to expect."

"Damn you man! You've had the temerity to speak to them about this?"

"And why not? It's what they want too."

"Indeed, do they?" Straeford's black brows rose disdainfully. "Well, I can assure you it is *not* what *I* want!" And the earl attempted to pass the stocky man who was blocking his exit.

"Wait," Loftus importuned. "Why don't you think about my offer and let me know your decision later?"

"There is nothing to think about. I have no intention of offering for a daughter of yours, and I may add that I find your tactics distasteful in the extreme. You led me to believe it was a business proposition you were considering—not a back door to the *ton!*"

With effort Loftus ignored the bitter thrust and stood his ground. "I'm having a dinner party Thursday. Come and meet my family. No obligation."

The earl did not reply but stepped around Loftus and crossed to the door, jerking it open. Then he swung around to face the merchant once more and demanded, "Who put you on to me?"

"Don't you know?"

Straeford slammed the door shut and stared at Loftus incredulously. "That interfering old troublemaker!" he stormed. "I should have wrung her neck when she was at Straeford last week."

"I wouldn't advise it, laddie. Lady Maxwell is the best friend you have . . . besides me."

"Damn you and Lady Maxwell!" Straeford shouted before slamming out the door.

Within an hour the angry man of war was glaring at Lady Maxwell in the comfortable drawing room of that lady's spacious residence on Grosvenor Square.

"So you've had your talk with Loftus," she claimed, reading the thunder in her grandson's face. She seated herself regally on a small settee before the fire and regarded him with interest.

He gave her a dark look and flung himself into a wingback chair opposite her.

"Well, will you take one of the cit's daughters, my boy?"

He jerked out of the chair and crossed to stand in front of her. "I ordered you not to interfere in my affairs! Yet you ignored my right to privacy and approached this . . . this merchant and dared to suggest a match between a daughter of his and myself . . ."

"Justin St. Clare," the lady claimed, cutting through his impassioned speech, "sit down and exercise some of that icy control you are famous for. Your conduct smacks of the very class you profess to abhor."

Lady Maxwell's tactic worked immediately. The earl stepped back a pace and waited for his grandmother to continue.

39

"That's better, boy. Now if you were thinking rationally and not letting emotion blind you, I'm sure you would realize this is the only alternative left you."

Straeford sank into the chair once more, nodding his head in reluctant agreement.

Some minutes passed without further exchange between them, but not wishing to let the matter close until she received her grandson's verbal commitment, Lady Maxwell broached the subject once more. "So you will marry a Loftus girl." It was more of a statement than a question.

There was a strangled oath from the earl before he replied curtly, "I shall have to, I suppose, before you try to arrange my entire life to your liking."

This mild satire brought forth a crack of rusty laughter from the old woman.

"Loftus has two daughters, a young dark one and an older blonde one. Which do you fancy?"

"How should I know?" He scowled and leaned forward, placing his elbows on his knees and his face in his hands.

"They are called Margaret and Marisa."

The earl leaned back rubbing the back of his neck and smiling at his grandmother's ingenuousness. "Am I to choose on the basis of name or hair color, Madam? It makes no difference to me since I must have one of them." He stood again and began pacing the room. "I told Loftus in no uncertain terms that I would have no part in his marriage scheme. Perhaps he will have second thoughts and I shall be relieved of the need to decide."

"Wishful thinking, my dear. He will accept your offer. Did I not tell you he is mad for the *ton?*"

"And his daughters seem to be too," he rejoined bitterly.

"As I begin to ponder it, Justin, I think you had best take the older girl. She is less likely to have romantic fancies. There was some talk of her and a man called Aiken a few years ago, but that's all past history. She's far likelier to be of a sensible turn of mind by now."

"Had her fling, has she?" he claimed cynically.

His grandmother ignored this thrust. "Both girls are beauties, but the older one's a biddable girl. Yes, Marisa will adapt to your ways quickly and make you a good wife."

"God spare me! I have no intention of remaining in the girl's company any more than is strictly necessary. I shall return to the army with all due haste."

"But not before you've done your duty by her."

The earl ignored her thrust as she had his. "I shall leave her *and* her good family in your capable hands, madam. You will share the responsibility of introducing them to the *ton.*"

Lady Maxwell opened her mouth to protest, but Straeford held up his hand and continued, "That's the price you must pay for your interference, my dear. Is it a bargain?"

"You forget one thing young man." Lady Maxwell smiled a trifle maliciously. "The heir. There must be an heir!"

"You try me beyond all endurance," Straeford claimed through gritted teeth. "I have not forgotten." He rose and bowed mockingly. "I trust you will leave that, at least, to me."

She cackled. "I hear tell, devil though you may be, women still want you. You'll get us an heir for Straeford, Justin. Then you can leave the chit and her family to me and fly back to your precious military life."

"We are agreed. I'll see Miss Loftus is initiated as wife and mother before I take leave of her." He smiled wickedly. "Mmh, I might enjoy this more than I expected —a beauty you say?"

"Justin," Lady Maxwell warned, "whichever one you take, she's not going to be one of your light-skirts —but your wife, the countess—don't forget that!"

Straeford scowled, engulfed by a sudden black rage. "How will I be able to forget it with you and Loftus *and* his daughter about my neck? Just remember, afterward, the family is your headache."

Lady Maxwell passed an uneasy night following the disturbing interview with her grandson. Now that the machinery for the marriage was set in motion she was suffering qualms of conscience. At heart she wanted what was best not only for her grandson, but for Loftus's daughter as well.

3

A pounding at the door in the hall beyond woke the earl from a drugged sleep. It took some minutes before Harding's excited words penetrated the fog in his brain.

". . . Dashrami's forces at Baklar!"

"Hold your fire, man. Did I hear you right? Dashrami . . ."

". . . attacked the garrison at Baklar and slaughtered half the outpost! A mere handful escaped."

"Good God! General Seton was supposed to be there."

"I know. He escaped."

"Escaped? General Seton? What are you telling me, Ed? Start again. My head . . ." The earl groaned as he massaged his aching temples.

"Look, here it is," Harding thrust a morning journal beneath Straeford's nose. "Read it for yourself."

Suddenly the earl leaped from the edge of the bed where he had been sitting. Taking the paper to the window, he thrust back the draperies so the early morning light made reading easier. He winced painfully, his head throbbing from the excess of the brandy imbibed the night before, but he read hurriedly, consuming the incredible facts before him.

"Attacked at sunset . . . a band of two thousand screaming rebels . . . two hundred British soldiers dead . . . General Seton and Major Sellers escaped to Calcutta. I'll be damned! The old fool must have bungled again."

"That's exactly what happened, Just. The garrison was undermanned."

"I can hardly credit Dashrami's luck. The dirty heathen must have nine lives!"

"It didn't take much luck to outmaneuver Seton. This time there's no covering the blunders. Sentries weren't posted properly, the call to arms came too late, muskets weren't ready—Seton will be disgraced."

"It had to happen. He's been going downhill for a long time. It's a wonder he got by thus far."

"He got by because you were there to see he did. Well, not anymore. He will have to face the consequences himself this time."

The earl rubbed the black stubble on his chin thoughtfully. The War Office would not be able to sweep this disaster under the carpet, and the press and the public were bound to hear the truth about Seton. How that would affect him depended on whether the board saw Nangore and Baklar as two separate incidents, or a developing pattern of incompetence on the part of General Seton.

"For once, my friend, fate is easing your way."

"At the expense of two hundred British lives, man! Don't forget that!" Straeford declared vehemently.

"Hell, Justin, I'm not forgetting it! But it happened, and your future looks better for it. I'm sure the board will decide in your favor."

A knock at the door interrupted their conversation, and Straeford's servant, Billings, entered with a breakfast tray. After serving each man a cup of coffee, he left them alone again. Straeford stared moodily at the cup in front of him until Harding asked, "Something else troubling you, Justin?"

Straeford took a gulp of black coffee before answering. "It's the Loftus business."

"Oh." Harding waited for him to go on.

"I'm promised to the merchant for dinner tonight to meet his daughters."

"Take heart, old man. Mayhap you'll like the look of them."

"What's that to say to anything?"

"A pretty face can ease many a sorry plight." Harding grinned as he bit into a warm scone.

"Egads, Ed!" Straeford jumped out of his chair and began pacing the room restlessly. "They are common cits! The man's in trade. Daughters of a climbing, grasping merchant. Can you imagine their style? Their mode of life?"

"You over-dramatize, Just. You are not the first man ever forced to search the merchant ranks for a suitable wife and fortune. Besides, you told me the mother was a Bradshaw."

"Who married beneath her," Justin snapped.

"Still, you may find the gods are dealing more kindly with you than you know, my friend. Take heart and keep an open mind."

"An open mind is an unguarded door through which any fool may pass," the earl retorted before dropping into his chair and returning to the topic of General Seton and the catastrophe in India.

The modest Loftus residence in Bloomsbury surprised Straeford. The air of simple dignity presented by an unadorned dark green door and shining brass knocker was altogether impressive. It was not what the earl expected and he regarded it favorably.

The butler's manner was quiet, the foyer sedate and the drawing room well lighted, simply furnished and filled with fashionably attired guests conversing in civilized tones.

It far exceeded Straeford's expectations, and yet he was not pleased. An atmosphere of quiet repose did not belie the fact that it was a marriage mart the earl was attending and that he was both the buyer and the bought.

Well, let's see the merchandise and get the business settled. He did not doubt that he himself would be found suitable.

Angus Loftus came up to his aristocratic guest, a

jovial smile lighting his blunt features. "My Lord Strae-ford, allow me to introduce you to my family."

It was a large family—not only Angus's children, but cousins, aunts, uncles, nephews, and nieces he met and whose names the earl scarce heard. But he did observe carefully the immediate progeny of the wealthy merchant with whom he might be forced into a family relationship.

John Loftus, a lad of twenty-one, greeted Lord Straeford with a direct look that revealed none of his inner feelings. He was exceedingly fair, tall and wiry, and his handclasp was firm. His simple black breeches and frock coat were bare of the flowing laces and stiff collars so popular among the young sporting set who aspired to join the ranks of Corinthians.

The older daughter, Marisa Loftus, shared her brother's fair coloring and modest style, but there was a deeper intensity to the blue of her eyes and her blond tresses, worn in charming coils that framed her lovely face, were more honey-toned than flaxen. She too met the earl with a cool gaze that revealed nothing of her thoughts, though hers was a greater stake in this meeting.

There was something familiar about the man, but she could not quite bring to the surface of her mind that frozen moment at the Inns of Court when they had briefly collided in the snow.

It was Margaret, the younger daughter, who obvi-ously was the scene stealer. Her flowing hair of dark brown was allowed to tumble about her bare shoulders in a most provocative fashion. Her blue eyes were bright and sparkling and eager to convey her lively interest in the handsome catch her father had snared for his daugh-ters. It was apparent from the onset that she was already measuring the breadth of those wide shoulders with a proprietary air, and preparing a mental list for the wed-ding invitations.

The family was an attractive group, the earl was relieved to discover. But that they were not of his class was uppermost in his mind.

The Loftus board was another unexpected bonus. The master set an ample table and his cook was excellent. The dressed fowls stuffed with truffles in wine sauce were superb, and the earl's wine glass was never allowed to empty of the rich, red claret that filled it.

It was Marisa who held the earl's attention though the younger Margaret, seated to his right, was a stunning coquette. Wherever she learned her maneuvers with the fan, she had learned them from an expert. And those dark-fringed eyes regarding him with sly satisfaction were nothing new to him. He had met that look on the faces of ambitious females in the past, but he did little more than nod occasionally to her animated attempts to draw him out. Instead he studied Marisa Loftus, seated at the foot of the table, with unconcealed interest until his attention was distracted by the mention of General Seton.

". . . General Seton's fiasco. Just goes to show the army don't know what it's doing if you ask me." A shrunken little fox of a man with darting eyes peered maliciously beneath bushy brows at the assembled table. "Win one day and lose the next. Can't depend on 'em, *I* say."

No one else dared speak out with Straeford present.

"Must be something wrong when a ragged band of heathens can get the upper hand and send our ruddy soldiers scurrying for cover, eh? What d'ye say, Denton?" He flung a challenge to a red-faced young man across from him who dived into his dinner plate and began to eat furiously. Others started conversing eagerly with their neighbors hoping the old fool would have the sense to silence himself.

The earl looked at Marisa Loftus, wishing to study her reaction. It did not matter to him what this assemblage of cits believed since they were beneath his contempt.

The girl's face betrayed no emotion—no curiosity or shame or fear—only calm repose. He liked that.

But she was watching him too, studying his reaction as well. Her blue eyes which were slightly tilted at the corners were regarding him steadily, and he was surprised to perceive a lurking disapproval in their depths.

Be damned with her disapproval! The girl piqued his curiosity. For all she was the daughter of a merchant, she presented a picture of aristocratic beauty. The features of

47

her face were well-defined—her brow smooth, her gaze forthright, her lips and cheeks sweetly curved.

The words of the troublesome old man penetrated Straeford's thoughts once more.

". . . only capable of abusing helpless natives."

The old devil was growing louder and more quarrelsome, and since no one answered him, he added one more thrust.

"Seems our military are bravest when ordering executions and slaughtering helpless prisoners, don't it?" He was staring directly at Straeford. —

"Why, Uncle Reggie, with all this talk about the military, of which we know very little, you have not eaten your dessert, and I know it is your favorite." Marisa Loftus intervened, attempting to cover her uncle's breach of etiquette. He had insulted a guest in her father's home!

Although Straeford appreciated Marisa Loftus's tactfulness, he felt little gratitude for her intervention. He had no wish to be defended by this woman. He had outfaced worse than this old coot in the past, but it was time he silenced the fool once and for all and put the girl in her place. Let them know how insignificant their opinions were to him.

"My good man, my only regret is that I have not the authority to order similar measures here at the seat of Britannia's rule and rid our kingdom of a passel of fools. I would greatly enjoy lining them up and giving the order to send them to perdition."

Forks clattered to their plates, and gasps were heard before silence grew heavy.

Straeford ignored their reactions save for Miss Loftus's, whose lurking disapproval had surfaced into open dislike.

At this breakdown in decorum, Marisa rose, cast the earl a frigid glance, and led the ladies to the drawing room.

Minx! Justin observed. This girl begins to interest me. Lady Maxwell was right. Without a doubt it will be the older daughter. No fledgling miss for me.

Coming into the drawing room a short time later, the Earl of Straeford observed the rest of the family with ill-concealed disdain. They had gathered into several small groups with the younger Miss Loftus already seated at the pianoforte, ready to play and sing. Her sister continued to pour coffee for the guests until the earl's penetrating gaze caused her to raise her head.

Again disapproval registered in her luminous blue eyes. He could handle that. It was no less than he was used to. And it might be worth a few nights' effort to master the boldness of that direct look of hers. No shrinking virgin to contend with here, but a desirable woman indeed. He'd like to see her with those heavy honey coils loosened and falling free. Her heaving bosom promised a ripeness that teased his imagination, and the girl's full red lips were tempting even though she held them stiff and prim when she looked his way—as she was doing now, as everyone was doing—father, brother, sister and guests.

Straeford ignored the mixture of fear and alarm on their faces and boldly strode across the room to Marisa. Bowing stiffly he offered her his arm, saying loudly for those nearby to hear, "Come Miss Loftus, let us get acquainted. I did not have the opportunity to speak with you at supper, and I have a preference for blondes."

A heated blush traveled from Marisa's bosom to her cheeks in a wave of hot embarrassment which Straeford regarded impassively.

She dared no longer look at him. What did he mean by accosting her this way? She wanted to slap his face, but her good manners forbade such behavior. Obediently she took his proffered arm.

Her obvious distress angered the earl. He hated his own rude behavior, but he hated this marriage auction even more. He could not stem the flow of his cruelty.

"I'll take this one," he claimed bluntly passing in front of Loftus and marching through French doors into the small salon beyond with Marisa firmly clamped to his side.

Angus Loftus too was suffering pangs of distress. The earl was being deliberately provocative. It would have given Angus great pleasure to show the arrogant devil the door. But ambition warred with pride and ambition won. He would not be provoked into hasty action.

"Meg, play something for our guests!" Angus demanded of his younger daughter who was staring thunderstruck at the earl and her sister as they left the room.

"Father, it ain't proper," John Loftus whispered into his father's ear.

"Quiet, puppy." Angus silenced his son.

The earl led Marisa into the salon, but she would not be seated as he would have her be. She preferred standing for this confrontation.

A branch of candles on a console cast flickering shadows about the small chamber as they regarded one another silently for some moments, each striving to take a measure of the other. The girl's slender form, simply draped in flowing amber satin, presented an image of elegant allure. The soft sensuous curves of her body tempted the earl, and almost drove his real purpose from his mind.

"Well," he demanded at last, "will I do?"

Marisa did not reply at once, but studied the arrogant face with its determined mouth set beneath those glittering green eyes and black brows. She felt a tremor of fear. Her audacious captor in his black silk jacket and black breeches that hugged his powerful thighs seemed a dark demon about to swoop down on her. She could believe those tales of cruelty that were whispered about him. He held his broad shoulders in a stiff military stance that bespoke unbending authority. His hands, like the rest of his physique, were slender but strong. In all he was a formidable specimen of manhood whose physical perfection attracted while his cold hauteur repelled. He looked so harsh and forbidding that all sense flew from her mind, and she had not two coherent thoughts to pull together since he had suddenly seized her.

"I . . . I am at a loss, sir."

"Come now, ma'am, you know why I am here tonight."

"Yes, I do . . . but . . ."

"Well, then."

"I . . . we . . ." Marisa stammered, horrified at her loss of composure. What was his power that paralyzed her brain? "You are . . . offering for *me*, my lord?"

50

"Indeed I am."

"What about Margaret? We thought she would be the one."

"I prefer you."

"But she . . . Meg's heart will be broken."

"That is not my concern."

His answer finally stung some sense into her. "How cruel you are!"

"Best know the truth from the start. I make no apology for my personal qualities."

"What other qualities besides cruelty do you profess to recommend yourself for matrimony?"

Her audacity surprised them both.

"Why, I offer . . ." and here a glint of humor flashed in his piercing eyes, "experience of command, wisdom of the world, and nerves of steel; all suitable accomplishments for the proposed state of matrimony, I daresay." His smile gleamed wickedly in the dusky room.

"I think you also offer arrogance, conceit, and self-consequence!" Marisa retorted heatedly.

"In large measure, my dear. In large measure."

"I do not think those qualities lend themselves to matrimonial harmony," Marisa claimed, hoping to discompose his galling self-assurance.

"Then what about a noble lineage, title to vast lands, and that most important consideration above all—entrée into the best circles of society? Does that lend itself to matrimonial harmony, do you think?" he questioned insolently.

Marisa bit back an angry retort, lest she get into deeper waters. But it was a visible effort as fear and anger struggled to express themselves.

"And what of you, my dear? What do you offer?" The earl came to stand before her, his eyes traveling the full length of her body and lingering on her heaving bosom.

"I make no offer, my lord. I have no wish to marry you!"

This time it was *her* words that startled coherence from Straeford's mind, and he stepped back and regarded Miss Loftus anew. Angry tears gleamed in her eyes, and for a moment her distress touched him. He turned and walked to the fireplace trying to sort out his thoughts. He had no appetite for this heartless bargaining. Women! Damn them all to blazes! It would be a relief to be out of the whole money-grubbing business.

But what of his home—his debt to his father and brother and the Straeford line? He turned to Marisa once more, but his guard was not securely set and for a moment the girl read something of the inner torment of the man. Without words, much of his early history communicated itself to her. Could this really be the slaughterer of innocent natives? She was not consciously aware of her thoughts, but Straeford in turn felt her softening toward him. He steeled himself against her tender feelings. He would have none of the female arts used on him.

"I will leave it up to you, dear lady. I will marry you, not your sister Margaret. Make up your mind to that! I bid you good evening."

Straeford took his leave of the Loftus residence stopping only long enough to notify Loftus that he had made his decision and the matter now lay in his daughter's capable hands.

"But you can't marry the earl," Margaret cried angrily. "Papa bought him for me. You have no right!" Margaret was pacing the room furiously. "Tell her, Papa. Tell her. Tell her!"

"Now, Meg, child, calm yourself." Angus was beside himself with chagrin. The Earl of Straeford had managed to turn the tables on him and rout his entire household. There was no quieting Margaret for the past hour, and she was insisting that he force the earl to marry her.

Loftus had been certain that the earl would prefer his younger daughter, Margaret. Her flamboyant beauty put most girls in the shade. And her youth, he felt, was an added attraction.

Secretly he admired the earl for choosing Marisa. Her quieter beauty was a durable loveliness that would improve with the years. No doubt Straeford had an instinct for quality. But what would Angus do without his good right arm? Drat the man!

It was this girl who had maintained the warmth of his home in the eight years since the death of Jennifer

Loftus, Angus's much loved wife. Marisa had left school a year earlier than was planned to return home and take up the duties of hostess for her father and mentor to John and Margaret.

A more efficient and loving daughter no man could have. So like his dear Jenny. The only trouble she had ever given him was the time she almost married the Aiken lad. But Angus had put his foot down. He would not hear of an alliance with a nobody ... same thing Jenny had done, of course, but that was different. Now he was going to see his offspring properly launched into the *ton* where they belonged.

"I do not like that man, Father." John added his disapproval to the broth of contention. "Neither Meg nor Marisa should be given to him."

"What can you object to? He has rank and lands enough to satisfy the ambition of any female."

"Whose ambition is it you wish to satisfy, sir? Surely not Marisa's!"

"Hush, John," Marisa cautioned, lest he go too far.

"I have ambition enough if she does not," Meg proclaimed vehemently. "I want him. He's beautiful!"

"Meg, darling!" Marisa placed a hand on her sister's shoulder. but it was angrily shrugged away.

"Don't 'darling' me, dear sister. Your sweet reason act doesn't fool me, even if it does papa. What passed between you two in that salon? I'll vow you threw yourself at his head."

"Margaret, be still!" Angus thundered at last. "I'll hear no more of your brazen talk this night. If it's Marisa the earl wants, then it's Marisa he'll have!"

"No, I say you cannot do this, Father!" John dared to contradict, although his father's temper when roused was fearful to behold. "He's a black-hearted devil. Did you not hear him at dinner tonight?"

"Damn your impudence, boy!" Angus roared. And John faltered under his father's towering rage as he had always done. "What mean you interfering in my plans for all of you? You do as I say as long as you reside under my roof! Or I'll throw you out—penniless—to go beg in the streets!" He swung about to include his daughters in his tirade. "And that goes for the two of you, too! Marisa

53

will marry the earl . . . and John, you'll take that commission in the army when Straeford arranges it. Then it will be Meg's turn. She'll have a season among the *beau monde* and find some other eligible lord to marry. I'll hear no more about it! My decision is made! Make no mistakes about it!"

Angus stormed out of the room, refusing to look at his older daughter, who had not voiced her feelings in the matter. This was what Jenny had always wanted for her children and Angus was going to see that his beloved wife's wishes were carried out.

4

A lady swathed in a dark veil scurried down the carpeted corridor searching for number 278. She tapped lightly on the door and waited breathlessly as she heard the lock turn and the door open revealing Lord Straeford's valet, Billings. Despite that gentleman's training, he could not prevent a look of surprise before he recovered his usual façade of cool detachment.

"Is your master in?" the mysterious woman questioned in a low, wispy voice.

Billings hesitated, not sure of himself. A woman was unheard of in the Stephens Hotel—at least a respectable woman—but something in the lady's manner forbore his immediate rejection.

"Who shall I say is calling, madam?"

"Tell him it is . . . Evangeline Seton."

"If you will kindly step inside and be seated, I shall make your presence known to his lordship."

Mrs. Seton arranged herself stiffly on the small divan before the fireplace, not allowing herself to relax, but sitting forward as if ready for flight on the moment. The room was silent and watchful except for the ticking of a carriage clock on the mantel which revealed the hour to be three o'clock of a gloomy winter afternoon.

Lord Straeford strode into the room, his forceful footsteps announcing the presence of a man used to command and authority.

"My dear Mrs. Seton, how may I be of service to you?"

The dark-clad woman jumped back at the appearance of the man she had forced herself to seek out. Raising the veil of her bonnet, she observed his dark, alert visage through faded blue eyes and understood immediately why this was the colonel her husband had come to hate. The strength of his character was plainly revealed in the firm, chiseled planes of his face and the depths of those somber green eyes. All that discipline acting in striking contrast to Horace's self-indulgence!

"I know it is improper for me to be here, my lord, but I . . . if you could spare me a few minutes?" She let the question dangle without completion.

"Certainly, madam. I am at your disposal." There was no warmth in Straeford's voice, but the rules of courtesy he stringently observed.

"My dear sir, I hardly know where to begin." She looked to his lordship to help her find her way.

"If I may assist you . . ." Straeford offered dubiously.

Evangeline Seton nodded, clasping her hands tightly in her lap.

"You came here because of your husband, did you not?"

Mrs. Seton nodded again, but waited for his lordship to continue.

"Naturally, you are concerned about the situation in India after reading all the reports in the press . . ."

"They give such dreadful accounts—forgive me, but it sounds as if such slaughter were done—"

"But most of the villainy is laid at my doorstep, dear lady, not at your husband's."

She looked at him directly, willing herself not to flinch. "Horace has written me some of the circumstances. I am aware that . . . that not all is as represented in the journals." Her voice was a whisper.

Lord Straeford shifted uneasily, wishing himself out of this devilish interview.

"Mrs. Seton, do not distress yourself over public opinion. The rabble is easily stirred by sensationalism and the press seeks to satisfy its base appetites. You must choose to ignore it, if you are to have peace of mind."

"Lord Straeford, were it for myself alone, or even my husband, I could put a brave face on it and persevere. But I—we have a son at Sandhurst whose future could be shattered were the full . . . truth to be revealed." She looked to the earl with eyes imploring his forbearance.

His lordship did not reply, weighing the full import of her words. The lady was begging him to cover for her husband. It was a brazen plea to make, and yet, surprisingly, he did not resent it. It only wearied him. This frightened little woman was too pitiful for any reaction stronger than tedium. She was merely trying to protect her son.

The irony stabbed him—that she should come to him, who had long ago lost faith in the maternal instinct. And as for Seton, the fool deserved whatever public obloquy resulted from this miserable investigation.

"Mrs. Seton, let me speak bluntly. I cannot deliberately falsify the facts." She glanced up in alarm at his choice of words. "However, I can assure you that I do not seek to harm your husband's reputation. If it be possible, I'll see the wretched affair speedily settled with as little damage to General Seton's record as possible. There is no good to be served in feeding the public lust for scandal. General Seton was not always . . . as he is today. I remember a better man in better days." Straeford watched the lady's face gradually soften and lose some of the strain and tension that fear had etched so unkindly there.

"God bless you, my lord. Whatever have been the differences between you and my husband, I can see that you are a good man. I shall never forget your kindness in hearing me out."

The earl raised his hand in embarrassed protest in an effort to stem her overflowing gratitude. "Please say no more."

Mrs. Seton took her leave minutes later, pressing her

thanks and blessings on the earl, whose only emotion was relief that the touchy business had been speedily concluded.

A letter summoning Lord Straeford to appear at the War Office arrived by special messenger two days later. The earl tossed it into the fire with a perfunctory curse. Was he never to have control of his affairs again? Between the Board of Inquiry, Angus Loftus and Lady Maxwell, his life was a constant tug-of-war, never leaving him time for his own pursuits—which were to restore Straeford Park and return to the front.

War! It was all he was suited for. In combat, life was reduced to its simplest terms—a brutal struggle for survival and victory. He understood it well. There were none of the perplexing quandaries of social masquerades that life in society presented. He preferred to feel the vigorous pulse of life surge through his veins when his mortality was pitted against the machines of war. There was an exhilaration in testing his physical strength and endurance against supreme odds. And if he were to die—so be it. Death held no fears for one who found little to savor in life.

Billings peered out of the window to the street below where a group of pickets was milling around the entrance to the hotel. He wished he knew who had instigated that action against his lordship. Damn the fools! If only there were some quick way to disperse them before the earl ventured out among them. Yet he knew no amount of coaxing would prevent his master from keeping his appointment at the War Office—which meant a confrontation between him and that nasty crowd below.

"Will you see that my horse is brought around, Billings?" the earl asked as he shrugged into his red military jacket.

"Let me bring your mount to the back door, my lord," Billings appealed to Straeford as he adjusted his sword hilt for him.

"Would you have me slink off like a coward?" Straeford demanded disdainfully.

"No, my lord, but it ain't cowardly to protect your life against hooligans."

There was a short burst of laughter from his lordship before replying, "Don't worry about me, Billings. I assure you I have no intention of risking my life. Now see to my horse, if you please."

Billings knew he was defeated and excusing himself, went about the business of securing his lordship's mount.

On reaching the lobby, Straeford nonchalantly surveyed the marching pickets in front of the hotel before going out into the street. The mock courage of the rabble stirred his contempt. Only get them alone and see how the coward turns tail and runs!

"There he is!" yelled one of the demonstrators, and immediately they surged around the earl, shouting abuse and waving their placards at him.

"Hang 'im!" cried the spokesman of the mob above its roar. "Hang the butcher!"

The earl did not acknowledge the hostile faces surrounding him but moved through the muttering pickets with a forbidding hauteur that forced them to step aside despite their mounting lust for violence. Reaching the stallion Billings held for him, Straeford was about to mount when a stone struck his head.

"Dirty blackguards," Billings shouted as his master staggered and blood trickled from a cut above his eye, "attacking the Earl of the Realm!"

The crowd shifted indecisively at such a reminder and was held in check long enough for Straeford to search its faces and find his attacker. A glint of recognition lighted his narrowed green eyes, and ignoring the rest of the pack who parted before him, his lordship stalked his assailant.

Coming face to face with Johnny Bedloes, the young man Straeford had drummed out of the corps several years ago, he stopped and glared into the hate-filled face. "I'm not surprised to find you here, Bedloes. You never did understand the responsibilities of leadership," Straeford taunted coolly.

Bedloes's self-assurance faltered under the earl's harsh stare and he shifted his gaze nervously from the man challenging him to the crowd and back again. He knew he was losing ground as Straeford pressed a silent war of nerves on him.

"You'll get your just deserts this time, Mr. High and Mighty. The people won't stand for a butcher doing His Majesty's business in the world."

The mob, encouraged by Bedloes's bluster, pressed closer around both men. Straeford stood his ground, however, and continued to challenge its leader. "Still trying to get others to do your dirty work for you, aren't you, Bedloes?"

The herd grew suddenly still, waiting to hear Bedloes's reply to the earl's insult. There was a hair's breadth between their loyalty to Bedloes and their respect for Straeford's obvious bravery, and the frightened rabble-rouser knew it. In desperation, he drew a pistol from beneath his jacket and leveled it at Straeford, who grasped his arm the instant the weapon appeared and jerked Bedloes's arm into the air before the gun exploded over the heads of the mob. The blast sent a ripple of alarm through the assembled crowd which bolted for cover like frightened hares. Wresting the pistol from Bedloes's frenzied grasp, Straeford threw his would-be attacker to the ground.

The earl had the situation well under control by the time Billings arrived on the spot with a constable and several Bow Street runners. The scattered pickets watched the earl dust off his jacket and mount his horse to ride off without a backward glance.

A couple of men crossed over to Billings and commented, "Ain't a nerve in his body, is there? That's one mighty cool customer."

"My master don't know the meaning of fear," Billings claimed proudly and haughtily walked away.

"Please be seated, Lord Straeford." Lord Carstairs indicated a chair in front of the heavy mahogany table at which he sat. General Belvoir was beside him. There were no others present.

"What we have to discuss with you today is of a very grave nature. It is a matter that must not pass beyond these doors." Carstairs studied the impassive face before him and then continued, "Perhaps we should begin with your reading this deposition sent to us from the surgeon general's office in Calcutta."

Straeford took the document presented to him, beginning to wonder at the strained manner of Carstairs. As he read, his expression turned grim and he recalled the worried face of the woman who had visited him in his rooms a few days ago. General Seton was dead of a self-inflicted bullet wound to the head. A suicide!

"You can appreciate the difficulties this presents, my lord." General Belvoir spoke for the first time. "And we have another document for your perusal before we can pursue this matter further."

Straeford allowed a look of surprise to cross his face. It was a letter from General Seton to Lord Castlereagh. In it, Seton fully exonerated Straeford of any wrongdoing in the battle of Nangore. General Seton explained the shameful part he himself had played in that ill-fated attack, and made it clear that had not Colonel Lord Straeford taken command and counter-attacked the next morning, the whole expedition would have gone down in bloody defeat. General Seton did not spare himself but laid the blame to his own disgraceful alcoholic excesses. Seton ended by recommending that the colonel be elevated to the rank of general.

At last Straeford looked up from the pitiful letter and somberly regarded the two gentlemen across from him.

"I am at a loss for words, gentlemen. Naturally, I am gratified that General Seton has made clear the situation at Nangore, but I deeply regret his final solution."

"Of course. We understand perfectly the conflict of emotions you must be experiencing. However, we hope to receive some guidance from you in the handling of this matter," Lord Carstairs said.

"I don't understand. How may *I* guide you?"

"There will have to be a public announcement of the general's death immediately. It can be handled one of two ways . . . er . . . we can present the full facts of the general's demise . . . or . . . we can merely report that he died of heart failure and let the matter fade as quietly as possible," Carstairs explained.

"We feel the decision should be left in your hands since you have suffered most from this whole unfortunate business," General Belvoir added.

"I appreciate your consideration, gentlemen. By all means let us salvage what little reputation we can for Seton. He was not always as he was at the end." Once again Straeford remembered Mrs. Seton and was relieved to be able to comply with her request.

"Very noble of you, Straeford. Very noble," Belvoir claimed heartily. "Naturally there will be a public statement clearing you of all wrongdoing in the Nangore affair, and the board will be dissolved without further meeting. How say you to that?"

"Whatever you decide, sir. I will be relieved to put it all behind me."

"Very good, my lord. I laud your discretion." Carstairs joined his praise to that of Belvoir. "Now, there is another matter . . . the promotion. We agree with Seton that you are deserving of it . . . but . . ."

"But the timing is inopportune," Straeford finished for them. "That the press and public would not look favorably on such a sudden reversal, I'm well aware."

"You are far ahead of us, dear sir. And your understanding is excellent. Be assured that the matter of your promotion would not be forgotten, but merely delayed until such a time that it may be accomplished without undue disturbance."

"I find no fault with that procedure, gentlemen."

"Excellent. I think we can expect to close this matter with a minimum of public outcry—especially since attention is so much focused on the European front at present," Carstairs said.

Straeford nodded his assent.

"Which leads us to our last consideration. We feel this would be a propitious time to transfer you from India to Portugal. Arthur Wellesley is preparing an expedition to that country, and we thought to send you along in charge of the 9th Brigade. How say you?"

"I say very good, gentlemen. It is exactly the course I would have chosen for myself had I the opportunity of doing so."

"Well then," Carstairs claimed, rising and extending his hand to Lord Straeford, "I say this was a most successful interview, and I give you my heartiest good wishes for your future success, Colonel."

"And I add mine to them." Belvoir rose, shaking Straeford's hand and closing the interview.

That evening over a supper at the Green Fox, the earl reported his interview to Harding and lifted his glass in response to his friend's toast of "Better days."

"That's a toast I'll gladly join, my friend. I did not look to see the Seton affair so neatly packed up and settled. It still leaves me dazed." Straeford's gaze turned inward as, with mixed emotions, he relived the morning's interview at the War Office. He was both saddened and relieved. "I knew Seton was headed for disaster—but never did I think he would end up a suicide, poor devil."

"Suicide is a messy business, Just, but it certainly resolved a touchy situation for everyone concerned."

"I wonder if Seton's wife would sum it up that way. She came to see me the other morning."

"Did she, by Jove! You didn't tell me."

"I had forgotten about her . . . a little broken bird of a woman . . ."

"Now don't turn maudlin, my friend. It ain't your style. Furthermore, 'one man's meat is another' man's poison.' You have come out of the wretched affair with your feathers all smooth and your future looking bright— leastways, as far as the army is concerned. From what you've told me, old Belvoir and Carstairs were falling all over themselves with encomiums. You'll get that generalship you place so high on your priorities. Just see if you don't."

Straeford regarded his friend thoughtfully. "There's a lot of truth in what you say, Ed. I came out of this one amazingly well, didn't I? Wonder if this augurs a change in luck for me. Could it be Dame Fortune is tired of the cudgel and will reveal the softer side of her perfidious nature to me for once in my life?"

"I say, old man, this is no time for disrespect! Dame Fortune has just winked your way and I, for one, think a celebration is called for. Another round of master Ruben's stout will fortify us nicely. Hey boy, over here," Ed called loudly to the potboy. "Look to your business and fill these disgracefully empty glasses with dispatch. We have some serious drinking to attend to this night." Harding's mood was verging on hilarity.

"Much more of old Ruben's stout and it will be bellows to mend, for you my friend." Straeford laughed, catching Harding's infectious mood of gaiety.

"A little more of old Ruben's stout and mayhaps you'll gain some proper perspective, old man. Life is not the constant call to arms you believe it to be. I drink to your future success—both in marriage and your career." Harding raised his glass. "There. Did I not tell you it would go well with you in this matter, old man?"

"Damn your hide, Harding, you need not have brought the marriage business to mind at present. I thought to enjoy this evening."

"Don't be such a sorehead, Just."

"If you only knew what a trial this marriage contract entails. The boy must be given a commission; the younger daughter a London season . . ."

"It's well worth it if Straeford Park is renovated."

"Yes," the earl agreed reluctantly.

"And you say your intended is a handsome wench. Wait till you get to know her better. I am anxious to meet her."

"And so you shall. This weekend Loftus and his daughter are to inspect the Park. I could not endure the whole time in their company without support. You must bring Ann to supper and see me through this ordeal."

"Somehow I feel the ordeal falls more to Miss Loftus than to you, my friend. Have some pity." Harding laughed.

"There's not a female that walks this earth who is deserving of *my* pity," Justin claimed ruefully.

"You'll change your tune one day, Just. I predict it with certainty."

"To blazes with you and your maundering, you simpleton," Justin replied with affection for his long-time friend.

5

From a hilltop vantage point hidden behind a cluster of trees, the earl could observe the manor house without himself being seen. Sitting atop his slender black stallion, he watched the slow arrival of the carriage carrying Loftus and his daughter. A sense of personal embarrassment was quickly followed by a sudden welling of anger as they stepped down from the coach to examine the austere and neglected residence. From such a distance he could not discern their conversation, but from Angus's gesticulations directed at various points of the house, it was clear he was evaluating his investment.

Annoyed, the earl decided not to ride down the hillside to meet his guests. Instead he swung his horse around and thundered off in the opposite direction.

It was left to Lady Maxwell to welcome her grandson's guests and explain that his absence was due to estate business. The visitors accepted her information, and she quickly ushered them into the drawing room where she launched into a rambling discourse concerning the heritage of the estate and the house itself.

The regal lady provided extensive details regarding

the historical background and the significance of the few furnishings that had not gone to pay some debt. A small oak table at the far side of the room, for example, had been part of the estate for over two hundred years. Its rococo design provided a hint of the glory which the house's former occupants must have known. Lady Maxwell pointed first to a small, ancient, threadbare tapestry depicting a faded pastoral scene and then to the family crest—a half moon with two dragonlike creatures locked in ferocious combat—which was engraved on the fireplace.

A long moment of silence followed Lady Maxwell's recitation, making Loftus uneasy, and he blurted out his intentions to have the Park renovated before the marriage took place.

"Ye needn't fret one bit about the property, madam. I'll see to it that it's put back in shape as it was meant to be. I mean to stand by my gentleman's agreement with the earl and make right certain that he and his wife-to-be will live in style and grace, just the way it should be."

Her father's pointed boastfulness embarrassed his daughter, who sought desperately to change the discussion. Her attention had been focused on the striking face that appeared in the portrait above the fireplace mantel and she seized the opportunity to make an inquiry regarding it. "The lady in the portrait . . ."

"The earl's mother," Lady Maxwell cut in and seemed oddly offended by such an innocent comment, but Marisa could not stem her interest. She was impressed with the great inner strength emanating from the woman's penetrating green eyes. This was not the face of a passive, domestic creature but of one who bore an almost ruthless vitality. It was not hard to detect many of the physical qualities in her son—the aquiline nose, the sculptured cheekbones, and the luxuriant black hair.

"She must have been a captivating person."

Lady Maxwell did not reply at once but fixed her gaze on the portrait for what seemed like an interminable time. The Loftuses exchanged puzzled glances as they waited for a response.

"Captivating? Is that the word you used?" She stopped to fidget with the black lace ruffle of her high-necked dress. "My dear, perhaps I should warn you about Lady Marian. The less said . . ." Lady Maxwell's voice stopped abruptly as she raised her startled eyes to acknowledge the fact that the earl had entered the room.

In an uncomfortable moment of silence, he presented himself to the trio with a sweeping gaze before making a polite but half-hearted bow to Miss Loftus. She nodded with a smile and he found himself looking directly into her large blue eyes. Even though she wore a simple morning dress of green chintz and her honey-colored hair was plainly coiffed in a smooth knot at the top of her head, he felt strangely attracted to her in a way he could not clearly fathom. This was a source of annoyance to him, but he attempted to cloak his irritation and exchanged pleasantries with the merchant and his daughter.

Through occasional glimpses she dared to make in his direction, Marisa studied the man who had been designated to become her husband. His presence in the room was a commanding one, and she could not help admiring this black-browed stranger's handsome appearance. A taut, lean, muscular body was plainly evident to her as she stole glances at his gleaming Hessians, buff pantaloons, and dark green jacket. Standing erectly in front of them, he seemed a towering figure of strength. He was truly a magnificent specimen of masculinity. Marisa thought. But under Straeford's steady regard she felt uncertain of herself, and despite her determination not to reveal her nervousness she stammered whenever she addressed him directly. It was those penetrating green eyes, his hand placed squarely on his hip, his defiantly confident pose that caused her to wonder whether she was capable of any speech at all in his presence.

Mustering her courage, Marisa struggled for any conversation that would relieve the tension she felt. "My father and I were admiring your property as we rode in, my lord. It's magnificence is still quite apparent."

One of Straeford's eyebrows arched sharply as he mocked her with his reply. "Yes, it is not unlike a beautiful virgin who has long since lost her innocence, wouldn't you agree?"

The Loftuses, as well as Lady Maxwell, stiffened,

but it was Marisa, goaded by his sarcasm, who replied. "I am sorry to say that I find your comparison vulgar, and I do not understand the inference you are making by such a statement."

"You may make whatever inference you wish from what I have said, my dear lady; however, I do believe we are all aware of the true significance of your visit here today. We meet simply for one purpose, and that is to permit you and your father the opportunity to assess the worth of my estate and current holdings in order to determine whether a profitable business arrangement can be consummated through the coming nuptials. Now that should leave no one in this room with any misunderstandings concerning the matter."

Loftus's face contorted in disbelief at this outburst. "My lord!" he exclaimed crossly as he observed his daughter crimson with emotion. But it was Lady Maxwell who reproached her grandson soundly for his unwarranted tirade. "Justin! Please remember that the Loftuses are our guests. This is totally uncalled for."

The dark fierce look faded at her reprimand. Perhaps he had gone too far. But it had helped to relieve some of the frustrations he was feeling. Did he or didn't he want to go through with this bargain? His personal pride was being torn in two different directions; on the one hand stood the restoration of his family's holdings, and on the other his betrothal to this merchant's daughter. What was the correct course of action, he wondered, as he met Lady Maxwell's indignant glare. He knew his remarks had embarrassed her.

"Your reprimand is well deserved, my dear Grandmother," he said, bowing deeply in her direction. "I do apologize to my visitors and hope that they were not unduly upset by my intemperate remarks. Now let me demonstrate that I can be civil. I believe luncheon awaits us. Miss Loftus." He held out his arm to her, which she accepted reluctantly, and escorted her across the hall where a cold meal was served.

The tense climate which Straeford's remarks had created was alleviated only slightly during the luncheon by the gallant efforts of Lady Maxwell, who amused

Loftus with some frivolous tales of her childhood. The earl, for his part, lapsed into silence while Marisa pushed her food about her plate and spoke in polite monosyllables when she was required to do so. She could not help but feel the lingering hurt of his earlier comments, and was truly worried about her future in the hands of such a man.

Quite unexpectedly Straeford interrupted Marisa's thoughts with an invitation to inspect the manor house. He had barely spoken to her at all during the meal and now this attempt at . . . what was it? she pondered.

The earl's hand rested under her arm as he guided her down lengthy corridors and passageways. His closeness to her caused Marisa to experience strange and conflicting sensations. Feelings of attraction warred with feelings of anxiety toward this temperamental man. A tightening of her stomach muscles confirmed her stressful state. She feared further antagonism from him and wanted to avoid it at all cost.

As they arrived in front of the large double doors of the library, he flung them open. It was an attractive room with high ceilings and shelves lined to the top with leather-bound books. French doors opened onto a veranda where a garden was visible. Drawn to this setting, Marisa was about to cross the room for a closer view when she felt the earl's steel-like fingers clamp tightly around her arm preventing her from going any farther. Her eyes closed in pain and then slowly opened to look at his somber face. Boldly, she stared directly into his disturbing green eyes in search of some indication as to the significance of his actions.

"You have no objections to my viewing this room or your gardens, do you?" she asked pointedly.

He regarded her warily for a moment and then released her slowly and nodded. "None whatsoever. After all, the residence will soon be yours as well as mine; however, the library is in a sad state of disrepair, and I would hate to see one of those shelves give away and come tumbling down about your head." His tone was mocking and sardonic. "Come, let me escort you to the ballroom."

When they reached that room, Marisa stopped on the threshold and asked archly, "I take it that I am allowed to enter this room."

Through narrowed eyes he regarded her before grasping her arm firmly and guiding her forcefully across the inlaid wooden floor, their footsteps echoing distinctly.

The large spacious chamber with its long windows covered in faded red and gold brocade draperies still had an air of opulence about it, and Marisa instantly recognized its potential. "Why, this room could easily be restored to its original beauty," she said enthusiastically. "It will be grand to entertain in such an elegant setting."

"Will it indeed?" he drawled. "I presume you intend to do a great deal of entertaining?"

Her blue eyes with their heavy lashes opened wider. "I should think that would be largely your decision, my lord."

A flash of anger went through the earl, and he glowered at her during a long moment of silence. Why did she have to look at him like that? Her innocence was almost ingenious, he thought. He'd like to slap her lovely face just to see if that innocent look were real or feigned. Instead, he folded his arms imperiously and countered with a dare. "But, of course! And if I do not wish to entertain at all, you will oblige me, naturally?"

"I surely hope that will not be so," Marisa replied cautiously, "but if that is what you wish . . ."

"You play the ingenue very well," he sneered, "but I'd prefer an honest coquette, my dear. Come with me. I think it is time we had a heart to heart talk before this farce goes any further."

Brusquely he led the way back to the drawing room and seated her in an armchair next to the fireplace. As he stood in front of her preparing to speak, Marisa noticed the striking resemblance between Straeford and the portrait of his mother which appeared above the fireplace mantel.

"You look so very much like her."

"How observant of you, but I prefer not to be reminded of the resemblance I bear . . . the former countess."

"Why ever not? She was beautiful." As the words

70

left her mouth, she remembered Lady Maxwell's warning and wished she had remained silent.

"You need have no fear of her beauty." The earl's voice was oddly hollow. "You possess enough beauty to rival hers, I'm certain. Just think, another comely Lady Straeford! It makes me wonder. Will you have as many lovers—or more?"

Marisa gasped and started to rise to her feet.

"Sit down!" he commanded. The dark violent look on his face held her prisoner. "You have no need to fear me provided that you adhere to the marriage agreement we are about to make. Have you and your father discussed the conditions that are attached to this agreement?"

"I . . . well, yes, to some degree." But now she began to wonder.

"That is well, for I expect your complete fidelity until I have an heir for Straeford. If you can remain faithful to me that long, then I shall look the other way afterward."

The matter-of-fact delivery of these slanderous words not only stunned the girl seated before him but left her momentarily bereft of speech.

"We do understand one another I trust," he added after a pause.

"No!" Marisa lurched to a standing position on shaky legs. "No, I am afraid I do not understand . . . what you are proposing here at all. In fact . . . I am deeply offended!"

"What's this? A little maidenly protest to salve your conscience?" A taunting smile crossed the earl's lips.

Fearlessly, Marisa faced him, and he noted the bewilderment in her eyes was now replaced by anger.

"How can you speak like this? This is a dreadful, loathsome mockery of a marriage you are proposing. My father and I had no idea that you . . ."

"I doubt that, my dear," he scoffed in a manner which consumed her with rage.

"As far as I am concerned," she said, wheeling to exit the room, "you may consider our . . . our betrothal at an end!"

The earl's strong arms locked around her waist, and

71

even though she struggled against his grasp, he whirled her about to face him and pinned her tightly against his chest. She was powerless in his grip, and she raised her head to demand that he let her go. Ignoring her remonstrations, his mouth descended slowly upon hers and held her lips in a searing kiss until her senses began to reel from lack of breath. When he finally released her, a devilish light gleamed in his narrowed green eyes and he appraised her triumphantly.

"How dare you!" She raised her hand to slap his arrogant face. Instantly his eyes grew glacial, and he captured her wrist in midair.

"Don't ever raise you hand to me again, woman!" He released her after a long, threatening glare.

Trembling, she backed away from him. "You ... you're a devil," she managed to say through quivering lips. Turning quickly, she fled from the room and disappeared into the corridor in search of her father.

Loftus was unconcerned when Marisa revealed what had happened. He stubbornly refused to heed the anguished pleadings of his daughter to do away with the marital agreement. The contract offer had been accepted and, but for a petty squabble, his most cherished ambition was about to be realized. At this point in the game, he was not at all disposed to let anything thwart his plans—especially not his own hysterical daughter nor that conceited toff.

"Look here, Marisa," he cajoled in his gravel-pitched voice, "this ain't no love match, y' know."

"Don't you think I know that?"

"Well, then?"

"He's suggesting that I ... I'll take ... lovers." She was blushing painfully at having to discuss such a topic with her father.

"But, my dear, that's to ease his own conscience, I'm telling you."

The bewildered look on his daughter's face told him he would have to be more explicit, and he was truly vexed at having to be so blunt with his own child. "I mean he'll probably have a ... a mistress. Most men do, you know. And he expects you to look the other way."

Marisa stared blankly in response as she tried to grasp the full meaning of what her father was telling her. He had never before spoken to her in this way, but she realized now that he was satisfied with the marriage even though everything in her cried out against such an arrangement.

"There's something more," she said, still hoping to persuade her father to reverse his decision. "I think he hates me. I can't say anything to him without arousing his ire. And the way he looks at me ... I ... I thought he was actually going to strike me. I don't want to go through my life with a man who feels that way about me. Please, Father, don't make me do this!"

"Now child, you're overwrought, just imagining things. Don't ruin a good thing for yourself and for me. Listen to me, my dear. I'll have a talk with him and get this straightened out. You'll see," he said patting her hand, "it'll all work out, and some day you'll be grateful to me for bringing the earl into your life."

"But, Father, I don't ..."

"That's enough, I say! I said I'll have a talk with the man and that's that!"

Marisa knew that further protest was futile. Her father was blinded by his own ambition and meant to have his way in this matter. Her objections fell on deaf ears, and she lacked the courage to withstand his demands. None of his children could, none of them doubted he would make good his threat to throw them out of his home—penniless—if they did not bend to his will. Fear of poverty was a powerful force in the whole family's behavior. It had been drummed into them by their mother at an early age. Jennifer Loftus had lived intimately with that fear as a very young girl, and she had instilled a respect for wealth in her own children. "The rewards of poverty are severely limited, and the virtues of being poor nearly always go unrecognized," she reminded them frequently.

Loftus, of course, had always supported his wife's attitude in this and reinforced her teaching through the use of vivid examples. One time he forced his own offspring to walk through the streets of the Rookery in order to witness firsthand the squalid conditions which the poor were compelled to face every day of their lives. The wretched spectacle of toothless, ragged men and women, filthy children, and screaming, undernourished infants burned in Marisa's memory.

Angus Loftus's object lesson was quite effective. He had early awakened his children to the evils of being poor because his own humble beginnings had kindled his present driving ambition. He took deep personal pride in the fact that he was a self-made man who had risen from a shopkeeper's apprentice to become a successful businessman with a variety of far-reaching interests. All of that was achieved through hard work, sacrifice and singleness of purpose. If a man could be measured by his achievements in life, as Angus Loftus believed, he had accomplished much and was entitled to be respected accordingly.

Respect was very important to Angus Loftus. He had demanded it from his wife and now he demanded it from his children. As an employer, he was known as a fair but exacting man who expected nothing short of total fidelity from his workers and rewarded them generously when it was forthcoming. That was a virtue he had carefully cultivated, and he was firmly convinced that it was the basis for his success. The notion of respect due nobility for mere accident of birth galled him. Loftus admired a man of action, a doer, the type of man he had fashioned himself to be, but he was painfully aware that the ultimate road to recognition and honor was not through his own capabilities. He and his family would be forever denied access to that kind of esteem and distinction unless he could make this alliance between the earl and his daughter work. He was determined that it would.

He found his future son-in-law lounging in the drawing room with a cigar in one hand and a snifter of brandy in the other, a classic picture of the leisured class he despised.

"Well sir," the earl said cynically, as though he had been fully anticipating Loftus's arrival, "have you come to join me in a gentleman's drink or have you come to inform me that you have had second thoughts regarding our mutual contract?"

Loftus struggled to control his temper before replying. "Look here, my lord, did you wish to scotch this whole thing by being so . . . so blunt with the girl? You know how women are."

"I daresay I know what any man needs to know about them and probably more than most. Your daughter's no child. She'll survive."

"Humh, you're a hard-hearted man, you are. I had a devil of a time convincing her not to jump the hoop."

"But you did convince her." The contempt in the earl's voice almost caused Loftus to reconsider.

"I believe she's willing to listen to reason. But may I suggest that a word of kindness would go very far in facilitating matters?"

Straeford sighed in resignation and heaved himself off the divan. "Very well. Where shall I find her?" He knew quite well that if he did not soften his attitude he might lose Loftus's daughter, and that would mean he would have to find another heiress—and soon. Straeford decided he had to comply.

Loftus had discerned the reason for the earl's quick capitulation but refrained from saying so. "I'll send her to the garden, my lord."

While Marisa paced about the garden, she tried to allay her inner turmoil by taking several deep breaths. Doing so, the fragrance of the flowers attracted her attention, and her eyes swept over the lush vegetation surrounding her. Mixed shades of delphiniums grew along a crumbling wall and clinging roses cascaded gently over its edge. Nearby white sundrops and candlestick lilies mingled together amidst the tall grass and uncut shrubs. The stone benches scattered in the small garden were virtually covered by green moss and tangled undergrowth. At this instant all she wished was to be left alone to drink in the beauty of this moment in time.

As she singled out a flower to inhale its scent, she suddenly became aware of his presence behind her. His catlike movements gave him the ability to come upon his victims unaware, she thought irreverently. It was going to be difficult to face him again after the way he had humiliated her earlier, but straightening her shoulders and promising herself not to be intimidated, she slowly turned to meet his gaze.

"Am I intruding? I was told I'd find you here," the earl said in a tone she hopefully perceived as conciliatory.

"You do not intrude, my lord," she said seating herself on one of the small benches. "I was just admiring the garden and enjoying the flowers. It's quite lovely here."

"Unfortunately it is in quite a state of disarray." He pushed aside some stray branches with the toe of his boot and crossed in front of her, his hands behind his back. "And the same applies to the whole place," he said in disgust. Marisa did not reply, fearing that anything she might say would trigger another nasty scene. Plucking a flower from one of the bushes, she pulled at its petals absentmindedly as he stared unseeing at the garden. The earl shifted his feet nervously during an awkward moment and then turned toward her with a look on his face which Marisa had never observed before. She sensed he wanted to apologize and make amends, but his pride made it difficult for him to do so.

"Look here," he said, "if my conduct earlier today offended you, you'll have to put it down to the fact that I am not used to the ways of the polite world."

She lowered her lashes, waiting for something more to be said. Was that supposed to be an apology?

"Well, now that that is settled . . ."

Incredibly, that was it! She was flabbergasted.

"I do believe it is appropriate at this time to seal our betrothal." He slid on the bench beside her, and instinctively Marisa jerked backward as he came near, causing him to laugh with scorn.

"Did you think I was about to kiss you again, my dear? I will if you wish, of course, but I merely planned on presenting you with this." He dropped a small velvet box onto her lap and when she did not respond immediately, he urged her to open it. "Come, come, my girl, let's be on with it. You won't be unhappy when you see it, I'm sure."

This was not the way she had pictured this event in her mind. How could he be so cavalier at a time like this?

How shabby he was in his approach toward her! Did the man have no sensitivity whatsoever?

Obediently, she opened the box to view its contents, and her eyes beheld a large, square emerald ring that was surrounded by diamond chips which glittered brightly no matter which way she tilted the box. Etched within the center of the stone was a crescent, the family symbol, and the rich luster of the gem gave off an almost hypnotic effect as it lay in the box. Marisa had never seen anything so exquisite.

"It's beautiful! But I thought . . ."

"Thought that all of the estate's jewels had been sold? No, not entirely. This particular piece happens to be entailed to the estate as are the necklace and earrings which complete the set. This is the traditional betrothal ring. Now it is yours as are the rest of the famous Straeford emeralds." He spoke in a bored manner, as if he simply wished to be through with the whole matter as quickly as possible.

"Well, thank you," Marisa replied with great sarcasm, snapping the box shut and holding it out in front of his startled eyes.

"What are you doing? I said it was yours." Straeford was clearly exasperated and harshness crept into his words as he grabbed the box, removed the ring, and held it out to her. "Here! Put this on!" he demanded.

Reluctantly, she extended her hand to accept the ring. She hated herself as the earl slid the emerald on her finger. It slipped sideways when he released it from his grasp and he swore under his breath.

"Too large by half, I see. Well, your father can have that remedied easily enough."

"But, my lord," she protested gently, "won't you be kind enough to have it adjusted, since I will wear it in your name?"

"My dear woman, I see no good reason why I must be bothered with trifling matters such as having baubles adjusted. After all, it is you who wishes to wear it. And since your father has sought this goal so eagerly for you, I am positive he will be more than delighted to perform this service."

Pulling her hand away from his with a sudden jerk

77

she retorted hotly, "Yes, I'm sure that he will take care of this as he has everything else up to this point."

The earl threw back his head and gave off a loud, sardonic laugh. "That's right, dear lady, your father is a managing man, as we have both discovered to our mutual chagrin." Even Marisa was forced to smile at the irony of it all.

The Hardings arrived for dinner that evening, and their natural congeniality did much to lighten the atmosphere within the Straeford household. The earl was always pleased to see Edward Harding. but his wife Ann was another matter. A pretty, round-faced girl with plump. apple cheeks and springy brown curls which bounced gingerly about her head, she had an amazing capacity to chatter endlessly in disconnected discourse. She was good-natured, to be sure, and in many ways quite entertaining, especially to Marisa, who found her interesting tidbits of gossip a welcome contrast to the day's events. Straeford on the other hand found his friend's wife overbearing and wondered why Harding had not had the courage to muzzle her when it was necessary. To Straeford. Edward's failure to properly harness his wife represented a flaw in his authority and quite possibly his manliness.

During dinner, the earl made a civil effort to mask his displeasure at the inane conversation conducted by his guests. When the women finally retired to the drawing room, he breathed an audible sigh of relief. How Harding put up with his Ann's incessant prattle, he did not know. Yet the poor man wore a lopsided grin on his face every time his eyes rested on his wife. If that were his own wife—he dared not think of the consequences. Lucky for him that Miss Loftus was at least not a scatterbrain.

"Cigars and politics," Ann was babbling on as they seated themselves in comfortable chairs. "Men will smoke and drink all night without paying one whit of attention to a woman's heart. The cads. But don't worry, ladies, I made Ed promise just one cigar and then they must come to join us."

"You haven't been married very long, have you?" Marisa inquired.

"Less than a year. You see, I was in India with my father until he retired from the army. That's where I met Edward and Justin."

"Oh, then you must know the earl quite well."

"Well, no, not really . . . I mean, well, no one really knows Justin, now do they? He's so stand-offish." She giggled guiltily. "Lud, I suppose that isn't the right thing to say, is it? I only meant that Straeford is somewhat of a mysterious devil." She clapped her hand to her mouth as if to grab the words she had just uttered.

"Ninnyhammer!" Lady Maxwell muttered under her breath.

"What did you say, Lady Maxwell?" Ann asked unblinkingly.

"I asked if Harding sails with Justin on the thirteenth."

"To Portugal, you mean?"

"Of course, Portugal. Where else?" Lady Maxwell was beginning to show signs of exasperation similar to her grandson's.

"Justin was able to have my husband assigned to his regiment, so he will be going, too."

"I'm sure that will be very difficult for you," Marisa sympathized, "especially with a child due in October."

"Yes, it will be, but I have my family, of course. Did you know that the army is allowing a certain number of women to travel with them? Space is being provided for some of the infantrymen's 'fancy pieces' while the officers are . . ."

"Saints above!" Lady Maxwell cried and her teacup clattered on her plate. "Spare us any more details, if you please."

"Lud, I am sorry, my lady. Did I cause a turn up?" Ann's cheeks flushed brightly. "Marisa, please excuse my rag manners."

"Not at all, my dear. I find this all very amusing as well as informative."

"Still, I should not have spoken of such things before an unmarried lady. Tell me, dear, when did you say the date of your wedding would be?"

Marisa was nonplussed by the sudden shift in conversation, but Lady Maxwell was not.

"She did not say since the earl will be away all summer, but my grandson is planning to take a leave of absence from his duties during the winter sometime when things are usually quiet."

"A winter wedding," Ann gurgled. "How nice. Will the Park be renovated by then so that you can honeymoon here? I for one think it's an ideal place, instead of some town teeming with other people. Here you can be alone together."

Marisa choked. "Another tea, Mrs. Harding?" Lady Maxwell inquired with exquisite timing just as the men joined them.

After a substantial breakfast the following morning, the Loftuses prepared to leave for London, and Marisa was relieved when Straeford spoke to her in her father's presence about pressing military business preventing him from calling on them before his departure for Portugal. He assured them Lady Maxwell would keep him informed about the progress on Straeford Park. And if all went well, he planned to return at the beginning of the new year or sooner. Since he had already insisted on a small wedding, arrangements could easily be made for it to be held shortly thereafter.

"The wedding." Marisa Loftus heard him say those words over and over again in her mind as the carriage rumbled homeward at the conclusion of the weekend visit. She wondered how long it would be before it became a reality. She wondered about many things associated with this marriage.

6

Straeford stood on the rocky, granite coast of Figueira da Foz watching the last of his brigade disembark from the transports. It had been a long stressful day with one of the boats capsizing in the churning surf, bringing death to three of his men. Calling to his aide-de-camp. Lt. Drake. the earl told him to report to headquarters that the last of the transports was being unloaded and the brigade was awaiting further instructions. The boy saluted enthusiastically, turned smartly on his heels and strode away. Looking after him, Justin smiled to himself. It was apparent that Drake was looking forward to his first military engagement. As a matter of fact, the earl, too, was yearning for the heat of battle. It was a relief for him to be here in Portugal serving under General Wellesley, a military acquaintance of his from India.

Straeford squinted as his eyes followed the hot rays of the sun dancing across the ocean in the direction of England. Lady Maxwell would see to things there until he returned to marry the Loftus chit. Reluctantly he had to admit to himself that his grandmother's choice had been a wise one. The family's lack of credentials gave him a decided advantage. If the Loftuses had been well connected, they might not have been so willing to concede to some of his demands. Yet he had not won on all counts. If he had, his future brother-in-law, John Loftus, would not be here right now.

It was evident to him as well as others that the boy was not adapting successfully to military life, and it was causing the earl considerable embarrassment since it was known he was responsible for the young man's commission. Why Loftus was not eager and willing to learn and assume his duties, as Drake was doing, was incomprehensible to Justin. But there was no time to contemplate the matter now, for Drake had just handed him a message informing him that the army would march in two days for Lisbon and the French.

It was a long, difficult trek across the land. Even so, under Wellesley's competent direction the army moved quickly, and within a week and a half they were three days from their ultimate destination. At that point they had reached the little village of Vimeiro where they were to bivouac for the night. The army had barely settled in when scouts informed Wellesley that the French were approaching the encampment. Quickly he assembled his officers and issued orders for the deployment of the troops.

Straeford's men were to guard the eastern section of the front. Since the attack was expected to be launched from the south, his brigade would actually be in reserve. Although he would have preferred to be in the thick of battle, the earl did not question his commander's decision and went about the business of preparing his men.

Sometime later, riding along the eastern ridge with Harding, he drew rein and raised the spyglass toward something glinting in the distance. An ironic smile twitched across his lips as he held the field glass out to his friend. "Take a look!"

The major brought the glass to his eye. "Frogs!" he shouted. "And they're headed our way!"

Colonel Lord Straeford was already scribbling a note to Wellesley and calling to Drake to see that the general got his message at once. Immediately after sending the young man on his way, Justin began shouting commands at his men and officers. They scarcely had time to obey before a group of French skirmishers swarmed over the hill and attacked. The British met them head-on to defend the summit. Volley after volley of rapid rifle fire smashed into the advancing French infantry columns finally forcing them to give way under the fierce onslaught.

Again the enemy advanced and once more they were cut down by bayonets and musket shot. Now the British pressed their advantage and drove the French back, breaking through their lines and rushing them.

In the melée that followed Straeford found himself in the middle of the battling armies. His cries of command were drowned out by the din of rifle fire and bloodcurdling screams coming from the frenzied mass of soldiers.

Although Straeford held his frightened horse rigidly in check, the animal plunged forward crashing into that of a French colonel. The Frenchman sat tall in the saddle, saber poised. Adroitly parrying his enemy's oncoming saber thrust, Straeford quickly took the offensive and attacked. Repeatedly their blades clashed and clanged in a death duel, and blood flowed from cuts each inflicted on the other. Equally matched, neither man could gain the advantage until the earl's mount was hit and collapsed beneath him. Instantly realizing he was going down, Straeford managed to fling himself free and land on one bent leg and knee in the midst of the seething turmoil. Assured of victory, a sneer of satisfaction crossed the French officer's face as he wielded his saber and bore down on the British colonel. Straeford steeled himself to receive the thrust, but as the officer leaned toward him to strike, he lurched sideways and sprang up to deliver a glancing blow to the left side of the Frenchman's head. Blood spurted from the wound and covered his face as he reeled in the saddle and fell across the neck of his steed. The crazed animal bolted into the swarming infantry and disappeared.

Immediately Straeford turned his attention to the continuing fracas only to realize that the French army was fleeing.

"Colonel!" Lt. Drake slipped from his mount. "Are you all right, sir?"

"I need a horse, Lieutenant," he said, ignoring Drake's question.

"Take mine, sir! I'll manage to get another."

Nodding, Straeford mounted, wheeled his horse about, and shouted orders to the disorganized men who were preparing to follow their retreating adversaries. The colonel and his men waited in vain for the command to pursue the enemy. Finally, it became apparent to Straeford that the battle was over, and that they were not going to follow the French and complete the job they had so successfully begun. The reason why would not be known to him until several hours later when he and some fellow officers shared a drink. Then he would discover that just as the battle began Wellesley had been superseded in command by a general who refused to pursue the French because he feared that the British forces were not strong enough to achieve a total victory.

During the interim Straeford directed care for the wounded and the dying. Going among his men to encourage and cheer the disheartened, Straeford disregarded his own fatigue and the painful lacerations inflicted upon him by the French colonel until he was satisfied that everything possible was being done for his comrades in arms. He also made a point of checking on John Loftus to assure himself that the boy had come through the battle unscathed. Only then did he submit to the ministrations of the surgeon and permit himself a few hours rest.

Several weeks later Colonel Lord Straeford sat behind a desk rifling through some papers and running an agitated hand through his wavy black hair. He, along with several other officers, had been assigned the duty of overseeing the evacuation of the French from Portugal.

"One blunder after another," he muttered under his breath. First Wellesley had not been permitted to complete his victory over the French, and then the new commandant had gone ahead and signed a treaty with the French allowing them to leave Portugal in British ships. "Insult to injury!" Harding heard him say as he came into the room. "Look at this!" Straeford thrust a sheet of paper into the major's hand. "Church plate, state carriages ... they're taking half the possessions of Portugal with them!"

"And to think we were within a three days' march of Lisbon. I just know we could have defeated them." Harding commiserated with him. "Wellesley must feel like hell. Rumor has it he's going home."

"It's no longer just rumor. Sir John Moore has already been assigned his command."

"Colonel, sir!" A breathless Drake stuck his bright blond head through the doorway. "I have a message from Admiral Cotton."

Straeford waved his young aide-de-camp into the room. After reading the message from the man responsible for transporting the French out of Portugal, he sat in contemplative silence until he realized both Harding and Drake were watching him. Looking up at them he demanded, "Well, why are the two of you standing around? The sooner we send those Frenchmen packing the better I'll like it!" With that, he jerked out of his chair and strode out of the building down to the waterfront to take a first-hand look at the progress being made in the evacuation. If everything continued on schedule, all would be completed by late tomorrow, and then the French would be the sole responsibility of the British navy. He took a deep breath of salt air and exhaled deeply as he viewed the activity about him. Unexpectedly his attention was drawn to a French officer whose head was swathed in bandages. Recognition was immediate. So the blow he struck had not been a mortal one. Instinctively Straeford felt his left arm where the Frenchman's blade had cut him sharply. He had been far luckier than his adversary.

Sensing Straeford's gaze, the Frenchman turned his head in his direction, and his good eye bore unblinkingly into the British officer's face. A swift, easy gait brought him to the earl's side. "Allow me to introduce myself, monsieur. I am Colonel Dubois." He bowed slightly. "And you, my lord?"

"Straeford," came the terse reply.

"Ah, I have heard the name." His small dark eye glittered coldly.

"You have the advantage," Straeford replied cynically, unmoved by the hatred he saw revealed in the man's face.

"You will know me next time, *n'est-ce-pas?*"

Straeford's eyebrows rose sardonically. "There's to be a next time, eh?"

"But of course. This," he pointed to his injury, "must be avenged."

Straeford shrugged indifferently. "Until we meet again then." With a slight incline of his arrogant head, he strolled away, dismissing all further thoughts of Colonel Dubois.

Ever since last summer when the Earl of Straeford and her brother John left for Portugal, Marisa Loftus had been following the newspaper accounts of the Peninsular Campaign, but not much was being written about the men in battle these days. Most of the news stories were concentrating on General Wellesley's decision to sign the armistice with the French. She wondered how that man was holding up under the barrage of attacks being made against him. If he were as arrogant and cold as Colonel Lord Straeford, there was no doubt he would survive. She sighed, putting the paper aside and picking up a length of red velvet brocade. Kneeling on the window seat, she held it up to the mullioned window of the gallery.

"Perfect," came Lady Maxwell's voice as she walked across the gallery to seat herself beside Marisa.

"Do you really like it, Lady Maxwell?"

"I couldn't have chosen better myself. You have an eye for color and design, my dear. Justin should be well pleased with your choices."

"Do you think so?" she asked teasingly, yet there was a touch of sincerity in her tone which was not missed by Lady Maxwell. "You know what I think, my lady? I think Lord Straeford wishes me to blazes."

Her ladyship frowned. "Now, my dear child, do not be put off by Justin's brusque manner."

"How can I not be?" Marisa asked honestly. "He's made his feelings clear to me. Your grandson views me as an interloper, an upstart, and he does not cavil to show his disdain for me. His behavior has been exceedingly rude and his manner arrogant ..." Seeing the dismay on

Lady Maxwell's face, Marisa fell silent, ashamed of her own poor manners. "Oh, forgive me, your ladyship, I had no right to say those things to you."

"No, do not apologize. I know how difficult my grandson can be, and I will not deny much of what you say about him is true. But, my dear child, there is another side to him. There is a fairness of mind and a generous nature beneath that cold, vain exterior." She held Marisa's gaze. "Believe me, it's there. Do you think I would let you marry him if I did not know it to be so?"

The sincerity with which Lady Maxwell spoke touched Marisa deeply. It gave her sagging spirits a lift. "Thank you, Lady Maxwell, you've made the prospects for the future seem a little less bleak."

"I want your happiness as well as Justin's because I've grown to love you as if you were my own granddaughter." The elderly woman smiled reassuringly and clasped the young girl's hand.

"You have become very important to me too, your ladyship." Impulsively Marisa kissed the lady's parchment-like cheek. Lady Maxwell appeared slightly flustered by such affection, but she quickly recovered.

"You are just what my troubled grandson needs. Someone who is sincere, honest and loving. Give him time to become accustomed to his good fortune. He's too intelligent not to realize it." The urgency in her voice and the tightening of her grip on Marisa's hand expressed the intensity of emotion she was feeling. It disturbed Marisa, who found it so uncharacteristic of this usually cool, self-controlled woman. Evidently the earl's welfare was extremely important to his grandmother.

Noticing the troubled expression on the girl's face, Lady Maxwell relaxed her grip on Marisa's hand. She had no wish to frighten her with her own anxiety. To lighten the mood, she waved her walking stick at the portraits lining the wall.

"Did you ever see such a motley crew? Come, let me introduce you to some of the saints and sinners." Marisa followed Lady Maxwell as she passed before the notables and continued to expound on their virtues as well as their vices until they stood before the portrait of the seventh Earl of Straeford and his wife.

"You were a very handsome couple."

"I used to think so," she smiled fleetingly, "but you and Justin will be a much more striking pair. I look forward to seeing a painting of the two of you."

Marisa smiled at the prospect. "I'm afraid I do not see the present earl sitting still for a portrait painter."

Lady Maxwell cackled as she pictured the scene of her scowling grandson sitting before the portrait painter. Then she led Marisa down the gallery to the figure of the ninth earl, a pale, green-eyed, light brown-haired youth. "Justin's brother Robert."

"He looks so different from the earl."

"As night is to day," Lady Maxwell agreed. "Not only in looks but in temperament as well, and yet they were devoted to one another."

"How did he die?"

Her ladyship did not answer immediately but stared at the portrait of her dead grandson as if willing him to speak for her. When she finally did reply, her voice was strangely hollow. "He broke his neck in a fall from a horse."

"How dreadful!"

"Yes, it was, but there are reasons why some things happen."

It was a strange comment for her to make, Marisa thought; however, she had little time to reflect on it as Lady Maxwell continued speaking.

"Although Robert was a nice boy, he was also shallow and self-indulgent like his mother. She dominated him completely and he was too weak to withstand her blandishments. Only Justin was capable of doing that. Naturally, that did not endear him to his mother."

Now was the opportunity Marisa had been waiting for. "Lady Maxwell, will you tell me about the earl and the late countess? Something about the kind of relationship they had. It's a question which has had me curious ever since I met the earl."

It took her ladyship so long to answer that Marisa feared she was angry with her. Finally, however, the elderly woman nodded her head affirmatively.

"Let us sit in the warmth of the sun. This room has

a chill upon it." An expression of distaste passed over her face, and she pulled the black lace shawl closer about her shoulders.

Was it the gallery or her own question which had produced Lady Maxwell's chill? Marisa wondered.

"Actually, child, it is not my story to tell," she explained after they were seated with their backs to a sun-drenched window, the rays filtering across the room to the still faces of the Straeford ancestors. "It is Justin's tale, and some day I hope he will see fit to confide everything in you. Nevertheless, I think it my duty to give you some idea of the situation. It had its beginnings so very long ago, but it still affects Justin's life today. You see, my daughter-in-law was not overly fond of children —even her own. And Justin incurred her wrath even more by being an inquisitive, independent daredevil." She smiled, remembering the bright little boy who always delighted her. "He was very much like his father." A twinge of pain seemed to cloud her dark eyes. "My son's marriage was not a happy one. Marian hated her husband, and she transferred that hatred to her own son because he was a constant reminder of the earl. So whatever affection she was capable of giving went to Robert, and Justin grew up without the love a child needs."

Marisa looked across the gallery at the portrait of Straeford at his mother's knee. It was intended to create a tranquil image, the child's look of innocence giving no hint as to the anguish he must have experienced according to Lady Maxwell's account. To Marisa the painting was a contradiction, the innocent young child a contrast to the impassive, enigmatic man she now knew. She was about to offer this observation but decided it better not to interrupt her ladyship's running commentary.

"Perhaps he would have adjusted to the lack of a mother's love in his life if he had not discovered as a young man her ... infidelities. I am afraid that was the last straw ... " She paused as if to go on, but thought better of it. "Well, maybe now you will have a better understanding of why he has neither love for nor faith in women."

This last disclosure disturbed Marisa greatly. If his

lordship's feelings were of such long standing, what chance did she have of altering them? And she said as much to Lady Maxwell.

"Don't think like that! You must not be discouraged." Her ladyship was vehement. "He can change and he will! What he has needed is someone in his life like you, a good woman who will give him compassion and love."

"Lady Maxwell!" Marisa rose to her feet and twisted her hands in agitation. "You don't realize what you're saying. There is no . . . love between your grandson and me, and I cannot promise there ever will be!"

There was a strained silence as the two women stared at each other. Then Lady Maxwell rose and took the girl by the shoulders. "Forgive an old woman for being so insensitive. You barely know Justin and I will have to be content to let matters take their course."

Marisa relaxed and then apologized for her outburst. "I . . . I overreacted, my lady, I did not mean . . . ."

"Never mind, child, there is no need to explain. It is I who said too much. Now I am going to let you return to your decorating while I go check with Bess about tonight's dinner."

With great dignity the elegant lady crossed the chamber. Pausing at the exit, she turned to face Marisa. "There is one thing more, my dear. Do my grandson a great kindness and remove the portrait of the late countess from the drawing room." Without waiting for a reply she stepped out of the gallery and only the sound of her tapping cane lingered.

The interview with Straeford's grandmother had done little to reassure Marisa about the earl and her future. The future Countess of Straeford felt as confused and uncertain as before. And at this moment she was exasperated, too. Stalking over to the family portrait, she glared at it. The serenity of the picture angered her for it was a lie. A deceitful lie! And as for that innocent looking little boy on his mother's knee, he was a total enigma. To listen to Lady Maxwell, he was the victim of an unloving mother who was responsible for turning him into the cold, ruthless man she knew. Even if that were true, could she give him the tenderness, understanding and . . . and love he needed to soften his outlook on life? But wasn't she jumping to conclusions? There was nothing in his behavior that suggested he wanted to change . . . except for that one evening at her father's home when she thought she glimpsed deep sadness behind his haughty manner. Possibly that was only her imagination, too. Wasn't he simply a professional soldier, a man of war, who was perfectly satisfied with his life and brooked no interference in it? She shook her head. It seemed doubtful that she would ever come to understand the man who was to become her husband.

Straeford glared at the top of the surgeon's balding head as he bent over him and dabbed at a wound on his right shoulder.

"Well, Nevins, will you finish up! I've got things to do."

"But, my lord," the doctor said as he lifted his eyes from his work, "I must make certain that the wound is clean. You were very lucky that it went through the flesh. There is less likelihood of infection, but there is still the possibility of fever."

"It was a mere scratch, so stop fussing and bandage me up, will you." He was anxious to see what his men were up to now that the fort was secured.

"Very well, Lord Straeford," the doctor muttered in annoyance, sighed heavily, and began dressing the wound. Nevins worked quickly and soon Straeford's shoulder was covered with a white cloth. "There, I am finished." With the help of Straeford's batman, the doctor gathered his equipment.

"Send Major Harding in on your way out," Straeford ordered Nevins.

The surgeon shrugged his shoulders. What good would it do for him to protest or suggest that his lordship should rest? The man was inhuman. Already he was rotating his shoulder and flexing his arm, testing its agility. Without another word, he left his lordship in the capable hands of Billings, who was helping him into his shirt and jacket.

Only after the door had shut on Nevins did Straeford permit himself to wince. He could trust Billings not to make a fuss over him and that was the way he wanted it. Fortunately the wound was not serious. Yet he could not help wondering how many more times he could cheat death. There was an urgency creeping over him to have the marriage sealed. With a son, an heir for Straeford, the line would be assured. All these years he had ignored the possibility of his demise. Now he suddenly felt vulnerable. What had caused this doubt? Perhaps it was a sense of responsibility which was stirred in him after his return to England and his ancestral home. The heritage that was Straeford was solely dependent upon him. And he was no longer so young to believe in his own invincibility.

"God, is it cold out there!" Harding stepped into the room shivering and clasping his hands about his shoulders. "Bet it snows before morning." He came to stand beside the small fire in the grate, holding his hands over it. "At least it's comfortable in here."

Straeford chuckled as he looked about the abandoned stucco structure he was using as a temporary headquarters. Through the cracks in its frame the wind howled, and a few pieces of dilapidated furniture were scattered about the room, yet the experienced soldier considered this more than adequate accommodations.

"Have the sentries been posted?" Straeford asked as he and the major accepted a glass of port from Billings.

"Uh huh, and the men are dividing the spoils."

Straeford frowned over his glass. "Who's in charge of the operation?"

"Markham." Harding began brushing off a chair that had only one armrest left.

"Don't get too comfortable, Ed. I want you to check on this detail for me. See how Markham is handling it. I don't want the men to get out of control. And see that they are ready to march in the morning. Our victory today was partly due to the fact that the French didn't expect to see us this far north. Now that they know we are here, they won't be caught napping a second time. Billings will go with you and report back to me."

"All right, I'll attend to it at once."

The door had barely closed after them when there

was a disturbance outside. Suddenly Drake came stumbling into the room with a *senhora* following closely behind him. The strong wind whipped wildly at her long black hair, and her dark eyes were flashing angrily. Although her black and red costume was torn, exposing much of her body, she radiated defiance with her hands on her hips and her feet planted firmly apart.

"I beg your pardon, sir . . ." a breathless Drake stammered and pointed to the woman, "but she demanded to see you."

"Senhor!" she shouted defiantly.

"Speak when you're spoken to, woman!" Straeford commanded. "Who is she?"

"Claims to be a Colonel Dubois's *lady.*"

"Dubois?! Does she indeed?" Straeford suppressed a smile. "Very well, Lieutenant, I'll talk to her . . . . alone."

"Yes, sir!" Drake seemed to be relieved to escape the woman's presence and swiftly left them.

Straeford sat on the edge of the rickety table while the woman remained standing. "Name?" he shot at her.

"Isabella Costanza." She tossed her head sideways and swept the tangled mass of hair behind her with one hand, then stared at him boldly. "I demand that you return me to Colonel Dubois!"

His face darkened. "Do you indeed? I think you've forgotten that you have been captured behind enemy lines and are now a prize of war."

"No matter." She gestured with her hands. "I am Dubois's . . ."

"Whore!" Straeford put in with contempt, shattering her confident demeanor.

"You bastard!" she swore and lunged toward him, swinging her long nails at his face. But he met the attack by blocking her arm with a thrust of his own, sending her to the floor. "I'll keeell you," she choked as her breath returned.

"I wouldn't try it!" He glared so fiercely at the disheveled woman that she remained where she was. "That's better. Now, we can get down to business."

"What will you do with me?"

"There's no policy governing . . . ladybirds." He let the statement hang as once again he seated himself on the edge of the table. His leg swung freely as he eyed her thoughtfully.

Isabella scrambled to her feet, a note of fear creeping into her voice. "You will not turn me over to your men?"

"That is one possibility," he threatened callously.

"English pig!" she swore and her hand went out to strike him. He expected her to attack him again and this time he grasped her wrist with an overpowering grip and yanked it behind her back, forcing her to her knees.

"Are you finished attempting to claw me, you wildcat?"

"*Sim,*" she screamed in capitulation.

Straeford stared at the woman huddled at his feet and nudged her roughly with the toe of his boot. "So you are Dubois's . . . woman." There was a pause. "He has spoken of me?"

"*Sim.*" She edged away from his encroaching foot. "He wears the black patch over the eye because of the English colonel, and he swears vengeance one day."

"Looks as if he's going to have more than one reason for vengeance, eh wildcat?" His eyes gleamed wickedly. Isabella feared her seductive charms held no sway with this man. If her beauty failed to arouse him, what would he do with her? A savage grin revealed white teeth against his dark face. "And now what's to be done with you? Shall I amuse myself with you first, or simply turn you over to my officers who then can give you to . . ."

Isabella let out a scream and grasped at his boot. "No, colonel, I pray you will not use me so cruelly. By the saints . . ." she pleaded.

"Let go of me, woman!" Straeford roared, pulling his boot free from her clutching hands. Disgusted and angry with himself for taunting his helpless victim, he waved an imperious hand at her. "Go!"

Confused and frightened, Isabella stared at him dumbly.

"We already have a number of camp followers," he explained. "One more won't make a hell of a lot of difference. Find yourself a protector. Now go!"

94

Slowly she came to her feet and studied this fearful man. She wanted *his* protection, not some lowly infantry soldier's. "You will not take me first?" she suggested warily.

He gave off a harsh laugh. "Not unless you wish it."

They stared long and hard at one another until Isabella, swinging her hips provocatively, sauntered to the door and waited there. When he did not speak, she opened it. Still he said nothing. Finally she spun around to face him. "I think, Colonel, I choose you for my protector, eh?" There was a challenging gleam in her eyes and a saucy smile on her lips.

Straeford raked her voluptuous figure, and then with an insolent shrug he said, "For a night—why not!"

Confident once more, she came to him. "You will want Isabella for more than one night, my Colonel. You will see."

"Undoubtedly one of us will," he drawled and bowed mockingly. How Colonel Dubois was going to react to the matter briefly crossed his mind as he took the woman into his arms.

It was just before dawn when Straeford woke with a ringing sensation in his head and a burning thirst in his throat. He shivered violently and then felt intensely hot. This was going to be some hell of a day, he thought. Nevins had been right after all. He had a touch of fever. As he rolled off the bunk, Isabella automatically pulled the blanket more closely about her in her sleep. After splashing some water on his face, he went outside in search of Billings, who came scurrying up to him.

"My lord, I'll have some coffee . . ."

"Never mind that now. I need that concoction—the powder and tea from India."

"Fever, my lord?" The little man tried not to look anxious as he observed his lordship. Straeford screwed up his face and ran a hand over it. Reluctantly, he nodded in the affirmative. "I'll see to it at once, my lord."

While Straeford waited for Billings to return, he looked out over the encampment. Most of the fires had died out, and the men were huddled deep in their blan-

95

kets. Even though the wind had died down, it was still biting cold, and the leaden sky hung threateningly overhead.

"We'll move out as soon as the men have been fed," he told Harding shortly after the major had joined him and Billings. The batman was urging a second cup of tea on his lordship, who declined. "That was quite enough of that vile-tasting brew, my good man. Now let us all get on with the business of this day."

Both Harding and Billings knew better than to remonstrate further with the earl.

Isabella stretched under the blanket on the bunk and rolled over. As she sat up, clutching the covers to her bosom, she faced Straeford's piercing stare. *"Deus,* but it is cold."

"Get your clothes on then."

"But first a kiss, *sim?"* She held out her arms letting the blanket slip to her waist, unashamed of her nakedness.

Ignoring her brazen gesture. Straeford picked up her clothing and threw it at her. "I said get dressed!"

Isabella pursed her lips but decided it was too cold to argue the point and quickly dressed herself. Then coming up behind Straeford, she encircled his waist and leaned against him purring. Unceremoniously. Straeford disentangled himself from her and told her to behave just as Billings entered with their breakfast. Isabella ignored the chair Billings held out for her as Straeford seated himself. Glancing at Isabella's stormy face, Straeford waved Billings out of the room.

"Come and eat. The food is getting cold."

"I do not care for food!" She stamped her foot.

"Suit yourself," he said and began eating.

Infuriated by his lack of interest. Isabella glared at him, but he seemed not to notice. Finally she gave up and came flouncing over to the table. Without a word he handed her a platter.

"I have been informed this morning, that the French are moving this way and should be here in a matter of hours. If you remain here . . ."

"Deus! You will not leave me behind?"

"I'm returning you to Dubois. Isn't that what you wanted?"

"Bah!" Her fork clattered to the plate. "That was yesterday. Today is different, *sim?*"

"No, it is not!"

"I stay with you," she demanded.

"No, you do not stay with me. I do not want you," he stated emphatically as he rose from the table.

"This cannot be true?"

"Oh, but it is. Look, if you don't want to hang around here, I'll provide you with a horse and . . ."

"*Diabo!* You heartless fiend! I give myself to you and it means nothing? You would abandon me?"

"Oh, come now, don't play me a Cheltenham tragedy. You offered yourself, and I accepted. If it's money you want," he delved into his pocket and held out some coins to her.

"I will scratch your devil eyes out!" She slapped his hand holding the coins aside and jumped at him. And for a third time she found herself knocked to the floor.

"Damn!" he roared, "do that again and I'll have you chained to the wall."

"No one uses Isabella! No one!" she screamed.

"Don't break my eardrums, woman. I can hear you." His white teeth showed a brutal smile.

"Dubois, he will drive a sword through your black heart. I swear it!"

"Give my regards to the Colonel when you see him," he jeered and strode out of the small house to meet Harding who had just reined in. "Well, Major, what did you find out?"

"You won't believe this, but it's Colonel Dubois, and he wants to meet with you."

"Dubois, eh?" Straeford was rather pleased by this turn of events.

"What will you do?"

"Meet him, of course. The men won't be ready to march for another hour. That should give me plenty of time to complete my business with the Colonel."

"You don't think it is some kind of trap, do you?"

"I should think not. I believe the man has a sense of honor, and I would imagine a flag of truce will prevent him from attempting to ensnare us." Straeford beckoned to his batman who was standing at a discreet distance waiting with his horse. "Billings, get the wench and follow us." Mounting his black stallion, the Colonel motioned to Harding and Drake to follow him.

They rode three miles from their protected campsite, situated in a valley of low-lying hills, out onto a plains area. There, two hundred yards from their adversaries, Straeford and his countrymen halted and waited for Dubois to detach himself from a group of soldiers dressed in blue and head towards them. Straeford, in turn, moved out to join the Frenchman. They approached one another and dismounted, each man holding the other in an unblinking stare. Straeford could see the hatred and jealousy etched in Dubois' drawn, grey face. He had seen that look before—the look of a disappointed man unable to accept responsibility for his own failures.

"So, Colonel, as you predicted, we meet again."

"C'est vrai, but still the advantage is yours. It is *I* who suffer the loss of honor. *I* who bear the disgrace of defeat in battle. *I* whose body is maimed . . ." he choked, unable to continue.

"Is this why you asked to meet with me? To air your grievances?" Straeford's evident disdain enraged Dubois all the more, but before the Frenchman was able to reply, there was the thunder of hoofbeats which drew both men's attention.

"Maurice!" a woman's voice called.

"Mon Dieu, Isabella!" Dubois whirled to face the woman he had been vainly seeking for days. "I thought you must be dead."

"No, no, *guerreiro minho,* I was at the mercy of the English pig!" she spat angrily and tossed her head in Straeford's direction, a gesture Dubois was quick to interpret. He turned purple with fury. "So, dog, you add insult to injury. You will answer for this with your life." The man nearly strangled with his frenzy. "I demand satisfaction! Choose now—pistols or swords!"

"Did I not tell you he would kill you?" Isabella crowed joyously.

"Sorry to disappoint you, madam, but I have no intention of duelling over you, now or ever. And since we are under a flag of truce, Colonel," Straeford faced the angry Frenchman, "you have no choice but to let me withdraw from this farce." So saying, Straeford swung onto his horse before Dubois could prevent him.

"*Sacre Dieu!* You will not abandon the demands of honor." Dubois was incredulous.

"You'll have to give me more reason than a mere woman to fight over, my friend."

"Mere woman!" screeched Isabella. "Kill him, Maurice, kill him now."

"Fight coward! Come down from your high perch and fight like a man," Dubois demanded.

But Straeford's response was only to laugh and ride away with Harding and Drake beside him.

"You'll pay for this! By the holy name of the *Bon Dieu* I swear you shall pay and I will have my revenge!" Tears from Dubois' one glittering eye were coursing down his face.

Isabella found release in a string of oaths and cursing.

"The time will come when he will regret his very life. I vow it on my own mother's grave," and turning his back on the disappearing horsemen, Dubois mounted his own mare.

"Maurice?" Isabella ran to him in alarm and clutched at his arm. "Wait for me."

"I want no man's cast-off—especially the Englishman's! Get away from me." He tried to shake loose of her, but she clung to him.

"No, Maurice, you can't do this to me. I, too, have been ill-used and seek revenge for my suffering."

Dubois tried to shake free of her again, but she clung more desperately. "Let me help you," Isabella begged. "Please."

Dubois paused. "Help me? How?"

The frantic woman grasped for a straw and found it. "The British occupy my country. With the aid of some of my countrymen it would be easy to spy on that devil, and one day when he is most vulnerable, we will strike," she promised breathlessly.

As Dubois hesitated, considering Isabella's offer, a cruel smile played about his mouth. and she knew she had won. "Come," he sighed, "I will wait for you."

7

Having just completed the last details involved with the removal of the Christmas decorations, a task that always saddened her, Marisa held up one of the ornaments in the air and reflected on the joy and warmth of the season. It was a pity its goodwill could not remain alive all year, she thought wistfully. During this moment of quiet she sipped a delicious hot cup of tea and thought about Christmas next year. Would that terrible war finally come to an end? How would her marriage to the earl change her life?

She was locked deep in the privacy of her thoughts when her solitude was suddenly broken by the noise of someone coming down the hallway. When she opened the drawing room doors to see who it was, she couldn't believe her eyes. There, standing in front of her as big as life, was her brother!

"John? Why, John!" She rushed into his open arms, hugging and kissing him. "You're home! Can it really be true?"

She stepped back for a moment to take a longer look at him, her face suddenly waxing serious. "You're so pale . . . and you look so thin." He appeared exhausted to her, his eyes bearing a gaunt look, his face sallow in appearance. Why, the war actually aged him, she thought, and an overpowering sense of panic seized her. "You haven't been injured, have you? You are all right, aren't you?" she blurted out, both hands clasping his.

"Oh, yes, I'm all right," he said, smiling weakly. "There's nothing wrong. I haven't been hurt in any way."

Marisa's eyes lowered in relief. "Come dear brother, please sit down. There is some hot tea and buttered scones for you here. We needn't talk at all about that dreadful war right now."

"But I'm afraid I must," he protested. "It's the only way I can rid myself of this nightmare. And a nightmare it certainly has been."

"Perhaps . . . perhaps we should wait for papa," she suggested, trying to divert his thinking.

"No . . . I . . . I couldn't face him, really. Not yet."

Marisa instantly perceived a tone of desperation in his protest. "Very well, dear, whatever you wish."

"Did you receive all of my letters?" He sipped a cup of tea and Marisa thought she saw his hand tremble but she couldn't be certain.

"Until November. Then they stopped coming regularly and we began to worry."

"That's when the warlords decided we'd been idle long enough," he stated with obvious bitterness. "Vimeiro wasn't enough for them, so they sent us into Spain to confront the French there. We got as far as Salamanca when the roof caved in. Napoleon's army outnumbered us so badly that all we could do was retreat as fast as possible to La Coruña where the fleet was waiting to transport us home. The French were at our heels the entire time."

Marisa looked intently at her brother but wished there were some way she could help him turn his mind away from his war experiences. Obviously, it was painful for him to relate them to her, but all she could do was nod sympathetically and listen as he continued.

"And finally, they caught up with us . . . It was horrible!" His voice cracked as he continued. "Guns and cannons exploding. Men shouting, running blindly, screaming, not knowing what to do or where to go. They began dropping like flies and then panic set in. The ranks broke completely, and it was every man for himself. We just couldn't stand up to their bombardments and we knew it. I tried to round up as many men as I could, and we made our way back to board the ships, leaving so many behind, wounded, crying out for medical aid, dying right there in front of us as we passed . . ." He buried his head in his hands and sobbed violently. Marisa, torn with pity, comforted him and helped him slowly regain his composure.

"I'm sorry, Marisa," he shuddered. "It's just that I can't get that scene out of my mind. It feels like it's locked in my memory . . . those dying faces and somehow here I am, alive. I don't understand any of it."

"John, you can't dwell on this thing." Marisa tried to soothe him. "Eventually it will pass away."

"No. I don't think it ever will. Not if I have to face anything like that again. And I . . . I don't think I can. No matter how father feels about it."

"I'm sure we'll be able to get him to understand your feelings," she said, trying to reassure him.

"He understands nothing—nothing but his own ambition!"

"Hush, John! You're very upset at this moment and this is not the time to discuss the problem of father."

A wan smile crossed his lips in reaction to her admonition. "Hmmph! The 'problem of father'? Now that's an interesting way of putting it, I must say."

"Yes, it is rather," Marisa said with an impish smile, hoping to coax him into a better mood. "Here, let me pour you some more tea before it gets cold."

"Not now," he said, holding his hand over the cup. "I can't stay any longer. I must see Ruth before father returns."

"John," she pleaded as he rose to leave. She did not want to broach another untimely topic, but there seemed no other choice. "Perhaps you should wait until you see father. You know how he feels about your *tendre* for Ruth."

Her suggestion set his eyes ablaze. "I won't be bullied by him anymore," John thundered. "I joined this

103

infernal army because of him, but I'll be damned if I will be forced into a marriage just to please him. Now maybe you intend doing that, but . . ."

"Please, John, don't say it."

"Hmm, come to think of it now, you haven't even asked after 'the great man'," he claimed with an accusatory tone. "That's how much you care about him, is it?"

"No, that's not fair, John! I was just about to question you concerning him, but I haven't gotten around to .it." Marisa's voice trailed off as she winced under her brother's sarcastic gaze. "Well? Aren't you going to tell me what has happened to him? Please don't taunt me this way! You know that I must find out."

"I'm sorry. I didn't mean to alarm you unnecessarily. Rest assured that he is quite all right. He has not been hurt. As a matter of fact, he is one of the few officers who can claim a victory in this disastrous campaign. His men annihilated a French fort near Taro, I understand, but even he had to give way under Napoleon's onslaught. It was just too overpowering, and so he brought his men home with the rest of us."

"So he *has* returned!" An anxious feeling swept inside her. Soon he would be back to see her, and the final wedding arrangements would be made. From that point on, she heard nothing of John's remaining conversation. She looked at him directly, nodded appropriately, and even contributed a sentence or phrase to his continuing discussion, but it was merely a mechanical ritual for Marisa. The thought of the earl returning had so seized her mind she was unable to respond accurately to several innocuous questions John had posed without her asking him to repeat them each time.

When her brother had finally gone, Marisa was left alone with a thousand thoughts whirling madly within her brain. When had he come back? Why hadn't she asked John? And where was he now? After all of these months, when would he see her?

Their meeting was not to occur until a full two weeks had gone by, and then it was due only to the efforts of Lady Maxwell, who had announced a small dinner party in their honor. It was not, however, the kind of reunion that Marisa had hoped it would be. She had devoted many hours to her toilette in anxious preparation for that evening, determined that when the earl saw her for this first time in many months he would be captivated by her appearance. And when she made her entrée that evening, Marisa did, indeed, radiate beauty. Her high-waisted gown of soft peach satin enhanced her pale yellow hair charmingly styled à la Sappho for this affair. Her firm, well-proportioned breasts arched impudently beneath her low, tight-fitting decolletage where, directly below, a ribbon cinched smartly underneath her bosom. A burgundy velvet Spencer with a high-standing collar completed her ensemble, and she carried a petite embroidered bag at her side.

Many male eyes lingered in her direction throughout the evening, but, unbelievably, the earl showed scant interest upon being reunited with his wife-to-be. At their initial meeting, he had greeted her with a formal kiss on the hand and had exchanged not more than a few brief sentences with her before he was off talking to first this lord and then that viscount, and so it went. Even during dinner, conversation was dominated by the gentlemen present so that no intimate discussion was possible between the two of them. Feeling uneasy in the company of these garrulous socialites, Marisa wavered between shyness and outright anger at her inability to communicate freely with her husband-to-be.

Alone in her room that night, she painfully reviewed the evening's frustrations over and over in her mind. Why, he hadn't even mentioned the forthcoming wedding at all, except in jest when several of the male guests saw fit to pelt him with quips concerning his "new duties" and his "demotion in rank." Of course, Straeford handled their barbs with his characteristic aplomb, but Marisa could not help feeling hurt by their insensitive attempts at humor. Much later that evening, she had sought in a very quiet way to talk to him concerning several details relating to the wedding arrangements. But he dismissed them with one broad sweep of his hand. "I'm certain, my dear, that you are an intelligent woman who is quite capable of attending to these trivialities entirely on your own. Can't you see that I have far too many matters of greater importance that will demand my undivided attention for some time? Now I do hope that you will care for these details independently of me and not trouble me needlessly. All I ask, no, demand is that the ceremony be simple, brief and devoid of any embarrassing theatrics."

Trivialities? Matters of greater importance? Didn't this marriage have any importance at all for him? Marisa gritted her teeth in disgust as she recalled how cavalierly he treated what she thought were necessary questions for both of them to resolve. From that moment on Marisa took no pleasure whatsoever in the wedding preparations. Although she longed to have a glorious, gala wedding, she knew it was impossible and resigned herself to planning a small, undistinguished affair.

Finally, on a cold and blustery afternoon in early February, the ceremony took place. The huge Gothic church remained largely empty for the occasion and, except for the lighted candles on the altar and the dim luminescence yielded by the small stained glass windows, the nuptial rites were conducted in an uninspiring state of semidarkness. The earl had insisted on a simple wedding and, according to his wishes, pomp and guests were excluded.

While Straeford, Ed Harding and the minister stood in front of the altar, Lady Maxwell and Ann Harding occupied the first pew and awaited the arrival of the bride and her father. Impatiently, the earl referred to a pocket watch from his vest and at that exact moment the south portico doors opened to let in a gust of cold air and the entire Loftus family. Hushed whispers were exchanged among all of them before Angus appeared to escort his daughter to the altar with a proud grin on his half-whiskered face.

Marisa wore a tight-fitting ivory pelisse with several short capes trimmed in ermine, her accompanying hat and muff matching the fur of her capes. She smiled demurely as she walked in a dignified cadence up the aisle with her father. Her dress was simple but elegant, and it both surprised and impressed Straeford. His bride might be a mere merchant's daughter but there was no denying that she had the beauty and quiet good taste of a noblewoman.

Never faltering for a moment on her way to the altar, Marisa gracefully accepted the earl's arm and together they faced the minister. Although she could feel her heart beating frantically inside, she appeared outwardly calm and poised as the ceremony began. She struggled bravely to maintain a placid, confident façade as her eyes glanced quickly at this tall, dark figure of a man who stood next to her, now gripping her hand firmly, almost painfully at this, the most important moment of her life. Then an eerie feeling flashed suddenly within her, making her wonder if she had ever even seen this man before—really looked at him. Actually, he was a stranger to her, and this was the first time that she became acutely aware of that fact.

The sacred words that would forever unite them one to the other echoed solemnly within the towering inner walls of the church. As their vows were exchanged, each phrase was magically repeated first once, then again and again, until the sounds of their voices became unintelligible, muffled noises which rose upward and disappeared somewhere within the dark spiraling arches of the Gothic structure. When the earl slipped a band of emeralds and diamonds over her delicate finger, Marisa wanted desperately to hear the strains of an organ or a chorus of angelic voices to glorify that instant. In just a matter of a few fleeting moments she had become a countess. But the ceremony was bereft of music, people, warmth and love, she reflected, only because this man decreed it so. How much more wonderful it might have been if only he . . . She was curious to know whether he felt anything at all with regard to this wedding, to its significance, to her. When her eyes turned to meet his, she could find no warmth within them. Instead, only a cool appraisal appeared, making her wonder if they always gleamed like chips of green ice.

No kiss was exchanged between them at the conclusion of the ceremony. They simply turned to those present, the earl receiving the outstretched hands of the gentlemen present while the ladies joyfully hugged the new countess and kissed her on the cheek. Expressions of good luck followed them outside in the cold February air which sent the entire wedding party scurrying to their carriages.

Inside the head coach, the newlyweds sat facing Lady Maxwell and Angus Loftus. "Fine service," Loftus pronounced as he rubbed his hands together to warm them. "Only wish you hadn't insisted on such a small one. Why, we could have packed that church and afterward there'd have been such a celebration, the whole town would have known about it."

"I believe the *Gazette* will provide adequate coverage of the whole affair. You needn't worry, my good man. Publicity will be ample," the earl sneered.

Lady Maxwell's timing and diplomacy prompted her to intervene. "I understand that you've provided a banquet for the occasion."

"Oh, it's quite a menu, all right," Loftus boasted, "but then, why not? After all, it's not every day my little girl gets married—and to an Earl of the Realm at that!" He patted his daughter's cheek and beamed with pride.

Embarrassed by her father's shallow comments, Marisa stole a quick look at Straeford to detect his reaction, but he was paying her father no attention at all. Instead, his face bore a glazed stare of indifference as he watched the winter countryside pass beyond the carriage window. She breathed easier, knowing that the earl held Angus in low regard and kept mental tally of the unpolished man's social blunders. Hoping to avoid any mortification her father might cause, Marisa found herself struggling to steer and control the conversation to protect her parent from the earl's disdain.

Angus would have been deeply hurt if he had known his daughter's concern on this matter, for he just assumed he was admired as well as loved and respected by all his children since he had dedicated himself to the goal of providing them with every advantage possible. The supper he had ordered for that evening was yet another example of his desire to lavish his family with all that his money could buy. It was an extraordinary banquet consisting of at least a half-dozen of the most delectable dishes, including turtle soup, crab salad, potato puffs, mint-glazed carrots, asparagus a la Polonaise, white breast of turkey and veal Marsala. Special servants had also been engaged for the occasion. Dressed in formal livery, they quietly served the meal with an almost military precision.

Marisa found it difficult, however, to enjoy her wedding feast to the fullest. Seated next to her new husband, she seemed unable to rid herself of the many doubts that nagged her regarding his true feelings for her and the adjustments she would now have to face as his wife. A magnificent multi-tiered cake was set in front of them, helping her to dismiss these thoughts for the moment. But when her father rose to deliver a champagne toast to the two of them, she was touched by his words and she found herself again searching the earl's eyes as they lightly tapped their glasses.

What Straeford thought of the whole affair she could only guess for his characteristically stoic expression remained etched on his face throughout the entire proceedings. Even when they were alone and on their way to their newly acquired home on Berkeley Square, he remained almost sullenly silent until the carriage pulled up before their residence. In his enthusiasm, Angus Loftus had even managed to acquire the mansion that had once belonged to Straeford's mother. He and his daughter had little realized the painful memories it held for the earl. It was an imposing structure, a three-story town house, with an iron picket fence surrounding it and two tall street lamps standing at either side of the entrance gate. When the carriage came to a halt, the main door opened and Jenkins, the newly engaged butler, smiled broadly to welcome them. Inside, they made their way along an elegantly decorated corridor to the drawing room where a cozy fire burned invitingly in the hearth's grate.

"The house has only been partially furnished," she said. "I hope that what I've done so far is to your satisfaction. Possibly you might even have some suggestions as to the rest of the decor . . ."

"I? This is *your* home, my dear. I shall be a mere visitor from time to time. You may do as you wish with it."

"But this was once your home." Marisa's brow wrinkled in a puzzled expression. Surely he recognized her father's efforts to restore completely everything that once had been Straeford's.

"I barely recall it and it holds no special significance for the Straefords. My father bought it years ago simply to please my . . . the countess because she felt she needed a home in the fashionable section of London. And now your father has seen fit to purchase it as a wedding gift." He gave a short laugh laced with irony.

Marisa seated herself in one of the mauve wingback chairs as Straeford poured two glasses of sherry from the crystal decanter set on a nearby table. As he handed her a glass, he proposed a toast. "Let us drink to our mutual good fortune on this our wedding night, my dear wife."

That was the first time she had heard him use that word and he said it with a peculiar ring, Marisa thought. Obligingly, she rose to lift her glass to his and, as she sipped her drink, her eyes received a penetrating gaze which made her instantly uncomfortable. It was a slow and complete appraisal of her entire body, and it caused her to turn away from him and fidget with her goblet nervously.

She was a remarkably beautiful woman. As she stood near the fireplace her ivory satin dress seemed to change colors in front of the flickering fire. Her delicate white neck and smooth shoulders were bare except for the tiny capped ermine sleeves and a single strand of pearls she wore about her throat. Her complexion was milky and translucent in appearance, her hair a glorious gold.

Straeford continued to survey her classic figure during a long moment of silence that made Marisa think her nerves would snap. She forced her eyes to meet his squarely.

"My lord," she said, swallowing hard.

He replied with a deep but unintelligible mumble that shook her confidence.

"My lord . . . I . . ."

"Yes, yes! We've gotten that far twice around." He seemed amused at her faltering attempts to get to the point.

"I . . . I must speak forthrightly with you." Her voice was now breathless, and her composure completely deserted her when his eyebrows arched arrogantly and that satanic glint streamed from his eyes.

"By all means, please do. Isn't that an essential ingredient of wedded bliss? An honest, straightforward discussion between man and wife."

His mocking manner was loathsome, but she had to make him understand her feelings at this moment.

"We barely know one another, my lord . . . and . . . well, two people thrown into a marriage like this need time to learn one another's ways and . . ."

"On the contrary, I think we know each other well enough at this moment to be able to share our marriage bed together. What is this talk about needing more time? What difference will time make?"

"I mean . . . we need more time . . . at least in our personal relationship . . . before we . . . become intimate." She didn't like the way her words sounded as soon as they left her lips.

"Ah hah! I see! You wish to renege on our bargain, is that it?"

"Why must you refer to it as a 'bargain'? I would respectfully remind you that this day we entered into a *marriage* . . ."

". . . of convenience!" he cut in quickly. Towering over her, he jutted his jaw directly toward hers and snatched her chin between his fingers. "And it is my convenience to consummate this marriage tonight. Now do be a good wife and go upstairs and prepare yourself appropriately as an obedient woman should on her wedding night."

He escorted her to the door and pronounced, "I'll be up shortly. Now do hurry and don't disappoint me."

Perhaps he was right, Marisa thought as she mounted the stairs. What difference would more time make, indeed? She could have a lifetime and still never be ready for his demands.

Inside her room, Marisa rummaged about a bureau drawer until she found a coarse muslin night dress, a garment she thoroughly detested. Much more suitable for his temperament, she thought, as she slipped into its long sleeves and buttoned the high neck. Hopefully, he would

111

find this more "appropriate" than the alluring sheer gown she discarded in her drawer.

Pleased with her act of defiance, Marisa seated herself before a vanity mirror to undo her hair and brush its long honey-colored tresses as she pondered his entrance at any moment. She must not be afraid, she told herself. But when the adjoining door between their bedrooms clicked open, her hand hesitated in midair before continuing its descent on the next downward brush stroke. In the mirror she could see his reflection. Wearing only his tight white britches, his athletic V-shaped body made her feel as though she were being stalked in a game of hunt. Suddenly she felt unable to move, and her mouth became dry as she stared at his approaching muscular image.

A long thin white scar ran through the curling black hair on his strapping chest while a newer red scar coiled along his right shoulder. She wondered how he had survived that chest wound, but as his hands touched her shoulders she saw the look of displeasure which kindled within his eyes.

"Is this what the fashion magazines are recommending these days for enticing men into your bed?" He examined her gown, mocking it as a travesty of modesty.

Marisa said nothing, but tossed an indignant frown in his direction as she rose to douse the candles on the vanity.

"Wait!" he commanded. His arm clutched her waist in a whiplike grip, and she remembered the strength and solidity of his arms which now grasped her with terrifying ease.

"I wish to see what I bargained for," he taunted, his words utterly distasteful to her.

She struggled to release herself from his grip and came face to face with him. Two strong hands tore at the front of her dress and Marisa reeled backward.

"I won't be humiliated like this," she said, her voice cracking. "You have no right to deal with me in this manner."

"Oh, but I do indeed, my dear spouse, have every right to do as I please, or have you forgotten your vows which you solemnly spoke this very day?"

"Why must you be so heartless, so insensitive?" she protested.

Seizing her arm with one hand, Straeford thrust a menacing finger at her with the other. "Now you listen to me and listen carefully. I do not take kindly to criticism from anyone. But least of all do I expect it in my own household and from my own wife. You should be clear on this point right from the start. I expect no defiance from you any more than I would from a servant. If you are going to have the privilege of bearing the Straeford name, then I am justly entitled to your obedience to my bidding. And my bidding at this moment requires you to remove that ridiculous and insulting piece of rag you are wearing. I expect you to do it right now!"

With shaking hands, Marisa slowly unbuttoned her night dress, realizing that she should have expected him to retaliate. Suddenly her hands were abruptly pushed aside, and before she could defend herself in any way, he clenched the front of her dress with both hands and ripped the bodice open with a sound that brought a sinking feeling to the pit of her stomach. She shuddered helplessly as he shredded the remainder of the garment from her shoulders and let it drop in pieces to the floor. Marisa shivered, aware of her nakedness, powerless to deal with the tears which now threatened to flow.

"That's better," her captor said, both hands on his hips. He walked slowly around her, surveying his spoils. One hand slid along her shapely form and stopped to cup her sculptured breast. And then the other reached about her tiny waist and drew her against his rock-hard body. She felt weak, near to fainting, when he lifted her into his arms and carried her to the nearby bed. Now, with his warm body beside hers, she was alarmed at the strange stirrings welling within her as his powerful hands stroked the lovely valleys and hollows of her form, boldly, shamelessly.

"Oh, please . . ." she pleaded, just as he brought his lips down on hers hard and bruising, blocking out her protests. But there was little she could do to resist his total domination over her and she feared that any serious efforts to do so might trigger that lightninglike anger which he had revealed only a few moments earlier. This was not at all what she imagined her first act of love would be like. He treated her roughly, with only one purpose in mind—his own lust, totally disregarding her feelings. It was all she could do to keep from crying out as she submitted quietly to her conqueror's hungry advances.

When he finally took her body for his own, Marisa groaned audibly, and she felt his searing movements halt briefly in response. It was only later, when his passion had subsided, that the earl realized she had been a virgin. Rising abruptly from the bed, he left the room without so much as a backward glance.

The devil take her! he thought. A virgin at her age? But how? There had been some talk of a lover. He poured himself a drink and flung himself into a chair. Why didn't Lady Maxwell warn him? Well, too late now. No sense trying to second-guess the whole matter. He just thoroughly, if not too gently, initiated her to the act of love.

A stifled sob came from the adjacent room and Straeford swore out loud. "Damn her! Damn her to hell!" No woman was going to prod him with pangs of guilt ever again—not as long as he lived. He'd finished with that years ago.

Weary from several sleepless nights before the wedding and then last night's ordeal, Marisa slept late the next morning. Her maid had not awakened her until his lordship summoned her in the hallway.

"Tell your mistress I wish to leave for Straeford within the hour!" he commanded sternly, sending Lucy scurrying to Marisa's room.

"Oh, do wake up, my lady. His lordship looks to be in a black temper this morning."

Marisa stirred and winced at the stiffness and soreness she felt. The previous night's events crept into her consciousness as she awakened to the sound of Lucy's words. She sat up with a start, clutching the bedsheet to her bosom.

"What did you say, Lucy?"

"His lordship said he wishes to leave for the Park within the hour."

"Within the hour! Oh, Lucy, why didn't you wake me sooner? Forget the hot chocolate and hand me that peignoir. Is my bath drawn? I must hurry!"

Slipping into her robe, Marisa noticed the torn night dress on the floor exactly where the earl had dropped it the night before.

"Here, my lady, let me take that." Lucy stooped to pick it up and bustled about her chores, but Marisa stood there locked deeply in thought. He'd done his worst to her last night, so what more need she fear? If last night's episode were a prelude of things to come in this marital arrangement, well, then she might never be able to breathe another easy breath the rest of her wedded life.

"My lady," Lucy interrupted her thoughts. "Are you all right?"

"Yes, Lucy!" she said resolutely. "I most decidedly am all right this morning. And do you know what I'm thinking? I'm thinking that I will have that hot chocolate after all."

"What? But, my lady, his lordship . . ."

"His lordship will wait, thank you," Marisa said pointedly as she eased herself into her chaise longue and folded her arms triumphantly.

When Straeford reread the note his wife had sent him through Lucy, he was wild with rage. She could not be ready within the hour as he had wished, the note informed him. Crumpling the paper in his hand, the earl hurled a curse in the air. Apparently this woman did not understand him, but he'd soon remedy that!

Straeford startled Jenkins by storming past him in the center hall and taking two stairs at a time. Without a knock he flung open the bedroom door at the exact instant Marisa was rising from her bath. Lucy quickly drew a towel about her mistress while the earl stood there, glowering.

"Wait outside!" he snapped at Lucy, who bobbed a curtsey and fled with haste.

Marisa tightened her hold on the towel and braced herself as he drew near.

"What is the meaning of this?" he growled, crossing in front of her and tapping the wrinkled note in his hand.

Marisa walked slowly to her vanity and seated herself calmly before replying, "I thought it plain enough, my lord."

"Did you, indeed?" he sneered. "Well, hear this, madam wife. You have exactly fifteen minutes to ready yourself."

Marisa surprised even herself at how composed she remained in the face of his anger this morning. "Fifteen minutes! Impossible! I'll never be able to . . ." But the earl cut her off immediately, his tough fingers grasping her chin with a stinging grip. "Then I shall leave without you and you may make your own way to the Park. Do you understand?"

Marisa lowered her eyes and nodded.

"I shall expect to see you at the allotted time." Without another word, he whirled on his heels and strode out of the room.

A full twenty minutes had passed when Straeford entered the center hall, fully expecting to see his wife cowering there. A scowl creased his face as he looked up the stairs and listened for some sign of her descent. A minute passed, then two more. Fuming inside, he paced back and forth impatiently in the hallway. Finally, when an additional ten minutes had gone by, he stamped his heel in anger and marched out of the house. With a violent oath, he leaped onto his horse and galloped away.

A full hour following the earl's angry departure, Lady Straeford finally appeared to enter her coach and make her journey to the Park by herself. There was no other choice but to follow the temperamental man she had wedded only twenty-four hours before. Her arrival there would probably end in another personal humiliation, possibly a public one, too, if the *ton* were ever to discover that he had left his wife before their marriage had even begun. But what alternatives did she have?

By the time the coach reached the entrance to Straeford Park, Marisa could feel her earlier confidence rapidly leaving her. As the wheels inched slowly toward the manor house and the coach came to a stop, she anticipated the earl's reception and prayed for her courage to return. The doors to the house swung open, and she hoped that her prayers would be answered.

8

It was Manners who greeted her at the door to Straeford and Marisa was thankful for that. His hearty welcome helped alleviate the tension that had been building up during the interminable ride to Straeford Park, and when she entered the entrance hall that was now brightly lighted and airy in contrast to its former gloomy atmosphere, it was as though she had forgotten the many improvements she had made to the manor house and was now seeing it for the first time.

Marisa looked with pride at the results of her painstaking efforts. A sparkling gilt chandelier reflected on the gleaming slate floor and highly polished oak paneling. A basket of carefully arranged flowers was set on a new center table constructed of Carrara marble, and the aged portraits were now replaced by a series of lighthearted drawings. Her many hours of planning had done much to inject vitality into the house and recapture much of its original flavor.

"So good to see the house once again," Marisa smiled as Manners helped her remove her redingote. "Tell me, is his lordship about?"

"Yes, my lady. I believe he is in the library. Shall I announce you?"

"N-...no...I'm quite fatigued from the trip. I believe I shall retire until supper. I won't disturb him until then."

Clearly the earl had no wish to see her any more than she cared to see him at that moment. He had not come into the hallway to greet her, and surely he had heard the carriage arrive. Was this war of nerves going to continue?

Marisa went directly to the white chamber, a room that was part of the master suite. Upon opening its door, her eyes danced with delight as they reviewed the wallpaper, the canopied bed, the brocaded draperies, all of which had been scrupulously selected to create a pink and fawn motif in a white background. A rich Persian carpet coordinated perfectly with the basic pastel shades of the room, and the Hepplewhite furnishings completed the total effect of warmth and elegance.

Pleased with what she had accomplished in such a short period of time, Marisa wondered if the earl would be appreciative of her efforts. She tried not to think of the confrontation the two of them would eventually have. Muttering to herself in order to allay her fears, she curled up for a restful nap wishing that all her problems would somehow just disappear. But instead of sleeping, she found her thoughts going back again and again to the problem of what she would say to him when they finally met. How did she get here in the first place? It all seemed like a bad dream, she thought, as she stared absent-mindedly out her bedroom window while shadows appeared, slowly elongated, and then cloaked the room in dusky silence.

When Lucy came in to dress her for supper, Marisa felt relieved since she had convinced herself that the anticipation of adversities was, perhaps, far worse than the realities she would have to face. Besides, there was no good reason for her to be fearful toward her husband. After all, what had she done? And if she acted timidly toward his threats and his rantings—well, she knew he would think even less of her. This marriage would have to be built on the basis of mutual respect or it would be a hopeless farce. Whatever the outcome, she vowed that she would, at the very least, carry herself with dignity and self-respect through it all.

To bolster her confidence, Marisa decided to dress herself with as much style as she could muster. She had learned a long time ago from her mother that the anger of most men was often a result of a woman's charm and grace. A graceful Empire dress of pink shot-silk seemed the perfect selection for the occasion. Its close-fitting sleeves and slim skirt edged with a delicate embroidery gave her a sense of refinement and self-assurance. In front of her mirror, she looked approvingly at its fit and toyed briefly with the Grecian ringlets and curls which Lucy had carefully fashioned. A simple silver chain around her neck matched her earrings and now she was ready, hoping that it was all worth the effort.

When she reached the last step of the staircase, the earl suddenly appeared and, to her surprise, merely harrumphed an unintelligible greeting in her direction. Perhaps he was going to be civil after all? Nattily attired in a forest green cutaway, matching vest and white pantaloons, he looked every bit the aristocrat he was, and Marisa could not help admiring his imperial figure.

Unexpectedly, he escorted her to the dining room where once again Marisa's decorative work was everywhere to be seen. When he had last viewed this room, it was gray and unattractive, but now it assumed the same style and color scheme as the drawing room. Each chamber displayed rich blue velvet draperies which swept dramatically to one side and were held in position by a leaf of gold. The overhanging cornices were intricately designed structures that resembled a royal crown, and clusters of delicate golden petals flecked the cream-colored wallpaper that had been chosen for the background.

The effect was striking, and Marisa could feel instinctively that he was impressed. But the earl said nothing at all as the two of them ate in silence under the watchful eye of Manners and the newly hired maid. It was only after dessert had been placed before them and both servants had disappeared that Straeford decided to speak. He found himself on the horns of a dilemma. Ever since he returned to the Park, he had been taken aback by the extraordinary transformations his new bride had accomplished. He was grateful for that, but he did not know how to approach her at this juncture, since he had every intention of raking her down good and proper for her earlier defiance. Manners had added to Straeford's perplexity by heaping lavish praise on his wife and pointing to minuscule improvement she had made when the earl completed his first tour of his ancestral residence. As if that were not enough, Bess also took up the cudgel on her behalf when he visited the completely remodeled kitchen. The relief and gratitude he felt at seeing Straeford Park restored to this degree continued to war with his rage at her defiance of him.

The earl drummed his fingers impatiently on the long rosewood table as he watched Marisa linger over her dessert, seemingly oblivious to his presence. Had he known the deep inner anxiety she was experiencing at that moment, he might not have given in to his mounting sense of frustration so easily. But he felt he could no longer continue with this game of silence.

"Well, madam," he said with resignation. "I suppose you win this round."

"I . . . I win?" She was totally mystified by his remark.

"Yes. I am telling you that I intend to overlook your act of defiance earlier today."

"But, my lord, it was not defiance that caused me to be so late this morning. It was simply impossible for me to get ready in the brief amount of time you . . ."

"Enough!" he cut in. "Regardless, and above all else, I expect to be obeyed in all things, madam. All things!"

A brief moment of silence followed his angry command but Marisa thought it wise not to say anything at that point.

"Nevertheless," his tone was much quieter now, "I prefer to overlook this morning . . . for I believe that you deserve some measure of gratitude for what you have done here at Straeford Park. The work of restoration has been accomplished with, I must say, extraordinary good taste." He came to his feet and nodded politely in her direction. "I think you should know that it's far beyond my expectations and I offer my sincere congratulations."

"Oh," Marisa jumped up and said hotly, "is that what you meant by my 'winning this round'? If so, I must reject your offer of congratulations. I am deeply sorry, but I do not view this marriage as some contest, some cheap sparring match where either you or I must win."

"Well, I'll be damned!" he roared in disbelief. "You dare to rip up at me after I acquitted you? Sad want of conduct, I must say to you, my dear wife."

Marisa saw some justice in his retort and paused momentarily before replying with some conciliation in her voice.

"I . . . I did not mean to be churlish. It is only that . . . well, I find it difficult to understand . . . you."

"There is no reason you should. You have only to obey me and hold your tongue more carefully in check in the future."

"So what you're saying is that you really do not intend to let me understand you, is that it?" she asked pointedly.

"My dear, this topic of conversation has now arrived at the point of boredom I must say. It now seems to me that it is time for us to adjourn to the drawing room." He opened the door with an air of finality, and Marisa discreetly accompanied him to the adjoining room. Once seated on a new blue and white silk sofa, she looked carefully at Straeford. He was moving about the room, examining its contents as if he were in a gallery. Then a curious look appeared on his face as he studied the Worthington landscape above the mantel.

"Why have you removed her portrait?" Clearly he was disturbed, and Marisa wondered whether Lady Maxwell had been wrong in suggesting that the portrait be removed. Perhaps the grand old dame was capable of dealing with her grandson's wrath concerning that woman and the dark mystery of the past that surrounded her, but Marisa knew that she herself was not up to it. It might be prudent, she thought, to let the blame for the removal of the portrait fall on the dowager's head.

"Lady Maxwell suggested it belonged in the gallery with the rest of the Straeford portraits."

"I see," he said thoughtfully. "Can't say I disagree.

And I suppose you will have your own portrait hanging there before very long. I daresay in time it will serve in a similar capacity."

Marisa ignored his cynicism and broached a related subject. "Lady Maxwell thought . . . that perhaps you and I . . . well, together we might have an oil painting done."

Raising his eyes suspiciously, the earl gazed at his wife for a long moment. Damn! she was a beauty just sitting there with her delicate white throat and high cheekbones, those large sapphire eyes. Yes, it dawned on him all of a sudden. Yes, a portrait should be done, and he visualized himself standing behind her, his hand resting on her creamy white shoulder. And suddenly he remembered her in all of her glorious nakedness the night before, and he found himself wanting her now, at this very second.

He walked close to her and drank in that subtle fragrance that captured his attention whenever she had been near him earlier that evening. It was still there, definitely noticeable, hidden somewhere about her lovely neck—an intoxicating scent that set off an impulse within him to seek out its source and devour it.

"Your lordship!" Marisa implored, seeing the passion stirring in his eyes. "I wonder if you heard my question to you?" She rose from the sofa, trying to back away as he advanced even closer, but soon found herself with nowhere to go.

"I did hear your question, and I will give it very serious consideration. Does that satisfy you?" he asked, taking her hand in his, pulling her tightly against him before she could think of anything to say in reply. All at once, his mouth pressed passionately against hers in a long and savage kiss, making Marisa's legs feel as though they were utterly helpless to hold her upright against his advances. She fell limp under the overwhelming power of his arms, and then his lips found their way to her cheek, her earlobe, her neck and the hollow of her throat, sending peculiar sensations soaring in her brain.

How different he seemed from the previous night. His hands were firm and strong, to be sure, as they moved incontestably from her back to her waist and then up again, but they also were slower, more sensitive to her emotions somehow. And Marisa felt herself no longer struggling against him and his touch. Now she sensed a sudden rising wave of desire surge deep within her own body as the pressure of his muscular thighs against hers grew more forceful. However, she found herself refusing to yield as he pressed even closer.

Marisa trembled, unable to believe that she was capable of these dangerous yearnings that tantalized her being. It happened so fast she was weak, and then panic seized her as she realized that they were still in the drawing room. "N- . . . no," she whispered urgently. "No, no . . . Please, stop. The servants . . ."

Straeford recoiled at her pleadings. "Of course. Tonight it is the servants. And what excuse will you use the next time?" Without another word, he lifted her into his arms, causing her to give off a muffled cry. It was impossible for her to think clearly as he swiftly took the stairs, her entire being firmly in his grip. Entering her room with a kick of the door, he dropped her on the bed and followed her down in single-minded pursuit of his furious passion.

He quickly satisfied himself and afterward, as she lay alone in tearful silence, Marisa chafed at the extremes in mood which his nature seemed to constantly exhibit. The tenderness she had experienced earlier in his arms quickly disappeared. Now, having had his way in bed, he was gone—where, she did not know. How could he be here one moment in the midst of blazing passion and then gone the next?

During the week that followed, Marisa found herself dwelling on the earl's traits more and more. She took careful note of how little time he seemed to spend with her. Except for an occasional morning ride on horseback and their evening meal together, they typically spent their days quite apart from each other's company. Even when they were together, it seemed their conversation was thin and superficial. Several days' careful observations made her arrive reluctantly at the conclusion that Straeford really had no use for women in his life, not even her except when it came to his own personal pleasure. Once that was achieved, he appeared to have little need for a woman's companionship. In fact, it seemed to her that he was avoiding her company at every opportunity.

Marisa's suspicions were confirmed at the end of that week when Manners announced that the earl had left for London. Without so much as a word to her, he had gone and didn't even leave her a note to explain. No, his lordship had not informed Manners as to the nature of the business, the embarrassed butler reported to her apologetically. And Marisa realized then and there how insignificant she really was in his life.

Lonely brooding hours linked one with another in a monotonous chain of uneventful days until Marisa felt her nerves were about to snap. Then, chiding herself for having been so slow in coming to grips with the realities of her marriage, she knew she had spent too many days nursing her own hurt pride. Once assured that all she needed was to revive her interests in the London house and to come by some more amiable company, Marisa sent for Foster Duncan, the interior decorator who had helped her enormously with the restoration of both houses thus far.

Duncan was an effeminate little man with a balding head and a thin, almost fragile body, but he was an animated talker and always had a great fund of witty stories at his command. When he arrived, he was wearing a bright red frock coat, a red and white striped waistcoat and pale pink trousers. Marisa never ceased to marvel at his audacity. She found herself amused by his countless eccentricities that seemed to offend or annoy others so easily. For some reason, she had a great deal of sympathy for this caricature of a man who spoke at an incredible rate of speed, flitting from topic to topic in such a disorganized fashion she wondered how he ever was capable of doing the intricate work he had done for her at Straeford Park.

He had been invited every day for the entire week because Marisa was anxious to complete the restoration of Straeford and to turn her attention back to the house in Berkeley Square. Dutifully, he arrived each morning from the village of Stray with his design books tucked under his arms and the sample fabrics which he loved to display in countless varieties and combinations. Each evening he would return to the inn at the same hour, but on his final night before returning to London, the countess invited him to dine with her.

Foster Duncan had done much to elevate Marisa's spirits over the past few days, and she genuinely appreciated his droll stories. What a comparison with Justin, she thought, as she observed the amusing little man, his mouth chattering on nervously. And just as he was in the midst of one of his favorite vignettes, the dining room door was thrust open unexpectedly and in strode the earl. Marisa sat there, too dumbfounded to speak while Duncan, a glass of wine to his lips, dribbled and then choked uncontrollably.

"Who the devil are you?" the earl shot out in a booming voice that literally terrified the little man. Duncan sputtered out his name and extended a hand weakly in Straeford's direction, but his gesture of courtesy was completely ignored. Dressed in his scarlet uniform, the earl towered over the two of them and glared at his wife, who had barely recovered her wits.

"Let me introduce Mr. Duncan, the decorator I hired to renovate the Park, my lord."

"Decorator?" he sneered, looking with contempt at the cringing guest.

"Uh . . . perhaps I'd better be going, Lady Straeford. I . . . I . . . I have all of your suggestions now. They're really quite good a . . . and I . . . I most certainly will get to work on them immediately." Then, turning toward the earl, he stammered, "G- . . . Good night, m- . . . my lord," and made a hasty retreat.

Straeford continued his steely glare at his wife, who was seething inside with so many strong emotions she didn't know which one was uppermost. "How dare you insult my guest like that!" Marisa was standing directly in front of him now, her hands placed squarely on her hips.

"Your *guest?*" He rolled the word insolently off his tongue. "How dare you consort with mincing fops such as that behind my back?"

"I beg your pardon. Mr. Duncan is a gentleman, I'll have you know."

"Have you forgotten your new position in society, madam? You are no longer a merchant's daughter but my wife. You are the Countess of Straeford now, and I will expect you to select your acquaintances in a manner fitting your title."

"You may hold your title and position in very high regard, my lord, but I must say to you in all honesty that I care not a twit for either at this moment."

"Indeed? I was under the assumption that you married me for both. Could I have been mistaken?" He paused, then added caustically, "Don't tell me now that it was for . . . love?"

Marisa could barely contain herself as she blurted out her reply. "No . . . no . . . never! Never could I love a man as . . . cold and as callous as you!"

"Well, then, if it wasn't for those reasons, pray tell what *was* it for?"

Marisa turned her head away, unable to withstand his relentless assault, but his stern fingers clawed at her shoulder and he swung her around to face him. "You're not going to tell me that you were forced to do your father's bidding, are you?" That was something he would not be able to accept, Marisa realized, and she stood there, numb, unable to reply. He could never understand the complicated reasons for a decision she herself did not totally comprehend, so what good would it do to try to make any sense out of it? Marisa just shook her head in answer to his question.

"Then admit it, woman, and be done with your prevarications. You married me for my title and all of the comfort and respectability that are attached to the same. Now perhaps you may not 'care a twit', as you say, for my good name, but rest assured that I will *demand* that you respect it. See here, there'll be no sluttish hole-in-the-corner affairs for you. At least not yet, anyway."

Marisa trembled with rage and, completely forgetting herself, slapped his arrogant face roundly with a sound that cracked. A dangerous glint smoked from his eyes as he retaliated with a sharp slap first on her left cheek and then on her right one. He could overwhelm her in an instant, and she knew it was foolish to have let this

126

happen at all. The fight went out of her and, covering her face with her hands, she sank into the nearest chair.

A brisk knock on the door brought an end to any further altercations, and Marisa was thankful that Manners had chosen that moment to enter the room.

"Beg pardon, your lordship, but I thought to clean up if the countess be finished." Manners eyed his mistress sympathetically. He knew he had failed her by not announcing the earl's entrance in advance, but he had been forbidden to do so once it became apparent she was entertaining a male guest.

"Yes . . . yes, Manners," she was unable to hide her tears, and she hurried away, grateful for the kindly butler's help. He cast an accusing stare in the earl's direction, causing Straeford to say in defense, "Acquit me, old man!"

Straeford stalked off to the library to pour himself a drink and sort out his thoughts. This woman brought out the worst in him, he was sure of that. He had never planned to strike her. It was the furthest thing from his mind. But where in God's kingdom did she get the starch to hit him? For that, she deserved much more than a slap, of course. And Manners? Why, that old fool! He was bewitched by her. That was obvious. It was almost as if he were going to receive a reprimand from his own butler! By God, the whole household would be on his neck in the next breath. Damn all women! Damn them all to hell! Nothing but endless troubles.

Marisa examined her cheeks carefully in front of her vanity mirror the next morning and found no bruises. Fortunately, he had not struck her very hard. Whatever possessed her to slap him first? She must have run mad. But then she remembered his rudeness to Duncan and his accusations and . . . well, wasn't she really justified? The contemptuousness of his behavior was just too much to bear.

Marisa lingered in her room until the hour they would normally spend riding together, and she wondered whether the earl would summon her at the appointed time. She had not gone to breakfast deliberately as a sign of her continuing displeasure toward him and his previous night's behavior. When Lucy came in to help complete her morning toilette the countess inquired, "Has the earl sent me a message this morning?"

"Why, no, my lady," the maid replied as she held out a peignoir. Then, sensing her mistress's curiosity, she continued in a soft voice, "I believe he has left the house already."

"I see." So he was going to punish her today by not having her ride with him, Marisa thought. She knew how anxious he was for her to gain skill in horsemanship. "One of the first prerequisites of a noblewoman is that she possess considerable prowess on horseback," he had told her the first day they had gone out together. He had been deeply disappointed by her lack of confidence in riding and he showed it. That posed a challenge Marisa was determined to meet. She was not yet able to meet it by herself, it was true. But his going off by himself without her this morning was a rebuff she was not going to take lightly.

"I'll wear my blue riding habit, Lucy," she ordered with some irritation in her voice.

"Without his lordship, my lady?" the tiny maid inquired sheepishly.

Marisa huffed with impatience. "Please remember, Lucy, not to ask me the wrong questions at the wrong time."

"Oh, I'm sorry, my lady. Please forgive me," Lucy said, knowing she had clearly overstepped her bounds.

Marisa wasn't sure whether she had been too harsh in her tone toward Lucy. The trouble with having servants, she thought, was that you can never conceal anything from their eyes. Your privacy is never your own, really. Her observation also made her pause to reflect on the real possibility that there might be very few advantages to being part of the nobility after all.

Tim, the elderly stable hand, was reluctant to saddle up the chestnut mare that Marisa's father had purchased especially for her. The earl had been in a black mood earlier that morning, and Tim figured it had something to do with the absence of the countess.

"Maybe I'd better ride with you, m'lady," he said

obligingly. "The earl wouldn't forgive me if you didn't have me as a groom." Marisa agreed but wished even more that she didn't have to depend on anyone but herself when it came to riding.

When the mare was brought out of the stable, Marisa's earlier courage began to wane immediately. Tim helped her into the saddle and a general uneasiness came upon her. She lacked security and equilibrium on top of this enormous animal that seemed to have a mind all its own. Every time Marisa rode her, the mare responded differently and today it shrugged more nervously than ever. Marisa grew increasingly tense, feeling her confidence slip away, knowing the mare was far from docile. She wasn't sure she would be able to go through with this after all as her horse darted nervously, lifting a foot, then stomping it with a menacing uneasiness that sent a flash of panic to Marisa's stomach.

Tim couldn't help noticing the fear in her eyes after he was mounted next to her. Leaning across his horse, he warned, "You're holding her much too tight, m'lady. Now relax or you might cause her to start."

Heeding his advice, Marisa loosened her grip slightly, and the two horses walked out side by side along the path. Gradually, Tim fell back a few paces to let her test her confidence. But as he did, she felt her hands grow damp and clammy as she instinctively drew more tightly on the reins. Tim gave her a warning call as the distance between them widened, and both horses quickened to a light trot.

"Wait up, m'lady," he shouted, not wanting her to get too far away. "Whoa! Pull up your reins and move back in the saddle."

She tried to follow his instructions, but her tense grip caused her to give the mare an unintentionally hard yank that startled the animal. Suddenly it reared high into the air, screaming primitively. Marisa rolled sharply to one side, totally off balance. She was certain she was going down and struggled to regain her proper position. But as she did, the spurs of her right boot dug hard into the mare's flesh and the animal bolted ahead uncontrollably, leaving Tim behind.

Terror struck, Marisa screamed as the frightened

horse galloped off in the direction of the forest, her hat flying off her head, her hair tumbling down about her as she swayed precariously in the saddle to avoid low hanging branches. Her hold on the reins was weakened by two quick and painful jolts in the saddle, and her heart fluttered when she realized her grip was slipping away. A look back gave her no sign of Tim. Where was he? How could she have gotten away from him so fast? Now she was somehow going to have to bring this panic-stricken horse to a halt completely by herself or lord knew what might happen.

Marisa was going to lose the reins, she just knew it. She could feel them slide further with each unexpected bounce from her mare, and she was powerless to stop it. In desperation, she let the reins drop and then clawed frantically at the horse's mane for something to hold onto in order to keep from falling. Woman and animal roared onward together, forming a dusty, thundering blur along the forest path. Toward what end Marisa could not know.

She was sobbing, oblivious to everything save her own fear, breathless and choking on words which she was paralyzed to release. Then for a fleeting instant something registered in her brain, a faint but dimly familiar sound that she was not sure she had heard at all. And then she heard it again, this time more clearly. Hanging on for dear life, she dared a quick look over her shoulder, fully expecting to see Tim. To her surprise, it was the earl, shouting unintelligibly to her amidst the deafening rumble of the horse's hoofs. Again and again he yelled out instructions to her, but as he inched closer, he saw her reins fluttering aimlessly beneath her, out of her reach. Even if she could hear him clearly, she was totally incapable of helping herself.

Straeford goaded his stallion ahead with a furious lash of his riding crop. He knew he would be unable to stop her horse, but if he could get close enough to her . . . Now his horse was astride hers, and he knew there was only one thing left for him to do. Leaning far to his right, he waited for just the precise moment, regulating his reins so that both horses swerved nearer and nearer to one another. And then, with a sweeping whiplike motion, his right arm encircled her waist, lifted her out of her saddle and clamped her safely on his stallion while her mare raced blindly ahead.

Marisa collapsed against him in a faint, her breath completely taken away. The earl brought his horse to a standstill and quickly carried her limp body to a nearby grassy clearing to make her comfortable and examine her injuries.

"M'lord! M'lord!" It was Tim, and he prayed that his mistress was unharmed for he knew that the earl was certain to be angry with him. "Be she all right, yer lordship?"

"Yes, she's all right. Just had the wind knocked out of her." Straeford looked down at the countess nestled in his arms. "What the devil happened here, man? Why was she alone? She could have been killed!"

"She got away from me so fast, your lordship," Tim protested weakly. "I tried to get to her, but I couldn't. Thank God you came along."

"Go fetch the other horse," Straeford commanded sternly, having heard enough of the stable hand's excuse. "I'll get the countess home by myself."

Marisa's eyelids moved slightly, and then she groaned. "Don't try to talk now," he said, comforting her. "I'll get you back to the house in a minute." He pushed her straying golden curls off her muddied cheek, and then she felt him lift her up once again. That was the last thing she remembered until she was awakened by soft voices in her own bedroom.

"She'll be coming around any time now." It was Straeford whispering to Lucy who hovered anxiously over her mistress. The earl ran his fingers gently along her face. "Have her rest until dinner," he said, turning to leave.

"My lord," Marisa's voice stopped him at the door. "Please don't leave," she importuned as she sat up in her bed.

"But my lady . . ." Lucy pleaded, "you must rest."

"Please, Lucy. I would prefer a moment alone with his lordship."

Straeford's hand remained on the doorknob even after Lucy had gone.

131

"Won't you close the door for a moment? I'd like to speak with you."

He seemed reluctant as he slowly seated himself on a tufted stool next to her bed.

"I . . . I want to thank you for what you did this morning . . ." She started to continue but he interrupted.

"What I want to know is why you did such a damn fool thing."

His response annoyed Marisa, but she was determined that he would not provoke her this time.

"I did behave rather foolishly, didn't I?" she agreed, folding her hands demurely in her lap while an ever so slightly reddish coloring appeared in her face. Her admission surprised Straeford and he asked more kindly, "Why didn't you tell me you were afraid of horses?"

"I did!" she said, this time more strongly.

"No, you are quite wrong, my dear. What you said was that you didn't ride 'well'."

"A slight deception," she smiled weakly.

"Women! Ever deceivers," he grumbled.

"Well, I didn't think you would approve if I told you I was afraid."

"I wouldn't. That's true. But that doesn't mean I expect you to lie to me about it."

"Perhaps you're right," she admitted. "Perhaps I should have told you the truth." Her willingness to admit her error helped to mollify the harshness in his stare.

"Why are you afraid?"

"Oh, it's really a long and unpleasant story I know you will not care to hear. I never have been able to speak of it with any ease."

"Why don't you try telling me. It might help you, you know." He was actually encouraging her, and this caused her to take a long suspicious look at him before continuing.

"A few years ago, a friend and I were riding . . . his horse was difficult to handle, a very temperamental animal . . . And . . ." She sighed to alleviate the rising tension in her voice. Marisa swallowed hard, and he could see her eyes growing misty as she continued. ". . . and his horse went wild. My friend was practically stomped to death in front of my eyes and there was absolutely nothing I could do to prevent it. He was so badly disfigured from the incident that he never again was quite the same. In fact, he was mentally disfigured as well, and he . . ." It was clear she couldn't continue, and the earl rose to pour her a glass of water from the pitcher on the bedside table. He sat on the bed next to her as she tried to regain her composure.

"You should not have waited so long to ride again. It gave your fears a chance to get a firm grip on you."

"I'm just wondering now if I'm ever again going to be able to ride. At this moment I don't think I could face it."

"Don't be foolish, my dear," he smiled reassuringly and reached out to touch her hand.

"I won't! I can't . . . not after what happened today. I'll never mount a horse again."

"Hmm, that's a pity," he goaded her gently. "The *haut ton* puts great store in a woman with a good seat, you know."

"I don't care," Marisa pouted. "What difference does that make?"

"I think I could help you overcome your fear if you would be willing to let me. Since you already know the fundamentals of riding. within a short time you could overcome this unreasonable fear. It's simply something irrational that you've got to get out of your head."

Marisa didn't care for the exact words he chose, but this whole thing seemed to be such a matter of great importance to him that she found it difficult to resist his urgings.

"Do you really think it's possible? I mean . . . you think you can actually teach me to ride without any fear? Oh, I don't think I can do it anymore."

"But of course you can. That is, unless you're the cowardly type."

His remark was designed to make Marisa wince and she obliged him. "I . . . I don't even know anymore. Tell me, why are you so anxious to have me learn to ride? Why is this so important, anyway?"

Straeford just shrugged his shoulders. "I suppose I just would not be able to stand seeing the Countess of Straeford accused of cowardice."

Marisa winced again at the challenge he reiterated and then took on a pensive look. "I think I would prefer to give this more thought. Yes, I'd like some rest now."

"Please do that," the earl said, rising to leave. "You know that I ride every morning and I'd like you to join me if you decide to take up my offer."

Marisa did not immediately respond to the earl's invitation, but within a few days they were riding together virtually every morning. Although her fears were still very real every time she approached the saddle, she felt some progress being made through their daily outings. Best of all, it was an opportunity to be with the earl in a situation where she could not help but admire his superior skills as a horseman. It was something he did naturally, effortlessly, and it was a source of unending pleasure to him. He loved talking about horses, studying them, analyzing their movements, comparing their dispositions. And he thoroughly enjoyed demonstrating his skills and knowledge to Marisa.

9

Since Marisa had accepted the earl's challenge to ride with him, things seemed to be going rather well between them, and she hoped that nothing would change that. Her hopes were dashed at the end of one of their morning riding sessions, however, when he announced that he had invited several guests for the weekend.

"It's the Hardings and two other couples," he said. "When I was in London, I spent my time with some members of Parliament and the War Office . . ."

Marisa stiffened as he provided her with the details. His mention of London only forced her to recall how he had abandoned her so soon after their marriage. She tried to rid herself of her pique, but it just would not go away. He took no notice of her mounting irritation as he continued his explanation.

"I found it prudent to invite two of them here. Relington and Clarkson. Both of them have influence regarding the military campaign being planned for this summer, and Relington's wife seemed especially interested in visiting the Park."

"Why?" she asked belligerently.

Straeford scrutinized his wife more closely. "Just curiosity I suspect. Of course, she is an accomplished horsewoman, and the Park has many trails. I'm certain she ..."

"I see!" Marisa cut in sharply. She was furious now and did not care if he knew it or not. While she had been sitting alone in the country, he had been gallivanting about London and planning to bring his friends here.

"You seem upset. Is anything the matter? You're not timid about entertaining my guests now, are you?"

"No, of course not ... It's just that I ... oh, never mind." She was hurt and found it frustrating to try to explain herself to him.

He frowned and was perplexed by her strange attitude. "Look, I'm sure Manners and Bess will be able to handle things for you."

"And how do you plan to amuse your guests?" she asked haughtily.

Straeford took stock of her carefully before answering. "That should be easy enough. It's only two days. We'll ride and play whist, and the ladies can entertain. You do sing, don't you?"

"A little," Marisa lied.

Straeford raised his eyebrows in surprise. "Then you must play the piano?"

"No, I don't," she answered curtly.

"Hmm ... I thought all aspirants to the *ton* acquired those arts."

"You forget that I am only a merchant's daughter, my lord."

"What is the reason for all this sarcasm I detect? What has you so high in the stirrups?" Straeford was becoming increasingly annoyed by her display of temper.

"To be perfectly frank, I believe I have discovered why you have cultivated so much of my time these past two weeks. I was foolish enough to believe that it might have been because you were genuinely interested in our establishing a good ... relationship. But that wasn't the reason at all. No, you had another motive in mind all the while."

"Oh? And what was that, pray tell?"

"You wanted to be sure that I wouldn't be the

136

source of any embarrassment to you since I am not able to ride well, and since your polite circle of friends puts so much store in that sort of thing. Unfortunately, you overlooked something as mundane as my ability to sing," Marisa retorted smugly.

"Why you shrew! I ought to throttle you!" Straeford stormed and took a threatening step toward her, which Marisa ignored in the heat of the moment.

"Perhaps you should have left that task to the horse, my lord."

"Vixen! I can see your father allowed you too much freedom of the mouth!"

"And your mother . . ." Marisa knew as the words left her lips that she was close to the edge of the earl's limits. She had even surprised herself with such an inflammatory rejoinder.

A dark scowl crossed Straeford's face and his voice took on a low, deadly tone as he crooked a menacing finger of warning in her direction. "You leave her out of this! And don't you ever dare use her name as a weapon against me in this house!"

Once again Marisa dangerously tested the limits of her husband's anger. "Why? Did your poor mother find it an impossible task to raise an arrogant, unfeeling son who had no consideration for anyone else save himself? She must have . . ."

The earl could no longer restrain himself. He roared and leapt at her, his fingers seizing the white column of her throat in an instant. Marisa gasped for breath and tried desperately to scream for help, but his grip was overwhelming, and in a split-second flash of panic, she thought she would lose consciousness. As her eyes closed in pain and fright, the viselike grip of his fingers relaxed around her neck, permitting her to breathe freely. Then Marisa felt herself being flung unceremoniously into a chair, and when she dared open her eyes again, there was the threatening and thunderous black face of the earl in front of her. "I warned you, madam," he hissed through clenched teeth. "You broach the subject of . . . the late countess, you do so at your own peril."

Too stunned to protest, Marisa lay inert against the back of the chair and stared wide-eyed at her husband, trying to control the impulse to run screaming from him. Her throat hurt where he had grasped it, and she massaged it slowly swallowing hard several times.

"There'll be no bruises," he pronounced impassively.

"I . . . I suppose . . . that makes it all right?" Marisa felt as if she were suffering from a sore throat.

"You'll feel no ill effects from my handling of you."

"Is that some kind of apology for your outrageous behavior?"

"Apology?" Straeford choked, flabbergasted by her temerity. "Well, I'll be damned! Now don't provoke me any further, madam, or I won't be responsible for my actions." A certain ruthlessness was evident in his gait as he strode to the other side of the room. He felt a need to keep her at a distance since he was unsure of his response if she continued to goad him.

"You would not treat me as you have just now if I were a man."

"But then, of course, you are not, are you?" His eyes roamed over her insultingly.

"Oh . . . if only I . . . I wish I could call you out and run you through," she claimed vehemently and stuck her chin out at him in defiance.

Straeford's eyebrows shot upward and then his chest seemed to quiver with suppressed laughter. "I believe you would." He found the defiant beauty before him rather amusing as her eyes flashed and her bosom heaved with anger. "I know no other woman who would have had the audacity to say so under the present circumstances, however." He had to admire the courage and indomitable spirit this woman exhibited, yet he was determined to bend her to his will.

Before delivering her parting shot, Marisa moved to the door and opened it. "You certainly live up to your reputation, Lord Straeford. You're as unprincipled a villain as everyone says you are."

"I'm glad I did not disappoint you, my dear." A sneer curled the corner of his mouth, and he cast a low mocking bow in her direction. "I wondered how long I'd have to wait to hear you utter such words."

Marisa's face burned as she whirled out of the room.

Having decided to avoid the earl's company completely in protest against his treatment of her, Marisa had remained in her rooms for the better part of the last two days. It was now late in the evening, and she closed the book that she had been attempting to read for more than an hour. Perhaps she would try falling asleep. For the second time that night, she blew out the candle and crawled into bed. Her mind was filled with the confrontations she had had with the earl since they were married, and sleep would not come. Suddenly the darkness gave way to the light of her bedroom door opening. As she sat up with a start, the tall dark figure of the earl leaned over her.

"What are you doing here?"

"Not very imaginative, my dear." He flung back the bedcovers, and Marisa tried to roll off the opposite side of the bed to get away, but he had already locked his arms about her and brought her struggling body back close to his, pinning down her arms helplessly to her sides.

"How dare you do this! How dare you come to me knowing full well that I detest your . . . demeaning attitude toward me. I will not be treated as if I were chattel."

"Will you not? Must I remind you, my dear, that you are my wife by legal marriage, and as such you are bound to obey me. And at the moment that requires you to perform your wifely obligations to me. I will not be ignored, nor will I have you overstepping my authority in any way."

Unable to find adequate words to describe her feelings, Marisa shrieked and struggled in his grip until she managed to release one arm to swing at his face, but Straeford laughed loudly as he brought it under his control with small effort.

"I won't submit to you! I won't!" She twisted violently and thrust her body into his, temporarily loosening his hold.

Yet it was pointless to continue to resist him for he soon had her in his power again. "My, my," he sniggered, "such a willing wife! Now I think it's about time that I put an end to your rebellious ways." His voice took on a more serious tone. "No house can survive with two masters, and it's time you learned which role is rightfully yours and which one belongs to me."

The earl seized her roughly and pressed his entire body against hers. "Don't fight me, Marisa. You'll only hurt yourself."

Knowing the truth of those words, she unwillingly capitulated. She forced herself to remain impassive to his fondling until his grip relaxed and his slow sweeping movements began to invade her very soul. Gradually he felt her stubborn defenses fade. The feel of his warm hands gently running through her hair and then slowly along her slender shoulders awakened a new alarming sensation within her, compelling her to respond to his commands to kiss his lips and to taste the danger of his hypnotic power which suddenly seemed to devour her. She felt her silky nightgown slide silently from her body under his careful guidance, and she became acutely aware of the hair on his muscular arms as they glided along her shapely form. It was a primitive but irresistible sensation, and she found herself giving in to the urge to run her own hands through the curly tufts of hair that appeared on his solid bare chest. Unwittingly her action drove his taut body to a fevered pitch. Needing immediate release, he found it in her and she surrendered to his sweeping passion.

Their desire spent, husband and wife lay next to one another, a warm glow still perceptible about them. Turning toward her, he grasped her white shoulders in his hands. "You learn quickly my little wife. If only . . ." He stopped in midsentence and seemed to smile sardonically. Then he left her to ponder what he had been about to say.

After he had gone, Marisa lay alone in the darkness for a long time thinking about the curious nature of lovemaking. Her husband had tapped sensations within her tonight she had never known before. And his physical being gave her a secret thrill that until tonight she never knew was possible.

Gathering her covers about her and readying herself for sleep, it occurred to Marisa that there were still many things to learn about this enigmatic man she had married.

To the young countess's relief, the weekend was progressing much better than she had anticipated. Their guests had arrived in time for dinner on Friday, and afterward Lady Relington, a tall, buxom, pale blonde in her mid-thirties, was only too happy to entertain the party with slightly naughty renditions of popular tunes at the pianoforte. On the second evening there had been a slight contretemps when the gentlemen joined the ladies in the drawing room and Marisa was asked to sing. That glib white lie she had told Straeford during their last battle had come back to haunt her, and her pleasure in singing was dimmed, for whenever she glanced at the earl, he was fiercely scowling at her. Even the warm praises afterward about her lovely musical voice could not ease her feelings of apprehension, and she was not surprised when Straeford approached her later to comment caustically that he should have expected as much from her since deceit was second nature to all women.

Instead of defending herself. Marisa bowed her head and asked his pardon. If she had planned it, Marisa could not have scotched his anger better. Baffled by the sincerity of her apology, he did not pursue the issue any further. Thus a major blowup was averted.

The party had just divided itself into two groups to play whist. To Marisa's disappointment, she and the earl were chosen to play opposite the Relingtons.

"Oh, do let us switch partners," Amanda Relington cooed. "It's so much more interesting that way. Don't you think so?"

"I'd like nothing better than to partner this adorable creature." Thomas Relington cast a lustful glance at Marisa, who lowered her long lashes and colored under his scrutiny.

"La, I do believe you have embarrassed the countess, Thomas." Amanda laughed maliciously. "You must get used to our ways, my dear. Airs just will not do in the polite world. Will they, Justin?" she trilled spitefully, laying her hand on the earl's sleeve.

Straeford ignored her gesture and addressed her husband instead. "I think it best we partner our wives this evening, Relington."

"If you insist, old man. Can't blame you for wanting to keep such a little beauty to yourself." Straeford directed him a dark quelling look and Relington slunk into his chair.

As the game progressed, Marisa gained confidence because she and his lordship were winning. It was exciting to discover they were a compatible team judging each other's moves accurately, and she smiled happily as the earl took the last trick of the round.

Growing cross with her husband's ineptitude, Amanda attacked him angrily when they were outbid for the next hand. "Thomas, you lunkhead! You've missed every one of my signals!"

"The luck's with our hosts, sweetheart," he appeased, knowing how his wife hated to lose at anything.

Their winning had to do with more than luck, Marisa thought. Amanda Relington was spending too much time eyeing the earl to be concentrating on the game, while her husband had imbibed too freely of the Straefords' excellent brandy. Raising her eyes from the cards, Marisa met her husband's sardonic gaze. Evidently he shared her opinion. Then he did something quite unexpected and winked at her. She could not believe it. It was as if some special affinity had just been established between them. The startling gesture diverted her attention from the game long enough for her to make an error which Amanda capitalized on immediately. Fortunately Straeford was able to cover his wife's blunder and regain the advantage so that in the end they were the winners.

Afterward as they began to move away from the table, Thomas Relington stepped in front of Marisa, detaining her. "Do you ride as well as you play cards, Lady Straeford?"

"Actually this is the only card game I know." She went to sidestep him and catch up with the earl and Lady Relington when Relington caught her hand.

"You are bound to be the toast of St. James this season."

"You flatter me, sir." She tried to politely disengage her hand from his, but he refused to relinquish it. Straeford looked back over his shoulder for her and upon seeing her engaged with Relington continued across the room with Amanda.

"My God," Relington slurred in a hoarse whisper, "Straeford doesn't deserve such good luck . . ."

"Lud," Ann Harding seemed to come out of nowhere. "I've really enjoyed myself today. What about you, Lord Relington?"

"Eh?" He caught himself up. "Yes, real fine day."

"Is everyone riding in the morning, Marisa?"

"I'm not sure if the Clarksons will be or not."

"I understand that Lady Relington is an excellent horsewoman. Isn't that right, Lord Thomas?" Ann Harding continued to insinuate herself upon them until Relington finally withdrew. "I queered his pitch, didn't I?" Ann laughed.

"And I can't thank you enough. His greedy eyes were . . . devouring me. I was extremely uncomfortable."

"He's a loose screw. Always chasing some female."

"I can't imagine his being very successful."

"There are some women who don't mind balding heads and paunches, but I ain't one of them."

"Ann, you mustn't talk like that," Marisa chided her although her eyes danced with merriment. "Think of poor Amanda."

"That one! Why she's nothing but a brass-faced monkey! Worse than her husband."

"I do wish the earl hadn't invited them here."

"But he had to if he wants a command for the summer campaign."

"Yes, he did mention something about that to me."

"Well, you know Amanda Relington practically invited herself to the Park when Justin was in London, and . . ." Ann stopped abruptly and then stammered, "Oh, I didn't mean to speak of that. I'm such a paperskull! Ed will have my head. Justin told him in the strictest confidence."

Marisa was not listening to Ann's protest. Her whole being was concentrating on the implication of her previous remarks concerning Amanda and Justin. "Just what is Lady Relington to the earl, Ann?"

"Oh, no, you are wrong! Justin is not a rakeshame, Marisa."

"But he is not above using people to gain . . ." she clapped her hand over her mouth remorsefully. "I shouldn't have said that."

"Perhaps we both said more than we should tonight, but that's what friends are for. And we are friends, aren't we, Marisa?"

"Of course we are, Ann. Your friendship is very important to me." They were clasping each other's hands when Edward Harding joined them.

"Hey, what are the two of you whispering about over here?"

"Fiddle dee dee, wouldn't you like to know?" Ann smiled mischievously and tweaked his chin.

"I think, my dear, that I should be much better off not knowing." He grinned and Ann made a face at him. "Now, be a good girl and wish our hostess a pleasant goodnight. We're the last to turn in."

After making a quick survey of the room, Ann kissed Marisa's cheek and whispered, "We shall talk another time." Then taking her husband's arm, they left Marisa alone. Watching them go arm in arm in perfect harmony with one another, Marisa felt a twinge of envy. Their love and affection for each other was evident in every look and action that passed between them. She sighed, her earlier optimism over the success of the weekend having completely vanished. Deciding there was little point in waiting for Straeford to reappear from wherever he had taken himself, Marisa went into the hallway only to quickly step back into the shadows as she witnessed her husband kissing the palm of Lady Relington's hand. As the earl lifted his head, Amanda traced the outline of his rugged jawline with her fingertips. Marisa closed her eyes wishing to erase the intimacy of the gestures from her mind. For one wild second she thought of confronting them, but when she opened her eyes Amanda was already going up the stairs, and Straeford was crossing to the library. She was tempted to follow him and denounce his

144

behavior except it would serve little purpose. Either he would laugh at her suspicions and deny them or abuse her and admit it. In either case she would be humiliated and it would change nothing, because he would do exactly as he pleased without a thought for her feelings in the matter.

A servant dousing the candles finally gave Marisa the impetus to move. Knowing that if she met the earl at this precise moment she would not remain silent about what she had seen, Marisa quietly tiptoed past the library and hurried upstairs to her own room.

The other riders galloped off around the bend leaving Marisa quite alone on the trail. Although her heart was heavy, she was trying very hard to enjoy the clear, bright day with its first signs of spring. Some early-budding trees and flowering forsythia were already announcing the advent of the new season. Soon it would burst forth in all its glory. Yet, no matter how she tried to concentrate on the beauty surrounding her, the tormenting suspicion of Straeford's infidelity clouded her vision.

Ahead, the rest of the party had reached the stony brook that bordered the edge of the Park.

"I don't see why we have to wait for your wife, Justin, obviously she wishes to be alone." Amanda was pouting. Straeford had not come to her room last night as she had anticipated he would. What was wrong with the man? Hadn't she promised to use her influence to see that he had a command this summer? If he thought a kiss on the hand was enough show of appreciation, he had another thought coming. Amanda nudged her horse closer to the earl's. "Lady Straeford is such a timid little creature for such a big brute as yourself, my lord."

Relington watched his wife, hoping she would not overplay her hand where the earl was concerned. He wanted Amanda to succeed in making his lordship her next lover. It would afford him a better opportunity in capturing the reluctant countess for himself. Unfortunately, he had his doubts whether his wife or he were going to be successful. So far the Straefords were not playing the game as he had expected they might.

145

"I'm going to look for my wife," the earl announced suddenly and galloped off before Amanda Relington could utter a protest.

"Wait for me!" she called after him and would have followed had not Relington grasped her reins. "Let me go!"

"Don't be a fool! Don't push your luck."

Amanda brought her riding crop down across her husband's hand and spurred her horse forward.

Galloping hoofbeats drew Marisa's attention, and she brought her horse to a halt just as her husband appeared over the crest of the hill and started down the rise toward her. "What kept you?" he shouted as he came in range. "I thought you might have had trouble with the mare."

The concern in his voice lifted her spirits. "Why no. I simply was enjoying the scenery. I'm sorry you had to come back for me. Are the others waiting at the stream?"

"It doesn't matter. It was time we were turning back." He was glad to see that the aloof look which had haunted the countess's eyes all morning had disappeared. "The sooner we return to the manor house, the sooner our guests will leave. I see you agree." A brilliant smile accompanied his last words as his wife beamed her approval. Involuntarily he took one of her straying curls in his hand and tucked it behind her ear, and then he lightly caressed her cheek with his thumb. The gentleness of his gesture brought a warm blush to her face. Shyly she met his emerald gaze only to be surprised by a look of uncertainty and tenderness glowing from their depths. Their brief interlude of quiet intimacy was ruthlessly shattered, however, by the arrival of Amanda Relington shouting Justin's name.

Her arrival brought an end to their pleasant exchange, and the trio of glum horsemen made their way back to the manor house hardly exchanging a word the entire distance.

Shortly after noon both the Hardings and the Relingtons departed for London. Only the Clarksons remained behind so that Straeford might have a private

146

conversation with Sir Francis, and they closeted themselves in the library leaving the two women alone together. Lydia Clarkson was a tall, thin lady in her fifties. She had spoken very little to anyone during the weekend, and Marisa doubted her ability to hold a conversation for very long with this austere woman.

"I'm sorry that your departure has been delayed, Lady Clarkson."

"Don't fret, my child, I'm sure Sir Francis will not be delayed by Lord Straeford for long. Wives must accustom themselves to their husband's ways. I'm sure you will adjust to the earl's behavior in time."

Marisa was surprised by the woman's strange comment. "I do not know what you mean."

"No, of course, you don't. It's simply intuition. You see, I knew the earl's father and Justin is very much like him."

Without thinking Marisa asked what her husband's father had been like.

"He was a difficult man to understand. Very proud and very aloof. He didn't care much for society, and spent most of his time away from home fighting in the colonies."

"That must have been hard on his family."

"Yes, very. Especially for his young and beautiful wife. She was alone so much of the time during her first marriage. How happy we all were for her when she married Ellsworth. She was truly happy. And then all those tragedies struck."

Marisa felt her heart pounding in her throat and ears and she asked almost inaudibly, "What tragedies?" and held her breath waiting for the answer.

"Why, losing her second husband and her eldest son so close together and in such mysterious ways. Then there was that final break with Justin. It led some people to say the most dreadful things about him."

In the name of loyalty Marisa could not allow this woman to say another word. "Lady Clarkson, I suggest we change the subject."

"Oh, of course, my dear, I didn't mean to upset you."

147

It was apparent to Marisa, now, that Lydia Clarkson meant to drop every word of venom she had just uttered. But why?

"Sorry, my dear," Sir Francis came into the room with the earl, "but this young man has been trying to convince me that one of the commands for the summer campaign should be his. And I had to explain my concerns to him. After all, Lord Straeford just came home in January in a state of exhaustion and . . ."

"That's not true, sir. It was a mild fever I couldn't shake because of our constant moving about. Once in England I recovered quickly enough."

This was all news to Marisa. Her brother John had led her to believe the earl was in perfect health upon his return from Portugal. If he were not, that would explain in part his neglect of her before they were married. It was becoming more important to her with every passing day that her husband show some tenderness to her.

"It is a family tradition." She heard Straeford saying.

"But you've just married a lovely young lady. Why would you wish to desert this winsome creature?" Clarkson lightly kissed Marisa's hand.

"Duty, sir," Straeford replied tersely.

"Very admirable. Yet I worry about a man who places too much emphasis on duty and forgets personal matters." There was a significant pause before he continued. "You're very much like your father, Straeford. And I would not wish you to repeat his mistakes."

Marisa held her breath as she watched the earl struggle to keep his temper under control. "You choose to use the term 'mistakes', but my father did not view his life in that way."

"Don't mean to speak out of turn—but family problems can interfere with a man's performance of duty . . ." Clarkson's obvious reference to Straeford's parents shocked Marisa.

At first the Earl went pale under his tan, and then he flushed hotly with anger. His voice was cold with hostility when he finally spoke. "My performance as a soldier has never been affected by personal problems!"

"Sir Francis," Marisa found herself intervening, hoping to prevent any further antipathy. "Didn't you tell us over dinner yesterday that his lordship is without a doubt one of Britain's 'winningest officers'?"

"Well, yes, I did," he admitted reluctantly.

"If that isn't the only criterion in considering an officer, certainly it must be one of the most essential." She did not look at the earl, who she knew was regarding her closely. "You must tell me if I am right or wrong, sir," she smiled sweetly.

Clarkson studied the pretty, intelligent face before him and then began to chuckle. "You know, Straeford, your wife would make a good diplomat. You're some advocate for your husband, my lady. And for you, I will promise to give the earl's request my utmost consideration."

Marisa graciously acknowledged this compliment to her, but she wondered how her husband felt about it. From his expression she could read nothing, but she suspected he was displeased. She anxiously waited for the Clarksons to leave before the earl's self-restraint gave way.

Fortunately, Clarkson, too, sensed the earl's disapproval and decided it was best to say no more on the subject and left as soon as possible.

After seeing the Clarksons to their carriage, Straeford returned to his wife who was standing near a window, a thoughtful expression creasing her brow as she absently played with a long strand of pearls about her throat. Leaning against the casement, her relaxed body revealed its curvaceousness beneath the aquamarine muslin, and desire for her stirred within him. He realized that his countess was not only beautiful but dangerous. She was clever and charming; a woman to admire but also be wary of. A most worthy opponent, he admitted to himself. Today she had supported him in his bid for a command. There could be only one explanation for that —she wished to expedite his departure. This weighed heavily on him in spite of his self-esteem, and he dropped into a chair dejectedly.

"Why do the Clarksons dislike you?"

He shrugged indifferently. "Lydia probably has poisoned Sir Francis against me."

149

"Why should she do that?"

"You mean Lydia didn't fill you in on the details?" he jeered. Leaning back he placed his elbows on the arms of the chair and steepled his fingers.

"No." Marisa began to feel guilty for having listened to Lydia Clarkson at all.

"Well, my lady, it's an old story, one best forgotten."

"Apparently they have not forgotten."

"No," he laughed mirthlessly, "Lydia would not forget. Let it suffice to say she thinks she has an axe to grind." He stretched his long legs out in front of him and closed his eyes.

Marisa thought he looked tired. Was he that concerned about his chances of receiving a commission, or was it something else? Had he been with Amanda Relington last night?

Straeford opened his eyes to catch his wife regarding him intently. "Is anything the matter?"

Marisa shook her head negatively. "I was just thinking . . . about the weekend."

"It was a mistake! Never again!" he declared emphatically.

Seeing his wife's eyes darken with anguish, Straeford realized she had taken it as an insult to her ability as a hostess. "It has nothing to do with you," he snapped, rising from the chair and striding across the room and back again. "I was referring to my own stupidity. Arranging a social gathering to further my career. I don't know why I let myself be talked into it." Then he added more for his own benefit than hers, "If I don't merit a command on my ability as an officer, I don't want it."

Although Marisa was relieved to know that she had not failed him, she was concerned for his self-reproach and tried to soothe him. "It's only natural to want to gain favor with those who can fulfill your most cherished desires."

Her solicitude touched him, but his pride made him resist it all the more. "And what do you know about my 'most cherished desires'?" he asked sarcastically. "A man desires many things." His bold gaze raked his wife, causing her to tense visibly. "Of course, a command for me

150

would also be nice for you, too. It would free us from one another without throwing you to the gabblemongers."

Her chin tilted with hauteur—any tender feelings she was experiencing toward him were erased by his unkind words. "Then I should pray very hard that you receive it."

"Pray it is not before you and your sister are launched into society," he taunted, although underneath it all, he was unaccountably hurt by her rejoinder.

"Since the season is about to begin," she said wishing to offend him as deeply as he had offended her, "and we are both anxious to put an end to this . . . honeymoon, I see no reason why we should not leave for London immediately."

He stiffened at her rapier thrust; nevertheless, he managed to bow extravagantly and smile cynically. "As you wish, madam."

10

Lady Maxwell inspected the Straefords approvingly as they stood before her in the morning room of her town house. The earl was superbly attired in buff pantaloons and a blue double-breasted coat by Weston, while the countess was exquisitely clothed in a high-waisted morning dress of mauve cambric edged with piping of green velvet. They were such a striking couple—Justin with his dark, chiseled features and autocratic bearing, and Marisa with her flawless ivory complexion and regal carriage. They were bound to be much admired as well as envied this season.

"Sit down, sit down," snapped the old lady in some exasperation. The recent gossip which had reached her ears spoiled her joy in them.

"I presume this summons was important enough to drag us here on our first day back in town," Straeford demanded as he seated his wife opposite his grandmother.

"Sufficiently so, I trust. Rumors are flying and I thought it my duty to tell you. What is this nonsense Lady Relington is spreading about the two of you?" She watched the expressions change on each of their faces. Marisa looked alarmed while Justin scowled.

"Since you seem to be in possession of some information we are not, perhaps you would be good enough to explain."

"Humph, so I will!" There was a lengthy pause before she continued. "Gossip has it that the two of you make your dislike of one another quite evident. I hear you are always stiff and formal with one another—when you are with one another; that you never deem to use each other's christian names . . . Need I go on?"

Blushing scarlet, Marisa cast her eyes downward, and Straeford, a thunderous look on his face, shifted uncomfortably in his chair. "The jade," he hissed.

"Fortunately for the two of you the town is still light of company, and Amanda's had few opportunities to spread her malicious lies."

"Then there is no need to fuss since little harm has come from her tale-pitching."

"Only if you behave more naturally with one another in the future. Oh, I know I can rely on Marisa to do her part." She reached across the intervening space to pat Marisa's hand. "It is this scapegrace of a husband of yours I'm concerned about."

"Grandmother!" Justin cried in mock horror. "Have you ever known me not to heed your advice? You know you are the only woman who commands my compliance and devotion."

"Then the bigger fool you, my boy," she retorted, meaningfully throwing the trio into an awkward silence which was only broken when the butler announced the arrival of the Fairfaxes, the first callers of the day.

Immediately Straeford bolted out of his chair prepared to make his departure, but his grandmother forced him to abandon his plan of escape by reminding him of the words he had uttered just moments earlier about compliance. Fuming, he subsided moodily into his chair, and introductions to the Fairfaxes were made. The party soon increased in number, and the earl found himself surrounded by eager faces wishing to make the acquaintance of the handsome nobleman with the dangerous reputation. With gritted teeth he bore it until he was rescued by Lady Maxwell, who asked him to escort her to the library.

He had barely begun a speech of thanks for his deliverance when his grandmother cut in and began berating him for his conduct toward his bride. Was he deliberately trying to hurt the girl by leaving her open to ridicule? Returning to the city without her, bringing guests to the country when they were supposedly on their honeymoon. It was unforgivable.

Her tirade continued until Straeford hissed in a scarcely controlled voice. "I need not explain my behavior to anyone, my lady. Not even to you!" With that he slammed out of the room.

Seeing the look on her husband's face when he returned to the morning room, Marisa did not question his decision to leave.

Hastily she said her goodbyes and followed her husband into the hallway. There they encountered a pale, shaken Lady Maxwell. Her appearance completely deflated Straeford's wrath. Encircling his grandmother's shoulders with his arm, he ushered her back into the library. After pouring her some Madeira, he knelt beside her chair, took her hand gently into his large, strong one, and whispered an apology. When the color returned to his grandmother's cheeks, he kissed them both.

Later the scene replayed itself in Marisa's mind. She had never witnessed this side of his nature before. His display of compassion and tenderness moved her deeply, and although she dared not tell him so, the idea nestled in her memory, and she treasured it in the days to follow.

Sitting in bed and drinking her morning chocolate, Marisa thumbed through a number of invitation cards that had arrived that morning. Ever since Lady Maxwell's soirée three weeks ago, it seemed everyone was mad to take her up. She was mindful of a deep sense of gratitude toward the dowager who had generously sponsored her introduction to the *ton*.

There was an abrupt knock on the door, and Justin strolled into the room, dressed for riding. "Good morning, *Marisa.*"

His pointed use of her first name these days caused

155

her some discomfort, which she tried to ignore. "Good morning, Justin." The intensity of his magnetic gaze from those splendid green eyes brought her to a blush as she remembered the night she had just spent in his arms. It had left her confused. The thrill of his touch, his lips upon hers, their bodies melting together as one had aroused a passionate response in her. Then all tenderness disappeared. Smiling coldly at her, he had whispered, "Ah, my Lilith," and taken her ruthlessly.

Looking away from his disconcerting gaze she asked, "Would you care for some chocolate?"

"No, I have already breakfasted and been riding." He seated himself on the edge of the chaise longue.

"Riding," there was a wistfulness as she spoke, "I have not been on a horse since we came to London." She hoped he might take the hint and offer to take her, but instead he countered, "Too many late nights, I suppose. I see your tray is full of more invitations."

"Yes, I'm afraid so, and I don't know which ones to accept."

"Complaining, my dear? I thought this is what you wanted."

"I'm not complaining. I just wish the pace were slower."

Marisa tossed her golden tresses and slid out of bed, affording him a view of her shapely body in a sheer night dress before she pulled on a peignoir.

How quickly they learned the feminine wiles, Straeford thought. Last night she had enjoyed their sexual activity a little too much. In no time one man would not be able to satisfy her. Lady Maxwell's impassioned plea of a few weeks ago had almost made him doubt his own estimation of his wife, but last night she had reaffirmed his original beliefs. Sitting back and crossing his arms, he eyed her smugly, and Marisa wondered just what he was thinking now.

"What are your plans for this evening?" he asked abruptly.

"There is a small card party at the Fairfaxes this evening, and then tomorrow we are promised to Lady Claridge . . ."

156

"No, not I, my dear, I have attended enough society functions in the last three weeks to last me a lifetime. You are well launched into the *ton* and can go on credibly without me at your side now. My defection will hardly be noticed."

"But . . . I . . . have already accepted the invitations in *both* our names."

"Then that is your problem. Doubtless you will manage. I am going out of town for a few days."

"Out of town? But . . . Meg is coming . . . and there is the ball we are to give." She was following him across the room and had laid a tentative hand on his arm. The unhappy look in her eyes gave him a moment's pause.

"Be assured I shall return before then."

The slight thawing of his tone gave her courage to ask, "How shall I get in touch with you? Where are you going?"

He stiffened and his eyebrows snapped together. "Where I go and what I do is no concern of yours!"

His belligerent statement hurt and angered her, and she turned her back to him. With that he stomped out of the room.

Why was he so cruel and unpredictable? These past three weeks he had been obliging and courteous, escorting her to the theater, a rout party, Vauxhall Gardens, and several other affairs. Then, when she was growing accustomed to his presence, expecting his support, he simply deserted her. Very well, she would manage on her own. Richard Foxworth would be only too happy to escort her to the Fairfax and Claridge parties. And she would also accept Relington's offer to ride with him in Hyde Park tomorrow after all.

"Would you care to handle the ribbons, Lady Straeford?" Relington asked as he tooled his horses through the park.

"Oh, I think not."

"I'm not such a Corinthian, my lady, that I would mind your driving my cattle."

"But I never have."

"Then it's time you did." Promptly he placed the

reins in her hands. "Steady does it," he encouraged as he leaned closer to her, but she was concentrating too hard on his instructions to notice. "Shorten the ribbon a trifle for the direction you intend going. Good, good. You have a light but firm touch, all to the good."

"I hope your tiger is not too nervous with me holding the reins."

"Hawley? Never consider him," he stated with insolence. "Ah, another curricle is approaching. Let us move to the right."

The approaching conveyance carried Carol Fairfax and her fiancé, Marc Belvoir. Drawing rein, the two couples conversed pleasantly, exchanging the gossip of the day, and then moved on only to stop again as more of their friends and acquaintances hailed them along their route.

The hour passed quickly and soon they were on their way back to Berkeley Square. As they approached her home, Relington returned to a topic which had been mentioned earlier.

"So, the earl is out of town, and you will be attending Lady Claridge's ball alone."

With some indignation she replied, " I assure you I will not be alone. Richard Foxworth has kindly offered to take me."

"Ah, and I was just about to offer myself as your escort."

"That is kind of you, but I'm sure your own wife would prefer you accompanied her."

He shook his head negatively. "That is impossible, dear lady, since Amanda left for the country quite suddenly yesterday." A meaningful look accompanied his unexpected words, causing a sudden chill to invade her entire being. With great effort she strove to control her chaotic feelings. Unconsciously, she twisted the straps of her reticule until Relington's hand rested on her agitated fingers, forcing them still. Unable to meet his gaze or speak without betraying her emotions, she continued to stare at their interlocked hands.

"My dear, it may be painful for you, but you must accept the truth . . ."

"No, I refuse to listen! Please say no more on the subject." She spoke in short, choppy sentences as she tried to collect her thoughts. "Thank you for the drive. There is no need for you to see me to the door. Good day, Lord Relington."

Relington watched her go. He was quite pleased with himself and this day's work. Already his words were having an effect on her.

Shaking with rage and humiliation, Marisa paced her room like a caged animal. So, her husband was with Amanda Relington! Soon every gossip in London would hear of it. Why had Justin chosen that vixen of all women to be his mistress? His mistress! Dear God, her husband had a mistress! And there was absolutely nothing she could do about it.

The pacing stopped. Her anger ebbed to be replaced by despair. In total dejection she leaned her head against the window pane, staring unseeing into the street below. The light went out of the day, and still she remained frozen in her misery.

"My lady," Lucy peeped her head around the door. "Shall I lay out your dress for Lady Claridge's ball?"

"I've decided not to attend, Lucy." Exhausted, Marisa slipped onto the chaise longue and rested her head against the pillows.

"But, your ladyship, everyone will be there. It's to be one of the grandest affairs of the season. 'Tis the *on dit* in the servants' hall."

"Oh, is it?" The countess permitted herself a half smile, slightly amused by her maid's remarks.

"No disrespect intended, my lady, but it would be corkbrained not to wear that pretty new yella concoction and go out for some fun."

Marisa was perturbed by the girl's unsolicited informality. She was about to reprimand her for the liberty she had just taken by addressing her in such a casual manner, when the girl added, "I'm sure his lordship wouldn't expect you to sit 'ome blue-deviled because he can't join you this night."

Under her lashes the countess surreptitiously studied the girl. What had she heard? Was her husband's affair already common knowledge? Would it be duly reported that she was sitting at home brooding over it? No, that would never do! Shaking off her lethargy, she rose proudly from the chaise longue. "I've changed my mind after all, Lucy; you may help me dress."

The countess wore a classical high-waisted gown with a low decolletage. The pale yellow skirt of chiffon was slightly flared at the back, and the long, close-fitting sleeves were transparent. The costume was completed with the Straeford emeralds which hung from her neck and ears. At the last minute she decided to slip the emerald ring she rarely wore onto her finger.

She was pleased with her appearance, and Foxworth's praise as he placed an appliqued shawl about her shoulders added to her confidence.

The countess was never gayer, flirting and dancing with every gallant who sought her hand, revelling in the attention accorded her and hoping Straeford would be apprised of her success. Until tonight it never occurred to her that her subdued reception by the polite world was in part caused by her husband's formidable presence. That was all changed now as her customary friends and acquaintances, the sedate matrons and quiet gentlemen, were replaced by the more dashing, reckless members of the *ton*. It was heady stuff to be surrounded by so many admirers and flamboyant ladies, and Lady Straeford sparkled for their benefit cavorting with Foxworth, toying with Relington, and captivating half the men at the ball. No one would accuse her of wearing the willow for a faithless husband.

It was just before the supper dance that Lady Maxwell finally cornered her and led her away to one of the withdrawing rooms where she mildly reprimanded her for her unusual behavior.

"What is the matter, child?"

"The matter?" Marisa prevaricated. "Why, nothing is the matter. I am just learning how to behave like any society belle."

"This is not like you, Marisa. Consider what you are doing before you regret it and make a mistake . . ."

"Regret . . . make a mistake?" she retorted almost

hysterically. "That is not putting it half strongly enough, dear lady."

"Straeford . . ."

"Straeford is . . . I do not wish to discuss him! If you will excuse me, I think I am engaged for this dance."

She took herself off and continued her madcap fling until the early hours of the morning when she returned home.

Lucy slipped the emeralds from about her mistress's neck, and waited to receive the other heirlooms from the countess to be placed in the jewelry box. Suddenly Marisa stumbled to her feet, a stricken expression distorting her features.

"What is it, my lady?"

"The ring . . . it's gone!"

"Oh, madam, no!" Lucy looked agog as her ladyship held her empty fingers out to her.

"I always meant to have it adjusted only . . ." she did not finish her thought aloud but it echoed in her mind. Only, I wanted Justin to make the gesture . . .

"What are we to do, my lady?"

"I must contact the Claridges . . . and Richard Foxworth. If I did not lose the ring at the ball, I may have lost it in the carriage. Quickly, some note paper."

It was after six o'clock in the morning when she received word from both parties concerned that neither was able to locate the jewel. Consequently, in the cold light of dawn, Marisa sat huddled in a chair, clutching at the shawl about her, racking her brain, trying to decide what to do next. Straeford would have to be told.

Seated on a footstool near her mistress, Lucy noticed that the countess was trembling and attempted to put her to bed, but Marisa rejected the idea. As exhausted as she was, she knew sleep was impossible unless she had come to terms with the calamity facing her. Suddenly a solution presented itself to her. She would go see her father and ask his advice. He might be able to help her.

Although it was barely seven o'clock in the morning, Lucy could not persuade her ladyship to wait a minute longer, and they were soon on their way to the Loftus residence in Bloomsbury.

Loftus was about to leave for his office in the city when his daughter arrived. Shocked by this unexpected visit, he quickly ushered her into his private study where Marisa's calm completely deserted her, and she buried her face in her handkerchief weeping softly.

"My dear child, whatever is the matter?" He was deeply concerned and expected to be informed of the most dreadful mishap. This was not at all like his daughter. What could it be to bring her here still attired in her evening clothes?

When she finally regained her composure and explained her misfortune, he was relieved. A lost or stolen emerald ring, even if it were an heirloom, seemed a small matter to him. Nevertheless, he assured her that if it had been stolen and not lost, he could probably locate it through certain business associates of his.

"It will take a few days to come up with it. In the meantime you go home and relax. Stop worrying." Angus frowned, not liking the unhappy troubled look in his daughter's eyes. Could one heirloom ring have caused that, or was there something more? Guilt was not an emotion he was familiar with, but niggling doubts about her happiness kept crossing his mind lately, ever since he had learned of Straeford's coming to the city without her. Impulsively, he kissed her cheek. "I've missed you, my girl."

"And I you, Father. Won't you come to visit soon?"

"You know my views on that, daughter." He suppressed his natural loving instincts as he was reminded of his goal. "I'm not a gentleman born, and I don't intend to interfere once my children are established. I'll be content to remain in the background." He tweaked her chin. "But that doesn't mean I won't pay you an occasional visit. You say the earl is out of town? When does he return?"

"Oh, soon." She flushed slightly under her father's scrutiny. It would be impossible for her to tell him about Justin and Amanda even though he was the one who had informed her of how it would be. Quickly she changed the subject, reminding him that John and Meg were to spend the next month with Straeford and her so that they might participate in the Season. Loftus was only too eager to discuss the future of his two younger offspring with her. He cautioned her to watch John closely because he was acting strangely and was not looking forward to the coming weeks. There were no such reservations where Meg was concerned. She was impatient for her entrée into society, and he expected her to be a tremendous success.

Meg whirled before the mirror in her pretty pink frock admiring her own dark beauty. "I still don't understand why the earl isn't here to accompany us to the theater. I hope he's not planning to renege on his part of the bargain."

In sudden irritation Marisa grasped her sister by the shoulders and shook her. "Haven't I asked you not to speak in such a vulgar manner?"

Meg shrugged loose of her sister's light grasp and pouted. "There's no need to get violent about it."

Disliking her own lack of restraint, Marisa held out her hand to her sister, who reluctantly accepted it. "I'm sorry, dear. Let us be friends. This is an important night for you, and I don't want anything to spoil it. Shall we go? John is waiting for us in the drawing room."

"I do hope he is not foxed," Meg whispered as they came in on their brother who was lounging on the settee. "It's becoming a most distressing habit."

Marisa did not comment, but she, too, had observed his increased reliance on spirits and even more disturbing was the change in his disposition. He was discontented and made little effort to hide it.

At their entrance he heaved himself to his feet and grumbled, "Don't see why I have to be dragged to the theater. Ain't Foxworth and Lady Maxwell company enough?"

"Oh, you are impossible. Ever since your return from Portugal, you've been acting like a bear." Meg stamped her foot in exasperation. Then, folding her arms across her breast, she taunted, "Do you know, Marisa, he's still mooning over the doctor's daughter?"

John's face suffused with color, and he shouted for her to keep quiet. Turning from them he went to the sideboard and poured himself another glass of brandy.

Marisa's heart ached for John, who had lost the

battle of wills with his father. He was still in love with his childhood sweetheart Ruth and wanted to marry her. "Meg," she admonished softly, "don't be unkind."

"Well, I think he is behaving foolishly. Here we both have the opportunity to marry into the *beau monde* and he's crying over Ruth. Let me assure you, I have every intention of gaining a title for myself."

Marisa was taken aback by her sister's self-assurance and warned, "These society matrons guard their families well and can be extremely difficult if they so choose. It might not be quite as easy to marry a title as you expect."

"You married a title! You were accepted by the *ton!*" she stated indignantly.

"That's because she's a *lady,* and you, my dear little sister, are not," John jeered and downed his glass of brandy.

Stung by her brother's taunt, Meg tossed her curls and replied with ill-humor, "I went to the same schools as Marisa. If she succeeded, so shall I. Besides, Richard Foxworth has told me I am a natural."

"Ha! That dandy! He only hangs around us because our dear father pays his bills."

"Nevertheless, he was instrumental in father meeting Straeford."

"Yes, and he fixed his own wagon there, didn't he? He expected Straeford to be dumb enough to choose you." John laughed gleefully as he crossed to her and pointed an unsteady finger in her face which she slapped away. Her cheeks burned an angry red. "Then Foxworth would have had clear sailing with Marisa, or so he thought. But Straeford saw through you in one night and took Marisa for himself, leaving you in the cold."

"You miserable lout!" Meg cried in fury.

"John, Meg, this will never do." Marisa stepped between them. "Let's remember we are still members of the same family. It would be a shame to let what is past come between us."

After a tense moment John smiled and took each of his sisters by the arm. "You're right as usual, good sister. Meg, I apologize. It is foolish for us to argue over what has already happened. Only the future can be altered."

Before Marisa had the opportunity to ask John what he meant by his last remark, Richard Foxworth was announced.

From the moment Lady Straeford's party entered the theater, Meg became the center of attention for a number of eager gallants. Her success that night was the preamble to a whirl of social activities that ran the gamut from Venetian breakfasts to midnight suppers at Vauxhall. The countess, as chaperon, was included in these entertainments and soon the admirers were dividing their time equally between the two beautiful sisters—and Straeford was not there to hinder their pleasure.

In her enjoyment, Marisa found little time to brood over her husband's defection or the missing emerald ring. It was Meg and John who occupied much of her waking thoughts. Her sister and brother were becoming difficult to handle. Meg's self-consequence was growing with every conquest she made, and she gloated over the attention accorded her, accepting it as her due. But it was Meg's increasing partiality for the Marquess of Alden, a known womanizer, that caused Marisa her deepest concern. When she attempted to warn Meg about him, her sister quickly retaliated, reminding Marisa of the frequency with which Thomas Relington visited the house. Although the countess went riding almost daily with Relington, she could see little comparison between the two situations. While there was no chance of her succumbing to Relington's blandishments, there was every danger of Meg—wild, young, impetuous Meg—submitting to the Marquess. Unfortunately she met nothing but stony resistance from her sister, who all but told her to mind her own business.

Then there was John, who had withdrawn behind a wall of silence and indifference, blocking out every overture from his sister. If possible, she was more worried about him than Meg because there was less and less communication between them, and she did not know what to expect.

The nagging state of worry and stress took its toll on Marisa's endurance, lowering her resistance. She came down with a spring cold that forced her to take to her bed for a few days, much to Meg's displeasure.

It was a relief just to lie in bed and not have to participate in the activities of another hectic day, although Meg was silently reproaching her for spoiling her fun.

"I think it was mean of Lady Maxwell to refuse to act as chaperon tonight."

"Meg, how can you be so selfish? That good lady has run herself ragged these past few weeks for us."

Meg pursed her lips and swung to look at her reflection in the mirror. "Well, I do wish you would contrive to see that I don't miss the opera," she said peevishly, fingering a straying curl.

Her attention was diverted from Meg by Lucy delivering a note from Richard Foxworth. "He has an important message for me and wants to come up to deliver it."

"Do you want me to leave?" Meg asked archly.

"No, of course not. I do not intend receiving a gentleman in my bedroom alone. Hand me my shawl, Lucy, and then you may show the gentleman up."

"I can't imagine what important message Richard could have for me."

"Well, you will soon find out, won't you?"

After that rather snide remark from Meg the sisters waited in silence for Richard Foxworth to be ushered into the room by Lucy. As always his dandified appearance brought an irrepressible smile to the sisters' lips. He was wearing a lavender jacket, pink striped waistcoat, and embroidered breeches. And as usual the starched wing collar of his shirt reached the middle of his cheek.

"Dear ladies," he smiled superciliously and bowed over Meg's then Marisa's hand. Straightening, he placed a small box in the countess's fingers. "For you, my dear Lady Straeford."

"Richard, you know I can not accept a gift from you."

"Believe me, this one you can. Please open it."

"Yes, do," Meg insisted and seated herself on the bed.

Puzzled, Marisa lifted the lid to discover an emerald ring winking at her, and although in her heart she knew it must be hers, she was afraid to believe it. "Richard, is it . . . ?"

"Yes, dear lady, it is the emerald you lost in my carriage."

"I thought you told my sister you searched your coach and could not find it," Meg interjected skeptically as she leaned over and lifted the ring from her sister's nerveless fingers. Then she slipped it on to her own hand and held it up to the light to admire it.

"What you say is true. It was mere chance which brought it to light. Yesterday as I stepped into my carriage, I noticed the carpeting had come loose. Naturally, I instructed my coachman to repair it. It was then that Freddy discovered the ring lodged beneath the flooring."

"It's too good to be true." Tears glistened in Marisa's eyes. "It is the most wonderful news. Isn't it, Meg?"

Her sister shrugged her shoulders indifferently and handed the emerald back to the countess. "In the future I would suggest you take better care of your belongings. I would have had it sized long ago."

"Yes, yes, I should have, and I will see to it as soon as I am over this cold." Gratefully, she clasped Foxworth's hand. "I shall never be able to thank you enough, dearest Richard."

"Lady Straeford, do not give it a second thought. My only wish is that I had discovered its whereabouts that night and saved you all this anguish." He bowed deeply and then kissed her fingers.

"Fiddle dee dee, it was nothing but a tempest in a teapot," Meg suggested petulantly. "And now, will one of you tell me how I may attend the opera this evening?" She gave Foxworth a speculative look.

"My dear child, I would be delighted to escort you, and I will ask my cousin Madeleine to act as chaperon. That is . . . if Lady Straeford consents." He raised his monocle and looked at Marisa, but it was Meg who made a smug reply.

"Of course, she will approve. After all, you are the gentleman who just saved her from the embarrassment of having to explain to Lord Straeford that she lost a priceless heirloom."

11

Restlessly Marisa tossed about, tangling herself in the sheets. The lazy day abed had brought on a sleepless night for the recovering countess, and the stillness of the house, after John and Meg's departure for their evening festivities, closed down around her. Throwing off the hot covers, she slipped quietly out of bed and into her robe. Then noiselessly she crept downstairs to the library in search of something to read. After placing the candelabrum on a table which sat directly in front of the window, she surveyed the room. Since Straeford had chosen it as his personal sanctuary, Marisa had rarely been inside of it. The moderately stocked bookshelves ran the length of one wall, and a large oak desk was placed squarely in the center of the room. The secretary arrested her attention because it was piled high with leatherbound volumes. Curious to discover her husband's choice of reading material she went to the desk and began reading the titles of the books strewn across it. Disappointment was immediate, because they dealt solely with military subjects: generals, wars, tactics and campaigns. Was that the only thing he concerned himself with? Discouraged, Marisa turned away and caught sight of another stack of books sprawled carelessly at the foot of an armchair. Slipping to her knees beside them, she was pleased this time to read a variety of titles on a number of topics. Perhaps there was hope for him after all. Picking up the book lying face down in the chair, she was more than surprised to see it was Camões's *The Lusiad,* the national epic of Portugal. Was it possible that Justin was actually reading this? But here was proof—the opened book lying in a chair in a room that he occupied almost exclusively. Making herself comfortable, she began to read.

> Like to a daisy flow'r with colors fair,
> By virgin's hand beheaded in the bud
> To play withal, or prick into her hair,
> When sever'd from the stalk on which it stood.
> Both scent and beauty vanish into air,
> So lies the damsel without breath or blood,
> Her cheeks' fresh roses ravisht from the root
> Both red and white, and the sweet life to boot.

Absorbed in the poetic beauty of the verse, Marisa was not aware of voices in the outer hall until the door was abruptly opened, and she heard Straeford saying, "You may bring me a decanter of port, Jenkins." Then he was standing over her—his booted feet planted directly in front of her. "Well, what have we here?"

"Oh, my lord," she cried and scrambled to her feet with his assistance.

"I saw the glow of the candles from the street and wondered who was in here."

His well-intentioned explanation was accepted coldly by his wife who was remembering her outraged honor. "So, now you know!" The frigidity of her reply immediately put him on his guard, and the rush of pleasure he had experienced at seeing her curled up on the floor with her unbound hair cascading down about her blue-clad form was forgotten, and he retaliated.

"Why are you in here without my permission?"

"I didn't realize this was restricted territory."

Her sharp retort not only surprised him but angered him as she stood before him with her hands defiantly on her hips. "It is, if I say so! These," he said thrusting a hand out indicating the dislodged papers and books, "are my personal belongings."

"I wasn't prying, if that's what you think." Her own doubt of the truthfulness of those words caused her to blush and noticing it he asked suspiciously, "Weren't you?"

"No, of course not," she persisted in her own defense. "I simply came in here to find something to read . . . and I just happened to catch sight of *The Lusiad*. I only meant to glance at it, but I became so absorbed in it that I couldn't put it down. Did you find it that way when you were reading it?" She forgot her anger in remembering the poem.

A slight flush rose under his cheeks before he had time to turn away and toss the book carelessly among the others on the desk. "I only read it to discover something about the nature of the people who are to be our . . . allies in the coming campaign. A mere practical interest. It had nothing to do with its poetry."

Marisa pursed her lips. Why did she persist in trying to locate a soft spot in this man? Indignant, she turned her back to him and walked over to the bookshelves and quickly selected something to read. She would have left him then without a word, but Straeford had no intentions of letting the interview end.

Blocking her exit, he drawled with marked cynicism, "Not much of a greeting for a spouse you haven't seen in weeks, m'dear."

"Funny, I was thinking the same thing." Her sarcastic rejoinder nonplussed him, and she made good her escape.

How dare she treat him in such a cavalier manner! Here he had come back ready to resume his marital duties, and she was acting the bitch. What could possibly be troubling her? For half a second he was tempted to follow her and find out, but instead he stormed out of the library, startling Jenkins who was carrying a tray with the decanter of port the earl had requested earlier.

"My lord," Jenkins hastily put the tray on a table and scurried after his lordship, who was heading for the front door. "Shall I call for your carriage?"

"No, I prefer to walk."

"But, my lord, it is not safe . . ."

Straeford's disdainful scowl was enough for the butler to fall silent. Shrugging his shoulders, Jenkins watched his master disappear into the inky black night. Far be it from him to protest any decision made by that man and incur his wrath. Better to pity the poor unsuspecting footpads who accosted Lord Straeford for they would be tangling with Satan himself. Sometimes he wondered why he had come to work for the Straefords. If it were not for Lady Straeford, he would certainly have given in his notice. Only she could have induced him to work in the house of such a blackguard. His unfortunate mistress needed the loyal support of her staff, and he was determined she would have that at least. After a heartfelt sigh, Jenkins finished dousing all but one branch of candles in the entrance hall, and then made his way downstairs to the kitchen where he would sit over a hot cup of tea until bedtime.

Being the only occupant of Berkeley Square to retire early, Marisa was the first one in the breakfast parlor the following morning. Left alone with her thoughts, they naturally turned to her husband. She had not planned what her attitude toward him would be upon his return, but now that an icy calm had asserted itself, she intended it to remain so. Only let him not seek her in bed! Knowing that he had a mistress, she could no longer tolerate such intimacy with him, even if the *beau monde* found it acceptable. What a mockery the polite world made of love! How they delighted in gossiping about deceived wives and husbands. It was such a distasteful subject to one of her middle-class upbringing. She did not fit comfortably into the fashionable world. The earl's reluctance for the match made even more sense to her now. Well, once John and Meg had their chance, and the earl left for Portugal, she would retire from this kind of life. If only there had been a child from their union, she would have been content. It would have given her life a purpose. At Straeford Park she could have taught him values she thought important. They could have explored the countryside and read together, and she would have tempered the Straeford character with softness. She would have raised a son capable of compassion and love as well as strength and courage—not like the present earl, all arrogance and cruelty.

"Good morning." Meg smiled pleasantly as she came into the room and began filling her plate from the sideboard.

"I didn't expect to see you up so early."

"I accepted Terence Fairfax's invitation to go riding."

"I'm happy to hear that." Knowing Meg had rejected several invitations from the Fairfax boy, this was an unexpected surprise.

"He pleaded so sweetly I just had to relent, but you know I prefer older, more sophisticated men."

That brought a smile to Marisa's lips; however, she made no comment. Her sister would change her mind many times about the type of men she liked before finally choosing a husband.

"Did you and Richard enjoy the opera?"

"Very much. But John must have enjoyed his evening even more since he still is not home."

"You mean he didn't come in at all last night?"

Meg's answer was negative and Marisa said thoughtfully, "Perhaps I should send a note around to Marc Belvoir . . ."

"Don't be silly! John is a big boy. Do you think he wants you checking up on him like some schoolboy? He's probably with some *chère amie.*"

"Meg! I will not have you talk like that."

"Oh, honestly, Marisa, you are such a prude sometimes . . ." She broke off as she spied the earl standing in the doorway. "Well, good morning, brother-in-law."

Marisa may not have known that John did not return to the house last night, but she was well aware of the earl's homecoming. The noises emanating from his room shortly after daylight had led her to believe he was foxed. If her suspicions were inconclusive then, they were confirmed now. He looked burnt to the socket.

After a terse greeting, he said, "If you don't mind, Miss Loftus, I would like to speak to my wife alone."

"Well, I do mind. I haven't finished eating, and I'm

famished." His sister-in-law was affronted by such a churlish manner, and Marisa could not blame her, but the countess, seeing the anger kindle in the earl's narrowed eyes, prudently intervened.

"Justin, won't you join us? The coffee is still hot." Quickly she poured a cup of coffee and brought it to him as he seated himself reluctantly at the head of the table. Their eyes met briefly and coolly. "I'll fill a platter for you." Without comment he accepted this service from her, and she placed a heaping plate of food in front of him.

He finally broke the strained silence by asking, "Is your London season everything you anticipated, Miss Loftus? Are the young gallants besieging you as they have your sister?"

Marisa almost dropped the knife she was holding. What caused him to make such a comment?

"I don't know about your wife," Meg was saying unabashed, "but I have no complaints about the amount of attention I'm receiving."

" 'Our Meg,' has already been termed a diamond of the first water by Terence Fairfax."

"Indeed!" Justin scorned.

"Oh, Terence," Meg sneered, "he's a fool. I'm not concerned with his comments."

"Why, Meg, he is such a nice boy, and it is plain to see that he adores you."

"I don't want him to adore me. I'm not going to marry someone as insignificant as he is."

"Of course, we expect you to marry someone you can admire and love."

"Fiddle dee dee, 'admire and love.' I want what you have, sister, a title!"

At her sister's crude remark, Marisa stiffened with shock while the earl sat back with an expression of cynicism on his face. His mocking gaze and Meg's insensitive hauteur almost sent the countess fleeing from the room, but she managed to control the urge.

"Meg, how could you?" Marisa whispered in a constricted voice.

"What did I say that was so terrible?"

Marisa could not reply, but it was unnecessary. The earl spoke with cold derision, "You are the complete 'cit',

Miss Loftus—what is known in the polite world as a 'mushroom'. With your want of conduct you'll be back in Bloomsbury before the end of the season."

Meg gasped, rising to her feet. "Why you hateful beast! I shall not speak to you again unless you apologize to me."

There was a bark of scornful laughter which pursued Meg as she raced out of the room.

In the hush that followed the outburst, husband and wife regarded each other warily. Marisa was at a complete loss for words while Justin was wondering why he had chosen to defend his wife in the confrontation with her sister.

"Well, now that we've gotten rid of her for the moment, perhaps we can talk."

"As you wish, my lord."

"Yes, it is my expressed wish!" he said sharply. "I was at White's last night, and I have learned a few interesting details about your... affairs during my absence." Marisa felt her stomach lurch. "It seems you have been the belle of the ball cavorting with any number of young bucks, and if that were not enough I was also informed that you have been seen every day for the past two weeks in the company of Lord Relington."

"What if I have?" She bristled.

Her defiance only heightened his own feelings of hostility. "I don't like it, and I expect you to put an end to it at once."

"Ohh," Marisa trembled with anger. "You ... dare to ... You hypocrite! You can spend a week in the country with Amanda Relington ..."

"What?" he shouted in astonishment. How did she know that that woman followed him to the country, and he had to send her packing? There was one obvious answer.

Seeing his surprise, Marisa grew hopeful. "You ... you weren't with her?"

"I suppose Relington told you that I was." He knew the workings of that man's mind. Relington wanted his wife, and by suggesting he was having an affair with Amanda, he hoped to achieve his aim. "Don't see Relington again! Ever!"

Marisa could not accept the fact that he could demand that she stop seeing Relington when he chose to ignore her question concerning his own behavior with Amanda. "Does that apply to you and Amanda as well?"

"Why you witch!" He reached for her, but Marisa expected just such a reaction from him and fled into the hallway where Jenkins was closing the door on Meg and Terence Fairfax.

"Ah, Jenkins, is my carriage ready?"

"It is, my lady."

"You will have to excuse me, my lord, but I must rush, or I'll be late for my shopping expedition with Lady Maxwell." She skirted around the butler who was holding her shawl, but Straeford was not to be outfoxed. "Here let me," he said, relieving Jenkins of the shawl. Smiling wickedly, he stepped up to Marisa and slowly slipped the shawl about her. Maintaining a hold of her shoulders, he whispered, "I can wait, my lady. Enjoy your morning with Lady Maxwell. It may be the last for some time." Only then did he let her go.

Although Marisa was frightened by her husband's threat, she had no intentions of cancelling her drive in Hyde Park that afternoon. Some perversity of will drove her to keep the engagement.

When she returned from shopping with Lady Maxwell, she was relieved to discover that the earl was not at home. Relington's arrival presented no undesirable confrontation, and Marisa was able to keep her resolve to disregard her husband's order; however, she was totally disconcerted when Straeford, upon his sleek black stallion, accosted them in the park.

"Ah, Straeford, heard you were back in town," Relington addressed him.

"And I just heard that you talked Kennington out of blowing your head off for your latest indiscretion in the boudoir."

"Oh, I say old man," Relington blustered, "someone's been pitching you gammon."

"Indeed?" Straeford raised his black brows.

"Nothing but a misunderstanding. Mountain out of a molehill. Talked myself out of that one easily enough," he laughed nervously.

"How lucky for you. I wonder how successful you would be at talking me out of it?"

"Justin!" Marisa whispered frantically, aware of the crowded park filled with members of the *haute monde* just waiting for some new scandal to titillate them.

"Deuce take it! Don't fly into a pucker, my good fellow."

"I'm not your 'good fellow', Relington."

"Yes, of course," Relington said soberly. "But really, Straeford, my behavior has been perfectly innocent. A perfect gentleman."

"Glad to hear it because I have a devil of a time listening to anything when I'm in a passion. By the way, old man, just how many men have you killed in duels?"

"Here now . . ." A lump in Relington's throat made it difficult for him to speak. "I ain't ever killed a man."

"Haven't you?" Straeford cast him a frigid glare. "You become used to death after the first half dozen or so."

"Are . . . are you threatening me?" Relington asked unsteadily while Marisa held her breath.

"Threatening you? What reason could I possibly have for threatening you?" Straeford queried as he allowed his cold emerald eyes to rest meaningfully on his wife. "Well, I've detained the two of you long enough. Enjoy your ride." The gleam in his eyes belied the feigned cordiality of his words. Then as he turned his horse away, he said to his wife, "I shall see you at home, my dear."

His warning was implicit and she was frightened. It was evident that Relington was having similar fears, for when they reached Berkeley Square, he excused himself from their drive on the morrow and made a hasty departure.

It was a relief to her to hear from Jenkins that Mr. Angus Loftus had arrived only moments earlier asking to see her, and that he was in the drawing room with the earl. Justin's wrath would have more time to cool down, and for this she was grateful.

"Father," Marisa held out her hands to him and moved into his arms, ignoring Straeford who stood before the fireplace. "What is it, dear?" she asked as they sat together on the sofa. "You look upset."

"What do you know about this?" He thrust a paper

into her hands which she read quickly. "I received it about an hour ago." At Marisa's silence, he accused, "You don't seem surprised by it."

"No, I think I was expecting something like this from John."

"For God's sake, girl, why didn't you tell me?"

"What could I tell you, Father? That John was unhappy? That he was resentful of your . . . interference in his life? These were things you already knew. Besides, he did not confide his plans to me. Even if I did know, I couldn't have informed on him."

"I expected more loyalty from you! I could have stopped him."

"How? By bullying him into a life he does not want! Father, be happy for John. He has married the woman he truly loves. Let him follow his heart."

"He can follow whatever he damn well pleases from now on! I wash my hands of him. Let him see what it is like to fend for himself." Abruptly he got up and started across the room.

"Father," Marisa hurried after him. "Don't make any decisions while you are so upset."

He shook his head vigorously. "I warned him just as I did you and Meg. He knew how it would be."

"Don't go like this." She grasped his hand but her eyes searched over her father's bent head for Straeford, and silently she pleaded with him for his support. "Stay for dinner. I don't want you to go home alone and brood."

"What you need is a good stiff drink, sir," Straeford said as he poured some whiskey into a glass.

"If I stay, you won't change my mind."

"And I for one would not expect you to," Straeford stated emphatically, looking at his wife. "It was your son's choice. Now let him live with his decision. Marisa, why don't you go change for dinner? I'll see to your father." He placed a firm hand under her elbow, propelling her toward the door.

"But . . ." Marisa resisted. She was not giving up on her father that easily.

"Don't push your luck, my girl," Straeford whispered as he thrust her out into the hallway. "You may pick up the cudgels on your brother's behalf another time if you must. You might learn the techniques of when to attack and when to withdraw if you live with me long enough." He gave her a sardonic look before stepping back into the drawing room and closing her out.

Wearily Marisa trod her way along the hallway to her bedroom. It had been a horrendous day. First there had been the trouble with the earl. Next came the news of John's elopement, and tonight it was Meg's outrageous behavior at the Fairfax soirée. She had flirted shamelessly with Marc Belvoir, driving his fiancée into hysterics, and if that were not enough, she had encouraged the attentions of the Marquess of Alden again. Even Lady Maxwell's stern lecture about propriety had not daunted Meg, for no sooner had they left the good lady at her home than Meg declared her intentions of continuing her flirtation with the Marquess.

All thoughts of her family deserted her as she came into the bedroom and saw the earl standing before her in the dim candlelight. "Why, Justin, you frightened me." She clasped her hands to her breast to quell her racing heart.

"And frightened you best be, madam! For I have come for your reckoning." He snapped a riding crop across his hand and took a menacing step toward her.

Gasping, she backed away from him, all the while staring at the whip in his powerful hand. "You wouldn't."

"Wouldn't I? You defied me at your own peril. I've been far too lenient with you!" The riding crop lashed against a gutting candle and sent it toppling to the floor, and a wicked smiled played across his lips. "There's no escape this time. No running away. No servants to the rescue. I've seen to that."

"Don't do this, Justin," she whispered as she cringed against the wall.

"Give me one good reason why I shouldn't."

"I have done nothing to deserve such a punishment."

"What do you call defying my order not to see Relington again?"

"I couldn't just cry off. There was no reason . . ."

179

"Reason!" he shouted. "There was every reason!" He closed in on her, and instinctively Marisa turned her back to him waiting for the cruel blows to fall, but nothing happend. A deafening silence stretched between them, and suddenly it was apparent to her that he did not intend to use his weapon. His threats and bullying were meant to frighten her into submission. Slowly shifting her position so that she could see him, Marisa could read the indecision written across his face.

"Will you not trust me, Justin? I have never given you reason not to. Why must there be this constant torment between us?"

In chilling derision he claimed "Because no man can trust any woman."

"Not *any* woman—do you condemn us all?"

"Indeed I do, madam."

"But that's so unfair. Surely you have known some good women . . ."

"None, I say. From the first woman in my life there has been nothing but infamy and lies."

His mother again. He is so convinced, Marisa thought hopelessly. What had that woman done to him? But this was no time to broach that forbidden topic. Best discuss their own personal relationship.

"Couldn't you give it a try at least?" He eyed her suspiciously. "I mean . . . why not give me your trust until I give you some reason to doubt my . . . faithfulness."

"Ha!" he snorted. "Do you think I am some dupe to be fooled by a soft wheedling voice and pretty speeches about fidelity from some hussy?"

"Oh," she cried recklessly. "And what of you? Impugning my good character when I have every reason to doubt your own faithfulness!"

A murderous light came into his narrowed green eyes, and he struck blindly, bringing the riding crop across her shoulder. She screamed, swerved away from him and grasped the bedpost for support. The taut silence that followed was finally broken as he threw the crop across the room and strode out of the chamber.

She slipped to the floor and let silent tears course down her cheeks. She hated him! Hated him! Never would she feel one ounce of sympathy for him again.

Whatever had taken place between him and his mother surely had to be all his fault.

She remained in her crouched position for some time, until she had finally exhausted all her tears and venomous feelings. Then Marisa relighted the candles, removed her dress, and inspected her bruised shoulder. A red welt burned across it. To ease the painful sensation, she held a damp cloth over the tingling flesh. Weary from emotion, she dragged her aching body to bed.

The first light of dawn was creeping into the house when Justin wove his unsteady way upstairs to stand beside his wife's bed. Focusing his blurry eyes on her damp lashes and glistening cheeks, an unfamiliar feeling of compassion welled up in him. He brushed aside the sleeve of her nightdress to reveal the livid mark on her white shoulder.

Instantly she was awake and even in her dazed state she struck out at him. Grasping her flaying arms, he threw himself on top of her and buried his face in her hair.

"Didn't want to hurt you. Never touched Amanda. Want you." His speech was almost incoherent.

The more she struggled to free herself of his enveloping arms the more tightly they coiled around her. His mouth searched for hers in the semi-darkness but she twisted and strained her neck to refuse him. His lips brushed her ear, then her neck and back again to her turned cheek as she continued to resist him. Finally his lips found hers, and her anguished "no" was barely audible under the pressure of his hungry mouth. It lingered against hers for what seemed to be an eternity, and she tasted the heavy spirits on his breath.

Inflamed by his need for her, his fingers burned against her flesh in searing caresses, and her frantic protests were ignored, as were her attempts to wriggle free of his weight. His assault on her weakening defenses continued until she was wondering how she had arrived at this state of desire she was suddenly experiencing when only moments before she was consumed with hatred for him. What kind of power was he able to wield over her? Now she realized that the rising tide of emotions swirling inside had erased all trace of reason. Marisa knew that the ultimate conclusion to their lovemaking was unavoidable, but the danger of his throbbing body next to hers was no longer something to be evaded. Instead, she found herself wanting him, and she murmured a breathless sound as his body took hers. Her arms moved instinctively about his muscled torso, and she held him tightly as a certain rhythm overcame both of them. Within the caverns of her mind, Marisa was aware only of a thrilling wave of sensations which threatened to drown her all at once. She gasped for breath and heard Justin moan a heavy sound, but her sense of fulfillment ebbed quickly as he rolled free of her to fall into a drugged sleep.

Marisa stared at the ceiling knowing that she was lost. She hated him and loved him at the same time. This arrogant devil was making her life a tender torment. And no matter how she might rail against him, she was trapped by her love for him.

Justin muttered in his sleep, and Marisa began stroking his black hair until he settled quietly against her, and she then drifted off to sleep.

Straeford woke to find his wife wrapped tightly in his arms, and he was content to let her remain so until his eyes rested on the purplish welt streaking across her shoulder. The sight of her sleeping peacefully in his arms after his brutal attack on her drove him from her bed in self-disgust. In the adjoining room he tried to reconstruct in his foggy brain what exactly had taken place between them, but he was unable to remember the events of last night clearly. A sense of shame made him decide to avoid her company. A harsh laugh erupted from him. Hadn't that been his resolve just a few weeks ago? But the blond witch had cast some kind of spell on him, dominating his thoughts until he had been lured back to the city. That meant nothing, he rationalized, he simply was determined to keep an eye on her until his purpose to have an heir was accomplished.

12

"I don't believe it!" Straeford roared out loud as he reread the letter Jenkins had just delivered to him. He shook his head repeatedly in disgust. "I never really believed he would take the coward's way out. What an outright disgrace!"

Crumpling the letter in his hand, he hurled it angrily to the floor. It was a communiqué from John Loftus stating that he had resigned his commission in the army and was planning to emigrate to America with his wife immediately. Straeford's contempt for his brother-in-law left him utterly speechless. It was more than he could bear to have his good name, so rich in heritage, associated with such a sniveling act. Seething inside, he stomped off to inform his wife of her brother's treachery.

When he found her, Marisa was seated at her escritoire. She, too, had received the same message from her brother and was attempting to collect her thoughts, knowing full well what her husband's reaction would be. Before she even had a chance to turn in his direction when he entered the room, he launched into a tirade.

"Have you heard the news about your brother?" He didn't wait for her reply. "Why, it's beyond belief! How could he so flagrantly cheapen his family's name? And now, of course, my name is implicated as well."

Marisa looked up at him in silence as he continued his condemnation of her brother. Pain and distress were clearly written on her face, causing him to pause for a moment. And although he sensed her hurt, another thought occurred to him—a vicious one, he realized, but his anger would not permit him any restraints at this moment.

"I'm not going to mince any words with you, madam wife. I hold that you were party to this defection!"

"I?"

"Yes, yes, you, my dear. Do you think I am ignorant of the fact that your new sister-in-law is related to Mark Aiken, your former lover, who now resides in America?"

Marisa reared back, speechless at his insult. Her face whitened with anger, and Straeford felt a momentary sense of triumph. "You know," he continued, "I'm rather curious about you and that person. In fact, I am prompted to ask you right at this moment—were you ever in love with him?"

Marisa shifted nervously in her chair. "I fail to see the relevance of that question, nor do I understand what difference that could possibly make any longer."

"Oh, no. You'll not evade my question that easily, my dear. As your husband, I am asking you for a direct and simple answer. Did you or didn't you love Mark Aiken?"

"Well, if you really must know the truth," Marisa sighed, feeling trapped, "I suppose I did love him. Now, was that what you wanted to hear?"

For some reason her reply left him stunned. It was not at all what he expected to hear, and her answer left him with nothing to say. But Marisa was too preoccupied to take note of the effect her answer had had on him. For the present, she was more concerned with the impact John's desertion would have on her father.

"Frankly, I'm very concerned about my father at this moment," she said, picking up the threads of the conversation. "I am just as upset about all of this as you are. But I know he is, too, and I must see him at once."

Marisa rang for Lucy's assistance while the earl silently returned to his study.

When Marisa met with her father later that morning, she found Angus somewhat resigned to his son's actions. After all, it was not a complete surprise to him. He knew of John's strong feelings regarding the military and had gone over that issue with him a countless number of times, all to no avail. Angus seemed to be yielding on this matter. Perhaps, his daughter mused, a reconciliation between father and son was still possible. The task confronting her, however, was how to bring them together. She knew it wouldn't be easy.

Seeing that her father might now be vulnerable, Marisa decided to visit John in Islington. But she found her brother much less amenable to a meeting with Angus for this purpose. He insisted that it was a road that both of them had traveled many times before and little was likely to result from another face-to-face encounter. It was only Marisa's forceful arguing of the point that this might be the very last opportunity in both of their lives to make their peace with one another that finally persuaded John to see his father the following weekend. However, he did so reluctantly and warned her not to expect too much from such a meeting.

Marisa accepted that she had accomplished about all that was possible on that account. Father and son would now have to come to grips with their problems on their own terms. The only thing she could do was act as their intermediary. The rest was up to them, and she prayed that the final outcome would result in a proper reconciliation.

During the days that ensued, Marisa temporarily put aside her concerns for John and her father and focused her attention on the ball which she and the earl were planning to give. It was going to be her first official venture as a hostess, and its main purpose was to provide Meg with a coming-out ball. This meant that everything had to be perfect. Ceaseless details consumed Marisa's every moment as she consulted with the caterer, the florist, the musicians, the seamstress and, of course, Lady Maxwell, who offered some helpful advice on every matter, especially the etiquette and protocol for the occasion.

From dawn to dusk each day Marisa was totally immersed in consultations of every sort and in checking off items on a long list of tasks to be done that she scribbled out each morning. The pace was frenzied by the time the afternoon of the ball arrived. For quite a few days she had precious little time for herself, and she was thankful that her servants had been so patient with her in this whole affair.

Now she was enlisting Jenkins's aid in a decision concerning where to place a large vase of multicolored flowers. "Mmm . . . Let's see now. How about on the mantel of the marble fireplace, Jenkins?" Marisa stepped back to judge its effect when she felt her foot come down unexpectedly on someone standing behind her. She stumbled clumsily and sent a basket of roses tumbling from the table which she tried to grasp in an attempt to regain her balance. Her fall to the floor was prevented by two powerful arms, and she did not need to turn around to see to whom they belonged.

"Oh, dear!" Marisa surveyed the blossoms strewn about the floor, and Straeford picked up the basket to help her retrieve them. Apologizing to one another, they simultaneously stooped to gather them up and accidentally bumped heads in the process. A surprised look passed between them before they burst into uncontrollable laughter.

"I would like to wager that we could not repeat that comedy of errors if we tried," Straeford said, tossing some flowers into the basket. "Well, that about does it. No harm done." Straeford offered a hand to help her up.

"Yes. That certainly does it, all right," Marisa said with irony as she looked at the tangled mass of roses. "How shall I ever reorganize these flowers?"

"Why bother? Stick them in a corner somewhere so no one will notice."

"Oh, I can't do that. Each bouquet has a specific composition to create a special effect. If you look at the

186

one in front of the fireplace you see that the darker, larger blossoms are at its base while the lighter shades are . . . " She stopped in embarrassment as she caught him observing her with a supercilious grin. "Dear me, I know you did not come to discuss the decorations. You did wish to speak to me about something, however?"

"I did," he replied, the grin fading from his face while her attention remained focused on the roses. "Your sister was good enough to inform me that I am expected to lead her out in the first dance this evening."

"Mm hmm," she mumbled, still toying with the flowers, her lips pouting as she failed to place a white bud in precisely the right spot.

Straeford watched her with some amusement until finally the silence drew her attention.

"Oh, forgive me. What were you saying?"

"I was about to say that I am sorry, but I don't dance."

Marisa placed a hand over her mouth. "Whatever will we do then?"

"I'm sure there are many young bucks willing to dance with that little minx."

Marisa wrinkled her nose at his reference to Meg. "Yes, I suppose there are, but you see that would not exactly be proper, now would it? Well, I guess we'll have to think of something, won't we? But it certainly is late."

To her surprise Straeford showed his concern by suggesting a series of bachelors who might oblige her, but Marisa had excellent reasons for rejecting each one. Finally, with some asperity, he capitulated.

"Oh, very well, I shall appear the jackanapes and dance with her."

"Oh, would you?" she responded enthusiastically.

"If I say I will, then I will. Besides, I've done just about everything else these past weeks, so why need I balk at a mere dance?"

Marisa mustered up all the gratitude she could. "It's very sweet of you to do that for me."

"I'm never sweet!" he retorted gruffly. "I simply do not wish to . . . upset protocol."

"Well, thank you anyway for doing something that is against your wishes."

He shrugged his shoulders uneasily and turned to leave, but she held him back with an outstretched hand and placed a short-stemmed rose in his lapel. Smiling coquettishly, she exclaimed, "I hereby commend you for valor, sir." She stepped back to admire him playfully, but he seemed unwilling to reciprocate.

"I think this flower would enhance your beauty far better," he said with a straight face as he started to remove the rose. But Marisa put her hand over his and admonished him lightly, "Sir, would you reject a medal for valor?"

Her direct appeal melted the coldness from his dark green eyes, and his hand gently squeezed hers before he lifted her fingers to his lips and quipped, "In that case, I must accept most graciously." Then he bowed and withdrew quietly, leaving Marisa with a fluttering heart.

When there was finally a break in the long line of guests entering the Straeford home that evening, Marisa leaned across her husband to press Lady Maxwell's hand. The dowager looked exceptionally radiant in a high-necked purple satin gown.

"Dear lady," Marisa smiled fondly, "how can we ever thank you? Everyone is in attendance."

"Oh, it's true," Meg bubbled. "The Seftons, Lord Alvanley, Lady Jersey . . . They all came."

"Just don't spoil it, my dear girl," Lady Maxwell admonished, "by playing up to Alden again tonight."

"What's this?" Straeford demanded.

"The chit's struck up an acquaintance with that scoundrel, Alden."

"Huh! The man's old enough to be her father," Straeford frowned. The dissolute Marquess most assuredly did not have marriage in mind, and marriage for Meg was part of the earl's bargain with Loftus.

"Oh," Meg stomped her foot impatiently. "I don't know why everyone is making such a fuss. I happen to like Ted and marriage to him is exactly what I want."

"You scheming vixen!" Straeford exploded. He was

about to give her a thorough tongue-lashing, but the sight of the Hardings approaching them made him stop short.

"Are we very late?" Ann asked in her usual breathless manner, kissing Marisa on the cheek. "You see, little Eddie has a head cold. Poor dear, I just couldn't leave him until he was fast asleep."

"I hope it's not serious," Marisa sympathized.

"No, it's not," the major interrupted. "Ann is panicking over a sniffle."

"Now, Edward, how can you be so unreasonable? Your infant son is suffering! The poor thing."

"This is not the time for a family spat, my love." Edward grinned and ushered his wife away just as General Wellesley made his appearance. It was obvious from Straeford's effusive greetings that this was a man he held in high regard. He shook the general's hand crisply and appeared anxious to launch into a protracted discussion with the esteemed military leader. But Lady Maxwell's signal to Marisa to begin the dancing prevented that from happening. Their guests now clearly established in the ballroom, the Straefords entered with pomp to initiate the festivities.

The ballroom presented a vision of fairytale loveliness. Pink velvet draperies fringed with silver tassels, walls flecked with pink and white wallpaper, mirrors reflecting crystal chandeliers and silver sconces—all of the appointments delighted the eyes of the admiring guests.

As he promised, the earl led Meg out in a quadrille while the crowd of onlookers admired. She was a pretty minx, he observed, in her high-waisted white gown of tulle and pink lacing. Yes, her provocative figure and haughty smile could be a serious temptation to any man. Although he pitied the poor fool who would end up being her husband, the earl was confident that it wouldn't be that lecher, Alden.

When the first set had ended, Straeford was not at all surprised to find Meg immediately surrounded by a swarm of young bucks eager for her hand. Relinquishing his charge, the Earl was about to make a quick exit for the card room when Lady Maxwell cornered him with the pointed suggestion that protocol demanded that he dance with his wife. A frown crossed his face and then, much to her surprise, he set off obediently in search of Marisa. The grand old lady's eyes followed him across the crowded room as he nodded casually and directed a few carefully chosen remarks to the dignitaries and acquaintances he brushed by. Lady Maxwell felt enormous pride in this complicated but handsome grandson of hers. When his mood permitted, he could be charming, and this was clearly one of those occasions. His dress for this evening emphasized his natural nobility and refinement. Tonight he was clad in black, except for his green silk waistcoat, and he wore a white frilled shirt with an intricately folded jabot that was punctuated with an emerald stickpin. He wears his title well, Lady Maxwell mused.

Finally, he found the countess conversing animatedly with Lord and Lady Claridge at the far end of the room. After a polite exchange of pleasantries, the musicians obligingly struck up a waltz, and Straeford used the cue to edge his wife away.

"You'll excuse us, I'm sure," he said to the Claridges, "but I do believe my wife has promised me this waltz." Marisa blinked at the unexpected request, but recovered quickly enough to allow herself to be led to the dance floor.

Straeford swept her silently about the floor and observed the light grow in her eyes as she relaxed in the security of his arms and her body swayed gracefully in unison with his. Her gown of sapphire blue emphasized the deep blue of her eyes. Her dress was edged in diamanté and banded tightly under her bosom so that long, sweeping folds of silk fell dramatically to her silver-sandaled feet. A diamond pendant hung low and nestled disturbingly between her breasts. She was stunningly beautiful, far more beautiful than Meg could ever be, he realized.

His arm tightened about her waist, and his cheek rested gently against hers. A captivating fragrance emanated from about her neck, and he found himself murmuring softly, "You're absolutely breathtaking, my dear . . . beautiful."

Marisa raised her eyes to meet his and found herself spellbound. His green eyes gave off a glow she had not seen before, and now she closed hers dreamily as the two of them continued to whirl about the floor in a wondrous vortex. The light from the crystal chandeliers shimmered against the silver-fringed drapes as they floated about the room in cadence to the soft music, their senses mutually submerged in the magic of this moment.

Again the earl danced with his countess to the strains of the musicians' violins, and when a brief intermission was announced they both sighed in disappointment. It had been exhilarating and neither of them wanted to stop. For a time, however, Marisa seated herself in a white tufted chair at the edge of the dance floor, content to have the earl at her side. When she was quickly encircled by guests, Straeford removed himself for a breath of fresh air.

The night was cool, and a soft spring breeze rustled pleasantly across the terrace. Straeford drew in some air and exhaled slowly. His thoughts were still focused on the glowing feelings that lingered from the dance, but a faint and indistinct sound somewhere below the terrace distracted his attention. As he descended into the garden, he heard a woman's voice more clearly. And then, when a man spoke, the earl knew they were both familiar to him. It was Meg Loftus in the arms of Ted Alden, and the sight of the two of them locked in each other's arms was quite enough to take the earl completely out of humor. Why, this rounder's philanderings were a direct insult to Straeford's family and, quite conceivably, a scandal could result if it weren't halted immediately. The earl strode up to them and let out a sarcastic laugh that forced them to part abruptly.

"Straeford!" Alden frowned, adjusting his disheveled neckcloth with an embarrassed look on his face.

"So the little minx has trapped you after all?"

"I beg your pardon? What do you mean by that remark?" Alden demanded.

"Well, why don't you ask her yourself?"

"I haven't the faintest idea of what you're talking about," Meg said in lame defense.

"Oh, don't you, miss?" Straeford sneered.

"No, I don't! Come, Ted, I think we should get back to the party. I do believe my brother-in-law is foxed."

"He doesn't appear that way to me," Alden said under his breath. He was bothered by the earl's inference and ready to stand his ground for the moment. "See here, Straeford, just what are you getting at?"

"I am getting at the question of when you and my sister-in-law plan to announce your betrothal."

"What! Now just one minute! A kiss in the garden . . ." Alden faltered, trying to complete his sentence diplomatically, ". . . Well, that doesn't signify any such thing."

Meg waxed silent following his weak reply, but Straeford probed further with a vengeance. "Are you telling me that my family's honor is so lightly taken?"

"Of course not . . . certainly not." Alden sensed that the earl's incendiary temper had been aroused, and the possibility of a duel between them over this matter flashed across his mind and forced him to couch his reply in guarded language. Of course, he had no intention of wedding a chit so free with her kisses.

"Look here, I didn't mean to . . . uh . . . take liberties, and I apologize to the . . . uh . . . young lady here if I misled her in any way." Alden dispensed an ingratiating gesture in her direction. "I . . . I was simply overcome with her beauty . . . just lost my head. Never meant any insult to Miss Loftus. I'm sure you understand, Straeford."

"Yes, I understand exactly. And I'm certain there will be no repetition of this in the future. I can rely on that now, can't I?"

"Oh, but of course. Yes, yes indeed," Alden replied penitently. "And now if you'll excuse me." He skirted around Straeford in an attempt to exit quickly and without further humiliation. But Meg would not permit it.

"Coward!" she yelled, flinging her reticule at Alden's retreating back and causing him to stumble. Straeford laughed derisively, but Meg shared little of his humor. "You interfering busybody! You sniggering, pompous . . ."

Before she could finish the earl's hands reached out to clench both of her arms with a rock-hard grip. For almost a full minute he shook her violently, and Meg gasped from shock and fright. She thought for certain that he had completely lost control, but finally he stopped to warn her once more about her flirtation with Alden.

"Do you think I'm going to permit some conniving little shrew such as yourself to plunge us all into a scandal?"

"Scandal? I could have married him!"

"Now listen to me. Don't delude yourself for one more minute. You're nothing but a spoiled brat peddling her wares for the first time to, of all people, an accomplished womanizer. Why, you fool! You gullible little wench! Did you really think for one moment that Alden had succumbed to you? Hah! How laughable! Why, he's managed to escape the wedding noose more years than you've lived."

"I . . . I don't believe you! You're lying. And you're jealous, too." Meg tried to wriggle free of his painful grip.

"Jealous?"

"Yes, jealous. Your actions tonight prove that to me. You're really sorry that you didn't choose me instead of my sister. That's the real truth, isn't it?"

Straeford's eyes turned to steel. He released his grip abruptly, causing her to reel backward. "You conceited little bitch!"

"Yes. Go ahead. Rail at me all you like, your lordship. But I've seen you watching me. Giving me that sidelong look now and then. Why don't you admit it? You made a mistake and now you're sorry."

"Even if that were true, just what difference could that possibly make now?"

Meg heard only the first part of his statement and threw herself into his arms. "Oh, Justin, if only you had chosen me. I could have given you everything you ever wanted in a woman."

"And what might that be, my dear, dear Meg?" he asked, a ruthless smile playing about his lips.

"This!" Meg pulled his head down to meet hers and kissed him boldly. She had not anticipated that his lips in turn would brutally clamp hard on hers and his arms would tighten like manacles about her small frame, holding her immobile until she felt she could no longer breathe. Groaning, then struggling ineffectually to release herself, she felt faint. Suddenly he thrust her away from him, and Meg found herself staggering toward a stone pedestal, gasping for air. As she turned to face him, she raised the back of her hand to her lips, her earlier insolence now entirely replaced by fear. Straeford's eyes had an ominous look as he hovered over her.

"Shall I take you here in the garden, my dear? What do you say to that?" He moved threateningly toward her, and Meg let out a screech. Flailing her arms wildly, she took to her heels and scrambled out of the garden, Straeford's mocking laugh echoing in her ears.

As soon as Meg re-entered the ballroom, Marisa knew that something was seriously wrong, and she whisked her misty-eyed sister off to the morning room for a quiet tête-à-tête.

"What ever is the matter, dear?" Marisa coaxed. "You can tell me."

"Your ... husband," she sobbed. "He's a brute ... a monster."

"Meg! What are you talking about? What has Justin done to cause this?" Marisa was both frightened and angered by her sister's unexpected outburst.

"Oh, Marisa, I didn't know ... he was so ... so terrible! You poor thing! Married to that incorrigible ..."

"Meg!" Marisa demanded, her patience now taxed. "For heaven's sake, tell me what happened."

"I taught her a damn good lesson. That's what happened." The sharp rejoinder came from the open door. Straeford sauntered into the room, a look of contempt undisguised on his face. Meg wailed and darted behind Marisa.

"Don't let him touch me!"

"Touch you?" he scorned. "Why, I'd rather pet a viper!"

"Justin!" Marisa was totally nonplussed by both of their reactions. "What is going on here?"

"I'll tell you what's going on all right. Your loving little sister got precisely what she deserved tonight. She learned that she can't always get what she wants by throwing herself at a man, be he unmarried or otherwise. Isn't that right, my dear sister-in-law?"

"Oh, I hate you! I don't know how Marisa can tolerate the likes of you for one second. I detest the ground you walk on."

"Meg, please," Marisa pleaded, stepping between the two adversaries, who had squared off with one another.

"So this is where you are!" All eyes turned to greet Lady Maxwell. "I've been searching frantically for the three of you. Have you lost every sense of social grace, closeting yourselves in here when you have a house full of guests?" She paused for a reply and, when no one enlightened her, she demanded in a louder voice. "Well?"

"We stand rightfully chastised, Grandmother," Justin finally agreed. "We were just about to rejoin our guests, as a matter of fact. Isn't that right, Meg?" He cast an intimidating look in her direction. "Why don't you run along with Lady Maxwell? The countess and I will follow very shortly. And mind you now, girl, behave yourself."

Meg made little attempt to conceal the sour expression on her face, but she nevertheless dutifully followed Lady Maxwell out of the room.

Now that they were alone, Marisa was bursting with curiosity about exactly what had happened in the garden, but Straeford spoke first.

"Marisa, the sooner you find an eligible husband for that . . . that sister of yours, the better it will be for all of us."

"But my lord," Marisa entreated, "I really don't think you understand Meg at all."

"Of that I am absolutely certain," he snorted.

"She's young . . . and, of course, very, very foolish and sometimes headstrong in many ways. But she is not an evil person, I'm sure you'll agree."

"I am not at all ready to agree entirely on that point, but neither am I prepared at this moment to discuss the matter at great length. Let's simply abandon this topic of discussion for the present," he said with an air of finality. Straeford extended an arm toward her and seemed anxious to put the whole matter aside. "Let us rejoin our guests. After all, it is our party, you know. And I fancy another whirl about the dance floor with you, my dear."

Marisa could not help revealing a look of amazement at the earl's unexpected demonstration of warmth and affection. "Hmmm . . . " she mused out loud. "It seems to me that I remember your telling me that you never danced."

"Oh, no, my dear. Not at all," he said good-naturedly. "What I said was that I don't dance as a rule."

"Oh, and what might be the reason for breaking that rule tonight?" she inquired.

"A beautiful lady is the only reason I should ever consider breaking that rule," he replied, leading her toward the ballroom.

Marisa sat in front of her dresser, staring absentmindedly in the mirror, pondering the night's events. All in all, it had been a rather successful evening. Every guest that had been expected had appeared, and by and large the food, the service, and the music all seemed quite satisfactory. The only incident that had marred the occasion was the unpleasantness between Justin and Meg. Poor girl, Marisa thought. The earl was no one to tamper with, and it must have been a jolt to her to experience his wrath so totally. But what caused him to be so openly hostile toward Meg? Marisa reminded herself to find out in the morning exactly what had taken place between the two of them.

Otherwise, Justin had been disarmingly amiable and charming to virtually every guest with whom he came in contact—and to Marisa as well. She had been utterly amazed and delighted at his invitation to dance. He was complimentary and flattering and, yes, even loving. Tonight he had been the way she hoped he could be, and she felt proud to be his wife. It was something she had never quite articulated in her own mind before, but now, right at this moment, a very good feeling about her marriage seemed to glow inside her.

A light rap came from the adjoining bedroom door, and before she could respond, Justin entered.

"I didn't want to let the night go by without telling you how pleased I was with the whole affair. You did a magnificent job." He bent over to kiss her lightly on the cheek and, as he did, Marisa clasped his shoulder with her hand.

"I'm so happy to hear you say that, my dear Justin. I was just sitting here thinking about..." Before she could finish her sentence, his mouth was pressed against hers, his hands gently fondling her long, silken hair. It was a long, tender, lingering kiss with their lips mutually exploring, lightly touching, barely meeting one another, and though he had not intended it to be a passionate act, Justin now found himself unable to stop. A familiar and seductive fragrance revealed itself from some point along Marisa's delicate shoulder, and he felt compelled to press her closer to him in order to drink in that mysterious scent.

Without uttering a sound, Justin lifted Marisa into his arms and, with a smile on his lips, slowly carried her to the nearby bed. The ease with which he lifted her gave Marisa a strange, conquered feeling, so strong were his sinewy arms, that she found herself consciously admitting that it was a thrilling sensation, too.

Still wrapped in his arms above the bed, Marisa felt her nightgown slowly descend to the floor. Gently, he lowered her disrobed body to the bed, and she shivered in anticipation while he put out the lone lamp on her dresser.

When he returned to her, his body was naked, and his strong hands found her in the darkness, warming her with hypnotic, repetitive caresses. It was different tonight. Somehow he was communicating a genuine desire for her in a way that made Marisa want him, too.

Afterward, Marisa cuddled next to Justin and drifted off to sleep, her hand caressing his cheek. She would later recall that secure feeling which enveloped her as she lay there, nestled close to his body.

It seemed much later, though it actually was not, that she felt his body stir, and she awakened to find Justin sitting up at the edge of the bed.

"Justin?" she called sleepily.

But he did not answer. Instead, he simply got up and left the room without a word, leaving Marisa in a state of bewilderment.

He, too, was uncertain about the significance of this

entire day's events. As he reviewed them in his mind, he sensed for some reason that they were out of character for him. He wondered what all of those guests must have thought about this new role he was assuming. Was his wife attempting to transform him into something . . . domestic or demeaning? Something less than he was before their marriage? Had he made a spectacle of himself? Even though there had been many enjoyable moments throughout the day, he could not shake loose the notion that he was now vulnerable to her, and that was a feeling he did not relish at all.

13

Straeford no longer attempted to deceive himself where his wife was concerned. His defenses against her were weakening with every passing day. Greatly disturbed by his susceptibility to her sweetness and unaffected charms, he withdrew from her behind a wall of icy indifference. Whenever possible in the following days he spurned Marisa's company, and if he was forced to be in her presence, his conversation with her was brief to the point of being curt.

Marisa bore up under this treatment of her as best she could, but it was causing her some sleepless nights and unhappy days as she tried to come to terms with Justin's erratic behavior. After shopping one morning, she arrived home in time to see her husband and Edward Harding entering the library. Immediately the major did an about-face, coming to her while Justin stood stiffly in the doorway watching them. They exchanged pleasantries until Straeford grew impatient and called to his friend. "Ed, I'll be in the library when you are ready." He bowed slightly to his wife and left them alone.

Harding was bewildered by Straeford's behavior and upon entering the library he exclaimed, "You're a deuced odd chap."

"How so?" Straeford asked as he handed him a brandy.

"Not my business, I suppose, but that was some greeting you gave your wife."

Straeford puffed on his cigar and leaned back in his chair before quipping sardonically, "Quite right, old man, it's not your business how I greet my wife."

"Well, blister me!"

"Take it easy, Ed, no offense intended." Straeford laughed and came to slip his arm about the major's shoulders. "I was only agreeing with you. You were the one who said it wasn't your business."

"Yes, well, of course." Somewhat mollified, Harding smiled sheepishly and quickly changed the subject. "So, what was the matter you wished to discuss with me?"

"I want you to read a draft of my will. The part pertaining to the heir in particular. Here." Justin thrust a paper into his friend's hand. Surprised by such a request and not knowing what to say or think, Harding simply began to study the paper in his hand. When he finally raised his eyes from the document, Justin could read the astonishment in them.

"Hell, Just, this is most irregular!"

"Will you do it?"

"Who's to say you won't be around to raise your own son?" Harding was highly agitated and he began to pace the floor, but finally he came to a stop and stared across the desk at his friend. "Besides, where does your wife come into it?"

"She doesn't! If I'm not here, I want you to raise my son."

Stupefied, Edward Harding groped for the right words to condemn Justin's heartless action. He did not wish to hurt this man who had suffered at the hands of his own mother; and yet he could never allow Justin's prejudice against women to crush that sweet girl who was his wife. "Just," he gulped, "two women could not be more dissimilar than the present countess and your . . . mother."

Straeford flung himself out of his chair and leaned across the desk toward his friend. "There is no telling for sure with *any* woman."

"I . . . I can't agree with you. Lady Marisa is a good woman, and I won't usurp her position. It ain't right to even think about it." The two friends glared across the intervening space at one another until Harding broke the strained atmosphere by moving around the desk to grasp Straeford by the arm. "Just, you know I'd do about anything for you, but don't ask this of me. I'd be happy to be your son's guardian if anything ever happened to you. You know that. But I would never take the child away from your wife . . . unless . . . and mind I say 'unless' I were to discover my judgment of Lady Straeford were in error."

Although the earl continued to argue the point for the next half hour with his friend, Harding remained adamant. There was no dissuading him and at times he waxed eloquent in defense of the countess until Straeford finally admitted defeat and accepted the major's condition.

"So, when is the happy occasion?"

Straeford blanched and looked a little foolish as he admitted, "Don't know yet."

"Don't know? But I thought that . . ."

Justin shook his head negatively and waved the document in his direction. "This is a precaution. You know how much it means to me to see the line secured. I didn't sacrifice myself for Straeford Park alone."

"Some sacrifice. That's some woman you've taken to wife."

The earl did not agree or disagree with Harding's evaluation.

After being summoned to the library by the earl, Marisa was briskly informed that he had been made a brigadier general and would be leaving for Portugal soon. Her heart plummeted to her feet. "When are you leaving?"

He smiled unpleasantly, interpreting her question as a desire to be rid of him. "Don't be quite so anxious for my departure, my dear. No definite date has been set as of yet."

"I didn't ask because I was anxious to see you leave," she protested, but he ignored her rebuttal.

"I have made some provisions for the future."

"Provisions for the future?"

"Yes, I have arranged for everything including our offspring." He observed his wife's heightened color and eagerly asked, "Is there the chance you are already with child, Marisa?"

"I . . . I do not believe so . . . Justin." His face fell, sending a pang of regret through her for having failed him.

"Well, the situation could change at any time," he continued matter-of-factly. "Therefore, I have taken the precaution of providing for my heir."

"I don't understand. Precaution? What precaution?" She was instantly alert. Knowing this man as she now did, nothing would surprise her.

Impassively he explained the condition of the will making Harding the child's guardian.

Marisa was relieved. "He is an excellent choice. I would gladly accept his advice."

He leaned back in his chair and regarded her closely, waiting for her reaction as he explained, "I don't think you fully understand, my dear. The will states that if Harding deemed it necessary, he would have the power to rear the child himself."

She grew deathly pale. "Why? Whatever reason could he . . . would you wish to take the child . . . from me . . . its mother?"

He clutched and twisted a pen between his fingers before replying, "There are mothers and then there are mothers, if you get my meaning."

"No, no I don't!"

"Let it suffice to say I am *protecting* the child."

"Against its *mother?*"

"Precisely!"

"Y—you are . . . unbelievable! Well, let me tell you, *Lord Straeford,* I will fight that document with every breath in my body!" She was standing defiantly before him, her chin thrust forward, her hands on her hips, and Straeford, observing her through half-closed lids, was filled with admiration for her. For some reason her attitude pleased him. No matter how he threatened her, she dared to challenge him again. If the situation weren't so serious, he would have been tempted to give in to her and forget the whole matter. Instead he decided to be conciliatory.

"Calm yourself, my dear. There will be no need to fight anyone as long as you are a good mother, and Harding is convinced you will be."

But Marisa was not to be appeased. "Then it is, obviously, you who is not convinced!"

Straeford shrugged as he came toward her. "Who is to tell with a woman?"

It was always the same motivation driving him. His mother. Oh, how she wished she could have done more than banish her picture to the gallery. If only she could send her memory into oblivion.

"Don't look so fierce, madam. I told you it is *only* a precaution."

"A precaution I find both unnecessary and insulting."

"Nevertheless, it will remain as part of the will!" Hard green eyes met cold blue ones, and she was goaded to rashness in an attempt to wound him as he had done to her.

"This is preposterous. It is all of no consequence since we discuss a nonexistent child!"

Her retort hit home for his eyes stabbed back at hers, and there was an ominous note in his voice when next he spoke. "Oh, but it is a matter of great consequence for I do not intend that you shall remain childless much longer." And before she could utter another protest, she found herself firmly clamped in his arms. "It was part of the bargain, Marisa. You remember our 'infamous bargain,' don't you, my dear?" he asked mockingly as his hand cupped one of her breasts.

"Yes, oh yes, how could I forget?" she cried in a frenzy. "But even you would not be so contemptible as to take me here, my lord Straeford, for the whole household to see."

"Oh, would I not? This is my home. And you are my wife!" The incredulous expression which streaked across her face brought a deprecating laugh to his lips, and he held her at arm's length, shaking her lightly. "No, Marisa, even *I* . . . with my blackened reputation, will try to refrain from such contemptible behavior . . . unless you provoke me further."

"Provoke you! It is you who has provoked me by your heartless insensitivity . . ." Instantly she found herself free of his hold and alone in the room, but she was too angry at the moment to ponder his sudden disappearance.

Devil! Devil! Devil! she cried to herself. Now he was plotting to take away her rights as a mother. Why, oh why, had fate given her a man so totally consumed with a need to protect his heritage, but with no need for her love?

To celebrate the tentative reconciliation between Angus Loftus and his son John, a family dinner was held at John and Ruth Loftus's home in Islington. Only Straeford had not attended the occasion. As far as he was concerned, John Loftus was a coward beneath contempt, and Angus Loftus was a traitor to his principles. It was just as well that he had not been there, Marisa reflected as she and Meg returned to the house on Berkeley Square later that evening, for his abrasive personality in their midst might have hampered the overtures being made between father and son.

And as if to further convince her of that opinion, Straeford, dark and brooding, met the sisters in the entrance hall.

Cowed by his austere appearance, Meg clutched at Marisa's hand. There had been a considerable change in Meg's attitude toward her sister and her husband since that frightening night in the garden.

"My lady," Straeford approached his wife ignoring his sister-in-law completely. "Will you accompany me to the drawing room?"

She knew it did not augur well to be addressed so formally by the earl, and Meg's apprehension did little to lessen her own qualms. Nevertheless, she gave her sister a fleeting smile of assurance and followed Straeford into the drawing room.

"I see you are wearing the Straeford emerald," he

remarked pointedly, surprising her by such an observation, but before she had the opportunity to reply she realized that they were not alone. A tall, thin, sober-faced man dressed plainly in dark brown and twisting a tricorne hat in his hand stood near the opened French windows which were letting in a cool spring breeze.

"Lady Straeford," Justin continued to address her formally, "this is Jeremy Clock. He has a story to tell you which I think you will find fascinating. Please be seated." She glanced at his stony face in puzzlement as he silently indicated a straight-back chair for her to occupy. "In due time your questions will be answered, my dear." A corner of his mouth turned up in a mockery of a smile.

After seating herself, Marisa realized she was directly facing Mr. Clock while the earl had positioned himself out of her line of vision. Although he could observe her clearly, she would have to turn her head in order to see him.

"You may begin, Mr. Clock."

"Well, it's like this m'lady. I be a Bow Street Runner." Some broken teeth showed a kindly smile.

"Bow Street Runner?" Marisa was mystified and spun about to face Justin whose set features revealed nothing.

"Continue, Mr. Clock." Straeford looked past his wife to the runner who shifted uncomfortably from one foot to the other. There was something about this handsome couple which disturbed him, and he wished he were any place but here.

"You see, ma'am, I be trackin' this gang o' jewel thieves. They been operatin' perty reg'lar . . . 'bout a yer. Verry clever slip'en val'bles an' gems owt ta country."

"Yes, I see, but I don't understand what this has to do with me? Justin, I . . ." She tilted her head in his direction.

"If you'll listen, I'm sure, Mr. Clock will eventually get to the point of his discourse."

The countess flushed at the tone of voice he used with her before this stranger, and Mr. Clock, sensing her embarrassment, rushed on.

"Last night we captured the lot of 'em . . . red 'anded, ma'am."

"Well, good for you," Marisa tried to remain polite amidst her growing frustration.

"T'wer lucky fer you, too, ma'am, cause we fount yor ring 'mong the stol't jewels."

"My ring?" She darted a look at the emerald on her third finger, left hand, as Justin held out another jewel with the Straeford crest etched in its center. "Mr. Thomas of Richardson's on Bond Street identified it as the Straeford heirloom and Mr. Clock was instructed to return it to me."

"But I . . ." Marisa was staring in horror from one ring to the other. When the significance of the two emeralds blazed itself into her consciousness, she lurched to her feet, almost oversetting herself in her agitation, but Straeford clamped a firm arm about her shoulders, steadying her. Then he turned to Mr. Clock and dismissed him. Being rather astute, Jeremy Clock could see that the lady was in for a raking-down. Hawking her jewels for paste ones! Well, a domestic quarrel was no place for the likes of him. Quickly the Bow Street Runner clapped his hat on his head and left the august couple confronting one another.

The breeze whispering against the curtains was the only sound to disturb the awful silence in the room. Straeford swore under his breath and strode away, leaving Marisa alone in the center of the salon. Suddenly he whirled round and faced her. "All right, what are you waiting for?" his voice cracked like a whip into the tension-filled air.

"Justin . . . I don't know . . . understand exactly how . . . this happened . . ."

"For God's sake, woman, don't feign innocence! What kind of a fool do you take me for? Just tell me who you gave the stone to. Who helped you replace the Straeford heirloom with paste?" He almost strangled with anger.

"You can't believe I had any part in this deception." But she could see that he did. "Of what are you accusing me?"

"Damn you! The evidence is before your very eyes." He stalked over to her, grasped her left hand, and held the emeralds next to one another. "Now, ask me of what

206

I am accusing you." In disgust he thrust her arm away from him. "Give me the name of your accomplice . . . or should I say lover!"

"Oh, no!" She placed shaking fingers to her quivering lips.

Although Justin would not admit it even to himself, he was blinded by the pain of her apparent infidelity and could not perceive the situation rationally. A seething black rage was engulfing him, and his harsh words would not be stemmed.

"So, you intend to protect this . . . swine. Who would have thought a conniving bitch such as you could show so much loyalty!"

The injustice of his attack finally overrode the limits of her endurance. "You have no right to speak."

"No right! Why you faithless slut . . ." Hatred blazed out of his eyes at her and he raised his hand to strike her defiant face. Bravely she stood her ground and his threatening gesture wavered, his hand fell to his side convulsively clenching and unclenching. "Get out of my sight, you perfidious bitch!" he rasped through gritted teeth, barely able to control himself. "Get out of my sight before I kill you!"

With as much dignity as she could muster from her shaking limbs, Marisa managed to cross to the door. Before she could escape from his presence, he hurled a final parting rebuff in her direction. "Go to your lover for all I care!"

Proudly she swept around and met his black frown with one of despair. "You have wronged me . . . grievously wronged me," she asserted quietly and slipped out of the room.

Meg was waiting for Marisa on the first landing and assisted her trembling sister to her bedroom. There Marisa collapsed into a heap and sobbed out a halting monologue of the accusations that Justin had launched at her. At its end she lay back drained, unable any longer to think clearly at all. Eventually needing relief from the shattering experience, she fell asleep, and Meg stole away.

It was shortly after dawn when Jenkins was forced out of bed to answer the pounding on the front door.

There he was confronted by John and Angus Loftus holding a cowering Foxworth between them.

"Tell his lordship we have come to see him on a matter of great importance," Angus Loftus bellowed as he pushed past the butler.

"B-but Lord Straeford retired not so very long ago, gentlemen, and I do not think he would wish to be disturbed at this hour of the morning." Jenkins was not a courageous man, and he had heard and seen enough last night to know better than confront his master in one of his black tempers.

"Either you get him down here, my good man, or I will!" Loftus roared.

The butler did not like the look in the eye of this man much more than that of his lordship. "Very well," he acquiesced and showed them into the drawing room.

After drinking heavily and pacing the floor half the night, Straeford was in no condition to face his father-in-law. Bleary eyed, unshaven and still wearing a dressing gown, he stormed into the salon and scowled at the assembled figures.

"What the devil is this all about?" he demanded furiously.

Angry color suffused the elder Loftus's face as he attempted to control the rage he felt against this black-hearted devil he had forced his daughter to marry. His life-long ambition to see his children marry well and establish themselves in society was causing nothing but grief and despair. He had almost lost his only son and he had sold his devoted daughter into bondage to this ... scoundrel. Swallowing hard, he forced back his outrage. "Lord Straeford, I believe you are under a misconception concerning a certain emerald ring."

"So, she ran to you, did she?"

"If you mean Meg ..."

"Meg? What does she have to do with this?"

"She came to me last night to inform me of your accusations against her sister!"

"I don't intend to discuss this matter with you, let alone Foxworth!" Straeford insisted darkly as he strode to the door.

"Just one minute, my lord," Loftus shouted before

Straeford could leave them. "Foxworth is directly involved in the disappearance of the emerald."

"Oh, he is, is he!" Justin made straight for Richard Foxworth who shrivelled in his chair. "So, you're the blackguard . . ."

"My lord Straeford," John Loftus stepped between the two men halting the earl in his tracks. "There has been a terrible mixup and if you will let Foxworth speak, I believe this whole unpleasant mess can quickly be cleared up."

"Do you now?" Straeford eyed his brother-in-law contemptuously. The slimmer, younger man neither flinched nor looked away, surprising Justin so much that he capitulated.

"Oh, very well. Let's have it. What cock-and-bull story is he about to tell me?"

Foxworth came abruptly to his feet and spoke for the first time. "N-no cock-and-bull-story, I swear, Straeford. Lady Marisa had no part in it . . . I was desperate . . . badly dipped, and Loftus," he eyed the older man resentfully, "refused to pay my debts any longer—now that my usefulness to him was at an end. He'd got what he wanted . . ."

"Richard, we are not here to discuss your grievances. It is my sister's integrity that we are discussing."

"Yes, yes, of course. I shall get right to the point. It was the night of the Claridges' soiree. You were to attend with your lady, Straeford, but you'd suddenly left town. Remember?" If he had hoped to disconcert his lordship, he was sadly mistaken. Straeford continued to stare questioningly at him. "Get on with it, Foxworth."

"Oh, very well," Foxworth pouted. "The evening of the party I escorted Lady Maxwell and your wife there and back again. It was on the way home that Lady Straeford lost the emerald ring in my carriage. I saw it as the answer to my prayers, a God-sent opportunity to get out from under the hatches. I couldn't stop myself. So I had a paste replica of the ring made up, passed it off to your wife as the real thing, and sold the heirloom. I never thought to be found out. It was just my luck that the jewel thieves were captured before they could unload it in Holland."

Straeford thrust an agitated hand through his uncombed hair. He found himself wanting to believe Foxworth, but he was not completely convinced. The man was a known liar and a coxcomb.

"My daughter came to me when she thought it was stolen, blaming herself for wearing it without having it sized . . ."

"Are you trying to tell me she never had it cut down?"

"All I know," Loftus said sincerely, "is that she begged me to locate it for her."

"Why couldn't she and Foxworth have planned it that way, so he'd get the capital, and she'd still have the ring with no one the wiser," Straeford calculated coldly.

"Are you suggesting my own daughter would perpetrate such a deceitful hoax on me?" Angus was flabbergasted.

"Women have been known to do much worse."

"No!" Foxworth cried. "I swear on my mother's grave it ain't so!"

"And I swear on my daughter's honor it wasn't like that!"

"He'll not believe any of us, Father," John's voice shook with suppressed emotion. "Perhaps the Claridges or, better still, Lady Maxwell might convince him, but not us. We're not gentlemen in his eyes, and therefore are incapable of his peculiar kind of honor. The only thing he'll understand is a challenge from one of us to defend Marisa's honor. Very well, my lord, consider yourself challenged."

"Wait now," Richard Foxworth intervened. "If anyone is to challenge his lordship . . . it must be . . . m-me. I-I'm the one responsible. I'm at your service, sir. Name your seconds."

Their audacity unexpectedly amused Straeford. The cringing dandy and the cowardly soldier stood belligerently confronting him while the elderly Loftus looked as if he were about to pummel him with his fist. "There will be no challenge, *gentlemen*," he emphasized just as a commotion in the outer hallway reached their ears and drew the attention of the four men.

"Forgive me, my lord," a flustered Jenkins peeked around the door, "but more . . . visitors . . ."

"Never mind, Jenkins, we'll announce ourselves." Lady Maxwell, followed by Meg, entered. "So what Meg has been telling me was true."

"Grandmother?" Straeford was once again annoyed and exasperated. "This doesn't concern you."

"That's where you're wrong, my boy. I can straighten everything out in a minute."

"This beats all! I have a quarrel with my wife and it turns into a family fracas. So, Grandmother, you too have obviously come to defend the lady—and Meg," he added with cynicism, "have you done your part by assembling the participants or do you also have something to say?" Meg remained mute as Justin looked around the determined group. "You know," a spark of mischief glinted in his eyes, "the only one missing is the lady herself. Shall I send for her?"

There was a chorus of protests which was finally overridden by Lady Maxwell who insisted that she be given five minutes to settle the misunderstanding.

"Very well, Grandmother, the stage is yours. Everyone is already aware of most of the scenario," he smirked. "I'm intrigued as to what revelations you shall divulge."

"Don't be flippant with me, Justin. I shall be as brief as possible. Your wife left the ring to be cut down to size at Hanovers'. It was they who informed her that the emerald was a fake. That's when she came to me, to ask my advice in telling you, Justin. She did not know whether Foxworth had exchanged the rings, or if it had happened some time ago. There was the distinct possibility that your mother might have used the genuine stone to pay off some debt. We decided to consult my solicitor and have him do some quiet investigating before we brought the matter to your attention, Justin. Of course, we did not anticipate this turn of events which brought to light the real culprit."

There was not a sound in the room from anyone when she finished her disclosures, and uncomfortably Straeford observed the people around him. While Foxworth hung his head in shame, Lady Maxwell looked uncertainly at her grandson, and Meg eyed him reproachfully; finally the hostile expressions of John and Angus Loftus jolted him into speaking.

"Apparently, I have been wrong," he stated in an arrogant manner revealing none of his inner turmoil and self-condemnation. "It seems I owe the countess an apology. So if you will all kindly return to your own homes, I shall get on with the business."

There were some angry protests from Loftus and his son, but Lady Maxwell quickly silenced them by insisting that there had been enough outside interference, and that a married couple had to come to terms with one another by themselves. Then she shushed Meg upstairs to bed and led the Loftuses out of the house before they realized what was happening. Only Foxworth was detained long enough by the earl to be given an ultimatum to either stay out of the Straefords' lives in the future or his life would be forfeit. Then he personally ushered Foxworth to the front door and thrust him out of the house.

Straeford paced the drawing room floor waiting for the Countess to join him. He rubbed the back of his neck and sighed heavily. What an embarrassing mess! How many times had he been proven wrong where his wife was concerned? And to think this time it was his in-laws, whom he held in such low esteem, that had shown him his error. Their attack had come as a complete surprise to him. He had no experience in his own life of such strong family loyalty. Familial affection and solidarity were not common among the aristocracy. Certainly they were middle-class values he could not fault, and grudgingly he had to admit his admiration. Until tonight he had cavalierly dismissed the Loftus family as beneath his consideration, but they had revealed character depths worthy of his respect, and he was surprised to discover his approval of them. John, the coward; Angus, the social-climbing cit and even Meg, the ambitious coquette, had shown strength, dignity and compassion tonight.

His wife's arrival put an end to his contemplations.

The Straefords stared at each other across the width of the room. Very apprehensive about the reason for this summons, Marisa held herself stiffly together, unconsciously clutching the top button of her blue peignoir until her hand showed white. Noticing her tense body and red-rimmed eyes, Straeford's feelings of guilt grew, and in a sympathetic voice he asked her to be seated.

Marisa eyed him warily wondering what kind of a game he was playing. She was not about to be lulled into a sense of peace by his pleasant manner. Refusing to move any farther into the room, she answered him. "I prefer to remain standing, if you don't mind."

"As you wish, Marisa. I just thought you would be more comfortable seated. You look as if you are ready to fall apart."

Although Marisa knew she looked dreadful, she did not think Justin's appearance was very much better, with his unruly hair and unshaven face; nevertheless she refrained from commenting on it, and remained where she was.

Justin took a step toward her and involuntarily she jumped edging closer to the door. She was hanging on to her composure by a mere thread and any further abuse from him would send her into hysterics.

Sensing her mood, Straeford backed away. "Will you stop staring at me as if I were a hunter stalking its prey?"

"I cannot help how I appear to you." There was still a touch of defiance left in her.

"I promise I shall stay over here if you will only sit down."

His attitude was confusing her, but realizing her knees were shaking and ready to give out, she decided to acquiesce and slid into the nearest chair.

"That's better," he smiled and seated himself on the edge of a table at the far side of the room.

"Last night ... I made some wild accusations against you ... which I regret."

Marisa was thunderstruck by his admission, and felt a sense of relief sweeping through her.

"I have since learned the truth from your father and Lady Maxwell. Foxworth has admitted that he tricked you."

Her relief turned to resentment. "I see. Now that

there is proof of my innocence you are ready to believe me. My own assertion was not good enough."

"Your anger is understandable. I should have given you the opportunity to explain. Will you accept my apology?"

"Oh, no, my lord," she jumped to her feet tossing her long golden hair behind her. "Not this time! You have insulted me every way possible in the last four months and . . . and I will not accept your apology just like that." She snapped her fingers in the air, her whole body quivering with the effort of her outburst.

Justin was quiet for a few seconds attempting to control his temper as pride warred with his determination to be fair. "If you think I'm going to go down on my knees and beg your forgiveness, you can forget it."

"Even that would not be enough." Her chin arched higher and she swept back a wisp of hair that had fallen across her eyes.

"I'll be damned!" he choked.

"Yes, yes, perhaps you will be!"

Surprisingly, her response amused him and his face quirked in a wry smile as he chuckled, "That is a distinct possibility, my dear."

His quixotic reply left her bereft of any further words, and she just stared at him as he came across the room to take her hands in his. "So, I am not forgiven. Shall we leave it at that for the time being? You . . . and I are too fatigued to discuss this matter any further at present. Perhaps we can try another time. Right now what we both need is some sleep. Come." He slipped his arm about her waist. Succumbing to his gentleness, she went with him unresisting to the bedroom where he surprised her further by slipping the robe from her shoulders and assisting her into bed. "I shall see that you are not disturbed in the morning my dear. Sleep as late as you wish."

Torn between a sense of guilt and a longing to comfort and be comforted, Justin leaned over her and brushed a light kiss upon her forehead, compassion welling up in him for his wife.

Fatigued by her emotional turmoil and unable to comprehend the mood of the stranger she had married,

Marisa simply closed her eyes and was immediately asleep.

Confused and depressed, Justin withdrew to his own room.

Sitting among the dowagers at Almack's and watching Meg dance with one gallant after another, Marisa wished her sister would soon make up her mind and settle on a beau before the Season was over and all the young men were off to Portugal with the army. Straeford, too, was scheduled to leave for the campaign in Portugal, but she still did not know when. Since the fiasco over the emerald ring she had seen very little of him. The countess shifted uncomfortably on a hard seat. She had gambled and lost with her angry decision to refuse his apology that night. She had hoped that Justin would at last open his eyes and see her as she truly was but he refused. A solution to their torment was not forthcoming. He made no further overtures to rectify the situation between them.

Marisa was not to know the restraint under which her husband was laboring to do what he believed to be the right thing. He felt his wife was justified in her attitude toward him. His treatment of her had been harsh and cruel from the beginning, and there was no guaranteeing it would not happen again. He believed his distrust of women was too ingrained in him to change even if he wanted to. In this bleak frame of mind he made no attempts to patch up his differences with Marisa.

Her reverie was interrupted by the arrival of Lady Maxwell.

"I wondered if I would find you here." The old dowager seated herself beside her granddaughter-in-law.

"Where else should I be when you worked so hard to secure us vouchers?"

"That's not what I was referring to."

"Oh, what did you mean then?"

"Justin leaves for Portugal tonight."

"No!" Marisa ejaculated before she could hide her shock. "He . . . he never told me." She was seized by embarrassment—embarrassment at such an insult. Why had he not mentioned it to her?

"I suspected as much," Lady Maxwell said with great exasperation. "I'm beginning to believe that grandson of mine is a dolt, after all."

"Ohh, he's much . . . much worse than that!" Marisa hissed vehemently under her breath.

"Let him go. You're better off without him." Lady Maxwell watched Marisa's face pale.

"Yes, yes, you're absolutely right. I am through with him." Marisa settled back in her chair to watch the young couples waltzing. Unfortunately it brought to mind a night not so very long ago when Justin had held her in his arms and her hopes had soared only to be cruelly dashed in the next instant. Yes, let him go without so much as a goodbye. She would be well rid of him.

"I suppose you will want all communiqués concerning him to continue to be sent to me then?"

"Wh-what communiqués are you referring to, Lady Maxwell?"

"Oh, you know, the usual war reports—if he is wounded . . ." Lady Maxwell smiled indulgently as she watched Marisa scurry across the hall on her way home.

Boxes and luggage were stacked in the hallway, and the earl, dressed in his scarlet uniform, was conferring with Billings when his wife entered. Catching sight of her standing motionless in her pink sarcenet gown Justin caught his breath. Their eyes met and locked in an unguarded moment of regret and yearning. Wrenching his eyes free, he frowned and demanded, "What brings you home so early?"

"You're leaving?" she asked breathlessly trying to control the tumult of emotions crowding her breast.

"I'd assume that's obvious," he drawled, hoping his ridicule would antagonize her into a like response and lessen the danger of any tender emotions erupting between them. That would only lead to the weakening of his resolve to put this episode in his life behind him.

But she persisted in a faint quavering voice. "And you weren't going to tell me?"

"How could I? You weren't here!"

"But all day . . . no message . . ."

Her bright blue eyes censured him unmercifully, and he found himself swinging away from her to give Billings some quick orders. Then he stepped around the many boxes to take her unresisting arm in his and lead her into the darkened library where a mere candle flickered on the desk.

He placed the desk between them and began toying with a pen before explaining in a more kindly voice, "There seemed no need to disturb you with my departure."

"No need? . . but I am your . . . wife."

"I don't see where that makes any difference under the circumstances. We both know this separation is for the best. So what does it matter how it is effected? And frankly, Marisa, I thought you would prefer it this way after our last unfortunate encounter. It would be foolish for either of us to say things we really don't mean . . . just because I am going away."

Marisa wrapped her arms about her waist and leaned weakly against the desk for support. He was scorning her attempts at a reconciliation. He did not want one, and he did not want her here now.

"Our life together has not been easy . . . for either of us. You will be the first to admit that, I think."

She lowered her head in acquiescence to his statement, and it only reaffirmed his belief that her injured pride over not being told of his imminent departure had brought her here tonight. He knew she would be relieved once he was gone. Straeford walked away from her into the darkened recesses of the room. Impulsively, her arms went out to him, but the figure in the shadows did not heed the gesture as he cast his eyes upward—anywhere but on this woman who caused him such torment.

A blanket of silence covered the still room as the two tortured figures struggled with their doubts and longings until Billings knocked on the door and broke the tension.

"All is ready, my lord."

"I shall be along directly," Straeford said as he moved out of the shadows and threw the pen he was still holding onto the desk. "Well, I am off."

"I shall . . . write." She made a last desperate effort.

"If you wish," he hesitated and then forced himself to add, "but there's no need to trouble yourself."

"It's no trouble. I should . . . like to."

Her solicitude made him extremely uncomfortable. "Yes, well, I may not be able to respond."

"I know you shall be very busy, but if time permits, I would appreciate a line or two—now and then."

"I'll see what I can manage. Goodbye, Marisa. Take care of yourself."

"Justin!" she cried as he wrenched open the door to leave. Swinging about to face her, his hand clenched the door jamb, holding himself in check. "Please . . . my lord, be careful."

Suddenly he crossed to her and, taking her hand in his, he kissed it. She placed tentative fingers on his bent head, and he jerked away and strode out of the library before he allowed any further demonstrative action between them to take place.

Straeford refused to look back as the carriage pulled out, and he held himself rigid until Berkeley Square was left far behind. Then with a sigh of relief he thanked God for Napoleon Bonaparte. The campaign would keep him from thinking or remembering.

Marisa had watched his departure from the window of the library. There was no backward glance, no smile, or wave of the hand to remember him by—just his brusque, controlled farewell. Silent tears coursed down her face as she fingered the pen he had been holding and she sat in his leather chair, wishing and remembering.

14

All during the crossing of the Bay of Biscay Marisa had fretted disconsolately. What would Lord Straeford say to her when he saw her in Portugal? She was mad to dare this journey without her husband's approval. And yet, when Lady Maxwell had suggested that Marisa accompany Ann Harding's party of wives traveling to Lisbon, something reckless had leaped in her heart and she felt she must go. Although she had fought against loving the man who made such havoc of her emotions, the truth could not be denied. She loved Justin helplessly. Why else had she suffered over the thought of his entanglement with Amanda Relington? And why such frenzy on the night of his departure lest he be gone without her seeing him?

But the parting had been so inconclusive. And in the six months he had been gone he had barely troubled himself to write a line to her. There had been no reply to her last letter.

And so she took Lady Maxwell's suggestion and came in haste to Portugal. She had not even waited for a reply to the note to Lord Straeford that apprised him of her coming. And Mrs. Harding had written to her husband, Edward, telling him of the countess's sudden decision. She also warned him that she was taking their son with her. At first Ann had considered leaving little Eddie at home with his maternal grandparents and his nurse. But she could not bear to be parted from the child, and, instead, brought him and the nurse and all his infant trappings with her to Portugal along with her newest and best friend, Marisa Straeford.

Valerie Claridge and the newlywed Carol Belvoir tried to dissemble their curiosity over Lady Straeford's sudden decision to accompany them, but secretly they burned to know the inside story of the Straeford marital relationship. The Earl of Straeford and his countess were considered an ill-sorted match by the gossip-loving *ton*. Much speculation flew among members of that élite sect in eager anticipation of discovering a juicy morsel to satisfy their avid hunger for tales of marital discord. During most of the journey Marisa had managed to turn aside her companions' subtle probings, and to keep her thoughts private.

Only Ann Harding knew what it cost the countess to chance the displeasure of that forbidding man Lady Straeford called husband. Having known Justin for a time when she lived in India, Ann believed the man to be of a hard nature whose consuming interest was the pursuit of war. That his lovely wife had lived in a state of anxiety ever since the news of the battle of Talavera reached London would never occur to such a man as Straeford, Ann feared.

The threat of more battles need not have troubled Marisa. Unknown to the British public, the Duke of Wellington had no thought for further engagement of the enemy. Talavera had been such a bloody battle so bitterly fought that both sides were forced to a standstill. However, Wellington had succeeded in holding his position and the French finally withdrew late in July of 1809.

But it was a fruitless victory. Wellington was beset by a host of calamities that cost him his hard-won advantage. First the Portuguese general, Venegas, did not appear as was planned; next, Soult was on the march again, and finally, Cuesta did not hold Talavera as ordered, but evacuated it instead. As with Oporto, the British were forced to call off pursuit of the French in order to regroup and recommence battle plans again.

No. Wellington was not about to engage again until he was quite ready. And when he did, it would be to fulfill a grand design he was constructing for the safety of Portugal and the destruction of the French. But the British government and people, and the Portuguese government and people, and even Wellington's own men were fretful and discouraged, wondering why the duke so often seemed to prefer caution to glory.

As the summer of 1809 wore on, there was hardly an officer who did not expect to embark for home. Wellington was under constant pressure to provide reasons why the British should remain in Portugal with the outlook so unpromising. Even the Military Secretary at the Horse Guards talked of sending Wellington to India should they evacuate Portugal. But the "Iron Duke" was not to be stampeded into hasty action. His was a campaign, for the present, of "knotted ropes." If anything went wrong, Wellington was heard to say that he "tied a knot and went on." He would wait his time. Nevertheless, the future success of his methods could not be discerned at that time, and dissension was rife.

The temporary cessation in combat was unknown to Marisa however, and she suffered visions of Justin wounded in battle. She wished him removed from harm's way, even though she knew her lord lived for war—that he found the pursuits of ordinary life dull and uninspiring —that a certain dark strain in his nature sought violence and conflict.

Still, she was sure there was another side to Justin— the one he concealed from everyone. Once she had seen a flash of his deeper and, she prayed, truer nature. That first night in her father's house she had received an intuition of his torment and yearning toward tenderness. Marisa had to discover whether her instincts about the man were true or not.

And what if she were wrong? What if there were no heart made for love and tenderness within the man, but only stone clear through, as he had done his best to convince her so far?

Instinctively, she turned away from that thought. She would face it, if it became necessary, in time. For the present, she only hoped he had received her latest letter and would be there to meet her when she arrived.

Straeford, in fact, had received all of his wife's letters but had not replied because he deliberately delayed reading them. One letter he had carried in the pocket of his tunic, and at stray moments when his hand inadvertently touched the thick parchment, he would feel a start of pleasure that angered him. Then he would grasp the missive as if to throw it away but could not bring himself to do so.

Eventually he did read it in the privacy of his tent at his outpost in the lonely Beira Valley, and as he read the softly flowing sentences by the flicker of candle flame, he was transported back to Straeford Park. He felt the warmth of Marisa reach out to him and saw the gleam of her smile, and wondered how it was that that white witch took such hold of his imagination.

She wrote that Meg had become engaged to the Fairfax boy and that every prospect for happiness now existed for the couple. But her most important information was that she was studying Portuguese and reading Camões's *Lusiads* in translation. "I believe the soul of a nation is expressed in its national epic," she wrote. Witch! What was her muse that led her so unerringly to those private pursuits that he felt were uniquely his own? He had tried to throw her off the scent that time he had found her among his books in the library at Berkeley Square, but obviously to no avail. No doubt she would discover the convent at Alcobaça too.

Not only had Marisa discovered the abbey in her studies, but she was planning to visit it as well. Straeford would have strangled her had he known.

The day Edward Harding received his wife's letter informing him of Lady Straeford's projected arrival, he went in search of Straeford and stuck his head in his friend's tent.

"Busy?" he queried.

222

"I'm trying to finish a dispatch to Wellington if I could only find ten consecutive minutes without some damned interruption," Straeford replied, not troubling to dissemble his annoyance.

"Sorry, old man," Harding rejoined without the slightest contrition and settled himself comfortably in a chair near his friend's desk. "Oh I say," Harding noticed the pink envelope cast unopened to one side of the desk. "You haven't read your mail."

Compressing his lips, Straeford grunted something unintelligible.

"But it's from the countess. Surely you want to know what she has to say."

"No, damn it, I don't!" Straeford exploded.

"Deuce take it, but you're a damn odd fish, Just. But do as you please." Harding walked out on his comrade.

Straeford watched him go, and then flicked his eyes to the pink envelope. Grinding his teeth, he went back to his report. An hour later he thrust back his chair, and cursing, stared down at the blank sheet of paper. He strode to the other side of the tent, stopped, came back and grabbed the pink envelope, ripping it open.

"My God!" She was coming to Portugal and it was too late to stop her!

Edward Harding and Roger Claridge acted as hosts to the party of British wives when they docked at Lisbon. The gentlemen met the ladies and their entourage at the quay with carriages ready to transport them to their hired villas which once housed the Portuguese nobility. Marisa and Ann were to share a residence that Harding had secured for them, as Valerie and Carol were to share another acquired by Roger.

Lisbon seemed a giant cauldron of teeming life. Brilliant sunshine flooded everywhere. Many of the narrow streets were crowded with barefoot *varinas* carrying creels of fish to market in baskest delicately balanced on their heads, and peddlers of every description were hawking their wares of birds and flowers and fruit. Soldiers also, both British and Portuguese, swarmed the streets, and none on his best behavior.

As their coach pressed on through Black Horse Square where the statue of Dom José in plumed helmet dominated the lower city, Marisa caught fleeting glimpses of broad, tree-lined avenues. Above them climbed houses and buildings that clung perilously to mounting hills. They reached daringly into a sky of such crystalline blue that it took Marisa's breath away.

The carriage ride was brief, and soon they turned through a pair of magnificent wrought iron gates. They followed a broad circular drive lined with tall cypresses and pulled up before a three-storied structure of white stucco topped by a roof of deep red tiles. Each window of the second story supported its own carved balcony over which flowed trailing vines and climbing red roses. The uppermost story displayed a gallery of columns and arches in shadowy recesses that suggested an aura of mystery and seclusion. The faint sounds of a mournful melody drifted hauntingly from the darkened corridors above.

"Hush," Ann whispered to her companions. "What is that sound I hear?"

"That's probably the gardener's son serenading one of the upstairs maids. You'll find the Portuguese to be a very musical people, my dear," Edward enlightened his wife.

"What a lovely sound," Marisa added her thoughts to the others.

Once inside, the sudden shift from brilliant sunlight to shadowy darkness almost blinded the ladies. Gradually they were able to discern the enchanting design of the home they were to occupy during their sojourn in Lisbon.

"It is breathtaking," Marisa murmured to Ann.

"I cannot believe my eyes," Ann rejoined eagerly. "It is a veritable palace."

The floor on which they stood was a tiled mosaic of geometric pattern in varying shades of sienna and green. Hanging from a high vaulted ceiling that reached the full three stories above hung an ornate lantern made of golden panes of leaded glass supported by a massive black chain riveted securely into the darkened ceiling above.

Sunlight could be seen gleaming at the other end of

the long central hallway which was lined with doors and arches that led into chambers beyond. An imposing carved staircase curved up to the second floor where a gallery circled above.

"But Edward, such a monstrously vast establishment you have chosen. Marisa and I shall be lost in these dark corridors. However shall I find the nursery?" She was breathless with excitement. "And all the marble and gold . . ."

"The Portuguese nobility go in for a rather ostentatious display, my dear. I'm sure you can accustom yourself to the grand style, can you not?"

"Well, dear husband, I should be needle-witted were I to complain of such luxury. What do you say to these sumptuous accommodations, Marisa?"

"I'm all agog," she smiled. "It is so good of you, Major Harding, to allow me to intrude myself into your plans."

"Nonsense, dear lady. I am delighted to be of service. As soon as Ann's letter reached me, I set about locating the best possible establishment."

"Nevertheless, I apologize for my rag manners in thrusting myself forward so unexpectedly, but my decision to accompany Ann and your son was made rather suddenly," Marisa continued to apologize.

"I'll hear no more about it, madam. There was no trouble in finding a large enough residence, as you can see. Many of the fine houses hereabouts are empty since the Regent and his court fled to Brazil. It was just a matter of choosing one magnificent villa from among a plentiful array. This particular villa once housed the Trudenjos family."

"Lud, you two, but I'm weary of your polite prattle. Is there a housekeeper or upstairs maid, Edward dear, who can see us to our rooms? I do hope Nurse has your son and heir comfortably settled by now. As for me, I vow I must have a bath and a rest before dinner. What do you say, Marisa?"

"My sentiments exactly, Ann. I feel such a shabby sight with the dust and stain of travel on me."

In truth, Marisa could barely restrain herself from

225

cornering Edward Harding and bombarding him with questions about her husband, but she knew that she would have to bide her time until the amenities of arrival were settled, and she could discreetly broach the subject. She yearned desperately for knowledge of the dark-browed earl, but must content herself to wait. She chided herself for a fool, and would admit to no one her bitter disappointment that he had not met her at the quay. Romantic folly surely, to dream that he would magically appear because she so ardently desired it.

Besides, their first meeting was certain to be anything but romantic. If the past were any guide to the future, she should be quaking with fear instead of teasing herself with fanciful hopes.

Dinner that night introduced the ladies to Portuguese delicacies—some of questionable desirability. The smoked ham and melon were delicious, as were the tawny peaches from Alcobaça served in creme.

Later, over coffee in the drawing room, the subject of Straeford was finally approached.

"Well, ladies, what news do you bring from London?" Major Harding asked.

"La, Edward, I scarce know where to begin with the latest tittle-tattle. You do know, of course, that Lady Claridge comes to Portugal to keep the eagle eye on Roger. The *on dit* is that he has found himself a dusky bit of muslin this side of the Atlantic, and she means to . . ."

"Ann, my dearest darling wife, the latest scandal broth is not the news which I seek to hear."

"Oh dash it, Edward, what else is there?" She was abashed.

"I was thinking more of the press and its attacks on Lord Wellington . . ."

"Really Edward, since when have you ever known me to diddle my wits over politics and war?"

"My dear Ann, such expressions you use! You are getting harder to follow with each passing year." His fond amusement touched Marisa.

"There is much in the journals that is vicious in the extreme." Marisa took up the conversation. "They say the duke will shoot any poor Portuguese peasant who does not follow his orders, and they cannot understand why there has not been further engagement of the enemy."

"As usual, they report what will create dissension and do not trouble themselves with truth or accuracy," Major Harding claimed with more heat than Marisa believed him capable of showing.

"I think they dare such slander because our government does not support the Portuguese effort."

"True. True," Harding agreed.

"Lord Liverpool's complaints are often written up, and naturally they stir the rabble to protest . . ."

"I see you exercise your wits over more than the latest scandal mongering, Lady Straeford." The major looked meaningfully at his wife, who pouted prettily.

"Fiddle dee dee," she smiled airily, ignoring his attempt to chide her, and tapped his arm with her fan. "Who gives a fig?"

Turning to Marisa the gentleman added, "Your grasp of the situation is very thorough, Lady Straeford."

Marisa flushed at the admiration in his eyes. "If I am so attentive to the press reports, it is only that they are my sole channel of information about matters that concern me deeply."

"I take your meaning, my dear lady. Let me set your mind at ease about his lordship. Presently he is stationed about one hundred miles from here in a mountainous area to the north."

"Does he know about my coming to Portugal?"

A slight flush stained Major Harding's cheeks as he recalled that afternoon in Straeford's tent. "I believe you may safely assume he is aware of your arrival . . ."

"I see."

Marisa's crestfallen face caused the major to wish he had spoken less frankly, and he tried to cover what he knew to be Justin's attitude on the matter. "Then again one can't be too sure of mail delivery in that region. And often there are enemy patrols to contend with—skirmishes, you know—and it is sometimes many days that men are away from camp."

These words caused Marisa such obvious alarm that

227

the major silently cursed himself for a blundering fool. "Lady Straeford, if I may speak openly for a moment . . ." He paused.

"Please do, sir. I look on you and Ann as my dear friends."

"You do us honor." Both he and Ann smiled warmly. "I do not wish to intrude in your private life, Lady Marisa. But if I could offer a few words of advice, or perhaps, of explanation . . ." She nodded eagerly. "How shall I say it?" He paused again. "Justin was forced to come to conclusions about life—and the fairer sex—at an early age, an age too young for proper understanding. A man's impressions undergo many transformations from the time he is a young man, transformations which Justin was not allowed to experience. There are some attitudes that, unfortunately, have become hardened in him, but that I feel one such as yourself may in time soften."

"Perhaps it is too late," Marisa replied softly.

"Do not believe it, ma'am. There is a warm heart beneath that thorny exterior. Just have patience, and you'll see it for yourself."

Marisa could not prevent the tremble in her voice as she spoke. "You give me hope when I am in sore need of it, Major. I shall hold to the thought you have expressed. I am deeply grateful to both of you. And now if you'll excuse me, I think I shall retire for the night. Thank you again."

Edward and Ann watched as Marisa left the room. They looked at each other silently, not daring to express the fears that fretted their innermost thoughts.

A Christmas reception and ball at the palace had the ladies in a state of high excitement. It was the first formal occasion to be held in honor of the wives from England, and each woman was determined to outshine the other. The remaining Portuguese nobility would be present, as well as members of the British Legation and officers of His Majesty's Royal British Army.

It was with a heavy heart that Marisa prepared herself for the glittering holiday affair. She allowed Lucy to arrange her blond tresses in a mass of tumbling curls starting high on her head and cascading down her back, in style imitating a waterfall.

She could not help being pleased with her reflection in the cheval glass. Her gown, which daringly revealed the creamy curves of her bosom, was a sea-green froth of spider gauze sprinkled with brilliants that sparkled and winked beguilingly with every movement of her graceful form. She would go to the ball and laugh and be gay, and Straeford be damned!

But why oh why had she received no word from that arrogant devil? Perhaps he would come to the ball and dance with her. For a moment her spirits rose as she entertained a fantasy of herself waltzing deliriously in his arms, his heart beating close to hers.

Ah well. She put aside the dream and greeted Ann, whose gown was a cerulean blue satin caught up with tiny velvet rosettes on the bodice and hem. Her soft brown hair was gathered in loose curls fastened with more rosettes, and she presented a charming picture of vivacious femininity.

Edward Harding was profuse in his compliments as he escorted the elegant pair to their waiting coach. After a short ride, they pulled up before a massive marble palace whose windows were ablaze with lights. No less than three flights of sprawling stairs led to a pillared entrance from which opened enormous gilded doors leading inside. Extending from either side of the central building were additional wings lined with rows of fluted columns supporting carved entablatures and tiled roofs which supported further ornate towers and domes.

Once inside, the Harding party passed through a long corridor lined with gilded mirrors which reflected a dazzling array of bejeweled ladies in modish gowns accompanied by elegant gentlemen in evening attire. The receiving line was headed by a member of the British Legation, Sir Arthur Ashington, in consort with Senhor and Senhora Almarez of the Portuguese Regency Council.

"I vow I shall never cease in amazement at the Portuguese display of wealth," Ann whispered confidentially to Marisa.

"One can't help being impressed," Marisa agreed.

The coffered ceiling of the main ballroom was gilded and painted in a floral pattern of roses and vine leaves that were repeated in side panels along the walls. Interspersed between these panels were floor to ceiling mirrors and glass doors leading to supper rooms beyond. The vast floor was laid out in a figured marble of polished moss green bordered in white, and the entire room was lighted by crystal chandeliers supporting huge clusters of candles. Urns and vases overflowed with red roses.

"Ann darling," a lady called to them just as they were taking seats along the wall.

"Lady Claridge, how good to see you here," Ann smiled happily. "Isn't this exciting, Marisa? All our friends from the crossing are here."

Lady Claridge approached them in the company of a pale, faded-looking woman whose face showed traces of a lost beauty. She stared hard at Marisa, who wondered at the lady's undisguised interest.

"Ann dear, I want you to meet an old acquaintance of mine who is living here in Lisbon. Adele Buxton, may I present you to Lady Straeford and Ann Harding, two of my companions who traveled to Portugal with me."

"How do you do?" The lady regarded them with an hauteur that was barely concealed.

"How nice to meet you, Mrs. Buxton," Ann claimed. "What good fortune for us to discover someone who is already familiar with Lisbon. There must be so much you can tell us about this fascinating country."

"There is not much to tell, really, not much that is fascinating, anyway. I find Portugal quite a dirty, inhospitable land."

"Oh," Ann replied stupidly. The lady's ungracious retort for once silenced the irrepressible Ann.

"Have you lived here very long?" Marisa picked up the limping conversation.

"Since last spring. My husband is with the foreign office and works closely with the Portuguese government here—if government it can be called." Again a sarcastic rejoinder.

"Well, well," Lady Claridge intervened nervously.

"Roger is with the foreign office, Adele. My husband finds the Almarezes and others to be quite agreeable."

"Really?" Adele replied haughtily. "I've met that handsome husband of yours, Valerie. He *does* have a winning way about him. Perhaps he is inclined to look kindly upon the Portuguese."

Marisa could hardly believe it, but the lady seemed to be deliberately implying something nasty.

"Why, they seem a charming people to me," interjected Ann Harding who noted the sudden frigid stare of Valerie Claridge.

"Oh, I don't deny their charm Mrs. Harding. As a matter of fact, some of the ... ah ... Potruguese *senhoras* are *very* charming."

Mrs. Buxton's pointed remark shocked both Ann and Marisa.

"Indeed." Lady Claridge drew herself up into battle stature.

"Oh Mrs. Buxton," Ann charged in indiscriminately, "it is not only the people, but their style of living. I mean they seem so free and easy in their way of life ..." Ann quit midway, realizing that she merely added coals to the pending fire, and looked about frantically for a way out of a situation that was threatening to become very unpleasant.

"Pardon me, Valerie," Marisa came to Ann's rescue. "Is not Sir Roger beckoning to you from across the room?" She was determined to avert the mischief Adele unaccountably intended. "Perhaps he wishes this dance with you. A set is forming for a quadrille at this very moment."

"Oh, indeed it is, Marisa," Ann joined in quickly. "And I believe we are promised for this one ourselves." She cast about a hopeful glance which was speedily intercepted by an eager youth from the British military, and soon the ladies were swept away from further exchange with the perplexing Adele Buxton.

From that moment on, Marisa barely had a moment to herself. She danced every dance—engaged by young men in scarlet uniforms, elegant Portuguese courtiers and charming English diplomats. The night wore on to the early morning hours, and she danced quadrilles, waltzes and a cotillion. Her radiant English beauty was much admired, and Marisa drank deeply of the heady wine of admiration.

· Two admirers escorted the countess to supper where she feasted on cold lobster and crêpes stuffed with deviled crab. She imbibed several glasses of champagne and felt her head grow light. What was happening to her? She had never relaxed her guard so greatly before.

Back on the dance floor once more she found herself in the arms of a Latin charmer whose flashing black eyes continually devoured her face. He held her far too closely, whispering soft endearments into her ear, and she did not discourage him. Whatever had gotten into her? she wondered. And later when Vargas led her into the conservatory to admire the orchids, she gave but little resistance to his advances.

As the gentleman's passion became less restrained, however, and he ardently crushed her to him in an impetuous embrace, her head suddenly cleared.

"Please, *senhor*. I beg you to let me go."

"Ah, *menina*. Just one kiss. My lips burn to press your sweet mouth."

"No, no. You must not."

"Ah, but you are cruel. You dance with me and smile so sweet. You come with me to the conservatory. And now it is no, no. I think you make a game with me."

"You are mistaken, *senhor*. I did not mean for you to think . . ."

But it was too late. Senhor Vargas's mouth was clamped to hers, crushing out all further protest—and for one foolish moment, Marisa melted against him. Then wrenching away suddenly, she fled from the conservatory so flustered she collided with several couples. In her confusion she suffered a further shock which set her legs trembling. For one terrible second she thought she had glimpsed her husband's dark head in the ballroom beyond. Her own head was whirling. She must be hallucinating!

Struggling to regain her composure, she darted to the

supper room seeking Ann Harding. When she found her friend, she begged that they leave and return to their villa.

Marisa fell into a dreamless sleep the moment her head touched the pillow, but she woke with a start when the first pale rays of December sunlight crept into her room. For some inexplicable reason, she could not sleep longer. A sense of unease troubled her mind as she lay in bed trying to discover its source. Last night had been wonderful. She never expected to enjoy herself so much at the party. Of course there was that shocking little episode with Senhor Vargas . . . but actually it was nothing—no need to dwell upon that trifling incident. Yet her peace of mind was unraveled, and she gave up trying to sleep and got out of bed.

Garbed in a rose satin dressing gown, the countess went in search of the kitchen. Perhaps a cup of tea would soothe her nerves.

She had almost reached the bottom stair when voices drifting from the library reached her ears. Even before the words became recognizable, she understood the reason for her early morning unease. It was Justin. He was here, and he was angry. Her heart gave a sudden lurch before her brain relayed the threatening message it received.

"I tell you, Harding, Ann never should have encouraged my wife to come to Portugal."

"It was not Ann who put her up to it, but Lady Maxwell. Ann merely assisted in accommodating your wife once the decision was made." Harding spoke in defense of Ann.

"That meddling old crone is at the bottom of this whole miserable affair."

"Come on old man, you make too much of this. What is so terrible about your wife's desire to be with you?"

"She has no business being here. Women and war do not mix. I cannot trouble my mind to dance attendance on her whims."

"I do not think you credit the lady's good sense. She does not expect you to 'dance attendance' on her."

"I wonder what she *does* expect. There is not a female alive without some ulterior purpose for her actions."

"Did you ever stop to consider that *love* may be her purpose?" Harding claimed quietly.

Straeford received that suggestion with a snort of derisive laughter. "Don't prate to me of sentimental nonsense, Edward. Love is a delusion for fond fools who beguile themselves and avoid facing the truth of female falsity."

"You're a bitter man, Justin ... and a *fool* who himself won't face the truth. The countess cares deeply for you."

"Have done, Edward. You'll not convince me it was devotion that inspired the lady. I was at the reception last night, remember? I saw her come out of the conservatory followed by that Latin cur."

"You place too much importance on a mere incident ..."

"Mere incident!" Straeford exploded. But he paused to consider. "This time perhaps ..."

"Justin, I will not hear you slander that lovely woman. She has done nothing to deserve such shameful words from you."

"Not *yet* she hasn't. And I mean to keep it that way—at least until the Straeford line is secured."

"Well man, if that is your aim ... she's here now. Perhaps you can accomplish your desires in that direction."

"I have no thought for such matters at the present. She must be sent packing as soon as there is passage back to London. And I shall advise that meddling old fool, Lady Maxwell, to guard her tongue hereafter."

"My friend, do not be so hasty in your decision. Give your wife a chance to express her wishes in this matter. You may live to regret your unjust treatment of her. Consider your wife's feelings for once."

"You are too soft-hearted, Edward. I tell you I do not want this chain about my neck at this time."

"What a cold-hearted bastard you are!" Edward claimed disgustedly. "She is too good for you. How you managed to inspire love in such as she is beyond me."

"Love!" Straeford mocked cruelly. "It is not love I seek but *fertility*. God grant the wench is not barren!"

A sudden crash in the hall interrupted their exchange. Marisa, blinded by tears, had stumbled into a console, overturning a vase of roses as she hastened to flee up the stairs to her room.

The men rushed from the library in time to catch a glimpse of Marisa's rose-clad form flying across the gallery above. Both men looked to each other, shock and guilt frozen on their stricken face.

Straeford recovered himself in a moment and charged up the stairs two at a time after Marisa's retreating form.

She slammed the door to her room and bolted it fast. Immediately Straeford began pounding on it, attracting the attention of the servants who peered around corners in petrified terror.

"Marisa, open this door at once and let me in," her husband demanded.

"Go away!" she screamed. "I will never let you in."

By this time Ann Harding had roused herself and come to her door to stare in amazement. Edward came to his wife and grasped her hand in his.

"Open now, I say, or I will break it down!"

"Go away! Go away!" The frenzy in Marisa's voice sent a premonition of alarm through Straeford.

He pounded once more, but the door remained fast. He lifted his booted foot, and with a mighty thrust he kicked the door down.

Marisa was standing in the middle of the room, the back of one hand pressed against her mouth, her eyes staring huge and wild. Her hair was tumbling carelessly onto her shoulders and streaming over her heaving bosom, and one shoulder was bare where the negligée and strap of her gown were falling off her arm. Marisa cast her eyes frantically about the room as if searching for a means of escape.

The look of her halted Straeford in his tracks. He recognized the sight of blind hysteria. He had seen it on the faces of battle-shocked soldiers before.

"Marisa," he called to her quietly and took a step forward.

"No—don't you dare come near me," she cried. "You'll never come near me again!"

He halted once more. "Of course, my dear. Of course. Whatever you say; only calm yourself and let me speak to you."

"Go away, go away." She began crying in terrible, wracking sobs that cut him to the core.

Straeford started toward her, but in a sudden shift Marisa sprang to the balcony doors and flung them open. Reading her frantic purpose and knowing that she was thinking to throw herself over the balcony, Straeford hurled himself at her in one desperate lunge and grabbed hold of her arm. But his grasp was not secure enough, and Marisa whirled and wrenched free. The force of her thrust was of such strength that she lost her balance and stumbled backward to the steps leading to the patio below. For one terrible moment she swayed precariously while time seemed to stop, and then, to Justin's horrified eyes, Marisa toppled backward, plummeting to the flagstones below.

His nerves jolted sickeningly at the sound of her body hitting the stones at the bottom of the stairs.

"My God!" he cried, stricken. "What have I done?" he groaned, racing down the steps and bending over his wife's crumpled form.

15

For three days Marisa hovered in the realms of unconsciousness and there was fear that the fall would prove fatal. She had broken her right ankle and that side of her face bore the marks of ugly red abrasions. Little could be done about the concussion. The full extent of that injury would be discovered if and when she regained consciousness.

To everyone's dismay, Straeford would not leave her side. He slept on a cot beside Marisa's bed and was often seen holding his wife's hand for hours during his long vigil. His remorse was unassuageable. He accused himself of being a black-hearted devil whose lot it was to bring grief and suffering to those connected with him. Searching his soul, he found only darkness and despair for himself. In blind misery Straeford prayed that Marisa would recover and give him a chance to redeem the damage he had done.

His prayers for her recovery were answered. When, on the third day, she opened her eyes and recognition registered in their pain-darkened depths, he knew a moment of gratitude so piercing it brought tears to his eyes.

Marisa gazed at his gaunt face, darkened by three days' growth of beard and stared at the tears welling in his hollow green eyes. She felt as one waking unto a frozen world barren of human feeling. His lordship's apparent grief and pain no longer touched her. It mattered not to her what he was feeling—for herself, she felt nothing. She closed her eyes and turned her head away.

And in that slight gesture, Straeford read the full significance of their future relationship. Lady Marisa, the Countess of Straeford, had severed bonds with the earl as surely as if a court of law had struck down the marriage tie between them. She would have nothing more to do with him, and it was no less than he deserved. His prayer for redemption went unanswered.

The countess's recuperation was slow and unsatisfactory. Dr. Lomas warned that her recovery would depend as much on keeping her spirits up as in assisting the body in its mending process. He noted his patient's lassitude as the days passed, and queried the earl cautiously as he attempted to combat the lady's apathy.

"The *condesa,* Lord Straeford, needs diversion. It is difficult being confined to one's chamber for such long hours. Perhaps you know of some interest that the lady could be encouraged to pursue while she is an invalid. Painting or needlepoint . . ." He looked hopefully to the earl.

"I know little of such female fripperies," the earl replied impatiently.

"It is not frippery to restore your wife's spirits, *senhor*. Your wife exhibits uncommon apathy, my lord. It hinders the healing greatly."

The earl saw his point and relented. "My wife, sir, had exhibited a recent interest in your national poet, Camões. It may be that she would wish to resume her studies of that particular writer at this time."

"Excellent idea! Mental stimulation—perhaps a change of environment—I shall arrange to have your lady spend some time each afternoon in the library, and we shall banish the dark shadows, you shall see." He was enthusiastic. "And, I think, a small glass of our good port to build up the blood and stimulate the appetite. Yes, yes, I think this is the very program to hasten your good wife's recovery. You shall see a change very soon, I am sure."

Lord Straeford did not reply, feeling little hope for the physician's eager program. He knew the deeper cause of Marisa's present state of apathy and secretly feared that her recovery depended upon removal of his person from her presence. He knew she wished him away, and he was caught in a bleak dilemma, desiring Marisa's recovery but fearing to withdraw lest it become a permanent breach between them.

Whenever he visited her for a brief period each morning, it was to exchange polite amenities as two strangers forced to endure the company of persons they merely tolerated but did not enjoy.

And what, the earl questioned himself, did he really feel for Marisa? What made him so reluctant to leave her side when a short time ago he wished to send her back to England?

The answer to that question troubled him constantly. Finally unable to hide from the truth, he was forced to admit that Marisa meant more to him than he had wanted her to—and probably long before the accident had occurred. She was his wife, and he would not relinquish his claim on her. He dared not ask himself if it were the threat to his rights as husband that afflicted him, or if it were something more. He would not allow the word "love" to break through the surface of his troubled thoughts.

Despite the physician's high hopes, Marisa continued to languish. Each afternoon Lord Straeford would gently gather Marisa in his arms and carry her slight body into the library where a cheerful fire leapt invitingly in the grate. But for all the solicitude showered upon her—Ann and Edward would often be present to alleviate the strain between the Straefords, and the cook prepared luscious delicacies daily to tempt the countess's waning appetite—Marisa seemed more and more to withdraw into a private world of shadows much like the midwinter world of overcast skies and barren countryside outside.

For his part, the earl grew restive. It was against his nature to stand by idly and watch a situation deteriorate. He was a man of action, and it went hard with him to endure helplessly as Marisa faded before their watching eyes.

The colorless days of January ran one into another with little change in the emotional atmosphere between the Straefords. It was apparent to those who observed them that Marisa had withdrawn from her husband. He could not rouse a show of interest from her even when he presented her with her own richly bound volume of *Os Lusiadas*. Despite his dutiful attendance on her daily, despite his patient forbearance, she remained unmoved.

The library was filled with late afternoon gloom; a flickering fire cast dancing shadows on the dark paneled walls, and from the corridors beyond the quiet room the mournful notes of a sad love song drifted hauntingly. Josefe, the gardener's son, was strumming his guitar. The Earl of Straeford paced restlessly about the room, pausing to stare out the windows at the wind-driven rain lashing at the sturdy casements. Marisa watched the fire and waited for the waning day to dissolve into the enveloping darkness of another nighttime.

"We cannot go on like this, Marisa." The earl spoke while continuing to stare out the window at the rain.

She did not respond.

Her husband shifted his weight and turned to regard Marisa's delicate profile sporadically highlighted by the fire. A terrible yearning seized him, and for one brief moment he considered throwing himself at her feet and begging her forgiveness. The moment passed, leaving him shaken, but clear-sighted at last.

He went to her side and knelt beside her chair. This in itself was uncharacteristic enough to cause Marisa to turn her head and look at him.

"Marisa," he began quietly, "I have come to a decision."

She waited for him to go on.

"I have exercised my wits constantly to devise a means of altering your outlook and preventing the slow decline you are entering, but in vain. Were it in my power to restore you to health and happiness, I would leave no stone unturned to do so. But you have made it abundantly clear, my dear, that I can offer you nothing of myself." He paused, but having made his decision, he continued.

240

"I finally realize there is only one thing I *can* offer you . . . and that is your freedom."

At last Marisa looked at him with eyes that showed awareness. "My freedom . . . I don't understand. What kind of freedom?"

"Total. Complete. The marriage shall be dissolved."

"Dissolved?" She was filled with awe.

"You shall be free to seek your happiness else-where." As he spoke the words that would part her from himself, his thoughts were bitterly ironic. At last, when he could admit his need of her to himself, he was offering her her freedom.

"But . . . I . . ."

"Well?" Straeford got to his feet and stood over her.

Marisa looked up at the earl and could not answer him. His proposal stunned her. In all these passing weeks, she had never looked beyond the next day. That Justin would always be her husband she had never questioned. She could not grasp the meaning of what he was saying.

"Well," he prodded again, much of his old arrogance bristling forth.

"What will I . . . you . . ."

"Do about Straeford Park?" Again he misread her concern for him as concern for his property. "I shall sign it over to you, lock, stock and barrel. It has never been anything but bad luck for me." The depth of bitterness in those words smote Marisa's heart. For the first time in weeks, she felt her heart move, if only momentarily. "What say you to my plan?" he went on relentlessly, although there was anxiety in his heart.

"I—I do not know. I . . . must think," she replied, flustered.

"You will have whatever time you need. I have some military matters to attend to and will be leaving for the frontier. When I return . . . you may advise me of your decision."

Two weeks passed, and nothing was seen or heard from the earl since that gloomy afternoon when he had presented Marisa with his stunning proposal.

During that time she was learning the use of

crutches, and it was Josefe, the guitarist, who assisted the countess up and down the stairs. Whatever its outcome, the earl's proposal had acted as a catalyst to stir Marisa out of her apathy.

She spent hours mulling over his offer to dissolve the marriage, alternately desiring and rejecting the idea. What of the scandal? What kind of future would it mean for her? Did she really want to part from him?

But, oh, to be free and retire from the demands of the world. She would seek solitude and follow her own private dictates with no need to consider obligations to others ever again. She had done that for her father and her husband and it had proved a disaster. Now she would satisfy only herself. The temptation was alluring.

The prospect of putting together a life of peace in the country with none to trouble her was more fantasy than reality. Deep within, Marisa knew there was no escape into a cocoon of safety such as she was spinning in the secret recesses of her mind. The daydreaming was a necessary interlude that fed the deeper springs of self, allowing nature to restore the wasted substance of her body and the depleted reserves of her spirit. Even if she were to part from Straeford it would not be to withdraw from life. She had too much love to give to truly desire isolation.

Besides, Edward Harding had impressed Marisa with a thought that had not occurred to her after Justin had offered her her freedom. Did Marisa realize, the gentleman had said, what it must have cost the earl to make such an offer? All of Lord Straeford's goals had centered on the restoration of his family estate and its good name. Think what the scandal of divorce would cost him, Justin's friend reminded her. Not that the earl would admit that he cared for the world's opinion. Never.

And what of the heir that his lordship so ardently desired? If the Straefords were to part, she could be sure Justin would never again pursue such a goal. His distrust of the female sex would be forever sealed.

Marisa tried to disregard this plea for her husband. It was just such reasoning as had ensnared her in the unhappy condition in which she had so recently been bound.

"Do not speak to me of pity for his plight, sir. It serves only to force me down a path I had hoped was reaching an end." But even as she spoke these words she doubted her own conviction.

"If you'll pardon so bold an interference on my part, my dear, I think it is time someone told you a little of the St. Clare family history. Perhaps you should be made aware of the causes of Justin's bitterness towards women." Edward Harding looked to Marisa and waited for her permission to go on.

She fidgeted with the blanket over her knees and held him off, not looking at him, listening to the clock in the hall chime the hour. But at last she relented and gave him a nod of assent.

"I will not trouble you with a prolonged tale of woe. Merely I wish you to know that Justin's was not a happy childhood. For reasons I do not understand, Justin's mother, Lady Marian, seemed unable to tolerate him as a lad. She preferred Robert to a degree that was unpardonable."

"Yes, I know. Lady Maxwell so informed me, but it hardly explains the misogyny of the man I married."

"That is true, I agree. And I would not want you to think Justin minded his mother's partiality toward Robert overmuch. I shared my childhood with the St. Clare boys, and Justin ever loved his brother. If anything, he felt his mother's preference to be perfectly placed."

"Now that I *do* find sad," Marisa commented quietly.

"Of course, I must admit, Justin was compensated by his father's love, and Justin idolized his father. He made his life a model of that man's virtues—duty to country and such. But a boy needs the gentling of his mother's love as well, and that, I'm afraid, Justin never had."

"Lady Maxwell did not tell me the whole of it, and now that you have opened Pandora's box," Marisa claimed in final capitulation, "you might as well tell me the whole story this time."

Edward smiled ruefully at this unflattering comparison. "No, even I do not know the whole, but I shall endeavor to tell you what I *do* know. However, it is much

243

more than I had planned to say." He paused, watching Marisa's reaction, and when she continued to listen expectantly, he picked up the thread of the story he had begun.

"As you have heard, Justin left home at the age of seventeen and returned at the time of his brother's death. There was a terrible row between Justin and his mother over Ellis Huxley, the man Lady Marian married following the death of Justin's father. Huxley had wasted the estate, and . . . was instrumental in causing Robert's death."

"You mean Lady Marian's second husband caused the death of her very own son?" Marisa questioned incredulously.

"Indeed I do."

"Dear Lord, how terrible. But how do you know all this?"

"As for the dissipation of the Straeford estate— Robert had taken me into his confidence and shown me proof of Huxley's chicanery. There was no question that he squandered it in reckless speculation and gambling. And I was present at that terrible scene when Huxley was killed and Lady Marian turned on Justin."

"Dear God," Marisa whispered, her eyes wide with wonder. "Lady Clarkson once intimated that there was a scandal, but it never dawned on me it could be so monstrous."

"Monstrous is a mild word for the infamy spawned by Huxley."

"You must tell me all of it now," she demanded.

Harding continued reluctantly. "Justin came back from India after receiving word from his grandmother that Robert was dead. Robert had already written to Justin concerning his discovery of Huxley's misappropriation of the family fortune, and Justin suspected foul play where Robert's death was concerned. He had no proof however, until Jem Cooper made an attempt on Justin's life."

"Jem Cooper? Who is Jem Cooper? I'm getting terribly confused."

"I'm not surprised—the whole affair was such a shocking tangle of villainy. Jem Cooper was a desperate rogue hired by Huxley to murder Robert and make it look like an attack by thieves on Hounslow Heath. He would have gotten away with it if he hadn't attempted murder a second time—with Justin as the target."

"This is beyond belief. I remember how Lady Maxwell reacted when I asked her about Robert's death. Now I understand her reluctance to speak. This is a dreadful story."

"It's only half of it, my dear. You see, Justin is a tough customer to tangle with, and in the outcome of that sorry episode, Jem Cooper was begging for his *own* life before your husband was finished with him. Cooper spilled the whole shameful plot and agreed to aid Justin in a counter-plot to entrap Huxley."

"There's not a man alive who can outsmart the earl."

Marisa's view of her husband's invincibility brought a smile to Harding's lips. "Be that as it may, Jem Cooper forced Huxley to meet him at Straeford Park supposedly to demand more money. Justin and I, who were in hiding, witnessed the whole transaction. Huxley was not so easily manipulated, however, and when he drew a pistol on Cooper there followed a struggle in which Huxley was mortally wounded. Lady Marian heard the shot—it was well past midnight—and came flying into the library . . ." Here Harding paused, as if reliving that fateful scene of disaster.

"You may as well finish it, sir. What happened then?" Marisa prodded.

"She was as a madwoman. Her unbound hair was streaming over her night dress, and taking in the situation, she flung herself on top of Huxley's body moaning with grief."

"Ellis, oh my God, Ellis," she cried. "What have you done? What have you done?"

"Mother, please," Justin leaned down to lift Lady Marian from the dead man's body, but she whirled on him and hissed, "Devil! Don't you dare touch me. You demon! You've killed him."

"It was an accident, Mother. I didn't wish him to die before he could explain to you the evil he has wrought."

"Liar! Murdering liar! You've always hated him and

wished him dead. And now you have killed him in cold blood. First my precious son Robert, and now my beloved Ellis. Oh God, I curse the day you were born. For the rest of my days I shall call for your black soul to rot in hell. Get out of my sight. I never want to see your face again."

"Justin was stricken, his face pale and grim, but he tried several times to tell her the truth about Huxley. She would hear nothing but kept insisting that everything was his fault. Somehow she tangled Robert's and Huxley's deaths together and held Justin responsible for all the family misfortunes. I think her mind must have snapped that night. She continued screaming curses and imprecations until Justin could bear no more. He left for London that very night and tried to put together a life for himself as the new Earl of Straeford. He even became engaged to be married. But his mother, who had been secluded at Straeford Park, suddenly appeared in town on the night of the betrothal party, and having drunk too much, she got hold of Arabella Stanton, and shocked the girl witless with lies about Justin.

"I can still recall the look on Justin's face that night at the Stantons'. He knew what was coming but bore it with a kind of hopeless dignity. I think it was then that he became fixed in his bitter attitude toward women."

"I do not think I can bear to hear any more," Marisa whispered, struggling to keep back the tears that choked her throat.

"We are almost at the end now. I may as well finish."

Marisa nodded him on.

"Arabella was entertaining at the pianoforte when I noticed a change in the atmosphere of the drawing room. It was as if a subtle tension laid hold of everyone. I looked up and beheld the former Lady Straeford standing in the doorway, and I knew at once that Justin was in for some rough going. She was dressed in stark black unrelieved by any ornamentation—she always said she hated the color—and her black hair, that lustrous dark mantle was gleaming on her shoulders. Her green eyes seemed to smolder with a dark fire that turned them almost black.

She stood there imperiously surveying the room until every eye was on her, and Arabella had ceased playing. Then the ex-countess walked over to Justin and sat beside him. Arabella, a pale little bird of a girl, resumed playing, but faltered several times and soon left off to go to Justin's side."

"You must introduce me to your betrothed, my son," Marian Huxley claimed in a deep contralto voice loud enough for those around her to hear.

"Of course, madam. I shall be honored," Justin replied impassively.

As soon as Arabella was presented to her, Justin's mother set about accomplishing her wicked purpose for the night.

"And have you been a long-time acquaintance of this returned . . . prodigal, my dear?" she queried.

"No, my lady, it is but barely six weeks since we met at Lord Broadhurst's."

"The marquess?" Lady Marian arched her brow in feigned surprise as Arabella nodded meekly. "I did not know my son traveled in such elect circles."

Arabella looked confused and replied vaguely, "We are related on my mother's side . . ."

"Ah," Lady Marian nodded sagely, "money on both sides. How fortunate."

Arabella's eyes flew wide at the lady's vulgar reference to her family fortune, and she turned a fiery red as she realized that many nearby had overheard her future mother-in-law's ill-chosen words.

"Arabella's brother was in my regiment at Kimballa," Justin intervened, trying to head off the mischief his mother was brewing. "It was through his good offices that I made Miss Stanton's acquaintance," he added drily.

His fiancée smiled tentatively, sensing the antagonism between mother and son.

"Again I say, how fortunate. And yet 'tis not surprising when one sees how destiny holds you in her favor." She inclined her head toward Justin. "To think, a mere soldier one day and earl the next." An ugly sneer had crept into her voice.

"I have never seen Straeford Park," Arabella interjected to no particular point.

"Oh, you must visit me and see for yourself to what purpose you can apply your ready fortune—my son may have the title, but he is quite penniless, as you know."

Miss Stanton could no longer doubt the lady's ill-will. She looked from Justin to his mother, her face now pale and frightened.

"I don't believe you are acquainted with Randolph Stanton, Mother. Allow me to mend that situation now." Justin rose to his feet, his face revealing nothing but polite courtesy.

"Tut, tut, my dear, I have not yet finished my little coze with your charming affianced. Not trying to prevent our getting to know each other, are you?"

Justin shrugged indifferently, and seated himself once more. "As you wish, madam. I am, as ever, at your service."

"Then be a good boy and take yourself off for a while, that we women may speak more openly to each other."

Arabella cast an imploring look to Justin, who smiled encouragingly at her. "Perhaps you ladies might enjoy some refreshment. A glass of ratafia, my dear?" he addressed himself to his future bride.

"Ratafia!" Lady Marian scoffed. "I should hope you might offer us something worth drinking. Is there no champagne to toast this memorable occasion?"

"What say you, Arabella? Shall I fetch you champagne as my mother suggests?"

"Yes, please," Miss Stanton whispered, wondering how she was ever to extricate herself from the clutches of this frightening woman who loomed so suddenly on the bright horizon of her safe little world. "Only, do not be gone long, my lord."

"I will be back within minutes," Justin promised as if giving his mother fair warning. He was leaving the field open for her to do her worst, but it was a temporary retreat.

"So sweet, dear Arabella. Young love is so urgent, is it not."

Miss Stanton tested another smile on the lady in hopes of warding off the unpleasantness she felt was coming.

"But love can be blind," Lady Marian continued driving toward her goal. "And I would not have you marry my son in the dark, as it were."

"I'm sorry, Mrs. Huxley, but I do not understand."

"Well, surely there must be things about Justin that you would like to ask me about him. After all, who should know him better than his own mother?"

"I . . . it never occurred to me to wish to know more than I do."

"Really?" Lady Marian trilled a light laugh. "But what *do* you know about him?"

Arabella blushed and began to stammer. She knew she was being pressed toward some revelation that she did not want to hear but had no idea how to handle this woman whom she already feared and disliked. "Well, I . . . I know that he has been in India for many years as a member of the British army," the young woman responded lamely.

"Ah yes, India. Justin was a mere lad of seventeen when he broke his father's heart and ran off. His father never saw him again."

"That is too bad," Arabella responded dully.

"Yes, too bad. And what of Robert, my oldest son? What has Justin told you of him?"

"Only that he is dead." Arabella was horrified at the lady's line of conversation, but too confused to do other than listen stupidly and wait for her to be finished.

"Do you know how he died?"

Arabella shook her head no.

"He was murdered." Mrs. Huxley delighted in the alarm that appeared in the girl's soft blue eyes. "And the perpetrator of that heinous crime walks among us free to this day."

"Oh no!" Arabella cried, attracting some considerable attention. "How terrible!"

"Yes, how terrible. But what if I should tell you I know who the villain is but lack the proof to bring him to justice."

"Oh, Lady Marian, please. I am dreadfully sorry for your tragedy, but can we not talk of something else. I . . . I am beginning to feel quite ill."

"Do not be such a poor spirited creature, my dear Miss Stanton. You will never endure the life you are choosing for yourself if you do not grow some intestinal fortitude."

Arabella no longer made the effort to respond with courtesy. She visibly crumpled in her chair as she fought to hold back the tears threatening to fall. "Mrs. Huxley, why . . . why are you telling me these things?"

"Why do you think, you silly child? I wish to save you . . . to prevent further tragedy. You are no match for my son. It would take a female of tremendous courage and cunning to endure life with one such as he."

"But it seems you mean me to connect Justin with Robert's death. Surely you are not suggesting that Justin had anything to do with it." It was a whisper.

"Not only do I suggest—I accuse him—of both Robert's *and* my husband's deaths!" Lady Marian's voice rose to a hysterical pitch, her eyes glittering wildly.

"How can you say such a thing!" Arabella was beside herself. She no longer whispered, but cried aloud, and those nearby began to stare openly. "It's not true!"

"Oh but it is true! Your future husband plotted the murder of his brother so that he might become the earl. And he killed my husband so there would be no one in his way to prevent him from enjoying the fruits of his villainy."

"No! No!" Arabella wailed. She jumped up, holding her hands over her ears. "You lie!" she screamed and ran sobbing from the room.

At that point, Justin came up to his mother carrying two glasses of champagne. He handed one to her and bowed. All eyes in the room were on the disgraced pair, but Justin comported himself as if nothing were amiss.

"I believe you requested champagne, madam." He handed a glass to her, and raising his own, he toasted, "To you, my dear. Your victory is quite complete." He knew she had won and he accepted it fatalistically.

Lady Marian drank down the glass of champagne. Then she nodded to those in her immediate vicinity and left on the arm of her son, who gallantly escorted her through the staring guests and out of the Stanton residence.

"Needless to say, the wedding was called off and Justin was branded a monstrous villain," Harding concluded. "He returned to India shortly thereafter. Although no one truly believed the charge of murder, a shadow of evil attached itself to Justin that has followed him ever since."

Edward Harding's revelations about the deaths of Justin's brother Robert and Ellis Huxley acted as an agent to stir into motion the conflict between Marisa's desires to stay with Justin and to part from him. Her womanly instincts to succor and comfort the man to whom she had pledged herself for life warred against a newly discoverd yearning toward independence.

Had she not given her lord all he deserved of her humanity? He had used her badly and did she not have some right to strive toward the possession of her own soul in peace and harmony? Yet, did any woman, once married, have that right?

Perhaps she was crediting herself with too much importance anyway. She had every reason to believe his lordship wished himself well rid of her.

And where was he, she wondered as January drew to a close. They would be married a year in February. Would he remember? And did she really care?

Marisa could not sort out her feelings concerning the earl. At times she felt she would go mad trying to understand herself.

It was the discovery of the pressed rose in her husband's volume of *The Lusiads* that resolved her dilemma. There it lay between the pages of verse lamenting the death of Inez de Castro. It was the same passage she had read so long ago in London when she first discovered her husband's interest in Camões. Only now the lines were underlined:

Her cheeks' fresh roses ravisht from the root.
Both red and white.

It was the white rose she had fastened to Justin's lapel the night of their ball, its fragile petals transparent as tissue paper, but carefully preserved. And inscribed in the margin were lines in the bold script of her husband's writing:

> The marble heart was pierced by
> A white rose and there
> Such tender torment abides—

A sob escaped Marisa's lips as the significance of her discovery made itself felt in her mind and heart. Justin had saved the rose she had so spontaneously bestowed on him that night. Not only saved it, but cherished it in one of his treasured volumes. The words inscribed pierced her heart with such tender pity that she broke down and cried and felt herself cleansed. She would stay to try again, if Justin so desired it.

16

The test of that decision was thrust on Marisa two days later when the earl returned from his recent mission to the Beira region. He had gone to inspect the conditions of his men and to personally question two French officers captured in a recent skirmish along the eastern frontier where Portuguese guerillas were harrying French outposts and patrols. The information obtained from the prisoners was extremely valuable. There was every possibility that the French would be sending in General Massena, the wily French Fox who had won so many outstanding victories for France, to lead the opposition against England's Wellington and the Portuguese coalition.

The earl came upon the household while it was still at breakfast. Immediately the easy conviviality shared by the Hardings and Marisa was frozen into a stilted exchange of pleasantries as all parties tried to behave with a nonchalance that none actually felt. Making their weak excuses and claiming various duties, the Hardings departed to leave Marisa and Justin to establish communication without the embarrassment of nervous onlookers.

The unhappy couple regarded each other through the extreme discomfort of confusion and misapprehension. Each mistakenly believed the other to wish himself free of the entanglements of matrimonial obligation. Yet each in his deepest heart did not want that final separation that would permanently sever the bonds between them.

For Marisa's part, she was ready to try to achieve a lasting relationship with the earl. Not only did she feel that it was her duty, she still yearned to bring happiness to this troubled man who had been hurt so deeply in the past. She could no longer be sure it was love that prompted her—at least not romantic love—but neither could she deny that this dark, tormented man had engaged her heart.

The earl's feelings at this juncture were both stronger and more confused than Marisa's. He was certain that he did not desire a separation from this woman who daily was becoming more important to him than he had wanted. Because of this, he feared the need he felt growing out of all proportion to his ability to control it. Marisa could enslave him, if she but knew it. He was in agony.

For both of them, these thoughts were not clearly articulated, and they groped through a fog of inner conflict compounded by unreasonable fears of rejection that neither could bear to sustain.

"You are looking very well, Marisa," the earl ventured at last. "I hope I find your health much improved."

"Thank you . . . Justin. I am much better. Dr. Lomas comes to remove the splint next week, I believe."

Lord Straeford was heartened by his wife's apparent willingness to converse with him. "That is good news indeed. You must be heartily sick of that encumbrance by now."

"It is surprising, but I have managed to get about quite well despite the clumsiness of it. Not that I don't wish to be rid of it. I just mean, I hobble about rather well . . . considering . . . Oh bother, you know what I mean," she claimed, flustered.

"I know . . . I understand. . . ."

They stared at each other awkwardly.

"Did you accomplish all your military objectives?"

Marisa questioned nervously, seeking a topic for conversation.

"Yes, I did. But you must not question me too closely on that score, my dear."

"Oh, no, my lord," Marisa claimed, becoming more flustered. "I do not mean to pry into secret matters. Please do forgive me."

"But there is nothing to forgive, child. Do not look so alarmed. Your question was perfectly natural."

"It is only that there is such disquiet these days. I hear rumors that the British army may withdraw and quit Portugal altogether."

"Never believe it," Straeford claimed emphatically.

"Major Harding says the Duke of Wellington is much criticized by the governments both here and at home for not engaging the enemy."

"The duke will fight only when he chooses and will not be stampeded into hasty action no matter what the pressures are from political factions. He is a man of singular self-possession."

"You sound convinced of his good judgment."

"I am absolutely certain the duke will lead us through to victory over the French. And now, my dear, let us turn our minds to matters that touch us more personally."

"Of course, my lord, whatever you say." Marisa felt her pulse quicken with apprehension. He was going to send her away.

The earl, however, did not speak. Instead he rose from the table and paced the room a few times, unable to make himself say the words that might send her away from him.

"Marisa," he began at last, "there is a packet leaving for England next week ... I ... shall I ... that is ... it is possible to reserve space for you ... if you wish it." His voice had gradually lowered, so that his last words were barely audible.

He is not sure he wants me to go, Marisa realized with surprise. Maybe he really wants me to stay. "Next week seems such sudden notice, Justin. I'm not sure which day the splint is to be removed, and I might need some time to ... adjust. I mean ... perhaps we should wait a little longer . . . unless you think it would be best . . ." Her voice, too, had lowered to a whisper.

She is not sure she wants to go, Justin thought, not realizing he was echoing Marisa. Maybe she really wants to stay. "That sounds very wise to me, my dear. We must be certain you are well enough to travel . . . if you should so decide. We shall just put off any decision for the present, shall we?"

"Yes, let us wait and see."

Golden sunlight streaming through the tall library windows created a false sense of early spring although it was still February. Marisa opened the library doors and stood on the threshold to stare at a scene she had never expected to witness.

The earl was leaning over a chair, dangling a piece of string before the bewhiskered nose of a tiny calico kitten. So absorbed was he in tantalizing the sprightly creature who swatted at the string with lightning-quick movements that he did not hear the door open. It was only as the kitten darted behind the settee and Straeford turned that he beheld his wife in all her amazement. Hastily rising to his feet and brushing off his coat to cover his chagrin at thus being discovered, he muttered an incoherent greeting.

Marisa, who thought to ease his discomfort, hobbled forward leaning awkwardly on her crutch and called softly to the kitten, who was now inspecting the satin ruffles at her hem.

"Wherever did you find this precious creature?" she queried with an eager smile.

The earl secretly rejoiced in his wife's friendly demeanor. He still could not believe that the distant apathy with which she was wont to regard him following her accident had really dissolved.

"One of my men . . ." Justin stopped midsentence to rush to Marisa and scoop her up in his arms. Just as he was answering her question, Marisa, who had leaned toward the kitten, lost her balance as the crutch slipped beneath her, almost causing her to fall.

"Can't have you breaking any more bones," he claimed hoarsely as he placed her carefully on the settee.

He was white about the lips, as the memory of that terrible fall for one hideous moment flashed vividly before his eyes.

For a few tense seconds neither Justin nor Marisa spoke. They had not been so close to each other for so long that it threw them into some confusion. Justin was still leaning over Marisa when the two looked at each other and their eyes locked in a hold neither could break. To overcome the unbearable tension, they both began to speak simultaneously and stopped suddenly. Then Marisa's lips curved in a smile of sweet friendship, and Justin, warmed by the glow of her natural goodwill, smiled too. It was little enough, to be sure, but it was a further move toward the harmony they both desired more than they knew.

As if prompted by the spirit of mischief, the kitten, appearing from nowhere, pounced onto Marisa's lap and began to play with the lace at her bodice.

"Oh you precious lamb," Marisa cried happily, catching the tiny creature to her face and nuzzling her nose in its fur. Her unaffected gesture touched a chord of memory from Justin's childhood.

"May I suggest a name for your new-found friend, my dear?"

"Am I to understand that she is mine?"

"But of course. I brought her here for you."

"Then I think you *should* name her."

"What would you say to Emily?"

"Emily? Such a ladylike name for such a naughty little minx. But I do believe you have struck the perfect note for her. She shall never live up to that prim-miss of a name. Do you have some reason for choosing to call her Emily?"

"I once owned a cat by that name. She was just such a minx as you so aptly call this one."

"Then Emily it is. I do thank you most kindly, sir, for my new little companion. I shall keep her in a basket in my room."

The earl regarded his wife speculatively, a wicked gleam lighting his eyes. "Perhaps you will allow me to visit her there sometimes."

Again their eyes locked in a long gaze. This time a

perceptibly rosy hue flushed Marisa's cheeks and she looked away. The countess had never looked so adorable to the earl as she did at that moment.

Justin knew he had gained an advantage with the introduction of Emily, but he knew also that regaining Marisa's confidence, if ever he possessed it, would be a slow and arduous task. He had stumbled onto good fortune with the kitten, but now he must make his way back to his wife carefully and skillfully. They had yet to openly confront the events of that terrible morning when Marisa had overheard the earl in conversation with Harding. He shuddered inwardly, wondering how he would ever bring himself to speak of that morning and beg Marisa's forgiveness as he so desperately needed to do.

Upon removal of the splint from Marisa's leg, Lord Straeford found countless ways of keeping himself in his wife's company. He was the constant cavalier who wooed his lady as never he had during their betrothal days. He read Portuguese history with Marisa and assisted her in translating the Camões epic. As the weather improved, he escorted her on brief sightseeing excursions to Lisbon's most famous historic sights. They traveled to Belem where Vasco da Gama made his long vigil prior to his momentous explorations. They toured the Geronimos abbey and studied the Manueline architecture, planning ventures to Alcobaça and Batalha should the future permit.

Slowly there arose between them a comfortable relationship that they had never enjoyed before. Each was finding delight in the other that neither had dreamed possible.

On the night of their first anniversary, Marisa and Justin planned a celebration party with the Hardings that would take them to the notorious Cafe Bruxa Negra in the antique Alfama district to hear native singers whom some called *fadistas*. The *fado,* or fate, theme was peculiarly Portuguese in style. The music evolved from the national characteristic of the Portuguese which placed heavy emphasis on fate or destiny in the affairs of mankind. The Portuguese seemed to have a deep strain of melancholy in their natures, Marisa observed, and it was reflected in the native music.

On the night of their expedition into Alfama, the Hardings and Straefords found it necessary to leave their coach and proceed on foot through a labyrinth of twisting narrow streets until they came to a shadowy doorway fitfully lighted by torches burning from brackets set in the stone walls.

Marisa and Ann pulled the hoods of their black dominoes down over their heads and clung excitedly to their husbands' arm as they followed a dark-skinned waiter in leather breeches and a black cape. He led them through murky shadows past tables lighted by glowing red candles to a section secluded by a lattice of woven ropes which was reserved for their party. They were served a light golden wine blended with herbs. The indefinable flavor of the wine suited the atmosphere of exotic and forbidden pleasure.

"Wherever did you learn of this shockingly wicked *taverna,* Edward?" Ann whispered confidentially to her husband.

"You will have to question Justin on that score, m'dear," Harding replied, mischief gleaming in his eyes.

"I have my sources," the earl claimed evasively, entering into the spirit of play.

"That sounds slightly sinister," Marisa added her part. "I can't believe my high-stickler of a husband trafficks with any but the most respectable elements of Portuguese society."

"Oh ho," Harding taunted gaily, "now that's what I call a testimony of wifely faith. You would do well to follow Lady Straeford's lead, dear Ann."

"But I trust you utterly, Edward dear. I know you would not cut a caper. I simply wonder that you *or* the earl would know of the existence of a hole-in-the-corner place such as this."

"You do not like it here?" Justin queried, deliberately seeking to rattle the easily flustered Mrs. Harding. It amazed the earl to realize that he actually found this woman, whom he once labeled a fool, to be the charming person his altered vision now proclaimed her to be.

"It looks positively evil—all the dark shadows and mysterious people lurking about. I adore it!" Ann whispered confidingly. "It's bang-up to the nines!"

All four broke into merry laughter and continued in their friendly raillery until their attention was captured by the *senhora* singing on a small stage at the center of the room. Dozens of candles lighted up her red satin dress glittering with spangles and fake jewels, but there was nothing fake about the alluring *saudade* melodies that poured freely from her sultry throat and the throbbing of the guitar accompaniment that wove a haunting mood of melancholy magic. The music was a dark poetry that echoed sad enchantments through the corridors of the mind. As they listened, Justin reached for Marisa's hand and raised it to his lips, kissing her fingertips lingeringly. She looked at him with eyes glistening, the Hardings momentarily forgotten. It was a gesture she would never forget.

The party grew very quiet and sentimental that night, an awareness of an unspoken communication having been shared through the hypnotic music of the *fadistas*.

It would have been a perfect evening had not the small party come under the observation of one whose heart bore a long-standing grudge of resentment toward the Earl of Straeford.

Isabella Costanza, who had sworn an oath of vengeance that ill-starred day Lord Straeford so arrogantly cast her off before the British army left Spain, had at last been presented with the object of her hatred. The dark fate which the Portuguese believed so inevitably intertwined in men's affairs had contrived to bring the earl within Isabella's sphere once more. She could still hear Dubois screaming his futile vengeance at Straeford's back as the arrogant Englishman rode away, leaving her and the Frenchman to grapple with their broken pride in that foolish arena where they had enacted that charade of honor. "Fight, coward!" Dubois had demanded in vain, and their mutual humiliation had lain in the dark recesses of their minds, festering, seeking a channel for expression that had at last been revealed. Isabella would do the Straefords a lasting harm and set the wheels in motion on the very night that Marisa and Justin had awakened to each other as lovers. She watched his group until they left the cafe and sent a spy to follow them on their return home.

But the Straefords knew nothing of the dark thoughts directed toward them, and when his lordship presented himself to Marisa within her bedchamber that night, he knew he need not fear her rejection.

Marisa was waiting for him in a gown of white lace, her unbound hair tumbling to her waist. The only light in the shadowy room was a soft glow cast by a gentle fire in the grate. She stood, with all the tremulous anticipation of a bride, in the middle of the room watching him advance toward her.

When he clasped her to his burning body, she answered his yearning with a yielding response that quickened his breathing.

"Dear God, how long I've hungered for you," he groaned and began kissing her lips with a tender possessiveness, as if learning anew the sweetness of her mouth. She could feel the ardor rising in him, but that he was holding back his passion and would not let it surge forth in full expression. He kissed her long and lingeringly before lifting her in his powerful arms and carrying her to bed.

"Marisa, I never thought to feel for a woman what I feel for you. The passion in me is a rage so consuming that it makes me tremble," he admitted.

"Justin," she murmured and caressed his cheek, "Justin, what is happening to us?"

He buried his head in her breast and they clung together momentarily.

"Marisa, before I make love to you, I must know that you have forgiven me for the pain and suffering I have caused you."

"Hush, dearest. Do not speak of what is past."

"But I must," he claimed harshly. "I must hear you say you forgive me before I can rid myself of the terrible burden of guilt I have carried since that fateful morning you fell down those stairs and nearly killed yourself. The image of your broken body is seared in my mind like a burning brand."

"Let it go, Justin. Do not torture yourself. You can see that my body is not broken—it is whole . . . and eager to be claimed by yours."

"Marisa," he cried in the throes of a passion he

261

could no longer stem. It swept them to a rapture neither had dreamed possible, a rapture such as the Creator had envisioned from the beginning of time when He ordained the wound of separation to be healed by the joining of man and woman. For just such loving were their bodies made—that the soul might blaze forth in the glory of physical union. So brief, so sublime, so exalted, so transient and fragile and shattering. The answer to the riddle of existence. Yet the very act created a hunger that only eternity could satisfy.

Marisa and Justin slept in each others' arms lost in sweet dreams. It was only in the morning aftermath, as Marisa cherished the tender memories of their night of bliss, that she realized his lordship, for all his lovemaking, had not told her he loved her. He had begged forgiveness and told her of his passion, but the words "I love you" she had yet to hear from the man who now held her heart in his hands.

While Justin and Marisa had innocently slept in each other's arms, the dark gypsy Isabella was sending word to Colonel Dubois at French headquarters informing him of her discovery. The English devil, Straeford, was now in Portugal, living in the Trudenjos villa in Lisbon. That very morning Isabella was visiting in the Trudenjos kitchens with her cousins Donato and Carmelita who served as footman and laundress to the establishment. It was not for family fealty that the dark-eyed camp-follower sought out her relatives, but to discover what she could of the Straefords—of their life style, their comings and goings, their habits, conversations, entertainments—for somewhere in the skein of the Straefords' daily living was the dark thread Isabella required to weave her web of revenge.

She learned that General Straeford, though spending much time at the villa, would, nevertheless, be gone for intervals of time that were increasing in frequency lately, and that the other gentleman, Major Harding, often accompanied the general. Further questioning revealed that Straeford's military headquarters were over seventy miles to the north in the Beira region.

The Straefords unwittingly played into Isabella's designing hands. The couple had accepted an invitation to visit the *quinta* of Senhor Joaquim Almarez and his wife, Maria, sometime during May. The country estate, between Villa Franca and Santarem, was not very far from French military encampments that had gone undetected by British intelligence. The projected visit would provide Colonel Dubois with a perfect opportunity for accomplishing his plans for revenge. Colonel Dubois was known as a daring officer who had made his reputation at the risk of his men's welfare in past skirmishes with the British, and he would get the Straefords in his hands whatever the cost. Dubois did not intend to let the old score of Vimeiro pass when fate was assisting him so readily. He had always known the day would come when he would confront the British *diable* again, and now he was ready.

While Dubois studied maps of the area around Santarem, Lord Straeford planned to take Marisa to Queluz. There they would tour the former country residence of the Portuguese court before the royal family fled to Brazil in 1807. Queluz was Portugal's Versailles, perhaps less splendid, but nonetheless a charming scene for royal intrigue and decadence. The ugly Carlota Joaquina, the Prince Regent's Spanish wife, had conducted many of her famous indiscretions there, begetting children by unknown fathers before her quasi-exile to Ramalhão.

Following the devastating earthquake of November 1755, the Marquis of Pombal had launched an ambitious rebuilding program in Lisbon that had transformed that city into a prime example of the "enlightenment" sweeping Europe at that time. Everything in Lisbon was rationally planned and built—residences, streets and squares—with slide-rule precision, as if envisioned by an 18th century philospher. The royal house at Queluz was undertaken during that fever of reconstruction, but unlike the classical designs of Lisbon, Queluz was a wonder of rococo fantasy, a sort of wedding cake in pink.

Justin and Marisa strolled through its many rooms on a sunny afternoon in April, admiring chinoiserie panels from Macao, marble statuary from Italy, porcelains from Austria, ceramics from Delft and tapestries from Spain. Queluz was like a museum of art from around the world.

They took their dinner in a small dining room outside Cintra which they approached through a garden patio overflowing with blossoming mauve bougainvillea, scarlet geraniums and pink camellias. Although the dining room was small, its interior features were cut on the grand scale. The fireplace at the far end of the room was tall enough to walk into, and the stone ceiling, decorated with blue and white *azulejos* in the form of scrolls and arabesques, vaulted high above them. Their meal was an exquisite collation of creamed vegetable soup, sole meunière and a dessert of the famed peaches of Alcobaça in a light custard sauce. They sipped a superb Madeira and sat enjoying the music of a strolling minstrel who plucked haunting melodies from his guitar as a mood of romantic enchantment settled over his listeners.

"I wonder why their music always sounds so sad," Marisa murmured dreamily. "The Portuguese seem to be a contented people, but their music is filled with melancholy."

"It is the influence of the *saudade*."

"I have heard that term used to describe the Portuguese temperament, but I don't know what it means."

"I think one could say it is a feeling for the poetry of loneliness. The essence of the Portuguese character is one of fatalism—they are a people entranced by the beauty of sorrow."

"But they do not seem unhappy," Marisa demurred.

"They are not, really. It is just their belief that life is colored by a darkness—that one cannot escape fate. It is a deep sense of the transitory nature of life—that pleasure is fleeting and therefore all the sweeter when it comes." Justin's green eyes burned into Marisa's, as if he were explaining more than his understanding of Portugal's *saudade*.

"Is that what you have learned through your study of Portugal and the Camões epic?" Marisa questioned softly, hoping to draw him out. "You speak as if you understand what you are describing from personal experience."

"I have always felt a sympathy for the darker currents of life . . ." and here Justin paused as if weighing his words carefully. He clasped Marisa's hand in his and went on. "It is only recently that I have come to appreciate that there exist those bright currents as well. It is a kind of painful awareness—an elusive joy that stirs deep within me and makes for me, at times, a . . . tender torment . . ." He stopped abruptly, as if embarrassed at his admission of gentle feelings. Never had Lord Straeford exposed his vulnerability to another.

Marisa was deeply moved and felt that a sacred trust had been vouchsafed her.

When they left the dining room to wander among the gardens, Justin plucked a velvety white rose and presented it to Marisa, claiming, "My dear, once you gave me a rose such as this. It has ever since been my image of you . . ." But whatever the earl was about to say was never finished.

"Well, if it isn't My Lord Straeford and his charming wife."

Marisa and Justin were accosted by Adele Buxton, the unpleasant woman she had met at the Christmas reception in Lisbon. Adele was in the company of a middle-aged lady, Evelyn Canfield, another of the recently arrived British wives. The tender mood of intimacy between the Straefords was shattered as the earl assumed his habitual manner of cold disdain.

The group exchanged polite greetings and his lordship would have immediately taken leave of the couple were it not for Adele's persistence in pressing conversation upon them.

"Your wife and I met at the Christmas reception, Justin. I looked for you there when I learned of your presence in Lisbon." Marisa was surprised at the familiar manner of Adele toward Justin.

"I chose not to attend," Straeford replied rudely.

"You were ever the lone wolf, were you not, Justin?"

Lord Straeford ignored her pointed remark and turned to her companion. "Have you seen much of the Portuguese countryside since your arrival here, Mrs. Canfield?"

"Not as much as I would like to, I'm afraid. This is the farthest beyond Lisbon I have come so far. But I have been to Belem and the Geronimos."

"You must get that solitary husband to bring you to

265

one of my evenings at-home, Lady Straeford. All the English community can be found in attendance," Adele said to Marisa.

"It is very kind of you, Mrs. Buxton, but my husband is often away on matters of duty lately, and it is not possible for me to plan very far in advance," Marisa answered vaguely, sensing that his lordship was not desirous of furthering the acquaintance.

"Your husband and I go back a long way together," Adele claimed in a rather sudden shift of topic.

"Oh, indeed," Marisa rejoined lamely, and looked to Justin who was regarding Adele with barely concealed contempt.

"Yes indeed," Adele stated. "You may not believe it, but . . ." she laughed superciliously, "it is only by the merest shuffle of the cards that I, myself, am not . . . the Countess of Straeford."

For a heavy moment nothing was said.

"What Adele refers to so charmingly," Straeford's voice dripped acid, "is the fact that she and my brother Robert were once betrothed." He did not elaborate, and Adele, who realized she had overstepped the bounds of discretion, held her tongue from further transgression. "And now, if you will excuse us, ladies, I don't wish to keep you from your tour. Charming to see you again, Adele. Your servant, Mrs. Canfield." Lord Straeford, a look of smoldering hostility on his dark brow, steered Marisa away with such a tight grasp on her elbow that she almost winced with pain.

17

Later that night, as the Straefords prepared to retire, Marisa forced herself to broach the subject of that strange encounter with Adele.

"Adele Buxton is a person whose existence I prefer to dismiss," his lordship stated with a finality that brooked no challenge. His face had not worn such a look of forbidding hauteur in a long time.

"Forgive me if I distress you, Justin, but you must allow me to speak."

Lord Straeford regarded Marisa coldly before shrugging his shoulders elegantly and claiming, "This conversation you press upon me may prove to be one you shall rue, my dear. Are you sure you want to pursue it?"

"No, I'm not sure," Marisa admitted. "And yet, look at us right now—such distrust and fear between us that it breaks my heart. Before Adele Buxton appeared this afternoon, I felt that at last we were learning to open our hearts to one another. Tell me truthfully, Justin, have you not felt of late that we were growing . . . closer?" She reached out a hand to him yearning to speak her love as she groped for the right words to thaw the coldness growing between them.

Lord Straeford, who had been pacing restlessly in front of the fireplace, stopped to look carefully at Marisa. There were tears shimmering in her eyes, and he could not ignore the pleading of her gesture toward him. With a groan, he clasped her harshly to his breast and murmured against her hair, "Ah, don't cry, dearest, please don't. What a vile brute I am to cause you more grief. Whatever you ask of me, I'll give it. Only never let me cause you pain again."

They kissed each other fervently as if swearing an unspoken oath of trust. Then Justin led Marisa to a small divan before the fireplace and settled her comfortably within the circle of his arm.

"And now, my dear, whatever you wish to know, ask it of me."

She sighed contentedly. "It does not seem so very important now that you are not set against me, Justin." Marisa nestled against his shoulder. "But I will finish what I started because it seems to me that there are matters concerning your early life that I need to know about to better understand you."

"And you really want to understand me?"

"With all my heart." She smiled tremulously at him.

"Then ask away, sweetheart."

Marisa thrilled at the tenderness in his voice. "I realize that you have been deeply hurt in the past." Marisa did not know how much to disclose of Edward Harding's revelations and picked her way carefully through a thicket of thorny topics. "Perhaps if you were to tell me some of the things that have caused you to develop such . . . cynicism about life, you might be able to exorcise the hold the past has on you."

"So you wish to redeem my black soul, my little savior?" he chided her. "But I would warn you that it is a hard-won cynicism I have achieved, and I would not part with it lightly."

"Well, I must try, nevertheless. I felt such bitterness surge forth when we came upon Adele today."

"Adele is a very minor character in the shabby little history fate has contrived for me." Justin drew Marisa closer and began to speak against her hair. He told her of Adele's perfidy in trying to lay claim to his affections before Robert was yet in the grave and of the love he bore his brother and the aching grief he endured on his death. He went back over the events of the attempt on his life by Jem Cooper and of his mother's deranged denunciation of himself on Huxley's death.

He could sit still no longer, an agitation seizing him as he recalled the incidents that scarred his soul. Abruptly, he rose. "My mother never forgave me for Huxley's death, but had he not died by accident that night, I would surely have killed the cur myself."

There was such vehemence in his voice that Marisa momentarily doubted her wisdom in forcing this discussion. But she did not stop. "Did your mother never become reconciled to you?"

"Never. But that is hardly a wonder. My mother hated me from the time I was born."

"Justin, surely she did not hate you as a babe." Marisa came to him and slipped her arms around his waist.

Straeford studied her upturned face before answering. "I am sorry to disabuse you of a favored notion about the maternal instinct, dearest, but my mother surely hated me as I lived. She did not want any more children after Robert was born. She told my father that she had done her part and provided an heir, and that there would be no more progeny."

"But why?"

There was a long pause as Straeford contemplated all he was about to reveal to this woman. Then, coming to a final decision to divulge all, he explained, "My mother married my father for money and position. She already had a lover. Robert was born eight months after the wedding—she claimed he was premature, but my father, who suffered doubts, wanted a son whose paternity was certain—that's how I came to bless the union. My mother felt I was forced on her, and she could not abide me for it."

269

"But how do you know all this?"

"My grandmother told me when . . . I returned for Robert's funeral."

"Why did you stay away in India so long?"

"I could not bear to see the lie my mother lived under my father's roof."

"Justin, you paint such a black picture."

Disentangling himself from Marisa's embrace, Justin began to pace again, trying to control the anguish that memory aroused in him.

He had been on his way home after a night of carousing with Ed Harding when he saw the light flickering in the summerhouse. Having heard that gypsies were in the neighborhood, Justin quickly crossed the stream and stealthily crept up to the house. He tested the handle to the door and slowly opened it and slid inside. Bright moonlight streamed across the room to illuminate the couple locked in each other's arms on the divan.

The strangled roar that erupted from him brought the startled couple to their feet as the wild young man lunged at his mother's lover. There was a brief but violent scuffle between them before Justin was flung to the floor where he struck his head against the foot of the divan, stunning him.

"Go! Go quickly," Justin's mother insisted as the man protested. "I'll handle him. Don't worry. Now go!"

He left, and Marian came to stand over her son, who was striving to clear his head and rise from the floor. His face was distorted with disgust and misery as he glared at the angry countenance of his mother, the countess.

"I'll kill him!"

"Fool! Why couldn't you mind your own business?"

"It is my business when . . ." he choked, "my . . . mother betrays my father so shamelessly in his own home!"

"Don't prate to me of betrayal when you play the sneak!" she scorned.

"I should kill you too!" He lashed out futilely.

His mother's jeering laugh tortured him and tears welled in his green eyes and spilled down his cheeks.

Angrily, he dashed them away. "Mother, why does my father's honor mean so little to you?"

A burst of laughter broke from her, and sweeping back her long black hair, she held him with her own glittering green eyes. "Which father do you mean? The one whose name you bear or the one whose loins sired you?"

Justin's head jerked involuntarily as the significance of that cruel denunciation was perceived. "You . . . can't . . . mean . . ." he hesitated, horror-stricken.

"Oh, but I do, my dear," she taunted. "You are a bastard!"

"No!" The word was torn from him.

"Yes! And if you dare to oppose me in any way in the future, I'll tell the man you call 'father' that the son he loves so well was sired by another. Do you understand me?" She grasped the stunned, heartsick boy by the shoulders. "You'll do nothing. You'll say nothing." Suddenly she delivered a stinging blow to his cheek which aroused him from his stupor and he tore himself from her grip.

"I hope to God that I never lay eyes on you again as long as I live!" he cried and flung himself out of the summerhouse with her laughter ringing in his ears.

"Justin." Marisa grasped his limp fingers in hers as he continued to stare into the fire unblinkingly. "Oh my dear, my dearest love." She kissed his cold hand trying to draw him out of the painful past. "We shall never speak of it again. It is over and done with forever. Your mother can hurt you no longer. We have each other and nothing else matters—whether you are the Earl of Straeford or General St. Clare." He looked at her uncomprehendingly, as if coming out of a trance. "We'll build our life together with a dozen children and live happily ever after." She smiled encouragingly.

"It really doesn't matter to you—about the title, I mean?"

"My darling Justin, you may renounce the title tomorrow, but I shall never leave your side. Never! Don't you know by now how much I love you?"

"God, I don't deserve you. But I need you desperately. I have been given a second life through you." Justin began to rain a storm of kisses upon Marisa's joyous face. The floodgates were down, and he no longer fought against the admission he thought never to make to any woman. "My dearest heart, I *love* you. I would die for you."

Their lovemaking was rapturous. Each burned with a new fire of devotion from which their very souls drew life. At last Marisa was ready to reveal the secret she had been carrying beneath her heart for many weeks:

"Justin, darling. I have news that I have been waiting to tell you when the time was right."

Justin rose above her and stared into her glowing eyes. "You are with child," he whispered hoarsely.

"Yes, my darling. I feel quite certain that I will present you with a son before next Christmas."

"Dear God, how perfect you are! To think this incredibly lovely body bears the fruit of my love." He showered her body with adoring kisses that suddenly awakened a raging passion within her. Marisa pulled him eagerly against her, demanding a violent union that left them both breathless and wondering.

The next morning all shadows were forever dissolved between them. The dark shadow of Lady Marian which had clung so tenaciously to Justin's mind and heart for so many years was at last cast out. Marisa's triumphant love had exorcised the incubus of hatred from her beloved's unconscious world where the hidden springs of despair had quietly seeped their bitter poison into his soul. Marisa's husband was cleansed and reborn, and the Straefords could not get enough of telling each other the wonders of their love. They had breakfast in their bed chamber, and the entire household was agog with the news that the earl had ordered champagne for breakfast.

"To the future Earl of Straeford," Justin toasted Marisa.

A slight shadow crossed the countess's face at her husband's salute.

"Do not frown, dear wife. Our son will be the legitimate heir, never fear."

"But last night you said . . ."

"I know, but I never did finish my tale. You see, when I returned from India and found myself to be the new earl, I told my grandmother that I would renounce the title. It was then that she laid to rest the lie I had been living with for six years. For my mother had deliberately lied to me. It was my grandmother who told me of my parents' early years, and how my mother was forced to bear me. My real father was the earl after all, and I his legitimate son. You see, I bear the family birthmark in the palm of my hand. Look—this small crescent on the heel of my left hand. All true St. Clare males have borne this very mark for generations."

"Why Justin," Marisa claimed in awe, "it is the same symbol that appears in the emerald. How is it possible you did not know this as a boy?"

"Another of my mother's tricks. Did you ever view the portraits of past earls in the long gallery at Straeford Park?"

"Why yes, one day with Lady Maxwell."

"Well, of the ten earls thus far, three have not borne this mark. Strangely, all three did not live very long. The third one was my brother Robert. The truth was withheld from Robert and me to protect him. I was left in the dark until Lady Maxwell enlightened me. Actually, it is such a small marking that I never noticed it." He smiled dazzlingly on Marisa. "Madam, I give you the next Earl of Straeford.

The first week in May the Hardings and Straefords took another nighttime excursion into Lisbon for the festival of São Matteu which was held outside the Castle of St. George. As they pressed their way through the teeming narrow streets leading to the hilltop where sat the castle overlooking the whole of Lisbon and the Atlantic Ocean below, they were jostled by throngs of noisy Portuguese whose irrepressible gaiety was infectious. The small group stopped to watch street dancers in peasant costumes performing to the music. The crowds clapped their hands and sang with loud gusto, encouraging the dancers to a frenzy of whirling and stomping that climaxed when

273

they leaped over bonfires to the frantic *olas* of the eager onlookers.

"Gracious!" Ann exclaimed excitedly, "it amazes me they do not land in the fires!"

"Especially the women. I do not see how they keep their skirts from catching in the flames," Marisa added.

"I'm sure they are well rehearsed," the earl claimed dryly. "They know what they are doing—it's not as spontaneous as it appears."

"It's a display for the goggle-eyed, just such as you two are," Edward Harding laughed.

"Oh pooh to your good sense," Ann replied. "Let Marisa and me enjoy the spectacle without your unfeeling lectures, gentlemen."

"I think we have just been set in our place," Lord Straeford told his friend with a laugh. "Come on, let's stop in one of these cafes and order some refreshments. I'm sure Marisa needs to rest."

"I need nothing of the kind," Marisa answered her oversolicitous spouse firmly, "but I would enjoy seeing more of the local color. By all means let us stop for refreshments."

They entered the Taverna da Noite and sat at a table before an open kitchen with a huge crackling fireplace and blackened walls hung with copper kettles. Sausages and onions dangled from heavy hewn beams above, and the tempting smell of spices mingled with those of wine to tantalize the strangers. They dared to test the house speciality of bananas flambé, a dish that proved more of a feast for the eyes than the palate. But it was all part of the night of Portuguese revelry, and the ladies enjoyed the display inordinately. Ann and Marisa were permitted a small glass of wine each, and before long the happy party was as noisily laughing and celebrating as the native Portuguese.

They were gathering their belongings in preparation for returning to the streets when an old gypsy with a black shawl over her head stopped at their table and asked to read the ladies' palms.

Both Edward and Justin were about to send the woman on her way, but Ann intervened, begging to be allowed to have her fortune told. The men shrugged their shoulders complaisantly, and once more they were seated while the gypsy studied Ann's outstretched hand.

"You are a married lady, *sim?*"the gypsy stated in a gruff, husky voice, her dark eyes shrewdly observing the open, eager face of Ann Harding.

"Indeed, I am."

"Brilliant deduction," Justin whispered to Marisa who cast a quelling glance toward him.

"You have a little boy—a son called Edouardo . . ."

"Oh yes," Ann breathed wonderingly.

The gypsy went on to tell her that she came from a distant land and would soon return there again. She predicted many more children and a happy life. Ann's eyes glowed with happiness, and she urged Marisa to have her palm read also.

The countess, who was of a less credulous nature than her friend, hesitated and looked to Justin for his opinion.

"Please suit yourself, Marisa," he told her. "I have no objection, as long as you take it for the nonsense it is."

"Very well. What harm can come of it?" Marisa held out her hand to the old crone who took it in her own gnarled palm and studied it for several seconds before making any comment.

"Well," Ann prodded her. "What do you see?"

The gypsy looked up at the group watching her and then back to Marisa's hand.

"I see—a long journey."

"Very original," Justin whispered to Ed.

"But not to the land from which you came. The journey will be to France."

"How lovely," Marisa responded, tossing her head at Justin. "I have always wanted to see France—but it must be some day far off, is it not?"

"No," the fortune teller replied. "Very soon."

"Oh." Marisa replied lamely, deciding the woman was a fraud after all.

"The line for the journey is broken—see. You will not go all the way. There will be much . . ." here the seer faltered . . . "woe. You should not go." She dropped the countess's hand abruptly. "That is all I can tell you."

275

Justin tossed the woman a gold coin, and dismissed her with a wave of his hand. She took herself off to ply her trade at a nearby table.

"Well, shall we be off?" Justin questioned his companions who seemed a little subdued after the encounter with the fortune teller. "Here now, what a sober crew you've become. Where are all those high spirits I was struggling to keep in check but a short time ago?"

The others picked themselves up and hastened to follow Justin from the cafe, but they were unable to strike the same note of abandon they had earlier enjoyed. They returned home sooner than they planned, not certain why the night begun so propitiously should have ended so disappointingly.

The weather in southern Portugal was already hot by mid-May, although the green countryside had not yet turned to the scorched earth of later months. Marisa enthusiastically contemplated her visit to the Almarez *quinta* the following week. Since Lord Straeford had been called away to headquarters farther north in the region of the Mondego River, he had agreed after much coaxing on Lady Straeford's part to meet her at the Almarez estate, instead of traveling there with her as originally planned.

The earl was concerned for his wife's health. Ever since he received the news of the coming child, he treated Marisa as if she were made of spun glass, and while his loving attention touched her deeply—never had she dreamed of being so cherished—she could not help chafing at the restrictions such constant watchfulness created. She must not tire herself by the exertions of walking overlong; she must retire early and sleep late; she must eat all that is healthy and nourishing, and above all, she must not worry about anything; she was to be happy and carefree—no discussion of the war conditions was allowed within hearing distance of the countess.

And yet, the war with France could not be obliterated from anyone's mind. The Straefords, along with thousands of their English countrymen, would not be in Portugal were it not for the French menace threatening to overrun the whole peninsula. It was because of the projected battle coming closer as months passed that

Lord Straeford was called away to one or another of the three outposts where British troops were encamped along the Mondego River in the upper Beira region. The three main regiments of the British army were separated by long marches between them, and Wellington himself frequently changed headquarters, occupying at different times Viseu, Celorico and Coimbra.

Communication was difficult, and Straeford's special mission was to hasten the network of communication between British military outposts.

If Lord Straeford had had his way, the trip to the Almarez *quinta* would have been cancelled entirely—but he could deny Marisa nothing these days and the doctor had assured him that the short trip by coach would not overtax his wife. Her pregnancy was sufficiently advanced and secure that she might safely undergo the journey. Besides, the doctor added, the country air in itself was guaranteed to be a welcome tonic for her ladyship.

Marisa would travel accompanied by Ann Harding and two maids, and every attention to her comfort and well-being was thought out well in advance. It never occurred to anyone that there might be danger in the form of enemy soldiers in a territory so near to Lisbon itself. But then, no one knew of Colonel Dubois's rabid interest in matters involving the Straeford household. The French were far to the north or safely in Spain for all practical purposes, and their existence was never considered as a deterrent to the trip—not by anyone assisting in preparations for the holiday.

"Villa Franca," Maria Almarez told Marisa at a recent dinner party in their home in Lisbon, "is the scene of the *festa brava* twice a year."

"The *festa brava?* I don't believe I have ever heard of it," Marisa replied.

"*Festa brava* is the running of the bulls. The countryside around Villa Franca is Portugal's breeding ground for bulls. When the festivals are held each year, a herd of black bulls is let loose to run through the main streets of the town. The people go crazy with excitment."

"How do they keep the bulls from running wild?" Marisa asked.

"Oh, the pathway, or *corrida,* is mapped out—all the

sidestreets are barricaded—but sometimes a bull escapes or breaks rank, and then the uproar begins. Some aspiring young matador invariably seizes the opportunity to display his skill with a cape."

"You mean there are people in the streets with the bulls?"

"But of course. Hundreds of men run in front of the bulls—it is a test of their bravery. They wish to display their courage to the crowds."

"Good gracious! Are there ever any accidents?"

"For certain. Sometimes very serious. Many a daring conquistador has been saved by friends yanking him to a balcony above in the nick of time," Senhora Almarez explained with a touch of pride in the manhood of her countrymen.

"Will there be such a festival while we are visiting in the area, Senhora Almarez?"

"It is possible. The festival dates vary from year to year. Would you like to attend one?"

"I don't know. It sounds terribly dangerous . . . and I shrink at the thought of anyone being injured. I'm afraid I always considered bullfighting to be a cruel custom."

"Ah but no, Lady Straeford. Not here in Portugal. In Spain, *sim*, they kill the bull, but in our country it is a sport of true nobility—a display of matchless equestrian skill. A *cavaleiro* fights the bull on horseback, and the animal is not killed."

"I didn't know that. I thought the animals were always killed."

"The Marquis de Pombal forbade it in the last century following the death of the Duke of Arcos in the bullring."

"I see. I'm so glad that the bull is not killed. I think maybe I would like to see the running of the bulls, after all."

The festival of the bulls was only one of the anticipated spectacles awaiting Marisa. She yearned to travel through the Portuguese countryside and see firsthand some of the sights that she had so far only read about in books. Her readings had taught her that Portugal was a fascinating land of such diversity that it defied a well organized plan of exploration. Some of its best treasures were tucked away in remote locations—a 14th century monastery or an abandoned Moorish castle—so that it would be necessary to set off in many directions to take in all the unique sights to be discovered in that enchanting land.

On the morning of their departure for the Almarez *quinta* Marisa was met with unhappy news. Little Eddie Harding had awakened with a fever and rasping cough. His mother would not leave him in that condition.

"But of course you can't leave him, Ann dear. I understand perfectly well." Lady Straeford tried to dissemble her disappointment, but Ann knew her friend well enough to discern the unhappiness underneath those kind words.

"I am so sorry, Marisa. I know how you were looking forward to this journey. I would dare to suggest that you go on without me, if I did not think your husband would object."

A sudden hope lighted Marisa's eyes but was quickly extinguished. "I would not leave you here to worry over Eddie alone," she sighed. "We must send word to Justin and Edward so that they will not be alarmed at not finding us at the Almarez *quinta* when they arrive there."

"Lud, that is true. And we'll have to send word to the Almarezes also."

"That's right, Ann. I'll see to the notes. You just take care of that little man of yours."

As Marisa wrote the notes, she could have wept with disappointment. Perhaps, if Eddie were to improve, they could still go. But no, it would be days before the child was fully recovered. By then all the schedules so carefully worked out would be thrown off.

Dr. Lomas came that same morning to see the child and pronounced his condition to be nothing more than a mild congestion that should clear by itself within a few days. He prescribed rest and a light diet, and by that same afternoon Ann was happily announcing her son to be much improved.

"It seems to have been a false alarm for the most part. I vow the little rogue is agitating his nanny to let him out of bed already," Ann claimed gaily until she caught sight of her friend's wan little smile. "Oh, I do so regret spoiling your plans, Marisa dear." She walked to the window and looked out. "And the weather is so fine. Just perfect for traveling . . . I know! Why don't you go on without me tomorrow morning! It's only one day behind schedule, and there is no need for both of us to miss the fun."

"But I couldn't leave you with a sick child."

"Oh pooh, you heard the doctor yourself. There is not the slightest need for worry—and if all goes well, I may follow you in a few days myself."

"Oh Ann, do you think I dare? I know Justin would not approve."

"Oh, bother Justin. He fusses over you like a hen with one chick these days. The trip will do you good. You take Lucy with you tomorrow and go."

"And you will come yourself as soon as you are sure Eddie is recovered?"

"I do believe I will. I'd like to see that *festa brava* myself, you know."

"Oh I can't be so selfish and leave you. I'd better wait until you can come too."

"You'll do no such thing. Now go find Lucy and tell her what you're planning. You did not post the letters yet, did you?"

"No . . . I'm ashamed to admit I was hoping for a change of some kind." She flushed with embarrassment.

"Well, it's a good thing you have not. Go find Lucy."

"Perhaps I shall tell her to be ready just in case I should decide to go—but I'll wait to see how Eddie is before I make it definite."

"Very well, dear. But I'm sure Eddie is fine."

The next morning the fine weather held and with a little prompting from Ann Harding, Marisa was packed and bundled off in the coach with Lucy seated at her side. She had expected to start earlier, but there was some trouble with a coach wheel, and by the time repairs were accomplished it was nearly noon. Momentarily Marisa hesitated, thinking to delay another day, but decided to be on her way before any more setbacks occurred. Two outriders accompanied the coach that Manuelo was guiding along the river road to the Almarez *quinta*. If all went well, they should reach their destination on the other side of Villa Franca by late afternoon.

Marisa felt guilty at leaving Ann behind, but she salved her conscience by telling herself that her friend was sure to follow within a few days. Little Eddie had been caught out of bed more than once before she departed that day, and Marisa knew the child was in no danger. The countess had a harder time quieting her conscience when she thought of his lordship's reaction to her traveling without Ann, but again she silenced her fears by reminding herself that Justin would be so happy to see her that he would probably forgo showing his displeasure. He could not bear to see her unhappy.

Lady Straeford stared contentedly out of the window, enjoying the passing scenery on the outskirts of Lisbon. The neat white houses with pink tiled roofs and painted green doors were colorful and charming. Each little domicile seemed to have its own pink walled garden over which trailed roses, fuchsias and bougainvillea in riotous colors of red and pink. As they traveled farther away from the city there began to appear that most characteristic structure of the Portuguese countryside— the windmill—whitewashed towers with rotating sails. The windmills had small clay vases attached to the ropes between the sails through which the wind passed playing a haunting, eerie melody. Marisa had read of them and was enchanted. What a curious mixture of lively gusto and poetic melancholy was this peninsular land and its people.

The sky was an incredible crystalline blue as puffy white clouds in fantastic shapes scudded by. The hills in the distance were still green but later in the summer much of the countryside would turn sere and brown from the hot glare of the sun relentlessly baking the exposed earth below.

The coach passed groves of olive trees shimmering silver in the bright afternoon glare and orchards of figs and peaches grew alongside the road. Gradually the countryside leveled out. The dusty road stretched flat and endless to the horizon with little more to see than countless miles of waving grass, and Marisa dozed in the drowsy warmth of the afternoon.

She was rudely jolted awake by the sudden lurch of the coach as it dropped down to the right side of the road. Lady Straeford found herself helplessly entangled with Lucy as they slid to the floor. For one breathless moment it seemed the coach must roll over, but it rocked precariously and then held still.

"My lady, oh my lady, what has happened? Oh my arm . . . I think it is broken . . . oh, oh . . ."

"Hush, you foolish creature!" Marisa commanded as she struggled vainly to regain the seat and heave herself to the door.

Manuelo and the outriders struggled from the outside and within minutes the door was yanked open, allowing the countess and her maid to scramble unceremoniously to the roadside where they stared in bewilderment at their damaged conveyance.

"What happened, Manuelo? Did we break an axle?"

"Não, não, senhora. It is the pin, see, the wheel, it has come off and rolls into the field. Josefe, he will get it for us, and we will soon fix it. Do not distress yourself, my lady. We shall repair it soon and be on our way once more."

"I pray you are right, my friend. I do not relish standing here in the blazing sun for any length of time."

"Desculpe me. I am a worthless ox. I did not think. *Hola,* Donato, pull down that box and place it beneath that tree *por la senhora, rapidamente."*

Marisa was too stunned by the confusion to notice the sly looks exchanged between Manuelo and Donato as they dragged a box from the roof of the coach to provide a seat for her to watch the act about to be staged for her.

The sun, which had seemed the harbinger of good tidings earlier in the day, now took on the aspect of a baleful eye glaring fiercely on the ill-assorted creatures struggling below. Lady Straeford removed her bonnet and fanned herself absentmindedly while striving to keep her thoughts from racing in helpless panic. What would Lord

Straeford say if he could see her predicament at this moment? What a storm of wrath he would raise.

"I knew we were risking danger when we set off this morning, my lady," Lucy claimed with the wisdom of hindsight. "There was an omen—I were warned and I paid no heed, and now see what catastrophe has struck us . . ."

"What are you babbling about, Lucy? Who warned you?"

"It were Old Teresa. She read my cards . . ."

"Cards!" Lady Straeford expostulated scornfully. "You have been listening to that addle-witted creature when I have repeatedly forbidden it." Marisa's anger was disproportionate to the cause. "Haven't I told you that it is all the veriest nonsense?"

"It weren't nonsense, my lady. Just see the fine pickle we're in—out in the middle of nowhere in a foreign land—God knows what evil awaits us—the gypsy saw a dark man on a black horse riding hell for leather . . ."

"Hold your tongue, you fool!" Marisa hissed. She felt as if a cold hand were laid upon her shoulder and shuddered involuntarily. For one brief moment nausea welled up into her throat and she feared she would be sick, but she swallowed hard and fought back the sudden attack of weakness. "If you can't say something sensible, don't speak at all."

"Forgive me, *senhora*," Manuelo interrupted Marisa's tirade of indignation. "But the wheel, it is worse that we thought. I have send Donato to Albuera . . ."

"What . . . where . . .?"

"Donato, he goes to Albuera, the next village, to get us help. Perhaps he finds someone to repair the damage . . . or perhaps he hires us another *coche* to take us to Villa Franca."

"You mean you cannot repair the wheel yourself?" Marisa asked foolishly. "It does not look so badly damaged to me, Manuelo."

"*Sim, senhora.* You are right. But the pin is lost, and the wheel will not stay on without it. You understand?"

"Yes . . . No . . . Oh, I don't know. It is so hot out here. How long do you think Donato will be gone?"

Manuelo shrugged his shoulders expressively and assumed a look of dumb uncertainty. *"Quién sabe?* Perhaps the *condesa* would be more comfortable waiting inside the coach once more? We will push the boxes under the wheel—so—and it will be safe for you to sit inside . . . I think. Do you wish to try this, my lady?"

"I might as well, Manuelo. I am afraid this box seat is growing very hard." Marisa attempted a smile, but was not very successful. Her thoughts were an incoherent fluster of worry over the child she carried, fear of remaining helpless on the open road, and perplexity about what course to pursue. Her body felt heavy with heat and discomfort, and she believed it probably would be better to wait in the dubious comfort of the coach rather than to continue on her unyielding roadside seat.

Once inside with Lucy, she fell into a fretful doze, unable to think her way through to a plan of action. Perhaps the Almarezes would send out a search party for her when she did not arrive this evening. They must wonder at her constant changing of plans . . . and would likely conclude that she had changed them once more . . . she was so weary . . .

The shocking noise of gunshots startled Lady Straeford from her reverie. Lucy screamed and threw herself into her mistress's arms.

"Lord save us! It's bandits!"

Outside there could be heard shouts and curses accompanied by the thunder of horses' hooves. It must be an ambush, Marisa thought. The door was suddenly wrenched open, not by the masked *bandidos* she had expected, but by a man in uniform, a uniform that turned her blood to ice! There was no denying the military blue of the French army. An officer of the *Grande Armée* was, incredibly, addressing her with the suave self-assurance unique to the French military.

"Mes regrets, madame, but allow me to inform you that you are now a prisoner of the Emperor of France, Napoleon Bonaparte."

It was beyond all belief! Enemy soldiers at her coach door claiming her as a prisoner of France! She must still be sleeping and this all must be a dreadful nightmare. Marisa struggled valiantly with her dismay and confusion, trying to collect her wits and behave with a semblance of British dignity.

"I do not understand, *monsieur*. We are not soldiers on a battlefield. What mean you by attacking stranded female travelers thus? What valor is to be found in the capture of mere women?"

"Forgive me, *madame,* but you are not, as you say, 'mere women'. You, dear lady, are the wife of one very important *général Anglais*—Lord Straeford, *n'est-ce pas?*"

"But . . . but how do you know that?"

"Ah, all in good time, dear lady. All in good time. You will understand everything when you are delivered into the hands of my commandant, Colonel Dubois." He bowed, then changed his manner abruptly. "Here you, get out of the coach at once!" He spoke sharply to Lucy.

"Oh no, no. My lady, save me. Please don't let them take me!" Lucy wailed in terror.

"What do you want with this girl, *monsieur?* I insist you leave my maid here with me."

"That cannot be. She must be returned to the Villa Trudenjos in Lisbon with your coachman. No harm will come to her."

"But I don't understand . . ."

"She and your driver are to be sent back that the alarm may be given."

"The alarm given?" Were they mad? The more he said, the less she understood.

"Yes, she is to bear the message explaining your whereabouts. She will be believed."

"Message of my whereabouts?"

"I do not have time for more talk now. You will be given the full explanation by Colonel Dubois *dernièrement.* Do you hear that, *ma'mselle?*" He turned to Lucy. "Colonel Dubois. Tell them at the Villa Trudenjos that Madame Straeford is now the prisoner of *Colonel Dubois.*"

Lucy only stared, her eyes wide with terror.

"Comprenez-vous? Do you understand?" he snapped at her.

The maid jerked her head in a convulsive nod of assent.

"Now get out and mount behind the coachman.

Vite, vite! Enough of this delay." He grabbed the girl's arm and jerked her rudely from the coach.

Lucy was by now sobbing and wailing loudly as she was torn from Lady Straeford's horrified embrace. Marisa rose as if to follow Lucy, feeling it incumbent on her to make some move in the girl's defense.

"Non, non, Madame Straeford. You will stay with us. Do not fear, That so gallant husband of yours will, no doubt, come to your rescue, eh?"

"So that is it!" Marisa claimed aghast. "I am to be bait in a trap set for my husband!"

"And so, now you begin to understand. *Très intelligent, n'est-ce pas?"*

"My husband will kill you for this—you and all your sneaking compatriots. It is your own destruction you engineer with the fiendish plot!" Marisa declaimed with a bravado she was far from feeling.

"Bravo, madame! You are a captive worthy of the pains we have taken to ensnare you." He bowed mockingly and the door slammed closed, leaving Marisa alone to battle her terror in private.

Dusk was falling and soon it would be nighttime. What was going to happen to her?

She had little time to wonder. Within minutes the coach began to move. Marisa could not at first comprehend how this came to be. The wheel was broken, was it not?

Or was it?

In a lightning shaft of revelation, Marisa realized that she had been the victim of a carefully laid plot to kidnap her. Manuelo had known all along that the French were waiting for her. He had the pin to the coach wheel the whole time. It was not lost. It was all a delaying tactic until the French should arrive.

And she had started out so trustingly. Oh the treachery!

And Justin! They were after Justin. Lucy had been given a message for him. They wanted him to know their plans.

The coach was jolting badly. They must have left the main road for a secondary one through the countryside. Dear God! Where were they taking her?

18

Her destination, had she known it, would have caused Marisa a rueful smile of irony. The Convent São Margite, one of the 12th century strongholds of the Knights Templar, was just such an historic landmark as the countess had yearned to explore. The Templars, who once immured themselves behind the convent's massive walls, had fought ferociously against the Moors at Santarem and were instrumental in ousting the infidels from Portugal. The convent contained some of the finest Manueline architecture of Portugal, including the lacy stonework of ornamental vines, leaves, rosettes and scrolls.

The Knights had transformed the convent, which once housed cloistered Cistercian monks, into a powerful fortress of thick stone walls and imposing battlements that jutted into the skyline above a prominent mountain ridge of the lower Serra da Estrêla.

On her arrival in the early hours of dusk on the following night, however, Marisa could barely discern the awesome outlines of her intended prison. The countess was ill and suffering from exposure. She had endured a journey that had transported her by carriage and then by flatboat up a stream winding precariously through steep mountain ravines.

The last stage of her journey had been accomplished via donkey through a precipitous passageway in the mountains—the only access to that elevated eyrie.

The countess was brought before her captor, Colonel Dubois, in a state of near collapse. The room in which she was deposited seemed to be a former audience chamber at whose far end a monstrous fire blazed in a story-high fireplace. The hall was lighted by flaming sconces that reflected deep, restless shadows up into the vaulted ceiling. It was an intimidating scene, but Marisa was beyond fear, so fatigued was she by her arduous journey.

"So, at last, I am presented the very charming lady, the Countess of Straeford," a silky voice murmured from the far end of the room where sat the man Lady Straeford's husband had so grievously wounded at Vimeiro. He studied his captive from a single dark eye, unconsciously fingering the black patch which concealed the scar that was, in reality, the underlying cause for the outrage Lady Straeford now suffered. Beside him stood a dusky gypsy whose flashing eyes surveyed the pale countess with withering scorn.

Marisa swayed and the room shifted out of focus momentarily.

"Here, you," the colonel motioned to a sergeant standing beside the heavily carved oak table where Dubois sat, "a chair for Madame Straeford. Please be seated, dear lady. I am sorry to see you have suffered from this . . . adventure . . . but you shall soon be made comfortable. We mean you no harm."

Marisa, who had sunk gratefully into the chair, did not reply at once, but took time to summon her remaining strength.

"*Monsieur,* you must tell me . . . please . . . exactly what you do mean by bringing me here thus."

There was a low murmur of laughter from Dubois's companion, Isabella Costanza, who tossed her dark hair haughtily and opened her mouth to speak, but the colonel intervened.

"Ah, that is a *longue histoire* that I must relate to

you at another time. For now you shall rest and perhaps partake of some refreshment, eh?" From the soft tones of his voice and the mildness of his manner, Marisa was having difficulty envisioning him as a villain.

"I cannot bear this uncertainty any longer. You must tell me *now* why I am here. You must!" Marisa claimed passionately, unmindful of the pleading that rang through her words and the continued scorn of the other woman.

"Please do not fret yourself so," Dubois advised. "The matter rests between your husband and myself—not you." For the present, Dubois was content to see himself as a kind of benign minister of justice. "It is a matter that has long required restitution. I repeat, no harm will befall you."

"What!" Marisa claimed fiercely, rising from her chair. "You plot to destroy my husband and *dare* claim that you mean me no harm!" She was trembling from head to foot and was forced to take hold of the chair for support.

"You will make yourself ill, *madame*. I beg of you to calm yourself." The colonel rose and came around the table to take hold of the countess's hand.

"Don't touch me!" she cried vehemently and wrenched her hand free before falling in a dead faint at the colonel's feet.

Isabella Costanza could no longer restrain her hysterical mirth, and her trill of pure malice echoed off the walls to be lost in the far reaches of the arching ceiling high above.

At the same time that Marisa lay in a swoon in that remote mountain hideaway, her husband was reading the message delivered to him in his tent just moments earlier by Josefe, the gardener's son from the Villa Trudenjos. Major Harding and Lord Straeford's Portuguese interpreter, Raoul Garcia, watched nervously as the general perused the epistle held impatiently before the flickering candle.

The sudden exclamation, "Oh my God!" which was torn from Straeford's lips sent a thrill of apprehension through the other two men.

"Justin, what is it?" Harding questioned anxiously, coming to his side.

"Dubois!" Straeford called in a strangled voice and jumped from his chair. "That dog from hell!" Justin raved, his face a mask of black rage and hate.

"Good God, man, what is it?" Harding shouted, beside himself with shock and fear.

"Marisa! Marisa!" Straeford stared blindly at Harding, not seeing his friend, but his wife's face frightened and terrified. He felt physically ill and the color drained from his face.

"Here, Justin, take this," Harding thrust a tumbler of brandy into his friend's shaking hand. "Drink it."

Straeford did as he was bid without thinking and heaved a shuddering sigh as he strove to regain command of himself.

"Now for God's sake, tell me what has happened," Harding demanded.

"Colonel Dubois . . . you know who he is?"

"Yes, the one you wounded at Vimeiro."

Straeford shook his head vigorously in agreement. "That devil's spawn has contrived to kidnap Marisa on her way to the Almarez *quinta.*"

"Kidnap Marisa . . . but what of Ann? They have her too?" Harding was aghast.

"No, no," Straeford answered impatiently. "Ann is still in Lisbon. Marisa was traveling alone . . ."

"But how did Dubois discover that your wife was traveling to Villa Franca? It makes no sense."

"More sense than you think," Lord Straeford admitted in a calmer voice, his mind already working ahead of himself. "Isabella Costanza acted the spy. She has been in Lisbon these last months and has kept Dubois informed . . ."

"Costanza? Not that camp-follower who was Dubois's woman?"

"The very one," Straeford replied ruefully. "Our sins find us out, don't they? My vile past is catching up with me." Straeford stared hard at his friend and thrust a hand through his black locks. "God!"

"Did they tell you where Marisa is being held? Do they want ransom?"

Justin nodded yes to both questions.

"Ah, now I see what it is all about. Dubois wants you as prisoner in exchange for your wife."

"Precisely."

"Where are they holding her?"

"In a convent north of Tomar in the Salvantos mountains . . ."

"The São Margite?" This came from Lieutenant Garcia, who suddenly burst into the conversation for the first time.

"That's it, Raoul. You know of it?"

"For certain. I am from Tomar. The Convent São Margite was a fortress of the Knights Templar, but it is now a ruin."

"Yes, yes. That's the one. Can you guide me to it?" Lord Straeford broke in eagerly.

"But of course."

"What are you going to do, Justin?" Harding demanded.

"I'm going there at once. Dubois has given me three days to get there and will permit one other person to accompany me in order that Marisa will have someone to escort her to safety." Harding tried to interrupt, but Straeford would not allow it. "There is only one passage leading to the convent and he has sentries posted to ensure that I come as I am ordered—without enforcements. There is no choice in the matter."

"Now hold on, Justin. It's not like you to act in haste. We must devise a plan . . ."

"There will be *no plan!* My wife's life is at stake! Don't you understand?" Straeford retorted violently.

"General Straeford, *desculpe me,* but if you will permit me to speak." Lieutenant Garcia paused. "There is more than one passageway to the São Margite. If we leave tonight we can be at Vilar Fuentes by early morning . . ."

"Vilar Fuentes?" Straeford queried.

"*Sim.* It is but a short distance from São Margite. It is a northern approach seldom used. Only a few local people know of it. We could surprise the French and break into the fortress before they knew what was happening," Garcia claimed, excitement gleaming in his eyes.

"My God, Justin. Do you hear? The very answer." Harding joined with Garcia hopefully.

"I dare not risk it. What if they were to discover us? They would kill my wife. No. I dare not." But there was not total rejection in Justin's voice, and both Harding and Garcia recognized Lord Straeford's desire to be convinced of a plan of rescue.

"Justin," Harding stated firmly, "You must dare . . . for the countess's sake. Only think what it would mean to her to lose you at this time in her life. And what guarantee do we have that Dubois really means to let her go once he has you?"

Straeford had no answer for that argument.

Throughout the dark of night, Straeford and Harding, in concert with Lieutenant Garcia, contrived a plan of rescue whose very daring purchased it a measure of success. It was almost certain Dubois's forces were limited, otherwise he could not have sneaked as far into Portugal as he had. A small band of handpicked light troops should do the trick for the British—a dozen men capable of doing the job of ten times their number. The whole of their plan depended on surprise and swiftness of attack. It was finally agreed that Harding would accompany Justin when he presented himself as hostage to Dubois. They planned their arrival for late in the afternoon of the third day of the stated deadline. The task of escorting Lady Straeford to the safety of Lieutenant Garcia's family estate near Vilar Fuentes would fall to Major Harding. Once the countess was removed from danger, Garcia and the select detachment would attack. The outcome was in the hands of fate.

By dawn the desperate party was already on its way through a valley in the Serra da Estrêla. They traveled by horse through forests of tall pines and scrub oak which impeded their pathway, often forcing them to waste precious time circumventing obstacles. Nevertheless, by dusk of the second night, they had arrived at the foothills of the Salvantos mountains in whose twisting folds lay the Convent São Margite.

Straeford and his men wasted little time once they reached this point. It was Lieutenant Garcia who led the party through the narrow defile between massive boulders that appeared impregnable. To the unpracticed eye there seemed no entrance to the fortress of rock and trees that presented its forbidding façade. But the young Portuguese showed them the place where an opening began behind a boulder that did not press against its neighbors as it appeared to do, but actually stood forward at least six feet, allowing a horse and rider ample passageway behind. From there on, the climb was steep and precipitous, but by no means impossible. From the midnight sky bright with myriad stars, an impassive full moon cast sharp shadows on the stealthy travelers wending their way through the mountain crags.

By midnight, after a particularly perilous passage over switch-back trails, they came to the crest of a ridge that overlooked the Convent São Margite below. The northern wall of the central abbey was actually the back of the mountainside, and it became obvious that no one would expect access to the convent to be possible from the north. Garcia, however, explained that a trail of gradual descent was there among the dense trees and thick brush, and that the men could negotiate it easily within a half-hour's time. From their position on the ridge above, the whole of the encampment was laid out for ready observation.

"It appears that their number is no greater than we had anticipated when we started out," Harding said to Straeford.

"I count a total of three sentry outposts by those fires," Straeford rejoined.

"They have no fear of discovery. They believe themselves unassailable except from the southern access," Garcia added.

"What we need is a diversion that will draw the main body to a single point and catch the scoudrels unaware," Straeford mused.

"They must have a makeshift magazine for ammunition down there . . ." Harding began.

"And an explosion, *senhor*," Garcia broke in eagerly, "it will do the work of a hundred men."

Straeford agreed. "Once Harding and I are within

the convent, lieutenant, I will negotiate to have my wife released and taken to safety. In the meantime you will move undercover and contrive to set up the magazine for the explosion. You must wait only till Major Harding has the countess well out of the area before you detonate. I shall endeavor to break free of my captors and join you in the attack. But whatever happens to me, Dubois must be destroyed. That dog must not be loose to menace my wife ever again."

The British patrol then settled themselves among the rocks and trees atop the mountain crest and snatched a few hours' sleep until dawn should arrive.

"My lord, behold," Garcia whispered, waking the earl from fitful sleep as the sun broke over the eastern ridge of Mount Salvantos. "That wagon beside the small buildings to the east of the chapel—the magazine, no?"

"By God, it must be! Those are powder kegs piled on it. They must be waiting to be unloaded." Straeford was as excited as his lieutenant.

"Won't they make a spectacular fireworks when they go off!" Harding claimed joyfully. "Our mission is assured."

"It looks promising, my friends," Straeford admitted. "But I wonder where that devil holds Marisa. May his soul rot in hell!"

"Come on, Justin. Let's get down there so we can arrive by the southern route the way we are expected."

"You're right. I want to be inside those walls by late afternoon. Let's go!"

It was three o'clock in the afternoon when Straeford and Harding, astride their horses, presented themselves to the sentries at the south portal. The gates swung open, and their horses' hooves echoed ominously over the cobblestone courtyard leading to the central abbey where Dubois and Isabella stood on a balcony watching their enemy approach. The raven-haired gypsy, her hands on her swinging hips, could be heard laughing derisively as she called out, *"Hola, general. Bem vindo!* Welcome to the Convent São Margite."

Lord Straeford glanced neither up nor down, keeping his stiff gaze straight ahead until he and Harding reined their horses to a stop and climbed down. Two guards emerged from the shadowed porch and searched the Englishmen for arms. Finding none, they led their captives to the audience chamber where Marisa had stood before Dubois just three nights ago.

The French colonel, seated at the oak table as before, studied the sedate approach of his long-awaited enemy. Dubois's single dark eye glittered with hate and scorn. Isabella, maintaining her arrogant pose, began to laugh again until Dubois hissed her silent.

Harding stood to Justin's left and felt himself grow cold at the unconcealed hatred radiating from the dark pair. They obviously believed themselves the unassailable victors in this bitter encounter.

There was a long silence before Dubois finally spoke. "So, at last," he purred. "Did I not promise you we would meet again?"

Justin disdained comment.

"Oh ho. The mighty Lord Straeford does not wish to speak?" Isabella taunted. "Let us hear what he has to say when his fine lady is brought before him."

"Quiet!" Dubois commanded.

"Bring the countess in," Isabella demanded, disregarding Dubois's command. "Let him see for himself that pale, whining creature he calls wife!" she spat.

"Did I not command you to silence?" Dubois roared and slammed his fist upon the table.

Straeford felt his heart sink to his boots at Isabella's description of Marisa, but he gave no sign of his inner torment.

"You and I are to settle a long-standing debt at last." Dubois resumed, choosing to play out the scene at his own pleasure. He had waited since Vimeiro to even the score, and many times when confronting his own disfigured image in a mirror, he had promised himself the exquisite pleasure of revenge. His plan had been worth every pain of its devising, and every day of its expectation. The prospect before him was sublime, and not one drop of pleasure would he deny himself.

The colonel stood up abruptly and came to stand in

front of Lord Straeford. He knew it would test the Englishman's endurance to remain impassive in so frontal an attack.

"Your lady, Madame Straeford, you wish to see her?" Dubois questioned smugly.

The earl stared rigidly into the sneering face. He felt Harding grasp his elbow in warning.

"Kill the English pig!" Isabella demanded. "Enough of this game. Run him through his black heart!"

"Did I not command you to silence?" Dubois whirled on Isabella and struck her a stunning blow across the face that sent her sprawling to the floor. "Guard. Throw the bitch out," he commanded. "Out of my sight, *salaud.*"

Isabella scrambled to her feet, screeching, "No, no! You cannot do this to me. I have as much right as you to be here. It was *I* who put you on to the trail of this *canaille.*"

"Out of my sight, I say. Take her away."

"No!" Isabella screamed over and over again as two men struggled with the clawing vixen and dragged her from the room.

Dubois waited until the sound of Isabella's voice no longer echoed through the corridors before resuming his game of protracted revenge.

"And now, *mon général de brigade,* perhaps you would like something to drink after your wearying journey . . ."

"Why don't we get on with the business at hand." The earl spoke for the first time, striving to maintain a calm demeanor.

"Oh, but surely you will not deny the amenities? Honor demands you do not refuse the hospitality of one gentleman officer to another, *n'est-ce pas?*"

Sensing that Straeford's endurance was running short, Harding attempted to stem the breach and force Dubois to release Marisa to him.

"It is growing late, Colonel Dubois. I would consider it a great courtesy if you were to allow me to get started with Lady Straeford before darkness falls. I must find my way to an unfamiliar destination from here."

"All in good time, major. All in good time," Dubois

replied, enjoying the sport of vengeance too much to quit just yet. "First-you must drink with me."

"Very well, colonel. I would be happy to partake of some wine—a Madeira or sherry would be welcome," Harding temporized, beginning to fear the disintegration of their carefully laid plan.

"Non, non, monsieur. Not wine, but brandy—*French* brandy—the very finest in the realm." He turned to one of his sergeants-at-arms. "Pour us some brandy. Three glasses. You *will* drink, Lord Straeford, *n'est-ce pas?"*

It was a threat, and Justin nodded calmly, though the blood raced violently through his veins. Damn this devil to hell! He would kill him or die in the attempt— only let them get Marisa safely from the scene. He accepted the glass and held it, waiting for the toast he supposed Dubois would make.

"To *Napoleon. Vive l'Empereur!"*

Neither man raised the brandy to his lips as Dubois downed his, and although they itched to pour the liqueur on the floor, they decided against such an insult. It would have infuriated Dubois all the more.

Then the colonel taunted, "You do not drink, eh? Well, general, you *will* before this contest is finished. Bring in the countess."

A terrible silence filled the room as they waited. Dubois never removed his gaze from Straeford. He wanted to see his hated enemy's pain. Dubois was amply rewarded when the door at the left opened and Marisa entered with a guard on either side. Although she walked unassisted, it was evident that she came forth at the command of nerves steeled to endure great physical stress. She held her head high, but the lady was pale.

For one brief moment, a look of such agony crossed the earl's face that it must surely have gratified Dubois for the rest of his life. His lordship moved involuntarily in her direction, but Harding again grasped his friend's arm and held him back.

"Justin," Marisa whispered softly and would have run to his side except for Harding's reaction.

"Ma chère comtesse, please be seated," Dubois offered suavely, choosing the role of the gallant once more.

Marisa shook her head, refusing the chair. Her eyes sought desperately to communicate with Justin, but he would not look her way again, and she held on to her dignity. Her brain was numb with fear.

Justin turned to Dubois, who had seated himself behind the massive oak table, enjoying his role of presiding potentate. The English were completely in his power, and it pleased him to toy further with their fate.

"Well, Colonel Dubois," Justin spoke levelly, "we have met all your demands. Will you now release my wife into Major Harding's hands, that she may be safely delivered to her destination before nightfall?"

"But why so hasty, *mon general?* Are you so anxious to part from your lovely wife already?"

A cold rage thundered in his ears, but Lord Straeford refused to be drawn into the trap Dubois was setting for him. Once he gave in to the desire to smash his fist into that sneering face, they were all done for sure.

"You spoke moments ago of gentlemen officers observing the amenities. I beg to remind you of the bargain made between us as men of honor: *Myself for my wife.*" There was a gasp of alarm from Marisa, but Justin overrode it and faced his enemy relentlessly. "I am here, sir, as you requested. What says your French honor to the matter? Do you release my wife as you gave your word to do?"

Colonel Dubois shifted uneasily before his foe's verbal assault. He was torn between the desire to hold all three prisoner, and the desire to maintain the image he had of himself as a man of irreproachable honor.

"Do not seek to maneuver me with clever words, *monsieur. I* will decide what is honorable or not honorable." However, Dubois was visibly wavering. He lacked the imagination for playing both villain and hero, and finally opted for the more flattering role. "Very well, since you are so *avide* for this final parting from your lady . . ."

"Dear God, no!" It was a cry torn from Marisa, who flew to Justin before she could be restrained.

One of the guards grabbed her roughly by the arm, and Justin instinctively slammed his hand against the soldier's arm, knocking him away from his wife. "Don't you *dare* touch her!" Straeford snarled and clasped his wife to his side.

"Don't send me away, Justin. Please, I beg of you, let me stay with you," Marisa pleaded.

"Dearest," Justin spoke urgently to her, damning the necessity that exposed his wife to the gloating eyes of his hated enemy. "Do not distress yourself this way. You must go with Edward now and be my brave girl." He pressed her to himself. "Do not give the dog more joy. I implore you," he whispered into her hair. "All will be well. Trust me."

"Ah, *adieux* are so sad, are they not? It breaks the heart," Dubois exulted. "But enough. You, Monsieur Harding, take the lady now and go," he snapped, suddenly weary of his sport and desiring to get to his disposal of Straeford. "I have other matters to attend to, and it begins to grow late."

Edward Harding came to Marisa's side and took her arm in his hand. "Come, Lady Straeford. We must be on our way."

Briefly she hesitated while desperate thoughts crowded her brain with impulses to cling and scream and resist, but she could not betray her beloved husband. She knew he needed her to be strong, and with tears streaming down her face, she cast one last yearning look at him before allowing Major Harding to lead her away.

The earl watched his wife's departure, his face white with the pain of letting her go so cruelly—believing it might be their final parting.

"Guards. Show our ... guest to his quarters," Dubois called to his men. "We must make him comfortable, *n'est-ce pas?*" The colonel could not restrain a laugh before dismissing his captive to confinement. "I plan some ... after-dinner entertainment for us, Lord Straeford. Perhaps you would like to ... refresh yourself before then."

Unwittingly, Dubois had played into Straeford's hands. Had he, at that moment, got on with the interrogation, Lord Straeford would have been in no shape for the events that were to follow.

Lord Straeford could not have been more pleased,

therefore, than he was the moment the door slammed shut behind him, locking him in a narrow cell that had once been a monk's austere chamber. He looked about, taking in the bare stone walls and the cot with its straw mattress. It was enough for his needs. He took out his pocket watch. Five-thirty. By dusk, Marisa would be safely ensconced with the Garcia family, and he would be ready for the final act of the drama. The French had not discovered the small packets of black powder concealed in his boots, nor the knife either. As soon as Straeford heard the explosion of the amunition dump, he would stage a small display of his own.

Meanwhile Edward Harding was explaining to Marisa that her husband was not as hopelessly lost to her as she feared. He told her about the planned attack. If all went as intended, her husband would be restored to her that very night. Lady Straeford tried to draw comfort from Harding's words as they rode away from the fortress, but in her heart were grave misgivings. What if the plan went awry and . . . she was unable to finish the thought. By the time they reached the valley, Marisa was barely able to maintain her seat on the swaying animal.

"Only a short distance now, my dear lady. If you could go on to the villa with Lieutenant Drake, here, I should very much like to return . . ."

"Yes, yes," she insisted, "leave me and go to Justin. Oh, Edward, save him for me, I beg you."

"I promise you before this night is over, you and your husband will be reunited." He kissed the hand she laid on his and spurred his horse toward the mountains again.

Marisa watched him go, praying fervently that he was right.

A thundering roar of explosions ripped apart the descending darkness just as Colonel Dubois was settling himself at a dining table laid with breast of capon and a bottle of chilled Chablis Blanc.

As soon as he heard the noise Straeford went to work in his cell. He poured the black powder from his boots into a hip flask and stuffed his silk handkerchief into the neck of the silver container. Extracting a length of rope from beneath the lining of his jacket, he tied the flask to the padlock on the cell door and inserted a fuse into the flask which he trailed along the floor to the opposite end of the cell. Then he overturned the cot and crouched behind it while he lighted the fuse and waited until the lock blew, taking most of the door with it.

The guard, who had run down the hall at the noise of the first explosion, missed the effects of the blast staged by his captive, for his life was soon dispatched by the sudden thrust of Straeford's knife between his ribs. Snatching the soldier's pistol and sword, the earl raced to find Dubois. It was the colonel's frantic shouts that identified his whereabouts to Lord Straeford.

"Sacré bleu! Qu'est-ce que c'est?" the stunned Dubois shouted, but his shout was drowned out by further blasts that seemed to mount in crescendo to the alarming accompaniment of ungodly screeches. Frenzied voices of French soldiers bellowing their shock and dismay filled the corridors inside the abbey while the courtyard outside echoed to the sounds of gunfire and the clatter of running feet. Two of Dubois's officers broke into the room raving in confusion that the garrison was under attack from the north, east and west. Sentries were dead; fires were burning and the situation was desperate.

"Impossible!" screamed Dubois.

"Not as impossible as it seems, my dear colonel." This last was spoken by the Earl of Straeford who stood in the doorway pointing a glinting pistol directly at Dubois's heart. The pandemonium caused by the explosions and guerilla style screechings of the British soldiers had thrown the French into a total rout.

"Diable!" Dubois roared, beside himself with rage.

"Do not fret yourself unnecessarily, *mon ennemi*— that score you desire to settle is no less desired by me. Stand aside," Straeford commanded the other two French officers. "Throw your weapons to the floor—now!" Straeford demanded as they hesitated, looking to the colonel for guidance.

"Do as he says," Dubois ordered.

Just as the men were divesting themselves of their

swords and pistols, Garcia appeared in the doorway behind Straeford in the company of Harding and two men in British uniform.

"The fort is taken, Senhor Straeford," Garcia exulted.

In the split second that Straeford's attention was diverted, Dubois lunged for a pistol and took aim at Straeford.

"Look out, Justin,' Harding yelled, and there ensued a mad scramble in which both French and English were firing at each ct..er at close range, filling the room with the crackle of gunfire and a blue haze of smoke. Dubois's aim was off and the ball merely creased Justin's left arm. The earl threw himself on top of the colonel and the two rolled together in mortal combat amidst a melée of flailing bodies and shouted curses. Dubois heaved himself above Straeford and clenched his hands around his enemy's throat, attempting to throttle the life out of him. Summoning superhuman strength, the earl maneuvered his knee into the colonel's chest and pushed with a force that threw Dubois onto his back. With a lightning thrust, the earl plunged his knife through the heart of his nemesis.

It all took less than five minutes. Dubois lay mortally wounded, and beside him lay two others dead—one French and one English.

"*Deus,*" Garcia breathed in horror, while Straeford swore a string of oaths.

"Damn his soul to hell," Straeford ended grimly. "My only regret is that I was denied the pleasure of killing him in a duel of honor." He paused. Then he knelt beside the body of the British soldier. "How many have we lost altogether, Lieutenant Garcia?"

"Two others, sir."

"What about the French?"

"Ten dead and two wounded—counting these."

"What about the woman? Did you find her?"

"*Sim,* she is being held with the others."

"We have a total of twenty-five captives, Justin." Ed Harding offered this information. "We're holding them in the chapel."

For the first time in days, Lord Straeford allowed himself to smile. "At their last prayers, eh?" He turned to

Lieutenant Garcia. "Raoul, I'll leave you in command. You have proven yourself a first-rate leader, and I shall recommend you for a promotion when I return to headquarters. However, I have business elsewhere that I would not put off any longer. And I advise you to release the woman. She can do nothing further to harm us."

"*Sim, vossa Senhoria.* I will take care of everything here for you."

"*Adeus,* my friend. Come on, Ed. I need you to show me the way."

It was on the stroke of midnight that the earl once more enfolded his wife in his arms and showered her tear-stained face with kisses, their tender torment over at last.

"Oh, my darling Justin. I have prayed so hard."

"Did I not tell you to trust me, my dearest?"

"But the odds were so great."

"Hush, my heart. You are safe in my arms and it shall remain so as long as we both shall live, my sweet, sweet salvation."

PULSE-RACING, PASSIONATE, ADVENTURE-FILLED FICTION